Sweet, Sexy

HEART

The Bradens & Montgomerys
(Pleasant Hill – Oak Falls)

Love in Bloom Series

Melissa Foster

A Note to Readers

Dash Pennington just might be my most swoon-worthy hero yet, and sweet, careful Amber is so very deserving of him. I had a blast writing about a man who knew what he wanted and was smart enough to realize he'd better do his homework and a woman who had been living within the confines of her comfortable shell for far too long. I knew it would take a special man to earn her trust, and the way Dash does it will leave you breathless. They're funny, super sexy, and beautifully perfect together. I hope you love them as much as I do.

If this is your first Love in Bloom book, all my love stories are written to stand alone, so dive right in and enjoy the fun, sexy ride. You will find a Braden family tree included in the front matter of this book.

The best way to keep up to date with new releases, sales, and exclusive content is to sign up for my newsletter and join my fan club on Facebook, where I chat with readers daily.
www.MelissaFoster.com/news
www.Facebook.com/groups/MelissaFosterFans

About the Love in Bloom Big-Family Romance Collection

The Bradens & Montgomerys is just one of the series in the Love in Bloom big-family romance collection. Each Love in Bloom book is written to be enjoyed as a stand-alone novel or as part of the larger series, and characters from each series make appearances in future books, so you never miss an engagement, wedding, or birth. A complete list of all series titles is included at the end of this book, along with previews of upcoming publications.

Download Free First-in-Series eBooks
www.MelissaFoster.com/free-ebooks

See the Entire Love in Bloom Collection
www.MelissaFoster.com/love-bloom-series

Download Series Checklists, Family Trees, and Publication Schedules
www.MelissaFoster.com/reader-goodies

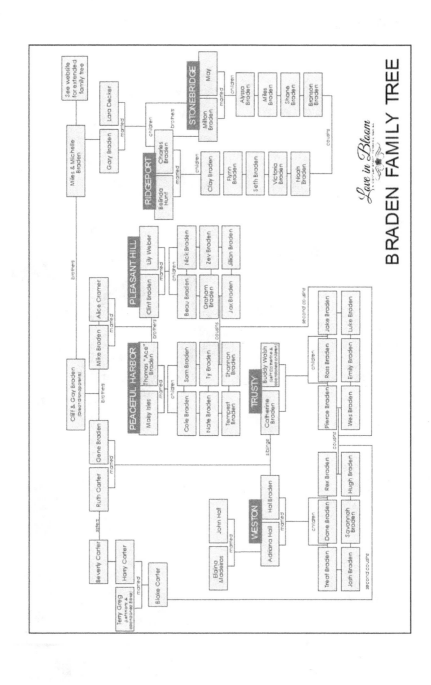

BRADEN FAMILY TREE

Chapter One

LIGHTS TWINKLED FROM the rafters and country music blared from a stage at the far end of the old barn as retired football star Dash Pennington and his old college teammate Sinclair "Sin" Vernon weaved around people dancing and mingling and children darting through the crowd with fistfuls of cookies. Women decked out in jeans and cowgirl boots eyed Dash suggestively. *Enjoy the visual buffet, ladies, because that's all you're going to get.*

Dash had been thrilled when his motivational speaking gig had been canceled. He'd jumped on the first flight out to see his buddy and had arrived in Oak Falls, Virginia, about an hour ago. This was just what he needed—a break from his crazy life and the skintight dresses and money-hungry claws of the plastic women in the circles in which he'd run for the last decade. He'd thought things would slow down after he retired from football, but he'd gone from one media circus to another with motivational speaking gigs, sponsorships, and the upcoming tour for his new bestselling book, *Capturing the Fire Within*, a guide for young men to find their paths and realize their dreams. The funny thing was, he was still trying to figure out his own path.

"This jam session is frigging awesome!" he shouted as they

walked past the stage where a group of twentysomething girls were singing with a band that looked more like a family reunion. A kid who couldn't have been older than ten or eleven was playing the violin beside a man who looked to be about sixty playing a guitar. A teenage girl was on drums, and a handful of other people were playing a variety of instruments. "How often do they do this?"

"Every few weeks." Sin raked a hand through his jet-black hair. At six foot three, two hundred and thirty pounds, he stood eye to eye with Dash. "The Jerichos invite everyone in the area to play music and dance. People bring food and catch up with neighbors. It's pretty cool."

"Kind of reminds me of home." Dash had grown up in Port Hudson, New York, which was a college town, not a rural area, but it had the same close-knit feel, and while they didn't have jam sessions, they had other community activities.

"Good old Port Hudson." Sin cocked a grin. "I need to take a trip out there soon to see how Dawn and Andi are doing, remind them what a real man looks like."

Dash narrowed his eyes in warning at the mention of his younger sisters, but it was all in good fun. They gave each other a hard time about their sisters often, but they also stepped in like protective brothers when necessary. "Speaking of sisters, did Kiki tell you she finally kicked that guy she was dating to the curb?"

"Yeah, last week. Thank God she listens to you." Kiki was Sin's younger sister. "I owe you one. Come on, let's find Amber."

"Right. *Amber.* The only woman on the planet not clamoring to get near me." Amber Montgomery owned Story Time bookstore and was hosting Dash's debut signing in a couple of weeks. She was the only bookstore owner who hadn't immediately agreed to host, which he found odd, considering how much attention his presence would bring to her store. It seemed like everyone wanted a piece of him. By the time she'd accepted, all the tour spots had been full. Dash had been curious about the holdout, and since Sin lived in the area, Dash had Amber's bookstore added as the first stop on the tour.

Sin looked at him wryly. "She's out of your league, man. But it looks like you've got plenty of fans. People around here don't usually gawk like this."

Dash glanced around as they moved through the crowd, noticing that, in addition to the women checking him out who probably had no clue who he was, guys were looking over like they recognized him, and a few cowboys were sizing him up. *Don't worry, I'm not here to take your women for a ride.* He'd learned his lesson about meaningless hookups when he was young and stupid, and he sure as hell wasn't going to screw over some random guy just to get his rocks off.

"Really? With you around, I'd think they'd be like this all the time." Dash wasn't kidding. Sin was impressive as hell on and off the football field. They'd met while attending Virginia State on football scholarships. After graduation, Dash had turned pro, and Sin had followed a coaching path, eventually becoming the athletic program director for their alma mater. A couple of years ago, Sin had taken over as the athletic director at No Limitz, the Oak Falls youth center. Dash had always admired his friend's determination to follow his heart instead of the money.

Sin gave him a don't-give-me-that-bullshit glance.

"I should've worn a cowboy hat to blend in. How about we don't mention football to your friends? Tonight I'd just like to be your friend, and when necessary, some guy who wrote a book."

"Yeah, I got that impression when you called. No problem."

As he followed Sin through the crowd, his attention caught on a beautiful brunette talking with a group of people. Her fingertips grazed the head of a golden retriever wearing a service vest. He had a fleeting curiosity about the dog, but he got caught up in watching the woman as she talked with the dark-haired guy beside her. A smile as natural and enticing as summer rain brightened her face, giving her an even sweeter girl-next-door vibe. As they neared, he realized her hair wasn't brown but more of a chestnut color, the long layers a little messy. The kind of hair that beckoned to be touched, the kind of easy smile he hadn't seen in a very long time. There was nothing overtly sexual about her simple peach sweater or dark skinny jeans tucked into scuffed brown cowgirl boots with pink designs that looked like old favorites, but he found her utterly captivating. He wanted to know who she was and what her voice sounded like. Was it as sweet as she looked? Was she? It had been a long damn time since he'd actually been *drawn* to a woman enough to want to know more about her.

The beauty shook her head, and her hair tumbled in front of one eye, giving her an alluring edge. She tucked that wayward strand behind her ear, her eyes sweeping over the crowd, colliding with Dash's, and holy hell, the air between them sizzled with a wild, frenetic energy. He couldn't look away, didn't want to, the need to meet her as real as the heat burning beneath his skin, and Sin was leading him *directly* toward her.

When they joined the group, Sin said, "The best thing about these jam sessions is seeing all the hottest ladies in Oak Falls in one place," startling the chestnut-haired beauty. She tore her gaze away from Dash, crimson spreading over her cheeks.

A familiar-looking dark-haired guy rolled his shoulders back and cleared his throat.

Sin laughed. "And the hottest *guys*. Sorry, Axsel."

"No worries. With a body like that, you're always forgiven." Axsel dragged his eyes down Dash's body. "And *hello*, gorgeous friend of Sin's."

Dash offered his hand. "Hi. I'm Dash. Where do I know you from?" In the next second, he recognized the man as Axsel Montgomery, the lead guitarist in the infamous band Inferno. "Wait, you're a rock star, right?" He started connecting the dots and wondered if Axsel was related to Amber.

"In *and* out of the bedroom," Axsel said flirtatiously, giving Dash's hand a squeeze. "And you have a great name. Short for *Dashing*, I assume?"

Dash laughed and shook his head, his eyes finding the brunette's again, causing a rush of heat to redden her neck and cheeks. She was adorably refreshing, in the sexiest of ways—a rarity in his world.

"Keep your trousers on, Axsel," Sin said. "Dash is straight, and I brought him along tonight to meet Amber, not to hook up with her brother. Dash wrote a book, and he's doing a signing with her in a couple of weeks." He motioned to the brunette, who was staring at Dash again. "Dash, *this* is Amber Montgomery. Amber, this is Dash Pennington."

It's my lucky day. "It's a pleasure to finally meet you in person, Amber." Dash held out his hand. "Shea had wonderful things to say about you." Shea Steele was his publicist. She'd told him that Amber ran the busiest bookstore in the area, and she was sweet, cautious, and definitely *not* his type. Shea couldn't have been more wrong.

The blond woman standing next to Amber, wearing about a dozen necklaces and a blouse with flowing sleeves, nudged Amber with her elbow, startling Amber out of her trance. Amber blinked repeatedly and shook Dash's hand. "Hi. It's nice to meet you."

Her hand was soft and warm, her voice as sweet as honey, and her gorgeous hazel eyes were as lost in him as his were in her. "I hear you own a great bookstore. I'm looking forward to getting to know you."

She continued shaking his hand. "I...*yeah*. Books...in the shop."

She was too damn cute.

A tall woman with thick and wild dark hair trailing over her shoulders from beneath a cowgirl hat stifled a laugh, and the blonde nudged Amber again.

"*Bookstore*, sorry," Amber said quickly, dropping his hand. Her fingers landed on the dog's head. "I own a bookstore. But you already know that. Oh my gosh. I better..." Her eyes darted around them. "Nice to meet you. I have to...do that thing. Over there." She pointed into the crowd. "Sorry. See you in the bookstore. Come, Reno."

As Amber hurried away, a thin blonde lowered her voice and said, "So much for flirting lessons."

Flirting lessons? That piqued his interest.

"You'll have to excuse my sister," the hippieish blonde said. "She's had a long day."

Dash watched Amber moving through the crowd. "No excuse necessary. She made a remarkable first impression." And he couldn't wait to see what her second impression was like.

AMBER HURRIED THROUGH the crowd until she was sure Dash couldn't see her and finally stopped to catch her breath. Reno, her seizure response dog, whined, and she petted his head. "I'm okay." She was trying to convince herself as much as Reno, who sensed her anxiety. She glanced over her shoulder to make sure she was in the clear and rose onto her tiptoes, leaning to the right to catch sight of that shockingly gorgeous muscled man talking with her mother and siblings. *Great.* They were probably joking about how flustered she'd gotten.

I have to do that thing? Ugh.

She was a total rambler when she was nervous. Even her *brother*, Axsel, had flirted better with Dash than she had. Everybody knew it, too. When her youngest sister, Brindle, and her besties, Lindsay Roberts and Trixie Jericho, found out that she'd been asked to host a book signing for Dash, they'd not only talked her into it, but they'd decided she needed flirting lessons. *A man finally caught your attention. You need him, Amb…Once you learn to use that to your advantage, he won't stand a chance,* Brindle had insisted. Lindsay had been dragging her out in the evenings, trying to teach her how to flirt. Last week she'd taken Amber to a meat market of a bar forty-five minutes away, where she hadn't known anyone. Talk about a fish out of water. Needless to say, Amber had drowned in embarrassment, while Lindsay had come home with two phone numbers and a date for the weekend. Their plan had become the bane of Amber's existence.

She was a professional bookseller and businesswoman. There would be no *flirting* with Dash Pennington, no matter what her friends thought.

She moved deeper into the crowd, wondering what Dash Pennington was doing in town so far ahead of schedule. She'd been looking forward to the jam session for weeks, and she'd been having a great time. Now she was a nervous wreck. She knew not everyone loved the nuances of small-town life, but it was the *only* life for her. Amber loved being surrounded by the people who had known her forever, had weathered the storms of her epileptic seizures, and had cheered her on when she'd opened her bookstore. *Nothing* compared to the safety of living in a community where everybody knew her name and her medical background.

Except maybe love…

Not that she had any firsthand experience with that. She reached down to pet Reno as the lights dimmed and the barn quieted. *At least I have you.*

Amber moved so she could see the stage just as a spotlight hit Nick Braden, Trixie's boyfriend, who lived in Peaceful Harbor, Maryland. Nick stood center stage in a black button-down shirt, jeans, and his ever-present cowboy hat. Trixie's four brothers were also onstage. To his left, Trace and JJ held their guitars, and to his right, Shane sat behind the drums, and Jeb was at the piano.

Even though Amber knew what was coming, she already had tears in her eyes.

Nick spoke into the microphone as he came off the stage, looking at Trixie like she was his entire world. Amber sighed, longing to be loved like that, wondering when it would be her turn. She was the middle child of seven, and in the past year and a half, three of her five sisters had gotten married, and Brindle already had an adorable little girl. None of them had even been looking for love, much less dreamed about a white wedding, a house full of babies, and building a life rich with family traditions, the way Amber had. She was happy for them, but she'd couldn't shake the niggle of jealousy.

Amber held her breath as Nick dropped to one knee in front of Trixie, professing his love for her. The barn erupted in congratulatory cheers. Tears slipped down Amber's cheeks, and she pressed her hand over her heart as Trixie and Nick kissed.

"That was pretty magical," a man said from behind her.

"It sure was," she said dreamily, wiping her eyes. "It was perfect. I want that *so* badly." She turned, and her mouth went dry at the smoldering dark eyes and panty-melting grin aimed directly at *her*.

Dash raised his brows. "So, you're a romantic."

She was *not* going to embarrass herself again. She wasn't a giddy girl, and he was...*too darn good-looking*. But he was still *just* a man. She touched Reno's head, centering herself as she straightened her spine and lifted her chin, hoping she wouldn't sound as nervous as she felt. "A *proud* romantic, thank you very much."

"A beautiful woman like you must have lots of men romancing her."

Laughter fell from her lips before she could stop it. "Hardly."

"I don't believe that." He cocked a brow. "Unless you run away from *all* men."

"I don't run away from all men." Amber had never needed thrills the way some of her sisters have, and in an effort to control her epilepsy, she avoided anything that created too much excitement or stress—like the ex-footballer turning her body into an inferno with nothing more than a little charm.

Amusement rose in his eyes. "So, you only run away from the men you Google?"

She was going to kill her gabby sisters. "I *had* to research you before I could accept the invitation to host." And she'd found out all she'd needed to know about him. He lived in New York City, had retired from football last year to pursue motivational speaking and launch the book he'd written, and from the *many* pictures she'd seen, he enjoyed partying with high-profile celebrities and gorgeous, leggy women. Mr. Tall, Dark, and Delicious was better suited for Sable, who loved a good challenge, than Amber, who had always preferred books and low-key gatherings to rowdy men and the drama that seemed to come with them.

She narrowed her eyes. "Why are you here, anyway? Shouldn't you be on your motivational speaking gig this week?" She'd seen his schedule, and between his speaking engagements and sponsorships, she wondered how he kept up. There were twenty-eight stops on his upcoming monthlong book tour, starting with her bookstore and taking him across the country with stops every other day, and some weeks there were daily signings, interviews, and television appearances. The man must run on all that testosterone billowing off him.

"So you *did* research me, quite extensively it seems." His lips quirked up, giving him a boyish expression that looked *really* nice on him.

"Of course I did. Did you think I was lying?"

"No. I had a nice chat with your sisters, their husbands, and your mother, who are all lovely, by the way, and according to them, you are honest to a fault. I respect that in a woman. So tell me, *Honest Amber*, why were you the only bookseller who didn't jump at the chance to host my signing? Did you read my book and hate it?"

"*No.* I really liked it. I mean, I don't know much about football, or the best positions, but I just skipped those parts."

He stepped closer, amusement and heat warring in his eyes. "I find hands-on experience is best when choosing positions." He leaned closer, bringing a gust of his spicy, masculine scent. "I'll be more than happy to help you discover which ones you like best."

The air rushed from her lungs. She didn't even know how to respond to that. His eyes drilled into her, and Reno whined, brushing against her leg. She petted him, trying futilely to calm herself down. He looked at Reno, and she braced herself for the questions that always came.

When his eyes met hers, they were filled with as much compassion as heat. "You okay?"

She nodded, wishing she were as sassy as her younger sisters Morgyn and Brindle, or as savvy as her older sisters, Grace and Pepper. She'd even take being snarky like Pepper's twin, Sable. Being *anyone* else would be better than her suck-at-flirting, blush-like-a-teenager self.

"It's *him*," a female voice said loudly.

Dash's eyes skirted to the right, the muscles in his jaw bunching at the sight of a group of women heading their way. Amber recognized them from Meadowside, the next town over, where her bookstore was located. Dash stepped back as they flocked to him, asking for his autograph as Sable's voice rang out from the stage, congratulating Nick and Trixie on their engagement. Sable was the lead guitarist and singer in the band Surge, and they began playing one of Trixie's favorite songs.

"Will you sign my address book?" A blonde shoved the address book at Dash and whipped a pen out of her purse.

Dash took them from her, but his eyes never left Amber as he said, "Sure. No problem. What's your name?"

"I'm going to…" Amber pointed behind her, walking backward.

"*Amber,*" Dash said authoritatively, taking paper from another woman. "Save me a dance."

Not only was he too darn aggressive, confident, and delicious for her, but women were *pawing* at him, and he looked all too comfortable with that, too. "I think your dance card is full. See you at the signing." She made a beeline for the barn doors with Reno, but even the cool October air stinging her cheeks wasn't enough to quell the heat thrumming through her.

Chapter Two

AMBER'S PHONE VIBRATED with *another* text from her mother as she turned down her parents' street early Saturday morning. Her mother had been texting all morning, asking where she was and when she'd get there. Amber was an early bird, and she tried to have breakfast with her parents often. Her phone vibrated again, and she gripped the steering wheel tighter. *Hold your horses. Sheesh.*

Her childhood home came into view. Sable's truck and Brindle's car were parked out front. Amber let out an exasperated sound. *That explains Mom's urgent texts.* She'd avoided her sisters' calls last night, not wanting to face their inquisitions about Dash Pennington. Hopefully he'd already caught a flight back to his big-city life. That man had gotten under her skin, dazzling her with his captivating charm and seductive eyes. She'd spent a fitful night replaying their brief conversation more times than she cared to admit, and when she'd finally fallen asleep, he'd bloomed before her, beckoning her into an erotic dream. He was the reason she was later than usual this morning. She'd gone for a morning walk to try to clear her thoughts of him. It hadn't helped, and even now, just thinking about him had her pulse quickening.

Reno perked up in the back seat, no doubt sensing the change in her energy.

That kind of excitement was the last thing she needed.

She parked on the street, curious about the black sedan parked behind Sable's truck. Her mother trained service dogs, and she wondered if one of the families her new pups, Merle and Patsy, was meant for was visiting.

She and Reno headed up the long driveway to the side yard to take a peek, and she gazed out at the gazebo, overcome with happy memories of the many times she and Pepper, the sister whom she was most like, had spent reading there as young girls. She touched her seizure-alert necklace, which Pepper had developed and patented when she was in graduate school, and got a little choked up, as she always did when she thought about her scientist sister being so consumed with giving Amber a sense of peace, she'd spent years coming up with a way to help her. She tucked those feelings away, remembering how Axsel would join them in the gazebo and play his guitar, while Grace, the oldest, practiced cheering in the grass or was off doing who knew what, and Morgyn and Brindle, the only two siblings who had gotten their father's fair hair and blue eyes, chatted endlessly about boys and clothes. Sable had almost never hung out with them. She was always tinkering with something in the barn, working on the old truck her father had given her at sixteen, or practicing with her band. It was no wonder she had become an auto mechanic and now owned her own shop.

Amber spotted her father heading up from the barn where her parents kept their horses and had facilities for the dogs. Merle and Patsy trotted happily beside him.

Reno's tail wagged.

"Go play," she said, releasing him from service.

He bounded across the yard, and all three fur babies tumbled in the grass. Amber waved to the fair-haired, patient and meticulous man who somehow had not only survived in a house bursting with estrogen but also always seemed to know exactly what each of his children needed. Amber had fond memories of taking secret walks with her father late at night when her sisters would sneak out to watch the Jericho brothers break horses before dawn. She had rarely joined them, and when she had, it was only because Brindle had been relentless in trying to include her in all of her rebellious fun. But most of the time, while her sisters were ogling shirtless cowboys at midnight rodeos, Amber and her father were taking moonlit walks, talking about her dreams of owning a bookstore and things she was going through with her friends. In the fall they'd collect acorns, and she'd keep them in jars with handwritten notes reminding her of the wisdom her father imparted during their walks. Her father still surprised her on occasion, showing up in the middle of the night for a talk and a stroll.

"How's my princess?" Her father leaned down and kissed her cheek, his familiar, comforting scent embracing her.

"Good. Whose car is out front?"

"Your mother and sisters invited a friend over for breakfast."

"How fun. That explains why Brindle and Sable beat me here. They never do that. Did Axsel come with Sable?" Axsel was staying with Sable while he was in town.

"No. I guess he stayed out too late last night."

"Sounds like Axsel. Which friend did they invite over?"

"Let's go see." He whistled, and the dogs bounded toward them. Her father lavished Reno with attention as Amber loved up the puppies.

She pushed to her feet. "Reno, *settle*." Her trusty pal came to her side as she stepped into the large kitchen, stopping cold at the sight of Dash sitting at their kitchen table in a white T-shirt and running shorts, bouncing Brindle's giggling seven-month-old, Emily aka Emma, on his lap.

Dash lifted his brows, flashing a victorious smile.

Butterflies swarmed in Amber's belly. Her mind scrambled to make sense of the handsome jock holding her frilly frocked niece in her parents' kitchen. There was a plate of crumbs in front of him. How long had he been there? Brindle sat to his right, and their mother sat at the head of the table, both of them beaming at Amber with a glimmer of mischief in their eyes. Sable stood with her jeans-clad hip parked against the island, arms crossed, a scrutinizing gaze locked on Dash. She'd always been Amber's most protective and untrusting sister.

"I had nothing to do with this," her father said for her ears only as he followed her in and went to sit at the table.

Amber knew darn well who had invited Dash over for breakfast, her matchmaking mother and youngest sister. Merle ran around sniffing everyone, but it seemed Dash's charm didn't just reel in women. Patsy went paws-up on his thigh, inciting more giggles from Emma and a warm feeling in Amber's chest as he kissed the pooch's head.

"Let the fun begin." Sable flipped her long dark hair over her shoulder, smirking as she bent to pet Merle.

"Hi, sweetheart. I'm so glad you're finally here." Her mother popped to her feet in her jeans and sweater and gave Amber a quick hug, whispering, *"I tried to hurry you up. He's the sweetest man."* Then, louder, as she went to make coffee, she said, "You remember Dash. When he told me about how much time he's been spending on the road with his speaking engagements, I thought he might enjoy a home-cooked breakfast."

Amber bit back her frustration and sat down across from Dash, taking in the homemade blueberry scones, pancakes, and plates of eggs, toast, and bacon on the table. "How nice," she said as Reno lay down beside her chair.

"Your mom is a wonderful cook, and I really enjoyed getting to know your family and spending time with this little one." Dash tickled Emma's belly, earning more sweet giggles.

Amber melted a little despite her frustrations. Why did guys look even hotter when they held babies?

"I looked for you last night." Dash held her gaze. "My dance card had your name written all over it, but you left me hanging."

She couldn't suppress an incredulous laugh and quickly cleared her throat to mask it. He'd probably danced with every single girl there. "Sorry. I had a few things to take care of at home."

"You did? Like what, honey?" her mother asked.

Amber put a scone on her plate, scrambling for a response. "I had a book club chat I didn't want to miss."

"That's okay, right, Emmie?" Dash made kissing noises at the baby, making him even more unfairly attractive. "I'm here until the signing." He looked up, catching Amber watching him, and his gaze warmed. "Maybe you can fit me in for a dance another time."

What was he doing there? Why was he so focused on her? She'd already agreed to host his signing.

"Look how much he loves babies, Amb," Brindle said, sounding like a salesperson instead of the high school English teacher she was.

"I wonder if he *has* any," Sable quipped.

Their mother glowered at her as she brought a pot of coffee

to the table and began filling their mugs.

"That would be a *no.*" Dash looked at Amber again. "But one day I hope to have a house full of them."

"Sounds like you and Amber have even more in common than we thought." Brindle kicked Amber under the table.

Ouch! Amber was going to wring her neck.

Sable sauntered over to the table, and their father gave her a look that said, *Please don't start something.* She'd been adept at ignoring those looks for as long as Amber could remember. "So, *Dash,* you said you were here for the next couple of weeks. Why Oak Falls? Should we expect a scorned ex to roll into town? A fiancée? Are you hiding out from a scandal?"

"*Sable,* he is our guest," their mother snapped.

"Yes, a guest we know very little about. Everyone's got dirty little secrets, especially sports figures." Sable drummed her fingers on her forearm, narrowing her eyes at him. "I'm just trying to find out what his is."

Dash didn't even flinch. "I came to see Sin. We're old college buddies."

"Ah, maybe *he's* your dirty little secret," Sable teased.

Amber stifled a laugh.

Their father turned a sterner look on Sable.

Emma reached for Brindle, and as Dash handed her to Brindle, he seemed to take Sable's taunt in stride. "Sin's a great-looking guy, but we're just friends. I am a little surprised that you'd think it would be a *dirty* secret if we were more than friends, considering your brother is gay."

"*Ohhh.* He got you, Sable," Brindle teased.

Their father nudged Amber. "I *like* this guy."

"Why are you telling *me?*" Amber bit into her scone as everyone else chuckled.

"For what it's worth"—Dash paused, and like metal to magnet, the heat of his gaze drew Amber's eyes to his—"my only dirty little secret is that I accepted this breakfast invitation with the hopes of seeing Amber again."

Amber's cheeks flamed and she tried to look away, but she was too busy trying to remember how to breathe.

"I hate to eat and run, but I've got to." Dash pushed to his feet. He was so broad and imposing, the kitchen that had always been spacious, even with all nine of their family members in it, felt far too small. "Marilynn, Cade, thank you for a delicious breakfast. Brindle, I appreciate you sharing your sweet Little Miss with me and, Sable, keep trying. You'll figure me out one of these days."

"You barely ate," Sable said.

"Running on a full stomach is never a good idea." Dash grabbed a faded Virginia State sweatshirt from the back of his chair, those dark eyes holding Amber captive. "I didn't want to miss a chance to see Amber again."

"You're welcome anytime, honey, but before you go, let me get you that body wash I told you about." Their mother hurried out of the room.

"Oh, yes, we can't forget that," Brindle exclaimed. "You'll love it. It's very…enlightening."

Amber gritted her teeth. Their aunt Roxie lived in Upstate New York and had gained quite a reputation for her homemade lotions, body washes, shampoos, and other toiletries, in which she claimed to add special love potions. Their cousins swore by them. Amber did, too, which was why when her mother hurried back into the room with a basketful of those products and Lord knew what else, she vowed to avoid Dash for the rest of his time in Oak Falls.

"Here you are, sweetheart." Their mother handed him the basket. "I threw in a few extra things I thought you might enjoy."

"That's very generous of you. Thank you. I look forward to using them."

Her mother gave a little shoulder wiggle and grinned hopefully at Amber, who was sure she had smoke coming out of her ears.

Dash turned his attention to Amber, too, causing a whole different type of smoke. "I'm tied up this afternoon helping Sin with a football clinic, but maybe you can show me around town tonight and we can make up for that dance we missed."

All eyes turned to Amber, and she felt her cheeks burn for the billionth time in the last twenty-four hours. "I...*no*...sorry. I'm really busy."

"Another time, then." Dash tossed her a sexy wink, thanked everyone again, and headed out the door.

As soon as the door closed behind him, Amber let out a breath she felt like she'd been holding for an hour, and the room erupted in chatter.

"Why did you turn him down?" Brindle practically shouted.

"He's a wonderful man," her mother said. "Persistent, too. I like that."

"He's a *sports celebrity*, Mom. They're as bad as rock stars." Sable said *sports celebrity* like it was a curse, and sat in the chair Dash had vacated.

"If anyone knows how bad rock stars are, it's you," Brindle pointed out.

"Exactly," Sable agreed.

Sable might be tough as nails, but she was built like a Playboy bunny, and she wasn't afraid to use *all* of her assets to go after what she wanted. Amber had no idea why Dash was even interested in her when Sable was more his type. She was single, gorgeous, and when she didn't have her protective sisterly claws out, she was usually up for a no-strings-attached good time.

Sable arched a brow. "Dash probably has five kids by five different women that he doesn't even know about because he's hopping from one bed to the next without ever looking back."

"Sable *Marie*," their mother chided.

"What? *Someone* has to look out for Amber," Sable snapped. "You and Brindle are practically offering the guy a dowry."

"Don't be so dramatic." Their mother sat beside Amber. "Dash is kind, and he's a gentleman, not some kind of sex-hungry pig."

Sable sat back and crossed her arms. "You're *not* this naive, Mom, which means you either have grandbaby-stars in your eyes, or you've lost your mind."

"She has not. Sin has nothing but good things to say about Dash," Brindle insisted.

Amber held her hand up. "*Stop.* I can't believe you all blind-sided me like that. I expect this kind of thing from Brindle. Every week she has the name of some guy she's found online for me to *chat* with—"

"You're welcome, even if you *never* do it." Brindle fluffed her blond hair over her shoulder with a proud grin, speaking animatedly to Emma. "Your auntie is missing out, isn't she? Your mama is a great matchmaker."

Emma giggled.

Amber rolled her eyes. "Mom, you gave him a basket of Aunt Roxie's love potions. Isn't that a little desperate? And, *Dad…?*" She gave him her most serious look. "I can't believe you fed me to the wolves."

Her father placed his hand over hers, giving it a reassuring squeeze and an apologetic gaze. "If I'd warned you, you would have gotten right back in your car and driven away, and then they'd be shouting at me."

"You did the right thing, Dad." Brindle looked at Amber as she pressed a kiss to Emma's forehead. "I don't see what the issue is. You've been drooling over Dash for weeks. He's the *only* guy you've ever gotten flustered over and the only man to pique your interest in years. He's finally here, and he's into *you*, Amber. It's your turn to have some fun."

"Our definitions of *fun* are very different." Amber popped a piece of scone into her mouth.

"Thank God for that." Sable pushed to her feet. "I have to get to the shop. I'm starting a rebuild on an engine today, and it's going to be a beast."

"Good luck, and thanks for having my back." Amber got up to hug her.

"Always." Sable narrowed her eyes. "And don't let them talk you into doing anything you don't want to do."

Brindle said, "You act like we're pimping her out for tricks."

Sable arched a brow, and they both laughed. "Love you, Brin, but give her a break, will ya?" She kissed Emma's head. "Take good care of my niece."

Sable left, and Amber sat down to finish breakfast. Her mother apologized for being pushy, Brindle urged Amber to step out of her comfort zone, and their father listened with amusement. By the time Amber finished eating, they were all joking around again. She helped her mother clean up and played with Emma, filling up on her sweetness, until it was time to head into Meadowside for work.

Amber drove through town, admiring the fall decorations

on the storefronts. She stopped at a red light just as Lindsay's grandmother, Nina, who everyone called *Nana*, and several of her friends rushed out of the Stardust Café, pointing across the street, gaping and giggling. Amber followed their gazes to the park, where Dash was doing pull-ups on a tree limb...*shirtless.* All his muscles flexed as he effortlessly pulled his beautifully sculpted body up time and time again, his skin glistening in the morning sun. A group of young mothers stopped on the sidewalk with their strollers, blocking Amber's view. She inched the car forward, catching sight of him again as he dropped to his feet and began stretching. Boy, he'd looked great in clothes, but nearly naked? Heat stirred low in her belly.

The blare of horns startled her out of her reverie. The light was green, there was a line of cars behind her, and Reno was on full alert in the back seat. *Oh geez!* She sank down in her seat, giving an apologetic wave to the people behind her as she drove away with her heart racing, images of a half-naked Dash Pennington searing into her mind.

"ARE YOU ALL set for tomorrow night's *Create Your Life* podcast?" Shea asked over the phone late Saturday afternoon.

"Yeah." The irony in his situation was not lost on him. He was motivating people to do more and follow their dreams, when he felt like he was a bystander waiting for a turn at the life he really wanted.

"Great. I rescheduled the Milas Corp's speaking engagements for next Friday. I emailed you the schedule, and we've got you on a flight to LA Thursday morning. I'll meet you for dinner, and we can go over the details for Friday."

"Jesus, Shea. You expect me to miss watching the game?"

"Seriously? Do you have *any* idea how busy I am?"

He laughed. "Why do you fall for that every time I do it to you? You know I don't care if I miss the game. It'll be good to see you." He grabbed a dark blue sweater from a drawer in Sin's guest room, where he was staying. "What time is my return flight Saturday?"

"I wanted to talk to you about that. I know you don't love celebrity events, but I really want to book you on *He Said, She Said, We Said* for Monday since you'll be in town anyway." *He Said, She Said, We Said* was an LA-based podcast featuring celebrities interviewing other celebrities. "And *The Tonight Show* had a cancellation. They can get you in Wednesday."

"Absolutely not." Dash pulled on the sweater and put the phone back to his ear, catching the tail end of what Shea was saying.

"...hottest show out there. It'll bring more attention to the book tour."

"We already have enough attention on the tour. You know I hate those kinds of podcasts where celebrities pimp each other out, and I'm not flying to New York next week." Shea had represented him for several years, and they'd become good friends in addition to business associates. Her tenacity had served him well, but she was fully aware of his plans to scale back. Not only did he need a break from the media hounds, but that morning had further piqued his interest in Amber. When she'd walked into her parents' house, her surprise had been as palpable as the electricity humming between them. He wanted as much time as possible to get to know her better. "I need this break, Shea. I'm going back to Oak Falls Saturday. End of story."

"*Fine,*" she relented. "I figured a few days with Sin was enough of a break. I had to try."

He sat on the bed to put on his shoes. "I told you I'm cutting back."

"Yes, *after* the tour. But I'm worried about you even doing that. You're a go-getter, and go-getters don't do well with too much downtime. Remember what happened to David Green." David Green had been one of the best tight ends in the country. He'd retired a few years ago and within six months had gambled away most of his savings, found his way to the bottom of too many bottles, and had tanked his reputation. Rumor had it that he was living hand to mouth in Mexico.

"I'm not a drinker or a gambler, and I keep telling you, you're wrong about me. You only think I won't do well with downtime because you've never known me to take any." But that was going to change. "I have to run, but Hawk texted earlier and said you booked him for the signing." Hawk was one of Dash's younger brothers, a sought-after photographer who did a lot of work with Shea's company.

"Your tour is a big deal, and I know how much you hate photographers. I figured if we kicked it off with Hawk instead of paparazzi, you'd be more comfortable. See? I've always got your back. I'll meet you for dinner in LA, and we can talk about some of the ideas I have for next year."

"*Shea,*" he warned.

"See you then," she said cheerily, and the line went dead.

Dash pocketed his phone, grabbed his keys, and headed out of the bedroom. Sin was in the living room, still dressed from practice in his sweats and T-shirt, looking at something on his phone.

"Hey, man. I'm heading out for a while."

Sin looked up. "I thought we'd grab dinner later, maybe meet the guys for a beer afterward."

"I'm going to see Amber. With any luck, I'll have to take a rain check on that dinner."

Sin's expression turned serious. "Listen, Dash. Things are different around here than they are in the big cities you're used to. Everyone knows everyone's business, and Amber steers clear of drama. She's the kind of girl who picks flowers in the park, brings you soup when you're sick, and sends birthday cards in the *mail*—not ecards or birthday texts. And she's a good friend. I don't want to see her get hurt. Word is spreading that you're in town. Tomorrow there'll be even more women from neighboring towns coming out to watch the big man in action and trying to catch your eye. If you want me to hook you up with someone who can show you a good time while you're here and won't bat an eyelash when you leave, I can do that. But Amber is not that girl."

There had been hordes of women watching them coach the clinic at the field today, and Dash couldn't have cared less. "What is it with everyone telling me Amber's not right for me? I told you last night that I felt something different with her and wanted to see how it played out."

"I guess I took *played out* to mean *for now*."

"You of all people know I'm not a dick. I get that Amber's a forever girl, not a for-now girl. I knew that last night when sparks flew between us and she bolted. And I'm not running, Sin. Have you ever seen me do that?"

"Can't say that I have. You're pretty careful not to get mixed up with women who are looking for more than you're willing to give."

"Exactly." Writing his book had made him feel a little like a fraud. He'd given up all of his dreams except football, and after watching teammates get engaged, married, and start families, he could no longer ignore the feeling that something important was missing from his life. He'd spent the last two years reevaluating himself and his endeavors. He was still trying to figure out exactly what was missing, but for what felt like the first time since he'd started playing football, he was following his heart instead of his head.

"Actually," Sin said, bringing his thoughts back to their conversation, "you didn't back off when I mentioned she had epilepsy, either. I'm sorry. I guess I'm more protective of her than I thought."

"I get it, and I'm glad you are. I don't know what this is yet. How can I? We've barely had two conversations, and she gets adorably embarrassed every time we talk. But I'm drawn to her in a way I've never been to anyone before. The whole time we were on the field today, all I could think about was getting cleaned up and going to see her. I haven't *ever* wanted to see a woman more than I've wanted to be on the field."

"You could have led with that." Sin's expression eased. "I had no idea you were that into her."

"This is a whole new ball game, but I appreciate you giving me the CliffsNotes on the rule book." He headed for the door. "I'll text you later about dinner."

DASH PARKED ON Main Street in Meadowside, a quaint small town much like Oak Falls, with old-fashioned streetlamps, dogwood trees lining sidewalks, and welcome signs on every door. He made his way to Amber's bookstore and found his face front and center on a poster for his signing in the front window beside a stack of his books, surrounded by fresh fall flowers, pumpkins, rustic lanterns, and other artfully displayed books. Acorns littered the floor of the display, and a miniature rocking chair with a cozy-looking blanket draped over the back held a stack of children's books beside a faux fireplace. There were fall-colored leaves in the back right corner and a nest with two birds in it, their heads touching. On the side of the display closest to the door, a tall WELCOME sign rested against a small wooden shelf littered with a mix of books and literary gifts. He pictured Amber meticulously setting up the display, placing each piece with the utmost care, until it was absolutely perfect.

A bell chimed as he entered the store, greeted by the scents of pumpkin and spice, and Amber's beautiful face as she looked over the shoulder of the petite blonde she was talking with in front of the register. A look of surprise washed away Amber's easy smile, and the blonde standing in front of her turned. He recognized Haylie Hudson as one of the mothers from the junior football clinic.

"Sorry to interrupt." Dash held Amber's gaze, enjoying the blush staining her cheeks as he strolled past several rows of bookcases. "I was—"

"Coach Dash!" Scotty, Haylie's son, ran out from behind a display, his sandy hair falling into his eyes. "Look, Mom, it's Coach Dash!"

"Hey, buddy. Good to see you." Dash glanced at Amber, but she quickly averted her eyes.

"Hello again, Dash," Haylie said flirtatiously, and held up a bag. "I just bought your book for the signing."

"Fantastic. I hope you enjoy it." Dash knelt so he was eye to eye with Scotty and noticed Amber's dog coming to her side. "You did great at practice today, buddy. Did you have fun?"

"Yes! I'm gonna be a fireman like my uncle Chet, but Mom says I can play football, too."

"That sounds like a good plan. Just be sure to keep your grades up. School is important."

"I will!" Scotty promised.

"Attaboy." Dash ruffled Scotty's hair as he pushed to his feet and noticed Amber watching him with a warmer, curious expression. It sure looked good on her.

"Can we get ice cream now?" Scotty asked his mother.

"Dinner first." Haylie glanced at Amber. "Chat soon?"

"Sure," Amber said sweetly. "Bye, Scotty."

"Bye, Miss Amber!" Scotty yelled.

Haylie slowed beside Dash as she headed for the door. "See you at the field tomorrow."

The bell chimed as they left, and his eyes met Amber's again, the air around them crackling as he closed the distance between them. "Nice place you've got here."

"Thanks." She petted her dog's head. "Are you...looking for a book?"

"I guess that would make sense, wouldn't it?" The store was warm and welcoming, with a dog bed beside the register and a nook of couches and mismatched armchairs in the rear, surrounded by more bookshelves and displays. To the right of the reading nook was the children's section, with a cylindrical bookshelf made out of stacked wooden crates, decorated with faux vines and flowers climbing up the sides. The top of the shelving unit was lined with potted plants and ivy, giving it a treelike appearance. There were dozens of small carpet mats, which he assumed were for children to sit on while they looked at books. The store wasn't just welcoming, it was homey, and Amber had obviously put her heart into every inch of it.

"But no, I'm not looking for a book. I'm looking for a bookstore owner." He stepped closer, and her breathing hitched. "Still busy tonight?"

She pressed her lips into a fine line. "Mm-hm."

"With what? Your book club?"

"Yes," she said quickly, as if he'd given her a great excuse. "That's exactly what I'm doing."

"You must have a very busy book club schedule. How about tomorrow night?"

"I can't." She continued petting her dog, but at least she wasn't looking away.

"Breakfast tomorrow?"

Her eyes widened. "Busy."

"Should I just meet you at your parents' house again?"

She laughed softly, walking over to a table displaying THIS MONTH'S PICKS, which included his book along with several others. "I can't believe you did that."

"I can't believe you won't go out with me. How about lunch tomorrow?"

She wrinkled her nose and shook her head.

"Book club again?"

She nodded, her smile widening.

"What kind of book club is it?"

"Erotic roman—" She blushed fiercely, her eyes widening. "*Romance*. It's a romance club. I mean a romance book club. We read love stories."

"You're getting more interesting by the second." He imagined sweet, bashful Amber getting all hot and bothered over erotic romance novels. "You know, *everything* is better in real life."

"*Oh my goodness,*" she whispered, looking away.

He stepped closer, so she had no choice but to look at him. "Come on, Amber. Let me take you to dinner. I'll show you a better time than you've ever had."

"That's what I'm worried about. I'm sorry, but you're just not my type."

"Are you kidding?" He couldn't temper his amused tone.

She shook her head.

"Wow, I've never been told that before." He raked a hand through his hair, trying to figure out why he wasn't her type.

"Sorry," she said sweetly.

He picked up one of his books and showed her the cover, which had a picture of him holding a football, smiling like he'd won the Super Bowl. "It's my smile, isn't it?"

"What? *No.* I love your smile." She quickly added, "I mean, it's a nice smile."

"I don't know. That doesn't sound very convincing. It's okay. I know my smile is a little ridiculous. My sisters give me grief about it all the time. They say I have a *toddler smile.*"

She laughed. "A toddler smile? What does that mean?"

"You know, the kind of smile that looks fake. It's too big." He smiled, showing her what he meant, and she laughed again. "So it *is* my smile. That's a little unfair. How can I fix that? It's the only one I've got."

"I *promise* it's not your smile," she said. "Your sisters are wrong."

"Are you *sure* I'm not your type? Because I see the way you look at me, and I can tell the difference between disinterest and desire."

"I'm sure." She lowered her eyes, her voice unsteady.

"I don't get it." And he wasn't going to give up. Not when her intrigue basically radiated off her despite her efforts to contain it. He picked up the romance novel displayed on the counter behind a ROMANCE OF THE MONTH plaque. The cover boasted a shirtless, chiseled guy looking seductively at the camera. "I can assure you that I'm *way* better at whatever the guy in this book does. You want romance? *Done.* Sexy stuff? *Never had a complaint.* Cheesy lines? *I can learn some.* You like the cover model, right? I've got great abs. Look." He lifted his sweater.

"What are you doing?" She turned around and covered her face, her dog moving with her, looking anxiously up at her. "Cover those things up! You're just too much, that's all."

He lowered his sweater and set the book down, suddenly very aware of the dog's reactions to the changes in her behavior. He was an idiot. Why didn't he recognize that earlier?

She peeked over her shoulder.

He held his hands up in surrender. "The coast is clear. No abs in sight. I'm sorry. Do I…cause problems for you? Physically, I mean? Is that why your dog is acting like that?"

She turned around, eyeing him apologetically.

"Sin explained that you have epilepsy and that the dog was a seizure response dog. I would have asked you last night instead of Sin, but you rushed away. I'm sorry. Should I have not asked him? I'm not well schooled in political correctness when it comes to things like this."

"No, it's fine. It's not like I try to hide it, and his name is Reno." She studied Dash's face for a minute. "You're just too much for me, Dash. I'm a homebody. I like book clubs and Meetings of the Female Minds, and having breakfast with my family."

"*Wait.* Meetings of the Female Minds? That sounds danger-ous." That earned him another sweet laugh.

"The meetings are *wonderful.* We have about thirty mem-bers. It's helpful to talk to women who have been married forever, or are divorced, or dating. We share advice and help each other learn how to navigate romantic relationships. Not that I have any to navigate, but one day I will."

That she would be part of that sort of group told him how important relationships were to her, and that made him even more attracted to her. "How do you know that relationship shouldn't be with me?"

She looked at him for a long moment before answering. "Because I like to be in control of my emotions, and I like my quiet life, and you're exuberant, and you have a magnetic personality that draws people to you. Women, especially, and I don't need that confusion in my life."

"That's where you're wrong. I think I'm exactly what you need."

"I…" She swallowed hard. "I need to get back to work."

He wanted to talk more, to prove to her that there was more to him than she thought, but now it was his turn to do some research. He needed to learn how to navigate Amber's world, to understand the connection between her reactions to him and Reno's reactions to her.

"I'll get out of your hair, but we're not done, sweetheart." He leaned closer and lowered his voice. "Not by a long shot."

Chapter Three

THE MORNING SUN beat down on Dash's shoulders as he ran through the park Monday morning. He'd mapped a six-mile route from Sin's place through the park and around town, and he'd run it again yesterday before the football clinic. Just as Sin had warned him, the field had been packed with female spectators, and the timing couldn't have been worse. He'd spotted Amber helping Brindle at the snack table near the field where Brindle's husband, Trace—a rancher and part-time football coach—was working with his team. Dash had waved, hoping to catch up with Amber when he got a break, but when he'd looked again, she was gone. After the clinic, he'd signed autographs, taken care of a few things with Sin, and then headed back to Sin's to finish the research on epilepsy that he'd started Saturday night after he and Sin had gone out to dinner. He'd learned that symptoms and seizures can vary greatly, but he'd gotten a much better understanding of what Amber was living with. He'd wanted to talk with her when he'd finished on Sunday, but he'd had that damn podcast, and by the time it was over, her store was closed for the night.

He wouldn't make the mistake of missing her again tonight.

He stopped to do pull-ups and noticed a group of older

women standing outside the Stardust Café watching him, just as they'd done the last two mornings. He finished his pull-ups, cranked out sixty push-ups, and jogged across the street.

The women scurried back into the café, and as he jogged by, he saw them gathered at the window. Chuckling to himself, he jogged backward and waved to them, startling them into giggles as they hurried to a table.

He pulled the door open and peered into the busy retro-style café, taking in the red vinyl stools at the counter, nearly every seat occupied, and the graffiti wall in the back. The older ladies who had been gawking at him, and several other customers were watching him from their seats. He called out, "Good morning, ladies."

"Good morning," the five women said in unison, giggling like schoolgirls.

He could see his own grandmother and her friends doing that. He loved his grandmother to the ends of the earth, but when she got together with her lady friends, they turned into whispering, giggling girls. "If you want a better view, meet me at the park tomorrow morning at eight, and wear your walking shoes."

Two of the women exchanged glances in a way that reminded him of his sisters when they were brewing up trouble. One looked like Helen Mirren, with short, layered, mostly white hair with a little blond mixed in, dressed in a smart pantsuit. Her partner in crime was an exotic-looking older woman with light brown skin, long silver locks, and almond-shaped eyes, dressed in dark pants with a bright yellow blouse and a colorful scarf knotted around her neck.

"We'd love to!" The Helen Mirren lookalike grabbed the exotic woman's sleeve, tugging her toward him. She must be the leader of the pack.

"Come in here, handsome," the exotic woman said.

He let the door close behind him, and the ladies took his arms, leading him toward the table where their friends were waiting.

"I'm Nina Bollard, but you'll call me Nana like everyone else does," the Helen lookalike said. "And this is Hellie Camden."

"That's me," the exotic woman chimed in.

Nana pointed around the table as she introduced her other friends. "We're the eyes and ears of Oak Falls, and we have gotten an earful about you, young man."

"And an eyeful," Hellie added, and all the ladies laughed.

"Sit down, darlin'." Nana pushed him into a chair. "We've got a few questions for you."

Oh yeah, they reminded him of his grandmother, all right. "Eyes and ears of Oak Falls, huh?"

"We've got the lowdown on everyone," Hellie said. "Are you looking for a date? We know all the single ladies."

"I can get my own dates, but thank you."

The women exchanged another glance, and Nana whispered, "If you swing the other way, Axsel is leaving town soon, but we could hook you up with him *now*. He's sweet, sexy, and you *know* he's alpha in the bedroom."

One of the ladies let out a little *roar*.

Dash laughed. "I didn't realize I'd come to such a matchmaking town. But it's not Axsel I'm interested in. What can you tell me about Amber Montgomery?"

"So, the rumors are true. You *are* shooting for the stars," Hellie said.

Nana patted his arm. "We don't give up secrets easily, especially about our Amber. She's everyone's sweetheart, and it's going to take a *very* special man to earn her heart. What makes you think you've got what it takes?"

He cocked a grin. "How much time do you have?"

AMBER BOBBED HER hips to the beat of "Dancing on My Own" by Robyn in her office Monday evening as she grabbed the basket with her stash of greeting cards off a shelf. It was almost closing time, and she had a busy night of writing cards and packing books planned. Her phone vibrated in her pocket.

She set the basket on the desk and pulled opened a group text from Brindle to Amber, Lindsay, and Trixie. A picture of Dash holding baby Emma popped up, and Amber's pulse quickened. Brindle must have taken the picture yesterday at the football field because he was wearing the same gray sweatpants and black T-shirt he'd had on, and Emma was wearing the same leggings and DADDY'S GIRL sweatshirt. Dash looked even better than she'd remembered. Even better than he had in her naughty dreams last night. His deep voice whispered through her mind. *We're not done, sweetheart. Not by a long shot.* In her dream, that same deep tenor had whispered about the dirty things they were doing.

Her cheeks heated with the memory, and she clutched the phone to her chest, looking out the glass partition into the store, as if Phoenix Majors, one of her part-time employees, could hear her thoughts.

She peeked at the picture again, and another message from Brindle popped up. *Amber, that could be your baby in your man's arms! He came looking for you after you left yesterday.*

A little thrill darted through her. She loved helping Brindle with snacks during Trace's practices, and she'd thought she could get a peek at Dash without him noticing she was there, but he'd caught her gawking at him, like all the other women had been, and she'd hightailed it out of there.

Amber thumbed out a response. *I'm not into harems.*

A text from Lindsay rolled in. *He can be my baby daddy.* She added a heart-eyed emoji. Another message popped up from Brindle with a peach emoji, immediately followed by a picture of Dash taken from the back, huddled with the boys he was coaching. Amber peeked through the glass into the store again, then quickly saved the picture to her Hidden Dreams folder on her phone. A girl had to have some inspiration.

Another message from Brindle popped up. *Amber, did he come see you again?* Amber wasn't about to admit that she'd spent far too much time looking out the front window, hoping he would come by and then immediately hoping he wouldn't. Why did *he*, of all people, have to have that effect on her? She thumbed out, *No. I told you I sent him away. What guy in his right mind would come back after that?*

Her phone vibrated with a text from Trixie. *Nick said you should stay away from him because he's a player. I told him to look in the mirror. Old dogs CAN change. I say go for it!*

Another picture of Dash popped up from Brindle, also taken yesterday. He stood with his hands on his hips, his movie-star smile radiating off the screen. She really liked his smile. It wasn't toddlerish at all. It was gorgeous, the kind of smile that said he had nothing to hide. Her gaze drifted lower, to the bulge in his sweatpants. *You couldn't hide that even if you wanted to.* She bit her lower lip. It'd been a long time since she'd been with a man. She didn't usually think about sex, but from the moment she'd first seen pictures of Dash online, she hadn't been able to stop thinking about him. He practically oozed testosterone, and after the things he'd said yesterday, she was sure he knew exactly what he was doing between the sheets. Not that she had the experience to match. Well, that wasn't exactly true. She had loads of sexy fictional experience, thanks to her book club, and one day, with the right man, maybe she'd get to try out those skills.

She glanced over her shoulder again and shamelessly saved the picture.

An eggplant emoji and heart-eyed emoji popped up from Lindsay, followed by *Dash has quite a fan club. I heard several ladies went walking with him this morning. Several SINGLE ladies.*

Better move fast, Amber, Trixie texted. *Lots of competition!*

Another message from Brindle rolled in. *Mom and Mrs. Jericho were there, too! Amber is probably the ONLY female around who doesn't want him.*

Amber groaned, thumbing out, *I didn't say I don't WANT him. I said he's too much man for me. You know I like low-key guys.*

"That's the last of the boxes."

Amber startled and spun around at the sound of Phoenix's voice.

Phoenix's eyes widened. "*Whoa.* If I didn't know better, I'd think I caught you sexting. Are you okay? Your face is really red."

"What? *Yes.* Fine. I'm just hot." She shoved her phone into her pocket, feeling it vibrate with more messages as she grabbed the basket and headed out of her office with Reno on her heels.

"If you say so." Phoenix was a freshman at the local community college, studying music and English. She looked rebellious with her dark eyeliner, short black hair highlighted with streaks of vibrant blue, and penchant for black jeans, rock-and-roll T-shirts, and black leather lace-up boots. But she was sweet, smart, and responsible, and Amber felt lucky to have her helping at the store.

Amber set the basket on the coffee table by the couches, hoping Phoenix would let it go. Thankfully, her phone had finally stopped vibrating. She needed to focus on the work she had to do tonight, not get anxious over Dash Pennington's hotness.

Reno lay down by the couch as Amber surveyed the boxes of books she needed to package for mailing. "Thanks for bringing these out from the stockroom."

"No problem. I put the labels and bookmarks on the supply cart. Thanks for letting me leave a little early. Are you sure you don't want me to come back after practice and help you get them ready to ship?"

"No, thanks. You know I love doing this."

"Yeah, you're weird like that," Phoenix teased. "See you tomorrow at Lyrics and Lattes?"

"I'll be there." Lyrics and Lattes was a coffeehouse in Wishing Creek, a neighboring town. Phoenix was a talented musician. She played several instruments and had recently begun playing at local cafés and pubs to make extra money. It had been a big step for her to play in public, and Amber tried to go to support her every chance she got.

After Phoenix left, Amber began looking through the basket of greeting cards, choosing a few to mail out to customers for birthdays and anniversaries, as she did every month. She heard the bell chime over the front door as she plucked out another card.

"We're closing in ten minut—" She turned, her words lost at the sight of Dash striding toward her in faded jeans and a gray sweater.

"Then my timing is perfect." He flashed that knee-weakening grin. "How's it going, beautiful?"

Chapter Four

AMBER COULDN'T BELIEVE he'd come back, but she refused to let him fluster her again. "Hi, I...What are you doing here?" The question came out too breathy. So much for not being flustered.

"You didn't think you could get rid of me that easily, did you?"

"I wasn't trying to get rid of you. I was just trying to keep you from wasting your time."

He stepped closer, his masculine scent taunting her. "Spending time with you is anything but a waste."

Oh boy, there went those butterflies in her belly again. He was too charming, and his eyes were beginning to look too honest, which meant she was losing her ability to think rationally. She needed to nip this in the bud. "Dash, I...We..."

"You're cute when you're flustered."

"I'm not flustered," she said too fast.

His eyes twinkled with a tease. "Sorry. *Nervous.*"

"You must think an awful lot about yourself if you think you make me nervous."

He arched a brow.

She laughed softly. "*Okay*, you make me nervous. Is that

such a big deal?"

"Yeah, it is to me. I like that you look at me like you want me, but you blush when I get too close."

"You're not helping."

"*You're* a big deal, Amber." He held up a beautiful bouquet, which he must have had behind his back. It was bursting with all of her favorite fall flowers—orange spray roses and gerberas, white alstroemeria, golden craspedia, miniature maroon carnations, grevillea, and a touch of blue thistle.

"Dash...?" Her eyes flicked up to his as he handed her the vase.

"Have dinner with me tonight. Let me put your fictional heroes to shame."

Yes, please. Oh no. What am I thinking? No. There would be *no* hero shaming. "Thank you for the flowers. They're lovely. *Gorgeous.* But I can't have dinner with you. I really am busy tonight."

"I was hoping for the swoony reaction you had the other night when your friends got engaged."

She winced. "I'm sorry. I don't mean to sound ungrateful. I really *do* love the flowers. They're all my favorites."

"I'm only teasing." His expression turned serious. "Actually, I'm not teasing. One day I hope to earn that dreamy-eyed reaction, because it was really something. So, tell me, my sweet romantic at heart, what's your excuse tonight? Book club again?"

"Yes, but for real this time." She waved in the direction of the boxes. "I have to package three hundred books so I can mail them tomorrow. They really *are* for the online book club I'm a member of. I give discounts to other members, and every month I get between three and four hundred orders."

"And you don't have staff that can do this for you?"

"I have a few part-timers, but I like doing it. I write notes to the members and send them bookmarks or other swag."

"A personal touch. Now, that's something I can get behind."

The heat in his eyes had her picturing all sorts of *personal touches.*

"I'll help you. Let's see what we're packaging." He grabbed a book from the box, sat his big body down on the couch, and kicked his feet up on the coffee table. Reno's head popped up as Dash opened the book and his eyes moved down the page. "Oh, *baby.* I see why you like to read these." His voice turned seductive. "'He guided her down to her knees...'"

His every word made her heart pound harder, her body burn hotter.

"'...holding her there with a smoldering gaze as she wrapped her fingers around his raging—'"

"*Stop!*" She snagged the book from his hands. "We're not reading! We're *packing.*"

"I'm just checking out the merchandise. That's my copy, by the way." He pushed to his feet and whipped out his wallet, dropping a twenty on the coffee table. "Hand it over, secret sexy reader."

She tried to glower at him, but she couldn't stop grinning. *Secret sexy reader?* As embarrassing as it was, that sounded cute. She kind of liked it.

"I can see why you like reading that stuff. That was pretty hot. Not nearly as hot as you deserve, but it's not bad." He took the book and set it on an end table.

"Oh, please." She put her hand on her hip. "You *know* you're not going to read it."

He stepped closer, so close she had to look up to see his face. His square chin was peppered with scruff, dark eyes drilling into hers. If she went up on her toes, she could press her lips to his as she'd done in her dreams. That single kiss had led to all of the other delicious things they'd done. Her loneliest parts clenched in anticipation.

As if Dash could feel the heat sizzling inside her, the edges of his lips quirked up. "I'll give you my rewrites when I'm done, and you can tell me who wrote it better."

Her mind sped through dirty scenes she'd read, instantly replacing the hero with him, causing her cheeks to burn.

"Penny for your thoughts," he said huskily, jarring her brain into gear.

She forced herself to step back, putting space between them. "Packing books. We're packing books."

He motioned toward the card she'd forgotten she was holding. "Is that card for me?"

"*What?* No. Sorry. It's for one of my customers, Hellie Camden. Her husband died a long time ago, and her wedding anniversary is next week. I send a card every year to brighten her day."

"Right, she spends the evening at the gazebo in Hemlock Park, where he proposed to her when she was twenty."

"How do you know that?" As soon as she said it, she remembered what Lindsay had texted about his morning *fan club*.

"I had breakfast with Hellie, Nana, and the rest of the dirty grandmas this morning."

"You had *breakfast* with them?" Was the whole town fawning all over him?

"I was running by the café when they invited me to join them. They're clever. They reel you in like they're offering you milk and cookies and a friendly chat, and then you find out they're plying you with whiskey and rum cake, and before you know it, you've told them your whole life story."

"That's them. I guess your fan club is bigger than I thought." She opened a box and put a stack of books on the table.

"My fan club?" He opened another box and began taking out books.

"I heard about the ladies who walked with you this morning, but you probably have gaggles of women chasing after you in every town you visit, and it's none of my business anyway." She pulled the supply cart over, and her eyes caught on the vase the flowers he'd brought her were in. It was full of acorns. Her heart skipped, and "Acorns," slipped out.

"I know it's probably not what you're used to. But my grandmother fills all of her vases with them. She says they're nature's magic because those tiny nuts transform into mighty oaks. Everything she says comes back to some sort of acorn metaphor."

Amber must have looked as dumbfounded as she felt, because he said, "It's silly, I know. But at least they're pretty."

"No, it's not silly. Did my mom tell you I have a thing for acorns?"

"No. She doesn't even know I collected them after our walk this morning."

Her throat thickened. "You *collected* them?"

"Yeah. In the woods by the creek. Why? A grown man can't gather acorns?" He shook his head. "*Damn.* I was aiming for romance, and you just shot me down."

"I'm not shooting you down. It *is* romantic. I'm just a little blown away. When we were young, some of my sisters—Brindle and Morgyn, mostly, and whoever they could swindle into going with them—would sneak out to watch Trixie's brothers break horses or have rodeos at crazy hours, like midnight or four in the morning. I never liked going, and my dad would come get me after they snuck out, and we'd go on walks, just the two of us in the moonlight. If I was sad, he'd say, 'Let's talk it out and set those bad thoughts free.' It always helped. In the fall, we collected acorns. If you look through the window to my office, you'll see a jar of them on the shelf behind my desk."

She pointed to the window, and he looked over, a smile curving his lips.

"I would write down snippets of wisdom he'd share, fold them up and put them in the jars with the acorns. He never called them nature's magic, but he'd say that life was like an acorn, and we needed to look deeper to find the seeds of wonderful things yet to come. I've never heard anyone else talk about acorns like that. That's why I thought my mom had said something."

"She had a lot to say, as did Nana and her tribe, but nobody gave away your secrets. And trust me, I tried like mad to get them."

She laughed softly and lowered her eyes. He was so forward and sure of himself, and she liked it. But why was he interested in *her* of all people? If Morgyn were there, her most ethereal and creative sister, who believed everything was guided by the universe and made a career out of repurposing and breathing life into inanimate objects, she'd say fate was dangling Mr. Delicious in front of Amber. But Amber knew better than to get tangled up with a guy who would be marching out of town before too long, probably with a trail of women following him like the Pied Piper.

"Are you sure you want to stick around and help me pack up books? You must have better things to do."

He held her gaze. "There's no place else I'd rather be."

The honesty in his eyes tugged at something deep inside her. She told herself not to believe it, that he was probably used to charming women's panties off and most likely saw her as a challenge. But it felt so real, she was having trouble convincing herself otherwise.

"Let's get started," he suggested. "I'll answer your questions about my fan club and anything else you want to know, and you can tell me all about yourself."

"I hate to disappoint you, but there's not much to tell."

"How about you let me be the judge of that? Come on, sexy reader." He rubbed his hands together, looking at the boxes. "Where do we start?"

She explained the process, expecting him to back out, but he remained on the couch, sitting beside her as she wrote notes to the members, inserted a bookmark, and wrapped each book in tissue paper, and then Dash put them in envelopes with the appropriate labels.

"So, what do you want to know?" He affixed a label. "How the walking group came about?"

"No, it's okay. I don't really want to hear about women chasing after you. I've seen enough of it."

"It's not like that."

She gave him a deadpan look.

"Okay, maybe it is like that for some women, but that has nothing to do with me. I'm not out there looking for dates." He leaned against her side with that charming smile. "I'm here looking at you, and trust me, sweetheart, there's no better view."

"I think you have those cheesy lines down pat." She picked up another note card, shaking her head.

"Mental note: *Sexy reader is not into cheese.* How about whipped cream?" He arched a brow.

She tried to hide how much she liked his ridiculous lines despite their cheesiness.

"I got to hang out with your mom again this morning."

"My sister told me. It's a little weird that she went walking with you. She rides horses and trains service dogs. She never goes out specifically to exercise like that."

"It was good for her to get out and talk with the other ladies. She had fun. We all did, and we didn't just walk."

She looked up from the note she was writing. "I'm afraid to ask what else you did."

"You really do have a dirty mind."

"I didn't mean it *that* way."

"Sure you did, but don't worry. I won't tell anyone." He chuckled. "We did calisthenics. Vertical, not *horizontal.*"

Ohmygosh.

"Talk about hysterical. The way those ladies bantered, I felt like I was in a frat house. And at the café, when I suggested that Nana and her friends join me tomorrow at the park, I asked them what they wanted to gain from exercising, and Nana said 'More stamina in the bedroom.' I'm all for a healthy sexual appetite, but I didn't need to know that."

"Nana is shameless." *Kind of like you.*

"I really like her. She told me about how she celebrates every little thing and that she's hoping to get her granddaughter Sophie and Sophie's husband, Brett, to move back to the area full time so she can see more of her great-granddaughter." Sophie was Lindsay's sister. She and Brett split their time between New York and Oak Falls. "I know Brett Bad and his family, by the way."

"You do?" She wasn't surprised that Nana had overshared, but she was surprised that he knew Sophie and Brett.

"My agent, Tiffany, is married to Brett's brother Dylan. I'm going to see them in a few weeks at a fundraiser for the Ronald McDonald House that the Bad family hosts. My buddies and I have been going for the past couple of years. We give to the cause, of course, but we also sign memorabilia for them to auction off. Every little bit helps."

She liked knowing that about him. "It broke my heart when Brett told us they'd lost their sister to leukemia when she was young."

"It's very sad. They honor her at the fundraiser. Speaking of fundraising, your mom said it costs thousands of dollars to train service dogs. I didn't realize that the families who get the dogs do fundraising to cover those costs."

"It's always been part of her program, although she's a softie. She's given dogs to people who didn't raise enough money to cover the training."

"She didn't tell me that. She's pretty amazing. I like getting to know her. She was careful not to talk about you in the group, but she did admit she's thrilled that Grace moved back home. She showed me a picture of Pepper, too. She looks more like you than Sable. She said she wants more grandbabies, and she's worried that your sister Pepper will miss out on the best things in life because she works so hard."

"She told you that about Pepper?"

"Yeah. You'd be surprised how people open up when they exercise with a group. It's like therapy. That's how I used to get my brothers and sisters to open up when we were kids."

"Really? How many siblings do you have?"

"Two brothers and two sisters. Breakfast with your family reminded me of being with them. We're always giving each other a hard time, but they're my heart and soul. I practically raised them after our father left."

His feelings for his siblings warmed her, but she sensed uneasiness when he mentioned his father. "Your parents are divorced?"

He nodded. "My father worked for my grandfather's real estate development company and had an affair with his secretary. When my grandfather found out, he fired him. My father took off with her shortly after. They moved to Florida, and I think a few years later they moved out West. We never hear from him."

"He just left and never looked back? That's awful."

He wrung his hands together. "He got in touch once, five or six years ago. He got into some shady business deals and needed money to get himself out of a hole."

"And he had the nerve to come to *you*? That's such a callous, hurtful thing to do. What did you do?"

"It did hurt, a lot more than I'd expected. For years I'd had a running dialogue in my head about what I'd say if I ever saw him again. I thought I'd make him apologize to my mom and my siblings, and I'd give him a piece of my mind. But when he was standing in front of me, he didn't even look like the same guy who had left us. I remembered him as confident and powerful, always dressed in a suit, reminding us how important it was to work hard and be a *man*. But he just looked *diminished*. I don't know if it was because I'd lost all respect for him or because life had beaten him down."

"It was probably both."

"Probably. Anyway, I didn't say the things I had planned. I didn't want anything from him other than his word that he'd never contact me or anyone in our family again. I gave him the money he asked for and said that was it. He wasn't getting another penny. It's shameful to have to pay off your father, but better me than anyone else."

Her heart broke for him. "I'm sorry. I can't imagine how awful that must have been. Not just the money part, but his leaving in the first place."

"It sucked, but we got through it, and we're all stronger because of it. When I look back now, as an adult, I'm blown away by how strong my mom was. She never let us see her cry, but I'd hear her late at night in her bedroom." His brows knitted. "She didn't just lose a husband—her whole life changed. She was a stay-at-home mom, and after he left, she had to go back to work, so I stepped in to take care of my brothers and sisters. We were all falling apart. I could feel my brothers and sisters pulling away, retreating into their own heads, and all I wanted was to hold us together. I would build obstacle courses in the backyard and drag them outside for competitions. That's when I discovered that group exercise was like therapy. They hated it at times, but I didn't care. I had a bigger goal, and it was the most important one I'd ever had. I'd have done anything to keep from losing them."

Amber felt like a veil was lifting and she was seeing him through clearer eyes. "You learned from your mom how to push past your own grief to help them. That says a lot about both of you."

"Any big brother would have done it."

"I don't think that's true. Are you the oldest?"

"Yeah. Harrison is two years younger than me. We call him

Hawk. He's a pretty well-known photographer. You'll meet him at the signing. He's coming to take pictures."

"It's nice that he's handling your kickoff. I'm looking forward to meeting him."

"Good, because I thought we could all go to dinner afterward." He must have seen hesitation in her expression, because he said, "Purely business, to thank you for hosting and to celebrate my first signing."

"A professional dinner. Okay, I can do that." *Even if my nerves are already catching fire.* "Why do you call your brother Hawk?"

"Because ever since he was a kid, he's looked at the world through the lens of a camera, and he always captures the most interesting views. We could be looking at the same thing, and what I see is never as striking as what he captures on film."

"Tell me about your other brother and sisters."

"Let's see. Damon is two years younger than Hawk. He tried my mom's patience every step of the way after our father left, starting fights, skipping school. I've cleaned up more of his messes than I care to remember. But he got through it, and he's a great guy. He still has a massive chip on his shoulder, but he channels his energy in healthier ways now. He recently took over our grandfather's business, and he's pushing it in a whole new direction. And then there are my sisters, Dawn and Andi." His expression warmed. "They're seven and eight years younger than me. Dawn is the host of *Just Desserts*, which is a baking show."

"You're kidding. I *love* that show. She's amazing. I tried to make the tiramisu crepe cake she made once because it looked delicious, and tiramisu is my guilty pleasure."

"Tiramisu at your service. It's nice to meet you." He held

out his hand, as if to shake hers.

She shook her head, but she was sure her amusement shone like neon lights in her eyes.

"Can't blame a guy for wanting to be your guilty pleasure."

Ohmygod. This guy… "You wouldn't say that if you saw the mess I made. I have no idea how your sister did it. There were *twenty-five* paper-thin crepe layers, and mine came out awful. She could probably make anything look easy. She's so vivacious, she makes you feel like you're right in the kitchen with her."

"That's Dawn. She can win over any audience."

"Sounds like she got her big brother's genes," she teased.

He brushed his leg against hers, and those butterflies swarmed again. "The only audience I want to win over is you, sexy reader."

"Stop making me blush and tell me about your other sister."

"But making you blush is so much fun." He laughed at her deadpan look. "You want to know about Andi? She's a lot like you. She's sweet and careful, and the smartest of all of us."

"I'll own up to sweet and careful, at least relative to Brindle and Sable. But the smartest in our family is definitely Pepper."

"We'll see about that. Andi is working on her PhD in marine biology, and she's a research assistant to Sutton Steele, the host of—"

"The *Discovery Hour* show," Amber exclaimed. "I know Sutton. I went to Boyer University in Port Hudson, and she was one of my LWW sorority sisters. The *Discovery Hour* is an LWW show. Wait, so is *Just Desserts*. It's on their lifestyle channel. But your sisters must not have been part of the LWW sisterhood, or I would probably know them." Everyone in Port Hudson knew of the Ladies Who Write (LWW), which wasn't a sorority, but more of a sisterhood, founded by a group of women who had bonded over their love of writing. They'd rented a house together, and later, three of the founding members had gone on to start LWW Enterprises, a multimedia corporation with offices across the United States.

"They weren't. I can't believe you went to Boyer." His eyes lit up. "I grew up in Port Hudson. My mom worked in the library for years before becoming a professor."

"I practically lived in the library. Maybe I knew her. What's her name?"

"Robin. She's tall, blond, and a *talker*."

"I think I knew her. This is crazy. If she's the Robin I knew, she was taking classes and wanted to be an English teacher. I remember wondering how anyone could work full time, go to school, and raise a family without losing their mind. She told me she had a family, but we didn't talk specifics. I didn't even know her last name. We talked about books and our futures, and LWW. She was very mom-like, and supportive of my dream of opening a bookstore."

"That's her. She was determined, and she instilled that same determination in each of us. She got her master's a few years ago, and now she teaches at Boyer."

"Wow, what a coincidence. I'm sure she doesn't remember me, but I'm so happy for her. Would you mind telling her that?"

"I'll do better than that. You can tell her yourself." He reached for his phone.

"*No.* Don't do that. She probably doesn't remember me, and then it would be awkward."

"Okay, but she's got a memory like an elephant. She'll be happy for you, too, making your mark on the world."

"It's hardly a mark on the world. Grace was a playwright in

New York, and she adapted our friend's novel into a screenplay. She and her husband are flying out to LA tomorrow for the filming of the movie that millions of people will see, and Axsel is a rock star with zillions of fans. He's leaving for an international tour tomorrow, and Pepper is changing people's lives with cutting-edge medical equipment. *They're* making marks on the world. I just own a little bookstore in my tiny hometown."

His brow furrowed. "What is it with you brushing off compliments?"

"I'm not brushing them off." She picked up a note card, focusing on that instead of the intensity of his stare. "I'm a realist. I know my store isn't that impressive to anyone but me."

"As I said before, let me be the judge of that."

Something in his voice brought her eyes to his, and she realized how much she liked the kind, funny, family-oriented man she was getting to know. In the next breath, his gaze turned darker, hotter, drawing her in and making her want to move closer. He was casting a spell, hypnotizing her with his charms. She forced herself to remain still, because she had a feeling that once she gave in to it, there would be no turning back.

DASH HAD THOUGHT he'd wanted to earn that swoony look he'd seen at the jam session. But seeing her fight her desire was quickly moving to the top of his Must Have More list. He'd never had a damn list about a woman before, but he'd never met anyone like Amber, and he wanted to learn everything there was to know about her.

"Tell me about you and your dirty bookstore. When you were younger, were you a hide-under-the-covers-with-a-flashlight-reading-naughty-books type of girl?" He leaned in. "Or did you discover erotic romance through real life with some lucky guy first, and move on to books later? Because if it's the latter, I sure as hell wish I had been that guy."

She swallowed hard, her eyes widening innocently.

It was just the reaction he'd been hoping for, but it backfired. Images of her in erotic positions assailed him. He wanted to feel her supple body beneath him, touch her soft skin, taste her arousal, and hear her cry out his name in the throes of passion. His cock hardened with the thoughts, and he struggled against the urge to pull her into his arms and kiss her until they both got carried away and fulfilled *all* their dirty fantasies.

Amber drew her shoulders back, tilting her head with a surprisingly sassy expression, stirring him from his reverie. "It was both. I used to steal my mother's romance novels and hide under my covers to read them, all in preparation for my wild college days. And they were *wild*," she said seductively. "Filled with orgies, bondage, and taboo sexual encounters with my professors."

Holy. Hell. "Really?" His voice came out rough with desire.

"No, you fool! Geez. Does *every* guy think women only care about sex?" She scribbled a note on the card she was holding and tucked it into a book.

"I didn't say that. I was just joking around. Well, except for the part about being your first hands-on erotic experience. I would have liked to have been that guy."

"What makes you think I *have* experience with that?" She was still smiling as she slipped a bookmark into the book and grabbed some tissue paper.

He liked seeing this playful side of her. "I just assumed that a beautiful, well-read woman like you would have already explored those areas."

"How about you get those packages ready instead of assuming?" She handed him the book.

As he put it in an envelope, he couldn't resist asking, "Does that mean I still have a shot at being the guy to show you the *ropes*?"

Amusement rose in her eyes.

"Yes, that pun was intended."

She leaned against *him* this time, with a glorious, seemingly carefree laugh.

"A'right, sexy reader, time to spill. Have you always wanted to own a dirty bookstore?"

"A bookstore? *Yes.* Dirty? *No.* That came much later."

"We'll circle back to the dirty part. But first, why books? Have you always been a big reader?"

She finished the note she was writing, and as she tucked it into a book, she said, "I fell in love with books in elementary school. At first it was because they were safe. But I quickly fell in love with the escape they brought."

"What do you mean by *safe*?"

She met his gaze. "They didn't get me too excited or make me feel out of control."

Ah, it was all making sense now. "Because of having epilepsy?"

She nodded.

"How old were you when you were diagnosed?" The second he asked, he realized he might be overstepping. "We don't have to talk about that if you'd rather not."

"I don't mind. It's part of who I am. I had my first seizure when I was eight. I was climbing the jungle gym when it hit, and I fell off. I was diagnosed shortly after."

"That must have been terrifying." He hated the idea of her suffering at all, much less as a little girl.

"I didn't remember what happened, or understand what was going on, really. Not at first. But I could see how much it had frightened my parents and everyone else. Everyone treated me differently after that."

He put his hand on hers, wanting to take her look of discomfort away. "I'm sure they were just worried about you."

"Some, yes, but it was like everyone was living in fear of my next seizure. It took a while to get the medication right, and I had another seizure on the bus, which was embarrassing. After that, a lot of kids kept their distance, and that hurt. Now I understand that they were freaked out by the seizure. It scared them because they didn't know what to do or how to help me, and I think they were worried that it might be contagious. Sable gave those kids a hard time."

"She's a tough cookie. She's protective because she loves you. I get that. I'm the same way with my siblings."

"I know. Don't take this wrong, because I *love* Sable, and I love that she has always, unfalteringly, taken care of all of us. But all I wanted was to prove that I was no different from anyone else, and that's hard when your older sister is scaring everyone off."

"Did you ever tell her that?"

"Eventually, but that made her feel bad, and I hated that, too." She gave a half-hearted shrug. "Anyway, I stopped doing things that could overexcite my body, and reading became my greatest escape. Eventually they figured out my meds, and I went years without a seizure. Then I had one when I was thirteen, and all that fear came rushing back."

"Thirteen? Puberty?"

She blushed, nodded.

"Sorry. I read up on epilepsy after Sin told me you had it, and that seems to be a common time for changes."

Disbelief rose in her eyes. "You read up on it?"

"Of course. I wanted to understand what you were dealing with."

"That was nice of you." She held his gaze for a moment, then focused on the note she was holding as she said, "Puberty is a common time for changes, which made it even more embarrassing. No girl wants people to know when her body is going through those changes, but there was no hiding it for me until they got my medications worked out again."

"That must have sucked. Young guys can be jerks anyway."

"None of them were jerks to me. They were nice, just uninterested. I don't blame them. Being a teenager is hard enough—why add a girlfriend with issues on top of it?"

"Because she's the hottest girl in school, and it's just a medical condition, not something to be afraid of."

"I think teenage Dash might have felt differently about that."

"No way. Teenage Dash was super cool. You would have been into him."

"If you say so." She laughed softly.

He really liked that quiet laugh and the way it lit up her eyes, which he noticed were more green than brown and had flecks of gold.

"What were we talking about before I told you my life story? Oh yeah, the bookstore." She handed him another book to put into a package. "I've pretty much always wanted to be surrounded by the magical world of books, and owning a bookstore became my dream. When I graduated from college, I took out a loan, which my parents cosigned for, and opened this store. I've never looked back."

"That, sexy reader, is brave and impressive."

"Says the football star, author, *and* motivational speaker."

"So, I'm a bit of an overachiever."

"Just a bit."

"And you're still trying to keep from getting overly excited," he said carefully. "Like pushing me away because I'm *too much*."

"You're a lot of man."

He liked her honesty. "And you're a lot of woman."

She rolled her eyes. "A little more packaging, a little less flirting."

"Where's the fun in that?"

They talked and joked around as they made their way through the boxes. Two hours passed in the blink of an eye. When Reno came over to check Dash out, he asked if it was okay to pet him.

"Yeah, please do."

As he petted Reno, he said, "Is he always on duty?"

"Sort of. He's always there for me, but I don't make him wear the vest unless we're going someplace where people need to be aware and he needs to be hypervigilant. He knows if he has the vest on, he can't play. But at times like this, it's fine."

"How long have you had him?"

"Four years."

"He's a sweet dog." He scratched Reno's neck with both hands, and Reno licked his chin.

"He's my little love nugget. My buddy, my confidence builder and smile maker."

"Lucky dog. Does he sense seizures?"

"I'm the lucky one." She petted Reno. "Some people say dogs can sense seizures, and others say they can't, or only a certain percentage of dogs can. I haven't had any seizures since I got Reno, so I don't really know. But he definitely senses when I'm nervous or excited, and stays closer to me."

"And what is he trained to do if you have a seizure?"

"He's trained to try to break my fall and keep a clear space around me so I don't hurt myself." She touched her necklace, a silver circle with a black button in the middle about the size of a silver dollar. He realized she'd been wearing it every time he'd seen her. "This is a seizure-alert necklace. Pepper developed it when she was in graduate school, and it's now sold all over the country. Reno is trained to push this button if I have a seizure. It has an internal GPS, and it alerts my family and emergency services to my location."

"That's incredible that your sister developed it, and it says a lot about how much you must mean to her."

Her expression turned thoughtful. "I get choked up thinking about it sometimes."

"I understand that. From what I read, if you have a seizure, it's best to be rolled onto your side so it's easier to breathe. Does Reno know to do that?"

"No, but I'm impressed that you do."

"I didn't read up on it to impress you." He put another book into an envelope, and as he affixed the label, he said, "I'm hoping to get to know you better and wanted to be prepared. I also read that there are different types of seizures. What kind do you have?"

"The big ones. Grand mal seizures."

"I'm sorry to hear that. I read that with most grand mal

seizures, it's not necessary to call emergency services unless the seizure lasts longer than five minutes, or if the person hurts themselves, of course. Is that right?"

"Yes, but since Reno can't tell time, he's trained to push the button right away," she said with a twinkle of a tease.

"*Touché.* That's a lot of responsibility for a dog. How long did it take to train him?"

"Two years. A lot of the dogs don't make it through the program because they don't have the right temperament, but Reno is my perfect partner."

"Do you take him everywhere?"

"Mostly. He's like a security blanket. I feel a little naked without him. It's the same with the necklace. I always wear it, even if I'm just hanging out with my family." She tucked a note into a book and reached for a bookmark. "But I don't bring Reno every time I go out with my friends, because they'll watch out for me, and I don't always make him wear his service vest. Like when I'm working here, he doesn't wear it, and he doesn't follow me around the store every minute. But if I'm going to a big gathering with people from neighboring towns who may not know he's my service dog, like the jam session, then he wears his vest."

"I see. Do you have to keep up with his training? Or will he know those tasks forever?"

"Training is a lifelong process. Like with people, he can forget things."

"Did you have a dog before him?"

"No. My mom has trained service dogs since the year I was diagnosed, but I didn't want anything else to signify that I was different in public."

"So why take on Reno?"

"You sure ask a lot of questions."

"I'm sorry." Damn, he didn't want to screw this up.

"No, it's okay. I don't mind answering. Most people don't want to know all the details. I got Reno because even though I had friends and I'd had short-term boyfriends, I was missing real companionship. I didn't think falling in love and making future plans was in the cards for me at that point. I was helping my mom train the dogs during Reno's last summer with her, and we became inseparable." She ran her hand down Reno's cheek and lifted his face to kiss his snout. He licked her cheek. "Like I said, he's my love nugget."

"And like I said, lucky dog."

As they finished packaging the books, he asked about the basket of greeting cards, and she explained that she sends cards to her customers on their birthdays and anniversaries. She was thoughtful, sweet, and smart. He wondered how the men in Oak Falls had let her slip through their fingers. Were they truly intimidated by her medical condition, or wasn't she interested in any of them?

It was nearly eleven o'clock by the time they finished and cleaned up. Amber went to put the supply cart in the back room with Reno in tow, and Dash checked out the rest of the store, noticing all of her personal touches, like the suggestion box, vases of dried flowers, and tiny elf and monkey figurines reading books, which were tucked into nooks and crannies throughout the store. Handwritten plaques called attention to certain books with comments like AN EDGE-OF-YOUR-SEAT THRILLER, A PERFECT BEACH READ, and FOR KIDS WHO LIKE TO LAUGH. Displays by the register boasted literary socks, candles, bookmarks, and other trinkets. This wasn't just a bookstore. It was the kind of place that made him want to kick off his shoes and stretch out on the couch beside Amber with a good book.

She came out of the back wearing her jacket, and he knew from the wariness in her eyes that the easygoing girl he'd gotten to know while they were busily packaging books and talking had become guarded once again.

He picked up the romance novel he'd purchased, and she said, "You're not really going to read that."

"I absolutely am, and I'm looking forward to it. I've got to see what kind of romance ideas you've been putting in your head."

She picked up the vase of flowers. "Maybe you can pick up some pointers."

"Right." As she set the vase by the register, he said, "You don't want to take them home?"

"I want to keep them here so I can see them tomorrow," she said a little bashfully. "They're all my favorites. How did you know?"

"I might have bribed the florist."

"Sneaky."

They headed outside, and she locked the doors. When she turned around, she looked at him the way she had earlier, like she wanted to kiss him or run away and wasn't sure which to do. It took everything he had not to go for the kiss.

"I'll walk you to your car." He put a hand on her back as they headed around the corner, and he made mental notes of her *tells.* The way she fell silent or rambled when she was nervous, and how she touched Reno in those moments, as if just doing so calmed her, and the tell he enjoyed most. Her stolen glances when she thought he wasn't paying attention, proving that she felt their connection just as strongly as he did.

She stopped by the only other car in the lot, a safe, reliable, blue-gray Subaru Crosstrek. It suited her perfectly. She put Reno in the back seat and attached a tether to his harness, then closed the door and looked up at Dash. Moonlight glittered in her eyes, and she fidgeted with her keys. "Thank you again for the flowers and for helping me with the books."

He stepped closer. "I had a great time. How about letting me take you on a real date tomorrow night?"

"Dash, you're a really nice guy, the kind of guy that is way too easy to fall for, but you're only here for a couple of weeks, and I'm not a short-term kind of girl. I think it's best if we just keep things friendly and not try to make it into anything more."

"Maybe you don't know what's best." He touched her hand, and she breathed a little harder. "Your words say one thing, but your eyes tell me another."

She opened her mouth to speak, and snapped it closed, as if she'd thought better than to say whatever she was going to say.

"Just say yes, Amber. You won't regret it."

"I can't," she said apologetically.

"Because you want to stay in control of your emotions, and you're worried I'll be too much for you? Or because I'm only here for two weeks?"

She lowered her eyes, and when they flicked back up to his, he saw her struggle, an inner fight to throw caution to the wind, and the strength of the woman who probably hadn't done that for so long, she might have forgotten how. "Both. You should ask out Sable or Haylie or any number of the other single women around here. We both know they'd jump at the chance for a few nights with you. Well, maybe not Sable, but there are plenty of others."

"They're nice, but they're not you. You're different, Amber, and I don't mean because you have epilepsy. I mean it in a broader sense, in the very best way. When I saw you across the barn at the jam session, you outshined everyone."

She let out a sound of disbelief. "I've never outshined anyone in my life, and that's okay. I don't need to stand out to be happy. I had a lot of fun tonight, and I'm sorry, but it's best if we just leave things like they are."

Every part of him wanted to push, to spout the reasons why she was wrong and change her mind. But he respected her need to be in control, which wasn't to say that he was giving up.

"Okay. Friends it is. But you're wrong about not standing out. You're more beautiful than any woman I've ever met, and it's not only physical beauty that makes you shine, which is why your beauty is so rare. It's what's inside that makes you glow. The things that can't be faked or made better with makeup or fancy clothes. You possess them in droves."

Surprise and disbelief brimmed in her eyes.

He opened her car door and waited for her to settle in before leaning down and kissing her cheek. "I'm not giving up on you, my secret sexy reader."

He closed her door and felt the heat of her stare blazing into him as he headed for his car.

Chapter Five

THE BELL ABOVE the bookstore door chimed, and Sable strutted into the store, drawing Amber's attention from the display of Dash's books she was restocking on Tuesday afternoon. Or rather, that she *had* been restocking before she'd gotten lost in thoughts of last night while ogling his picture.

"I had a feeling that literary baller who's got all the women around here following him like he's the world's most talented gigolo giving out freebie coupons was the reason you were so quiet at breakfast this morning." With her cowgirl hat and boots, Sable looked more like a rancher than an auto mechanic or musician. She planted a hand on her hip, the knowing look in her eyes telling Amber not to even bother trying to deny it. "I know you get bummed when Axsel leaves town, and now Grace and Reed are gone, too, and that trips you up a little. But not like this."

Their family had gotten together for a farewell breakfast at their parents' house this morning to say goodbye to Grace, Reed, and Axsel. Even though Amber was glad her siblings were living full, happy lives, she hated goodbyes. Last night's goodbye to Dash had been even worse. She'd tried to cheer herself up by wearing her favorite caramel-colored sweaterdress with the black and tan scarf and all of the other accessories Morgyn had made for her. She'd even worn the thigh-high boots Brindle had given her last Christmas. She felt cute in the outfit, and it usually made her feel good all over, but it hadn't helped. She'd still spent all day wondering if she'd made a mistake telling Dash she couldn't go out with him.

Sable crossed her arms. "What'd he do?"

"Nothing." Amber set down the book she was holding, her eyes darting to the flowers. *Everything.*

"Uh-huh. And I'm a virgin."

"Why is everything about sex all the time?" Amber hadn't meant to snap, but she'd kept her frustrations buried all day around customers, and she was sick of it. "Even when it's not about sex, it's about sex."

Sable's eyes narrowed. "What are you talking about? Did he try something with you?"

"*No.* He gave me flowers with *acorns* in the vase and spent hours helping me get books ready to mail out." She couldn't control her angry tone and began nervously straightening the books on the table. "He told me all about his family. He practically *raised* his brothers and sisters after his crappy father abandoned them."

Sable put her hand over Amber's, stopping her from shuffling the books around, and glanced at the flowers by the register. "Those the flowers?"

Amber nodded.

"Your favorites."

"He bribed Twyla." Twyla ran the flower shop.

"Son of a bitch," Sable said under her breath. "He's savvy. Gotta give him that. But you love flowers, and you sound mad. What did he really do?"

"I'm not angry at *him*. I'm angry at *life*. Everything he said last night about his family and who he is spoke to me here." She put her hand over her heart. "I never feel that. And we laughed, Sable. A lot. You should see how he looks at me, like I'm a goddess or like he's seeing the sun after years spent in the dark, and he makes me want...*you know*."

"Wow, he's really got you fooled."

Amber glowered at her. "Just for one minute, can you take off your armor? Please? Last night when we were talking, for the first time *ever*, I forgot that I wasn't just like everyone else." It was only for a little while, and when she realized it, it had scared her as much as it had intrigued her. But it was so freeing, she couldn't stop thinking about how good it had felt. "I finally meet a guy who piques my interest enough for me to want to get to know him better, and not only is he God's gift to women, but he's only here for a couple of weeks." She huffed out a breath. "It doesn't matter. I told him I wasn't interested."

"You probably did the right thing."

She said it so casually, it pissed Amber off. "How would you know? You've never opened your heart to any man. You don't know what it feels like to hear things that make you want to know more about someone. Like who was taking care of him when he was taking care of his siblings? And why didn't he go to Boyer if he grew up in Port Hudson? Which he did, by the way. His mom worked at the library when I was there. I had no idea she was struggling. She was so confident and happy. It's no wonder he's the same way. But I can't help wondering if it was hard for him to go away to college and leave them all behind. Or if he welcomed the break after having so much responsibility."

"You *really* like him," Sable said softly.

"No kidding. But I can't like him, Sable."

"Why? Just because he's prancing around like the Pied Piper with a magical skin flute and you're pure as winter snow?"

Her sisters thought she was *pure* and naive, but she'd been with men. She just didn't flaunt it the way some of them did. "That's part of it. You know I don't do well with stress or competition."

"No, I don't. I know you avoid it like the plague, but owning this place is stressful and you've never let that get in your way. You worked your ass off to make ends meet the first few years, and you still do. You blow away your competition. The Oak Falls bookstore closed *because* of your success."

"That's different."

Sable studied her face for so long, Amber finally groaned and threw her hands up.

"I need to get my things. I'm going to see Phoenix play tonight. Want to come with me?" She headed for her office, and Reno got up from his bed beside the register, ambling after them.

"I can't. I've got band practice." She followed Amber into her office, and her expression turned to one of surprise. "I'm such an idiot. This is about *sex*, isn't it? That whole rant about sex? It has to be."

Amber grabbed her jacket from the rack in the corner. "I don't know anymore. I just know it feels like I made a mistake telling him I wasn't interested, but I also think I did the right thing."

Sable picked up the jar of acorns from the shelf behind her desk. "How did he know about the acorns?"

"He didn't. His grandmother filled her vases with them and said they were nature's magic."

"Are you kidding me?" Sable scoffed and put the jar back on the shelf. "The guy's as soft as you are."

"No, he's not. He's *very* alpha, trust me. He's just got a big heart beneath all that bravado."

"Well, if anyone could see that in a person, it's you." She took Amber's jacket from her hands and held it up, helping her put it on. Then she took Amber by the shoulders, and with a serious expression said, "Listen to me, because I'm only going to say this once, and I might rescind it in five minutes."

Amber leaned in to her sister. "Do you know how much I love you?"

"How could you not? I've always got your back. Listen, if Morgyn were here, she'd tell you that those acorns meant something more than a coincidence."

"And you want to tell me they don't. I know how you feel about him, Sable."

"But what you don't realize is that how I feel doesn't matter. Lord help me for saying this, but this is your life, Amber. You're allowed to have fun with it, break rules, and have wild sex with ex-football players if you want to."

Amber felt her cheeks burn.

"I don't want you to get hurt, but if you want this guy that badly, go for it. Fuck him six ways to Sunday."

"Sable!" Amber whispered harshly.

She rolled her eyes. "I mean *have your way with him* six ways to Sunday, okay? Just do it with your eyes open. Not literally. You know what I mean."

"I don't know if I can do that without getting hurt, even if I go in with my eyes open. And I mean that literally, because can you imagine how hot he must look while he's…?" She giggled, unable to believe she'd said it. "My heart is different from yours,

Sabe. I can't do those things without my feelings coming into play."

"I know. But some heartbreaks are worth it, which is why if you choose to go that route, I'll be here when he leaves town to pick up your pieces and put you back together."

Tears welled in Amber's eyes.

"Oh God. Here we go." Sable pulled her into a tight hug. "No waterworks, okay?"

"Sorry." Amber stepped out of her embrace and wiped her eyes.

"Just do what feels right to *you*, because at the end of the day, that's the only thing that matters."

If only that were true.

It didn't matter anyway, because this time she was sure he wouldn't be back.

WISHING CREEK WAS about half an hour outside of Oak Falls, and Lyrics and Lattes was located off the beaten path in an artistic hub. Brick shops were separated by concrete alleyways with clear plastic arches overhead to protect them from the elements. The sides of the buildings were decorated by local artists with murals, ceramic and clay planters, framed pictures, photographs, stone and metal sculptures, and more. Just being in the area made Amber feel like she'd traveled far away from her safe little town, but not far enough to cause her to worry.

She pulled open the door to the coffeehouse and stepped inside with Reno, who was wearing his service vest. They were greeted by the din of the crowd and the welcoming scents of fresh-brewed coffee and food presented as creatively as the art on the walls, most of which was for sale. Tall, thin windows overlooked the alleyways, and a high shelf decorated with colored bottles ran around the perimeter of the room. All the stools at the coffee bar were occupied, along with most of the mismatched, colorful chairs surrounding mosaic tables scattered around the room.

"Hey, Amber." Jolene, the energetic fortysomething artist who owned the coffeehouse hurried over, her dark ringlets flouncing around her face. She knew better than to try to engage Reno when he wore his service vest. "You look ready for a hot date. Who's the lucky guy?"

"Unless you've got one tucked away somewhere, it's just me tonight."

"I'll keep my eyes peeled for a decaf French vanilla latte." Jolene winked. She'd once asked Amber what kind of guys she liked to go out with, and Amber had said, *Men who are like decaf French vanilla lattes—sweet, smooth, and always satisfying,* and decaf French vanilla latte had been code for Amber's type of guy ever since. "Come on. I saved your favorite table. Can you believe this crowd? Phoenix is really reeling them in."

"I'm happy for her. She practices all the time." Amber followed her to the table. One of Morgyn's repurposed pieces hung on the wall beside it. Morgyn had cut along the length of an old rusted handsaw blade, meticulously creating silhouettes of trees and birds out of the metal. It had taken her weeks to get it right, and it was one of Amber's favorite pieces. When Morgyn brought it to the coffeehouse for Jolene to sell on consignment, Jolene had purchased it on the spot, keeping it for herself.

"Are you eating tonight?" Jolene asked.

"Yeah, but I need a minute."

Jolene put a menu on the table. "Take as much time as you'd like. I'll be back in a bit."

"Go under," she said to Reno, and he lay down under the table as Amber hung her jacket on the back of her chair and sat down. It had been busy at the store, and with her mind wreaking havoc with her about Dash, she felt like she hadn't had a minute to relax.

This was just what she needed. She opened the menu and scanned the dinner options.

"Amber?"

The familiar deep voice sent a shiver of heat down her spine. She glanced up at Dash's handsome face and couldn't suppress the smile tugging at her lips.

"Are you stalking me?" he asked coyly.

That took her off guard. "No. I came to hear Phoenix play. She works for me. What are you doing here?"

"Having dinner with a friend."

A pang of hurt washed over her, and she looked around to find his *friend*. Her eyes caught on a pretty blonde watching them. Amber tore her eyes away, disappointment burrowing deep inside her chest. "Shouldn't you sit with her? It's a little rude to leave her alone."

"I agree." He pulled out the chair beside Amber.

Her eyes darted to the blonde, then back to Dash. "*What* are you doing?"

"Having dinner with a friend." He cocked a brow. "You said you wanted to be friends, right?"

"But your *date*?" She glanced at the blonde again.

He followed her gaze. "You mean that blonde? I have *no* idea who she is." He draped his arm across the back of Amber's chair, leaning closer, his piercing eyes making her stomach flip-flop. "I came here to see *you*. I had a great time last night, and I wanted to see you again. But don't worry, there's no pressure to be more than friends. I'll take whatever time you're willing to share."

Her chest fluttered, and she reached down to pet Reno, but he was too far away. She patted her leg. "Reno, come." Her trusty companion sidled up to her other side. "Lie down."

As Reno obeyed, a spark shimmered in Dash's eyes. "You can command me like that anytime."

Thankfully, Jolene appeared with a glass of ice water and set it down in front of Amber. As she guzzled it, Jolene looked curiously at Dash. "If you tell me what your friend looks like, I can send her over when she arrives and bring your dinner over, too."

Amber gasped. "You *are* meeting someone." She tried to pull away, but his hand curled around her shoulder, keeping her close.

He looked at Jolene, his smile never faltering. "Amber *is* the friend I was hoping to meet, and yes, you can bring our dinner here."

Our dinner?

Jolene raised her brows at Amber. "I guess there *is* a lucky guy tonight after all. What can I get you to drink?"

"More ice water, please. A pitcher would be nice."

Dash chuckled. "I'll have a dirty chai latte." He turned a darker look to Amber. "I like my drinks like I like my women, sweet and spicy."

His gaze slid slowly down her body to the slice of bare thigh between the hem of her sweaterdress and the top of her boots. If he kept this up, her cheeks and her panties were going to burst into flames.

"Amber, you *are* a lucky girl." Jolene took the menu. "I'll be back with your drinks."

"You ordered us dinner?" Amber asked the second she walked away. "How did you know I was going to be here?"

"A gentleman doesn't reveal his sources, and yes, I ordered us dinner. I figured you might actually stick around if you knew I had dropped a few bucks."

"That wouldn't make me stick around."

"Then what would?"

She shrugged one shoulder, gathering the courage to be honest instead of pushing him away. "*You.* The fact that you figured out where I was tonight and thought to order dinner, even if it was a ploy that kind of sounds like a bribe."

"What if I didn't have to figure it out? What if someone told me? Would you still stick around?"

She tried to read his expression to see if that was the case, but he just looked relaxed and happy to be there with her. "*Did* someone tell you?"

"No. I was sneaky all on my own. I'm just trying to figure out the rules of dating a secret sexy reader."

Knowing he'd tried to find out where she'd be tonight made her feel all kinds of good. She'd been pursued by a few guys throughout the years, but not like this. "I don't date often, so I'm making up the rules as I go along."

"Then I look forward to making them up with you," he said as Jolene arrived with their drinks.

"One dirty chai latte, a pitcher of ice water with an extra glass in case *you* need cooling off." She set the glass in front of Dash. "And I brought *you* a decaf French vanilla latte on the house." She placed the latte in front of Amber, giving her an approving look before walking away.

Dash eyed Amber curiously. "Is that your favorite drink?"

The butterflies were back, fluttering madly as she threw caution to the wind and said, "Sweet, smooth, and satisfying. What's not to like?"

DASH WOULD GIVE her *satisfying* if she'd give him the chance, and around her, he didn't have to work at being sweet or smooth. Amber wasn't like other women, swept up in the glamour and glitz of the spotlight his celebrity often earned. She brought out the regular guy in him, a side of him very few people ever saw. The side that didn't feel the need to live up to the superstar hype. As they ate dinner and listened to Phoenix play, he admired the artwork on the walls, which had Amber raving about Morgyn having made the piece behind her. She told him about Morgyn and Graham's whirlwind relationship and Grace and Reed's history together. She was so happy for her sisters and passionate about family, it brought out that side of him, too. He liked who he was with Amber, and if her gorgeous smile and easy laughter of the last two hours were any indication, she liked that guy, too.

He ate a bite of the strawberry cheesecake they were sharing for dessert, listening to her rave about *The Greatest Showman*. How was it possible that her favorite musical was his, too?

"I watch it at *least* three times a month. Have you seen it?" She ate another forkful of cheesecake.

He was glad she wasn't one of those women who survived on kale and energy drinks. "Yeah. Hugh Jackman is always incredible, but—" Her tongue slicked across her lower lip, and she closed her eyes, making an *"Mm"* sound, sending his mind down a dark alley. She was a sensual eater; it had been inescapable during dinner. Pleasure had risen in her eyes with nearly every bite, and she'd made those sexy noises, offering him tastes and coaxing him with *You've never tasted anything this good.* The trouble was, the only thing he wanted to taste was the beauty whose innocent eyes were locked on him.

"But what?" She tilted her head, looking at him with an innocent curiosity, completely unaware of the effect she had on him.

He cleared his throat to try to clear his thoughts. "But I can take or leave Zac Efron."

"Why? Because he's got a bigger fan base than you?" she challenged.

He chuckled. She'd challenged him several times tonight, and he loved her feistiness. "I don't give a damn about fan bases. He's just not a great singer."

"Are you *kidding*? He's got an amazing voice," she said vehemently. "When he sang 'Rewrite the Stars,' I would have given anything to be the one he was singing to. It was so romantic. You know what that song's about, don't you?"

He did, but he loved her enthusiasm and egged her on. "Not really."

"Seriously? It's about how she thinks they're not meant for each other, that their love isn't in the cards. And he believes they *are* meant for each other. He says he'll rewrite the stars for her. I think you're just jealous."

"Hardly, and you wouldn't say that if you'd ever heard me sing in the shower."

"Oh, I get it." She lifted a forkful of cheesecake, with a tease in her eyes. "This is when I'm supposed to jump at the chance to hear you sing in the shower. Sorry, my dashing friend, but that's *not* happening."

"You wouldn't say that, either, if you'd ever seen me in the shower."

"Nice try. Did you like the movie or not?"

"It took me a minute to get used to all the singing, but yeah, I really liked it."

"To get *used to* the singing? That's the best part. Every song tells a story and brings the characters to life."

"I agree with you about that. It was the first musical I'd ever seen, and I just had to get used to it. It's a powerful movie, and the songs definitely drive the messages home."

Her whole face lit up. "So, you *did* like it!"

"I'll never admit this in front of my buddies, but I've watched it about a half dozen times."

She let out a little squeal, leaning closer. "It's so much bigger than a romance, isn't it? It's a love story about a man and his outrageous vision, and how that vision impacted the lives of everyone around him. That's why it's my absolute favorite movie."

Her passion made him want to be one of her favorite things, too. "That's what I like most about it, too. It makes you think." *Like you. You're sweet and good, and you make me think about what I really want and what's missing in my life.*

"Exactly," she said breathily. "It celebrates being different and inspires people not to give up on their dreams."

It took everything he had to keep from sliding his hand to the nape of her neck and pulling her into the kiss he so desperately wanted. But he'd told her he was cool with being friends, and he didn't want to screw this up by taking away her control, so he held still and let those feelings come out in words. "You inspire me, Amber, and I'm not giving up on the dream that one day you'll go out with me."

Her lips parted on a sigh, heat and emotions swelling between them. Her breathing shallowed, and her eyes said, *Kiss me.* It was torture not to lean in and take that kiss. A minute passed, three, maybe more, and neither said a word. Desire pulsed like thunder between them. He knew she needed control, but he also knew she might be too shy to close the tiny gap between them and take the kiss they both wanted. Just as he was about to lean closer, she sat back and her eyes darted anxiously around them, briefly meeting his. "It's late. I should get home."

Still stuck on the heat crackling around them, it took him a moment to react. "Okay. I'd like to follow you back and make sure you get home safely."

"I don't know if that's a good idea," she said softly.

"I'm not looking for anything in return, or expecting you to invite me in, but I'd never forgive myself if something happened to you on the way home and I wasn't there to help."

She let out a small, relieved sigh. "Okay."

He paid the bill and followed her back to her place. Never in his life had he been so aware of the emotions coursing through him. Dash climbed from his car, taking in Amber's simple yellow cottage with a peaked roof over a postage-stamp-size front porch and the white picket fence that bordered the front yard. A stone walkway cut through pretty gardens, flower boxes graced every window, and a cozy side porch with a hanging wooden bench swing was tucked between the house and the carport where Amber parked. It was the smallest house on the street, but it had the same unique charm as Amber, making it stand out from all the rest.

Amber climbed out of her car, gorgeous in a suede jacket over her short clingy sweaterdress, which showed off her curves, and those thigh-high boots that had been taunting him all night, telling him his secret sexy reader probably had more sexy secrets. He couldn't wait to discover them.

"Go potty," she said to Reno, and he trotted around to the back of the house.

"I don't have to go right now, but if you insist." Dash pretended to reach for his fly.

She laughed. "You're not very well trained, are you?"

"I think the NFL might say otherwise. You must love your commute to work. What is it? Five minutes?"

"About that. I prefer to walk when I can."

"Is that safe?" He put a hand on her back as they made their way to the front door.

"Yes, very. And I have Reno to protect me."

"He's not much of an attack dog, but he could probably lick someone to death." He looked up at the house. "This is a cute place."

"Thanks. It was poet Jandolyn Meyer's house."

"I've never heard of her."

"Nobody has. She wrote poems for the Oak Falls newspaper in the early 1900s. I wrote a paper on her when I was in high school. I fell in love with her words long before I was ready to buy a house, and luckily, when it went on the market, it was in really bad shape. Nobody wanted it because it was so small and the lot is half the size of the others on the street. When I finally had the means to buy it, I didn't care how much work it needed. I knew it was meant to be."

As they stepped onto the porch, he said, "You're loyal. I like that."

"Loyal to a *house?*"

"To yourself, and the things that make you happy." *At least most of them.*

Reno came around the side of the house and sat in the grass.

"Doesn't everyone do that?" She gazed up at him, desire revealing itself again in the shimmering heat in her eyes, her shallow breathing, and the way she leaned in just a little.

If he wasn't looking for her tells, he might have missed that last one. "That depends on the person and the part of themselves they're being loyal to. Sometimes people hold back from the things that would make them happy because they're afraid to feel something or of getting hurt or hurting others. Seeing you makes me happy, so I show up like I did tonight, and I had a great time."

"I did, too," she said breathily.

"But kissing you would also make me happy, and I'm afraid it might scare you off." She breathed harder, her eyes never leaving his, giving him hope that he was getting through to her. "What are you afraid of, Amber?"

"Getting hurt."

Her vulnerability made him want to take her in his arms and protect her from the world. He took her hand in his. "I will never hurt you. Give us a try, and I'll show you what type of man I am."

She seemed to think about that for a moment. "Our lives are worlds apart, and you're only here visiting."

"Then give me a reason to come back."

Seconds passed in slow motion as she went up on her toes, closing her eyes as her soft lips touched his, sweet and tender, like a whisper saying, *Please come back.* As their lips parted, her eyes fluttered open, the green light in them as clear as the heat thrumming between them. His arm circled her, drawing her closer as their mouths came together, slow at first, giving her time to pull away. But she grabbed hold of his sides, kissing him harder, and he was right there with her. Their kisses were urgent and lustful, like ravenous animals who had been starved for too long. Their tongues searched and delved, and she made noises similar to the sexy noises she'd made over dinner, but they were sinfully different, full of longing and pleasure. Her mouth was sweet and hot, and her kisses were so damn perfect, he wondered how he'd go a minute without one. She grabbed hold of his shirt with both hands, stretching higher on her toes, kissing him harder.

Oh yeah, baby. I knew we'd be perfect together.

He backed her up against the door, his hands moving down her hips, around to her ass. She arched into him, moaning, grabbing at his back and arms, kissing him feverishly. He devoured her, groping her ass, lost in the lusciousness that was Amber Montgomery. Their bodies took over, obliterating all sense of time and space as their bodies gyrated, mouths feasted. She fisted her hands in his hair, keeping him from pulling away. She needn't have worried. He'd never experienced anything as exquisite as kissing her, and he never wanted to stop. He heard a sound in the distance, but she guided his mouth to her neck, and everything else failed to exist.

"Feels so good," she panted out. "I need to kiss you more."

She yanked his hair, reclaiming his mouth, and holy hell, he'd found his *wild thing*. He deepened the kiss, but slowed them down, wanting to savor the taste of her, the feel of her body vibrating with need. He framed her face with his hands, threading his fingers into her hair, and tilted her face up, kissing her softer, more sensually, earning more of the moans that made his cock ache to get into the game. The sounds of car doors closing rang out, and their eyes flew open as Reno barked. Red-and-white lights flashed against the house, and a look of horror rose on Amber's face.

Dash spun around and found an ambulance and another car in front of the house, Amber's parents rushing toward them with an EMT and a paramedic, and Reno barking up a storm. *What the...?*

"Honey, are you okay?" Marilynn asked. Then she put out her hand, focusing on Reno. "Reno, *settle*." The dog plopped to his butt and stopped barking.

Cade stopped in the middle of the yard, a look of relief accompanying a "Thank God."

"We got a distress call that Amber was having a seizure." The burly paramedic peered around Dash. "You okay, Amber?"

Dash looked at Amber, trying to figure out what was going on, but she was nervously patting down her tousled hair with one hand and tugging the hem of her dress with the other. His eyes caught on her necklace, and he realized they must have accidentally pushed the button. *Fuck.*

"Yes. *I'm fine.* Sorry." Amber's voice was shaky, her cheeks beet red, and her lips swollen from the force of their kisses.

Aw shit. "Amber, I am *so* sorry."

She gave him a troubled smile.

"Must have been a hell of a mouth-to-mouth resuscitation," the paramedic said.

"*Boyd!*" Amber snapped, looking like she wanted to climb into a hole.

Dash put his arm around her, locking eyes with Boyd. "We must have pushed her alert button by accident. I'm sorry. It won't happen again."

"Oh dear. A kissing emergency. I guess Pepper needs to get back to work on making that necklace Dash proof." Marilynn covered her mouth as laughter bubbled out.

"Mom!" Amber glowered at her.

Dash tried his best to stifle his laughter.

"We're just so relieved that it was a make-out emergency and not a seizure." Cade barely got the words out before he started laughing.

"Dad!" Amber exclaimed, and an incredulous laugh tumbled out.

"I'm sorry, honey. You're right. It's not a laughing matter." Her father tried to school his expression.

"It's a kissing matter," Boyd said jovially, and her parents burst into laughter again.

Amber glared at Boyd, but she was smiling. "Watch yourself, Boyd Hudson, or I'll tell Janie you're giving me a hard time."

Boyd held up his hands in surrender. "You know I'm only teasing. No need to call my wife."

Dash tightened his hold around Amber. "A'right, that's enough," he said firmly. "The show's over."

"Hey, Amber," the EMT called out as they headed back to the ambulance. "The good news is that you'll be the envy of every woman within a fifty-mile radius tomorrow."

Dash gritted out a curse as Amber's parents hurried toward them with Reno, and Dash and Amber stepped off the porch. Her parents embraced her, apologizing again and reassuring her that the laughter was just their relief coming out. Marilynn pulled Amber aside, talking in a hushed tone, and Cade gave Dash a serious papa-bear gaze. "I guess you won my princess over after all."

"Yes, sir, and I'm sorry about this incident."

He crossed his arms, nodding. "Tread lightly, son. You just opened up a whole can of worms that she's spent a lifetime avoiding."

"I know that, sir. I assure you it won't happen again."

"Good, because I'm getting a little old for doling out beatings."

Dash chuckled, but Cade gave him another stern look, which wiped the smile right off his face. Marilynn said she'd see him in the morning at the park, and as her parents headed for their car, Dash turned his attention to Amber, who looked like she'd been put through the wringer.

He gazed into her eyes and went for humor, hoping he hadn't just ruined his chances with her. "How's that for an unforgettable first kiss?" Her half-hearted smile crushed him. "What can I do to make this go away?"

"Nothing. It'll be fine. I'm going to take a hot bath and pretend that whole fiasco never happened."

"How about you remember the good parts?"

"They'd be hard to forget." Her eyes glittered again, but her underlying unease was unmistakable.

"Who knew you were such a little wild thing." He gave her one last kiss and headed down the porch steps, taking a second to love up Reno. "I'd better figure out how to save my reputation before everyone in town thinks I'm easy. Before you know it, my name will be all over bathroom walls. *For a good time call…*"

She laughed as she unlocked the door, and Reno trotted up the steps to her.

"It's all your fault, wild thing," he called out from the

driveway. "I don't know how you'll sleep with that on your shoulders."

"I think I'll manage." She waved and disappeared into the house with Reno.

Yeah, but how will I?

Chapter Six

AMBER WAS A mess, and she had half a mind to call Sable and give her grief for it.

The ideas Sable had planted in her head had seemed *really* good in the moment, and Amber had let herself get carried away with Dash. Not that she regretted those toe-curling kisses, but she'd never in her entire life gotten so lost in a man that he'd blurred out the rest of the world. When they were making out, she'd been vaguely aware of flashing lights but had stupidly thought they were the *fireworks* Brindle and Morgyn swore Trace and Graham caused when they kissed. Amber had lived under the radar for so long, she'd forgotten how awful it felt knowing that people might be whispering about her. She was *not* cut out for a fiasco-riddled life. She'd spent a fitful night vacillating between preparing for an onslaught of gossip and reliving Dash's incredible kisses. She'd walked to work to try to rid herself of her nervous energy and had even come up with a number of retorts to shut down the grapevine.

But it hadn't helped.

She'd been on the same emotional roller coaster all day, anxious one minute and excited about Dash the next, which was a problem in and of itself. She hadn't heard a peep from him since he left. If the situation were reversed, she would have called, or at least texted, to make sure he was all right, especially since he knew how much she hated being gossiped about. But as morning turned to afternoon and hours passed without a word from him, she became convinced that last night's debacle had scared him off. She should have known better. It was one thing to go out with a woman who had epilepsy and claimed to have things under control, but being with a woman who sets off alarms that bring paramedics and parents rushing to her side was a whole other ball game.

She was stupid to have thought that after everything he'd told her, he was different. A dull ache took root in her chest, making today that much worse.

Her phone vibrated, and she pulled it out and saw Brindle's name on the text message. Steeling herself for an onslaught of teasing about her seizure alarm going off, she read the message. *I heard you had dinner with a certain hot jock in Wishing Creek. I want details.* She added an eggplant emoji. Amber stared at the message, wondering why Brindle hadn't said anything about the aftermath of that wonderful dinner. But she didn't want to think about it, much less talk about it, and she tried to play it off casually, thumbing out, *I was there to see Phoenix, and he happened to be there. It was dinner between friends, nothing more. I'm swamped, can't text.* She sent the text and shoved her phone into her pocket.

For the rest of the afternoon, every time customers came into the store, Amber held her breath, waiting for inquisitive or judgmental looks and whispers, but not one person said a word about last night's events. Not even Nana when she'd stopped by to pick up a book for her husband and had gossiped about neighbors and friends. After *that*, Amber wondered if she'd woken up in an alternate universe.

As she finished setting up a new children's display in the back of the store, she thought about the lack of gossip. It should probably make her feel better, but it only confused her. Had she been out of the loop for so long that she'd become blind to the gossip?

A horrible thought struck her.

Brindle and Trace had been on-again, off-again lovers for years, and when Brindle had gone to Paris alone to figure out her life, Nana had started a Facebook poll about their relationship. It had taken over several social media platforms with a Team Trindle hashtag. Had everyone started gossiping online again?

Amber whipped out her phone, quickly navigating to the Oak Falls Facebook page. Her heart slammed against her ribs as she scanned it. There were pictures of Dash at the football clinic with the kids and at the park exercising with a ridiculously large group of women, most of whom were openly gawking at him. Someone had even posted pictures of him from the jam session, his arms around groups of young women and men, that killer smile beaming at the camera. She continued scrolling and saw the announcements she'd posted about his book signing and the contest she was running for decorating next month's front window display and was relieved that there was nothing about her and Dash.

She debated checking Dash's Instagram feed and wondered if he had an assistant handling it. Although when she'd researched him, he'd posted nearly every day. She'd seen selfies and pictures with gorgeous women and attractive guys in bars and restaurants that definitely weren't professionally taken. Her stomach twisted as she realized he hadn't taken any pictures of them when they were together. What did that mean? She wasn't important to him? Not worthy of his page? He didn't want people to know about them?

That made her feel sick to her stomach. She purposefully hadn't looked at his feed since he'd arrived in Oak Falls. That was part of her ignore Dash plan, which she'd failed at epically. But now she felt an unyielding need to check his page and see what he'd been posting.

Her pulse quickened as she touched the Instagram icon and navigated to his profile. The most recent post was a picture of the WELCOME TO NEW YORK highway sign with the caption *Goodbye, small town, hello, Big Apple! Home sweet home.* She checked the date, and her chest tightened. It had been posted earlier today.

He'd left town without so much as a goodbye? She really *had* scared him away.

That dull ache turned to a stabbing pain, her gaze drifting to the beautiful flowers Dash had given her and the acorns in the vase. She couldn't believe the thoughtful man who'd collected acorns and filled a vase with them would leave town without saying goodbye. She rechecked the date on the post, and sure enough, it had been posted today. She checked his other recent posts and saw one from last night at midnight with the caption *Small Town USA* and several pictures he must have taken earlier in the day of himself and a group of women at the park, including her mother, and of him and Sin eating lunch. There were pictures of the Majestic Theater and artwork from one of the Wishing Creek alleyways. He'd posted just past midnight the night before last, too—a picture of an acorn lying on the forest floor with the caption *Sometimes it's the start of something new, and sometimes it's just a nut.*

Her mind traipsed back to the night he'd given her the flowers, when they'd shared so much of themselves, and she'd told him she just wanted to be friends, driving that stabbing pain deeper. She continued scrolling through earlier pictures of Dash with kids from the football clinic, and him and Trace, and other friends of hers. She found a picture of him and Sin arm in arm outside Sin's house dated last Friday night, which he must have taken before the jam session, with the caption *Let the good times roll.* The picture posted the day before was of Dash with a gorgeous blonde on one arm, a brunette on the other, and a group of people gathered behind them.

She scrolled back up to the picture of the highway sign, hurt and anger whirling and tangling insider her, tightening into a painful knot. To think she'd worn one of her favorite short dresses today in anticipation of seeing him again.

The bell rang above the door, and as Amber came around the display tree in the children's area, her mother came into view, leading Patsy on a leash. She looked cute in an oatmeal sweater and jeans, her dark hair pulled back in a ponytail.

"Hi, honey."

Amber adored her mother, and she could probably talk to her about anything. But she wasn't even comfortable talking about intimate aspects of her personal life with her girlfriends. There was no way she wanted to discuss last night, or the fact that she was probably being ghosted, with her mother. She silenced a groan and mustered a smile. "Hi, Mom."

Reno lifted his head from his bed by the register and looked at Amber.

"Go visit," Amber said, giving him the okay to socialize.

Reno soaked up her mother's attention, and then he and Patsy got busy sniffing each other. Her mother often brought the dogs she trained into town for socialization. Reno knew not to run around the store, and he was a good role model for her mother's pups.

Her mother admired the flowers Dash had given her. "These are lovely. Did you pick them up at Twyla's?"

"Uh-huh." It was only half a lie, but Amber didn't want to bring up Dash. "Where are you headed so late in the day?"

"I took Patsy to the dog park. I was just on my way home and thought I'd see how you were doing after *last night*." She lowered her voice when she said *last night*.

"Can we not talk about that?" Amber started straightening displays, as she'd been doing all day. Nothing in the store was out of place, but she needed to keep her hands busy.

"I'm sorry." Her mother followed her around the store, speaking in a hushed tone. "I assumed it was okay for *us* to talk about last night. Just not anyone else."

"What do you mean?"

Her mother's brow furrowed. "This morning at the park when Dash gave us a stern talking-to, I assumed that didn't apply to you and me."

Amber stopped fidgeting with the books, giving her mother her full attention. "Mom, what are you talking about?"

"Nancy and I have been exercising with him and some other ladies in the mornings. He didn't tell you?" Nancy Jericho was one of her mother's best friends.

"He *did*, but just…What happened? What did he say?"

Her mother exhaled loudly. "Don't ask me how, but one of the ladies heard what happened last night, and she asked Dash if you were okay. He forbade us, in no uncertain terms, from talking about the two of you. He said anyone who wanted to gossip should leave the group right then. And let me tell you, darlin', he was adamant. He made us all promise to shut down any rumors if we heard them."

"That doesn't make sense," she said, more to herself than to her mother.

"Of course it does. He likes you."

Amber scoffed. "A guy who likes you doesn't ghost you." She walked away, but her mother stuck with her.

"I don't know what that means."

Amber spun around, hurt clawing its way up her chest. "It means he left town without even saying goodbye, Mom, and I *don't* want to talk about this."

"What do you mean he didn't say goodbye? He told *us* he was leaving town."

"That's just *great*. You guys rank above me, and I'm the one who kissed him." Amber breathed deeply, futilely trying to calm down. "He blew into town, pursued me with his charm and that ridiculously engaging smile, talking about his family and collecting acorns, and he convinced me that he *really* liked me." Saying it aloud drove the hurt deeper and made her feel stupid for falling for him. "I can't believe I bought it. I played right into his hands. And last night I thought we'd actually connected on a deeper level while we were out, and I let myself..."

"Open up to him?" her mother suggested carefully.

She nodded. "That's not easy for me, and last night was really hard and embarrassing. He had to know that today would be difficult for me."

"I think he did. That's why he told us not to gossip."

Amber shook her head. "I don't think he said the things he did to protect me. I think he was protecting his own reputation. He made a comment last night about it, but I thought he was joking. He probably didn't want word to get out about what happened. And here I was, waiting all day to hear from him, thinking he'd walk through the door any minute. When it hit seven o'clock, I finally checked his Instagram account. I guess it took the ambulance and the embarrassment for him to show his true colors, because he's back in New York, like the last couple of nights never happened." Tears sprang to her eyes. "How can it hurt so much so fast?" She wiped her eyes. "Did he say how long he was going to be gone? *Wait*. Don't tell me. If I'm not worth a goodbye, I don't even want to know."

"Oh, baby girl. I'm so sorry. He didn't tell us when he'd be back. He said he'd let us know when we could reconvene."

Amber crossed her arms, steeling herself against the anger and hurt consuming her. "What's wrong with me, Mom? Sable kisses guys and doesn't care if she ever sees them again. Why can't I be like that? It takes a lot for me to *want* to kiss a guy. It takes moving heaven and earth for me to actually do it, and yeah, it happened pretty quickly with Dash, but I really thought…" She looked down, trying to keep her tears at bay.

"It didn't happen that quickly, honey. It only feels fast to you because you've always led with your heart, and because of that you take your time to think things through before moving forward. If your sisters were in your shoes, most of them would have been lip-locked with him last Friday night. And don't get me started on your brother. He would have had the man's trousers around his ankles in the men's room at the jam session."

"*Mom.*" Amber felt her cheeks burning.

"Why do my children all act like sex is only for young people? I'll have you know, your father and I—"

"*Don't.*" Amber covered her ears.

Her mother tucked Amber's hair behind her ear like she'd

always done in these mother-daughter moments, looking at her with so much unconditional love, it brought a lump to Amber's throat.

"You listen to me, Amber Mae. There is *nothing* wrong with you. That man should be an actor, because he had us all fooled, and believe me, you do not want to be like Sable. I wouldn't change a thing about my confident, tough girl, but I don't think she's as unaffected by her actions as she appears."

"What makes you say that?"

"A mother knows these things. But this isn't about your sister, honey. If Dash really…*ghosted?* Is that the right word?"

Amber nodded.

"If he ghosted you, he is *not* the man he appeared to be, and he is *not* worthy of my beautiful, smart, big-hearted girl." Her mother pulled her phone out of her pocket. "I'm going to call Sin right now, and—"

"*No*, you're not." Amber took her mother's phone. "I'm an adult, Mom. I can handle this. It's not a big deal."

"Isn't it, sweetheart?" Her mother's gaze softened.

Amber relented. "Fine, it's a big deal to *me*, but I guarantee you nobody else would feel this way if it happened to them. It hasn't even been twenty-four hours. I hardly ever date, so what do I know? Maybe guys never call the day after. Maybe I'm being overly sensitive."

"No, you're not. You're doing what we taught you to do. To know your self-worth and not settle for anything less than you deserve. It's not about the number of hours that have passed. It's about how his lack of action makes you feel. The right man will know in his heart what you need, and he'll see to it before he does anything else."

"Those men only exist in romance novels."

"Thirty-plus years with your father tells me you're wrong, and I think Grace, Morgyn, and Brindle would give you an earful about just how wonderful their men are. Do you want me and Patsy to hang out with you tonight? We can watch a Hallmark movie and pig out on Chunky Monkey ice cream."

"I appreciate the offer, but I've got some bookkeeping to do, and then I'm going to walk home and snuggle up with the one guy who never lets me down."

"Is your father coming over?"

Amber smiled, feeling a little better. "No. I mean Reno. Thanks for talking me off the ledge."

"I didn't talk you off the ledge, honey. You hadn't stepped onto it yet. You were still deciding if Dash was worth climbing up or not. And right now, I'm sure glad you're not Sable."

"Why? At least she wouldn't be sad."

"Because she'd push *Dash* off the ledge, and we'd be having a hide-the-body conversation instead of a my-heart-hurts conversation."

THE REST OF the evening dragged by. The bookkeeping took twice as long to do half as much work because Amber's mind kept trailing back to Dash, her hopeful heart not wanting to believe she'd misread him so badly. She finally gave up on getting much done and headed home just before ten o'clock.

The moon hung high in the blue-gray sky, casting dusky light on the sidewalks as she turned off Main Street toward home with Reno ambling beside her. A car turned down the street, its headlights illuminating their path. It slowed to a crawl beside her, and she looked over. Dash's smiling face came into view, sending her pulse into a frenzy, then tightening the knots in her belly.

"Hey, beautiful, want a ride?"

He sounded happy, as if he hadn't let her down. Was he really that clueless about her feelings? It was ten o'clock at night. In what world was that an appropriate time to show up to see a woman after a date that had gone haywire? "No, thank you."

"You'd rather walk?"

No. What she wanted was answers. Why hadn't he reached out to her earlier? Why had he taken off? What was he doing back in Oak Falls? But her mother's words halted those thoughts—*The right man will know in his heart what you need, and he'll see to it before he does anything else*—bringing others. Was it fair to expect him to know what she needed after knowing her for only a short time? *Ugh.* What was she doing? She was *not* going to be one of those women who rationalized being low on a man's priority list.

Holding her head high despite the ache in her chest, she stared straight ahead as she made her way down the sidewalk. "Yes. I like walking."

He continued talking through the open window, the car barely crawling along the curb. "Are you okay? You seem annoyed."

"I'm *fine*." She hated acting this way, but hurt could turn even the nicest of girls into witches. "It's late. You should go on your way."

He threw the car into park, but she kept walking. He caught up to her on foot, blocking her way. "Amber, what's going on?"

The concern in his voice and confusion in his eyes had her throat thickening, but she didn't hold back. "I thought we connected, and that's on *me*, but I'm worth a two-second text. Especially after a night like we had that ended so embarrassingly."

"A two-second text?" He looked at her like she was crazy.

Her heart sank. "You sound like it's asking for the world. I guess we're just too different. Like I said before, you're a big-city guy who's used to women waiting around for you, and I'm a small-town girl who wants a guy I can rely on. A guy who will worry about my reputation ahead of his own. And before you say anything, my mom told me what you said this morning to the ladies at the park. Don't worry. As near as I can tell, you scared them silly, and your rep isn't tarnished."

DASH COULD SEE how difficult it was for Amber to say all that she had, and hearing it stung. But that didn't change the urge to bend over backward to take away the sadness in her eyes. The trouble was, he'd thought he'd already done that. "Wow. I don't know what's worse—that you think so little of me or that the letter I left you wasn't enough."

She shook her head. "Letter?"

"The one I put on your car this morning before I went to the park."

"You left me a letter?" Her brow wrinkled. "Oh my gosh, *Dash*. I'm sorry. I never saw it."

Relief swept through him. "I was wondering what the heck was going on."

"Sorry. What did the letter say?"

"Romantic things that I hoped would leave you as excited to

see me tonight as I am to see you." He drew her into his arms. "Because you, Amber Montgomery, are worth way more than a two-second text."

A nervous smile played on her lips. "I didn't want to believe that I'd misjudged you, but then I saw your post on Instagram about going home to New York, and it seemed like you were done with us, with Oak Falls."

The emotions he'd been wrestling with all day rushed out. "How can I be done with the woman I can't stop thinking about? The secret sexy reader whose kisses left such a mark on me, I've been getting turned on just thinking about them?"

She blushed fiercely.

"You have done something to me, Amber. You brought out a protectiveness I've only ever felt toward family. The idea of anyone gossiping about you made me crazy, and you're right, I probably did scare the ladies this morning. But that wasn't my intent, and I sure as hell didn't ask them not to talk about us to protect *my* reputation. I wanted to be sure you were respected and that you didn't have to deal with any gossip while I was gone."

She looked like she might cry and lowered her eyes.

"Amber." He waited for her to meet his gaze. "I didn't go to New York because I was done with you. I went because I want *more* time with you. I have to leave for LA in the morning, and I didn't want to go before giving you something I had back at my place in New York."

"You went all that way just to get me something?"

"Do you really think I'd leave the greatest woman I've ever met empty-handed and expect her to wait for me in a town full of burly cowboys?"

She laughed softly. "That was a smart move, because guys

are lining up at my door as we speak."

"Then I'd better up my game." He took her in a slow, sweet kiss, and as their lips parted, one look in her trusting eyes drew out more of his emotions. "I was on the road for twelve hours, and all I could think about was getting back to you and doing more of this." His mouth came hungrily down over hers, and just like last night, they quickly got lost in each other. She went up on her toes, and he deepened the kiss. When she went soft in his arms, he remembered they were still standing on the sidewalk and drew back, leaving her dreamy-eyed.

She sighed, and it was the sweetest sound he'd ever heard. Her fingers curled into the front of his jacket. "I really am sorry I underestimated you."

"It's okay. I can see why you were worried. I fumbled my romantic attempt, and I'm sorry about last night, but honestly, I think we're lucky the neighbors didn't call the fire department, because we are nothing short of combustible. I'm sure there was smoke from the inferno that is *Dash and Amber*."

She laughed. "That would have been even *worse*. I hope you know you don't have to give me presents to get me to wait for you."

"I was only kidding about that." He cocked a grin. "We both know I'm way hotter than any cowboy."

"Hey now. Don't get all cocky on me, or I'll have to prove you wrong."

He tightened his hold on her. "Are you *trying* to make me crazy?"

"Maybe I'm hoping you'll try to convince me otherwise with more kisses."

"Oh *yeah*, my sweet wild thing." As he lowered his lips to hers, he said, "You're going to make me crazy all right."

Chapter Seven

AFTER SEVERAL SCORCHING-hot kisses, they made their way to Amber's house. She sent Reno to do his business and snagged the letter from beneath the windshield wiper on her car. Grinning like a Cheshire cat, she clutched it against her chest and sang, "You wrote me a letter," as they headed inside. *Man,* he loved that.

Reno trotted in after them, and Dash took in the hardwood floors running through the cozy living room, which was as warm and inviting as Amber. An earth-toned couch and matching armchair sat across from a painted brick fireplace. Dried flowers in pretty vases were artfully placed around the room, and magazines and paperback novels littered the top of a sleek coffee table. Beyond the living room was a small dining room that led to an open kitchen with the same soft lines and simple elegance as the living room.

"Nice place," he said as they took off their jackets, and *holy hell.* He couldn't take his eyes off Amber in a flouncy short black floral dress that showed off her long legs and tied at her waist. The dress had bell sleeves, and ruffled socks peeked out of the top of her black cowgirl boots. It was the kind of devastatingly feminine outfit that many girls would turn their noses up at for being too *country.* "*Damn*, sweetheart. That dress and those boots…"

She smiled a little bashfully as she hung their jackets in a closet by the door. "Do you mind if I read the letter real quick?" She was already tearing open the envelope. "Make yourself comfortable."

He'd stayed up half the night reading and rereading the letter, contemplating the intelligence of putting his feelings in writing. If Amber were anyone else, he'd worry that the letter might end up as front-page news in a rag magazine. But if she were anyone else, he never would have written it in the first place.

As she read, every word played out in his mind.

My sweet wild thing, I'm sorry about the alarm and all of the embarrassment of last night, but I'm not sorry about kissing you. I sure hope you've changed your mind about being just friends, because after last night, I know without a doubt that friends won't be enough. I've been feeling incomplete and unsettled for a long time, but I've had a hard time figuring out exactly what was missing from my life. Now I know it was you. I've spent so much time in a world where everyone wants something from me, and nobody is who they claim to be, I wasn't sure an incredible woman like you even existed. How did I get lucky enough to stumble into a barn and meet you? You are the realest, most honest and challenging woman I've ever met, and you have reminded me of the man I was a very long time ago. I hope you'll stick around and see what else we can discover together. I'm heading to New York for the day, but I'll be back tonight and would love to see you if you're not other- wise occupied. D.

She lowered the letter, gazing at him with the dreamiest expression he'd ever seen. "Dash...?"

"Now, that's the swoony look I was hoping to see." He went to her, and she set the letter on the coffee table as he gathered her close.

She wound her arms around his neck, eyes full of wonder and growing darker by the second. "Did you mean all of that?"

"Every word. I know it's fast, but I don't want to play games—"

"I don't either," she said breathily, pulling his mouth down to hers.

He stopped short of kissing her, answering the question in her eyes as he took her necklace off and set it on the coffee table. Then his mouth caught hers in deep, passionate kisses. His heart beat furiously against his chest, and he felt hers hammering out its own frantic rhythm. One hand moved down her back, clutching her ass, and his other dove into her hair, angling her mouth beneath his, intensifying their kisses. He wanted to lift her into his arms and find her bedroom, but this was sweet, careful Amber, and he didn't want to rush her. They stumbled to the couch, devouring each other like they may never get another chance. He leaned into the kiss, taking her down onto her back. Her body was soft and eager beneath him as they made out like teenagers home alone for the first time. She felt like his first special girl, and he realized that was *exactly* what she was.

His hand skimmed down her side to her bare thigh, and she made a pleading, moaning sound into their kisses. The salacious sound shot through him, and he rocked his hard length against her center, the friction sending fire through his veins. The couch was too small for a big guy like him, but he wasn't about to complain. He cradled her beneath him, and in one swift move shifted them onto their sides, laughing into their kisses.

"Much better." He palmed her ass. "Mm. *Lace.*"

He nipped at her lower lip, giving it a gentle tug. Heat flared in her eyes, and he crushed his mouth to hers. The feel of her soft skin against his hand drew a groan from his lungs. She arched against his arousal, and he clutched her ass, holding her there, grinding slowly. He fought the desire to tear down her panties, knowing she needed control. Instead, he pushed his hand beneath her panties, holding her bare ass. Her skin was hot, her noises needy. When she whispered, "More," urgently, he was so fucking glad, "Thank God," slipped out, and they both laughed.

He moved his hand between them, teasing her through her damp panties, earning whimpers, her breathing hitching with every stroke. He tried to take things slow in case she changed her mind, but he was burning for more and slid his hand beneath the edge of her panties. She kissed him harder, rocking her hips forward. *Fuck yeah.* They were on the same page, and he didn't hesitate again. His fingers slid through her wetness, earning a long, surrendering sound that pounded through him. He intensified their kisses as he teased her, making her wetter, and shifted her onto her back beside him as he dipped his fingers inside her. She gasped, her sex clenching around his fingers. He stilled, but he didn't withdraw. "Do you want me to stop?"

"*No.*" Trust brimmed in her eyes. "It's just been a long time."

His heart swelled with the honor of that trust. Swamped with new, *raw* emotions, he kissed her slow and deep, loving her with his fingers. But as happened with them last night, he got lost in her, kissing her deeper, more possessively. He quickened his fingers, earning whimpers and moans as he stroked over the hidden spot inside her. His thumb moved to the apex of her sex, expertly teasing the sensitive bundle of nerves that had her grabbing his arm for leverage as she met each stroke with a rock of her hips. Her kisses turned desperate. "Come for me, wild thing," he said more demandingly than he meant to, and reclaimed her mouth ravenously as she rode his fingers. Her thighs flexed, fingernails digging into his skin through his shirt. Her head fell back, and his name flew from her lungs like a plea. *"Dash! Oh God…"* She writhed and bucked, her body quivering around his fingers, a stream of indiscernible sounds filling the room.

As she came down from the peak, he rained kisses over her cheeks and lips. Her skin was warm and flushed, her lips swollen from their kisses, and she was absolutely stunning. He lowered his lips to hers, taking her in a languid, sensual kiss, wanting to be closer, to know *all* of her. To hear her hopes and dreams and soothe her fears and insecurities. Her eyes fluttered open, full of lust and something much deeper, heightening his desire for all those things.

AMBER WAS FLOATING in a post-orgasmic haze. Dash began moving his thumb over that magical spot again, but her nerves were too sensitive, and she bowed off the cushions, grabbing his wrist. "I don't think I can survive another…"

A devilish glimmer sparked in his eyes. "Then let's make it a phenomenal death."

He took her in a deep, passionate kiss, and all thoughts of stopping went out the window. She wanted this, him, *more*. He trailed kisses down her neck. *Feels so good.* She breathed harder as he dusted his lips over her chest, igniting flames beneath her skin. *Don't stop. Please don't stop.* He moved the neckline of her dress to the side, revealing the edge of her bra, and pressed a kiss to the swell of her breast.

"*Mm.* Pink lace on my girl. Life just got even better."

His girl? She loved the sound of that.

His warm breath coasted over her skin as he pressed another kiss there. *Mm. So nice.* He moved lower, untying the bow at her waist. His eyes flicked up to hers, his fingers hovering over the front clasp of her bra. A single nod was all it took for him to unhook the clasp, and then that magical mouth was on her bare breast, licking, sucking, his teeth grazing her sensitive skin. She arched beneath him, grabbing his head, holding his mouth there. "Don't stop."

He did as she begged and gave her other breast the same attention. Every suck took her closer to the edge. Her body vibrated from her head all the way down to her toes. He kissed a path down her belly, her ribs, her *hips*. It hadn't just been a long time since she'd fooled around. It had been years since a guy had—

Her thoughts fractured as his lips touched her inner thigh, sending ripples of heat skating up her core. He did it again, and her eyes slammed closed. Oh, how she loved that! His hand moved down her leg, and her nerves caught fire. She felt him shifting, sitting up, sending cool air sailing over her legs. Her eyes flew open, and she found him reaching for one of her boots. He took them off, leaving on her socks. His brows knitted, and his chin fell to his chest.

"Don't laugh at my ruffles," she warned.

His eyes found hers, the emotions in them bowling her over. "I love your ruffles. Don't *ever* stop wearing them."

The desire in his voice sent thrills rushing through her. His lips touched her leg again, kissing his way up her body, whispering against her skin. "So pretty...So special..." He pressed a kiss just below her belly button. She inhaled sharply, and his gaze found hers.

"You're so feminine, wild thing, *you* do me in."

His deep voice, his words, the depth of his stare, all of it, all of *him*, did *her* in.

He hooked his fingers into the sides of her panties, drawing them down and off. Then his rough hands skimmed up the outsides of her legs, his eyes locked on hers as he kissed her inner thighs. Lord have mercy, the fire in his eyes made her ache with anticipation. She curled her fingers into the cushions as he splayed his hands over her thighs, opening her to him and lowering his mouth between her legs. She held her breath, readying herself, but he didn't touch her. His mouth hovered there, his hot breath teasing over her wetness as his mouth moved up to her clit, then lower again. He slicked his tongue beside her sex, and she moaned, rocking up. He did it again, earning another sharp gasp. His hand moved up her body, and he teased her nipple as he continued masterfully taunting her with his erotic torture. She clawed at the cushions, panting, writhing, *mewling*, need strung so tight she feared she'd burst. He hadn't even touched her where she needed it most, and the pleasure was so exquisite she didn't want it to end, but she also wanted more.

"Dash, *I can't...take it.*"

He pressed a kiss to the apex of her sex, and her hips shot

up. Just when she thought she'd lose her mind, he slicked his tongue along her sex, sending electrical currents racing through her. She whimpered, and his mouth came greedily down where she needed him most, feasting on her, thrusting his tongue into her and using his fingers on that other magical spot while squeezing her nipple. She was lost in a sea of sensations. Her skin was on fire. Her entire body felt like one giant nerve ending. He moved his mouth higher, using his tongue and teeth on her clit as his fingers entered her, moving in and out in a hypnotizing rhythm. She clawed at the cushions, blinded with pleasure, rocking against his mouth until her toes curled under and she surrendered to the ecstasy consuming her. He stayed with her, keeping her at the peak and loving her through the very last shiver.

She melted into the cushions, trying to catch her breath as he kissed his way up her body, gently clasping her bra, righting and retying her dress. Lord, this man…

He gathered her close, brushing his lips over her cheeks as she lay in his strong, safe arms, happiness wrapping around them like a ribbon, and then he kissed her. The taste of him mingled with the lingering taste of her, and the world came back into focus. She realized he'd given her *everything*, and she'd left him high and dry.

"Dash," she whispered, "Do you want me to…?"

"No, babe. Once you get started, I'm not letting you out of the bedroom for a week. I'll never make my flight in the morning."

She giggled.

"You think I'm kidding? I need to clear my schedule when I get back. I think a week ought to do it. You've got staff to take over, right?"

"A *week*?" *Holy cow.* "I barely survived tonight."

"Told you I was better than any old cowboy."

They talked and kissed until long after midnight, reluctantly giving in to what had to be the end of their evening.

"I wish I wasn't leaving tomorrow." He took her hand as they made their way to the door. "I'm having dinner with Shea tomorrow evening. Can I call you after you get off work?"

"I'd like that. Do you have my cell number?"

"No." He pulled out his phone and typed in a code. "Here, put your number in while I get your gift from the car."

She'd forgotten all about the gift. "A gift and mind-blowing pleasure? I might never let you go."

"I'm counting on it." He gave her a quick kiss, then jogged out to his car.

She put her number in his contacts and watched him carrying an enormous picture up the walkway. "You went to New York to get me a picture?"

"This isn't just a picture. It's an autographed movie poster for *The Greatest Showman*, signed by the entire cast and the director."

He turned it around, and her jaw dropped. "Ohmygod, *Dash*. Look!" She pointed to the signatures. "Hugh Jackman! Zac Efron! Zendaya! Where did you get this? *Wait*, you said it was in your house. I can't take this from you!"

He laughed. "Yes, you can. I want you to have it."

"But you love the movie, too."

"Yeah, but that light in your eyes? That adorable giddiness you're trying to hold back? That's *way* better than this."

"You're crazy!"

He set the framed poster down and hauled her into his arms. "I'm crazy about you, Amber. Every little thing about you, from your ruffled socks to your love of acorns."

She buried her face in his chest. "I saw your acorn post. I figured I was the *nut* you were referring to."

"That sexy little brain of yours shouldn't go straight to the negative. I couldn't stop thinking about you, so I posted the acorn. I know you don't like drama, so I kept everything about *us* off social media. That acorn was my secret message to my secret sexy reader."

"But I told you I only wanted to be friends that night, so the *nut* made sense."

He shook his head. "It's not about the words; it's about symbolism. You said you wanted to be friends, but your eyes told me otherwise. I was hoping you'd see the symbolism of looking deeper and seeing the start of something new between us. I guess I really do suck at doing romantic stuff."

"No, you definitely do *not*. I just stink at interpreting it."

"Maybe we can both work on that. A couple of weeks ago I posted about the signing, and I'll do that again to bring exposure to your store. But *this*. You and me?" He touched his forehead to hers and lowered his voice. "This is ours. It's private and special, and while we figure out what it all means, I'd like to keep it out of the gossip magazines. Please don't think that I'm not posting about the amazing woman I met in Oak Falls because of anything other than wanting to protect what I hope will become the most important thing to both of us."

She had a feeling it was already well on the way.

Chapter Eight

"HI. THANK YOU for returning my call," Andi said into the phone. "I've been trying to reach you. Hold on just a second, please."

It was late Thursday afternoon, and Dash was in LA. He'd called his sister to check in while getting a quick workout in the hotel gym before meeting Shea for dinner. Through his earbuds, he heard Andi telling someone she needed to take his call and would be back in a few minutes. He pumped out another set of curls as he waited.

"I'm sorry to keep you holding." Andi sounded overly professional.

"No worries." Dash could tell by the cadence of her voice that she was walking. He pictured her in one of her many proper business outfits, stick-straight posture, long dirty-blond hair hanging down her back, and black-framed glasses perched on the bridge of her nose, so different from bubbly Dawn, who lived life on the fringe.

"*You* are a godsend," Andi said in a hushed tone.

Dash bristled. "What is going on? Is someone giving you trouble? I can get Troy's old man there in two minutes flat." He'd grown up with Joey and Troy Stewart in Port Hudson.

Joey had gone on to play for the Jets and Troy had been Dash's teammate on the Giants, but their father still coached football at Boyer University.

"I'm on a date with a guy Becca knows, but his idea of good reading material is a comic book."

Becca was a co-worker of Andi's at LWW who dressed like a pinup girl and could give Sable a run for her money in the sass department. Dash liked her, save for her constantly setting up his sisters on dates. "She should know better."

"No kidding, but you know Bec. She refuses to believe that I like brains over brawn."

"That's just one more reason you should get into your field instead of wasting your talents as a research assistant to a woman who's faking her way through her career."

"Sutton's learning the ropes, not faking her way, and you know I love my job. Besides, not all of us need to plow into our careers headfirst like you. It's not like I'll ever leave Port Hudson."

Same conversation, different day. His sister wanted a family and a career, but more than anything, she wanted to remain in their hometown. The trouble was, she would never have the career she wanted if she stayed there. His thoughts turned to Amber and how much she loved Oak Falls. "I'm not saying you have to go far, but you'll never find the career you want there."

"Calm down, Mr. Motivation. I've heard it a million times, and I know you want what's best for me, but even *I* don't know what that is right now."

"Yes, you do. You've wanted to be out there saving sea turtles since you were a kid. I told you I can have Clay put a good word in for you with his brother Noah or his cousin Dane. That's one phone call and two great options. They could probably hook you up with something at the Real DEAL or with Brave." His ex-teammate and buddy Clay Braden's brother Noah and their cousin Dane were co-owners of the Real DEAL, a total immersion exploratory park for kids that included educational exhibits and hands-on activities, in Colorado. Noah ran the marine biology lab, and Dane, the founder of the Brave Foundation, which used education and advocacy programs to protect sharks and the world's oceans, ran the marine activities and exhibits.

He heard his sister sigh as he set down the weights he was using and began doing push-ups.

"I'll think about it," Andi said.

"Mm-hm." He knew she was appeasing him. "I just don't want you to lose sight of your dreams. If you wait too long to gain the experience you need to get your foot in the door, you'll get locked out of your field. You'll get a rep as the girl who played it safe for too long."

"Says the guy who is currently trending on Twitter as *hashtag Dash Pennington Reads Porn*. Do you really want to talk about reps?"

"What?" Dash snapped.

She giggled. "I guess you haven't been on social media since your flight. Some guy got a picture of you on the plane reading an erotic romance novel and posted it."

"Shit." He'd wanted to see what Amber was into and had been reading the novel he'd bought from her. "It's not *porn*. It's a love story." Those were words he never thought he'd say.

"I read hot romance. I know what it is. I just have two questions. Why is my badass brother reading it? In *public*, no less. And why are you breathing so hard? You're not reading it *now*, are you? *Ew.*"

He uttered a curse as he pushed to his feet and wiped his face with a towel. "I'm in the hotel gym, getting my workout in before I meet Shea for dinner."

"And the answer to my other question?"

"Research."

"Research? Did you get a complaint in the bedroom? Don't tell Damon, or you'll never hear the end of it."

"I didn't get a complaint. *Jesus*, Andi."

"Just making sure you're up to par on all the latest moves?" she teased.

He gritted his teeth. "Listen, how are things with you? I wanted to check in, but I don't have much time. I need to call Dawn before I hit the shower."

"I'm fine, except for my loser date."

"Good. Get rid of him fast. Tell him you have to take care of something for work."

"Yes, Dad," she teased. "Why were you really reading that book?"

"Goodbye, Andi."

"Wait! If you really want to impress women, check out *Crazy, Sexy, Sinful* by Charlotte Sterling—"

"I'm hanging up now. I love you." They'd grown up with Charlotte in Port Hudson, and now she lived in Colorado and was a bestselling romance author.

"I love you, too. Remember, *Crazy, Sexy, Sinful!*"

"I don't want to think about Charlotte writing romance. Bye, Sis." He ended the call and sent a text to Shea. *You might want to check out Twitter. I've been outed. Sorry.*

His mind returned to Amber. It never drifted far. He'd sent her a text first thing this morning saying he'd had a great time last night, and she'd teased him about having dreamed about

Zac Efron. She was a feisty one. He wondered if she'd seen the hashtag, and if so, whether she'd gotten a kick out of him reading the book.

He navigated to Twitter, took a screenshot of the picture and the ridiculous hashtag, and thumbed out a text to Amber. *Looks like I need lessons in how to be a secret sexy reader. I hope you're ready for the rewrites.* He added the screenshot and sent it to her. As he navigated to Dawn's contact information, Amber's response rolled in. *Brindle and Lindsay showed me. I can't believe you're reading it! Maybe I should tweet about what you're really into.* A picture of her leg from the knee down popped up. She was wearing a pretty pale green sock with a lace ruffle at the top.

He typed, *Only yours, my fiercely feminine wild thing. I have to finish my workout and get ready to meet Shea. I'll call around 11 your time. Can't wait to hear your voice.* He sent the message, and for a moment he stared at it. The last line had come so naturally, he hadn't even thought about it. He chalked that up to just another of the many ways she'd affected him. His gaze moved to the picture of her leg and the pretty sock, but he was thinking about her smile, her laugh, and how much he'd hated that she'd spent yesterday thinking he had ghosted her.

He'd make damn sure she never worried about that again.

Another text appeared from Amber. *Me too.* She added a kissing emoji. Hell if that little yellow image didn't make him miss her even more. He glanced at the clock and realized it was after five. He needed to get a move on and quickly called Dawn.

She answered on the second ring. "Hey. I have a bone to pick with you."

"Please tell me you have your pepper spray." It was after eight o'clock in New York, and he could tell by the way she was panting that she was out for her evening run.

"Nope, and I'm wearing a shirt that says *Easy target. Nobody cares if I go missing* across the chest."

"You're a pain in my ass."

"You're welcome. Now, that bone I need to pick—"

"If it's about the hashtag, I don't want to hear it."

"I'm way past the hashtag, and I have a lot of questions about *you* reading romance. But first I want to know why you didn't stop by to see us when you were in New York yesterday."

"I was only in the city for an hour to pick up a few things, and I guess if you saw the hashtag, you know I'm in LA now."

"That's old news. Everyone in the world has probably seen the hashtag and knows you're in LA. But next time you're in New York, I expect a call."

He smiled to himself. He'd raised his siblings to speak their minds, and Dawn was tough. But after knowing how bad Amber had felt when she hadn't seen his letter, he cut his sister some slack. "Sorry."

"If you had called, I would have told you that Mom has a boyfriend."

"What do you mean, a boyfriend?"

"I realize it's an unfamiliar term for you, but for the rest of us, a boyfriend is a man who regularly takes a woman out on dates and diddles her fiddle."

"That's our *mother* you're talking about." He paced, rubbing a knot in the back of his neck.

"If you think Mom isn't getting it on, then you're living in a fantasy world."

"Would you *stop*?" He shook his head to try to delete that thought, but it stuck like glue. "I know she went out with a guy from the school a few times, but she hasn't said anything to me about having a boyfriend." He'd called Coach Stewart to check out the guy, and Coach had assured him that Mitch Grayson was a stand-up guy.

"That's him. Professor Hottie Pants."

Dash gritted his teeth at the nickname. "Have you met him?"

"Yes. I had dinner with them last night. He's a total geek with a pocket protector and everything, but a hot geek. I asked him if he had a son Andi's age. She'd love this guy. I like him, and more importantly, Mom likes him."

"I just talked to Andi. She didn't say anything about this." A text from Shea popped up, and he quickly read it. *Already on it. In a meeting. We'll talk at dinner.*

"Andi was worried you'd freak out."

"That's ridiculous. Mom's allowed to have a social life." Even if he didn't know how he felt about it.

"The last time you met a guy Mom went out with, you scared him off."

"That was five or six years ago, and any guy who gets scared off by a few questions has no business going out with our mother." The last thing he wanted was for a guy to go after his mother or sisters, thinking he could get to Dash's money. "This guy must be something special if he caught Mom's attention after all these years."

"It was *four* years ago, and Mom has gone out with other guys since you scared that last guy off. She's just too smart to tell you about them."

"Are you shitting me? Someone's got to check out the guys she goes out with. Did Damon or Hawk know about the other guys?"

"I don't think they care as much as you do, but I don't think she introduced them to anyone. This guy is different. She lights up whenever she talks about him. I think she's going to introduce him to everyone."

He didn't have time to argue with her about his brothers, much less to get too deep into this conversation. "I'll call Mom tomorrow and get the scoop."

"Ask her about the diddling," she teased.

"You're making me lose my appetite. Listen, you know that favor I texted you about this morning? Did you have time to take care of it for me?"

"Yes. I got it out right in the nick of time."

"Thanks. You're the best."

"I want you to know that I'm taping this conversation and sending a copy to Andi, Hawk, and Damon, so they're aware that I am *the best*."

"Smart-ass. I'll say I was coerced. I've got to go. Love you."

"*Wait!* Why *were* you reading romance? You were looking for pointers, right? Wait until I tell Damon!" She cracked up.

Christ Almighty. His sisters were going to be the death of him.

"KISS HIM ALREADY!" Amber yelled at the Hallmark movie she was watching while she waited for Dash's call.

Reno lifted his head from where he was sleeping at the foot of the bed.

"Sorry, buddy." She reached down to pet him, then settled back against the pillows, eating another spoonful of ice cream as the couple in the movie leaned in so close, she found herself leaning forward, too. *Come on. One kiss. Just do it!*

She groaned in frustration as they said good night with nothing more than a wanting look in their eyes. She'd always loved Hallmark movies, but she was beginning to see why her sisters had a hard time watching them. Had Dash ruined them for her? She couldn't stop thinking about the way he'd kissed her like he never wanted to stop and touched her, unhurried and greedy, as if he were savoring every second of it. She closed her eyes, and his face bloomed in her mind, his dark eyes full of desire, just as they'd been as he'd lowered his mouth between her legs. Her entire body shuddered with the memory. She'd been revved up all day. All it took was one thought of Dash for her body to go into some sort of sexual frenzy. She'd never reacted so viscerally to a man, much less thoughts of a man, and she had no idea what to do with the sexual energy that clung to her like a second skin. It had been embarrassing at work. It wasn't like she could disappear into her office and whip out a vibrator to ease the tension.

Who was she kidding? A vibrator couldn't butter her biscuit the way Dash could.

She ate another bite of ice cream, thinking about the dirty romance movies her sisters and friends watched. She'd never been too curious about them, because she'd always felt like her sisters and friends were miles ahead of her with their sexuality. They'd *owned* theirs since they were teenagers, while Amber had been a late bloomer and she'd never really learned to *own* it. But with Dash, she seemed to have skipped over owning it and had charged into uncharted territory, not only relentlessly replaying the dirty things he'd done to her but also fantasizing about the wicked things she wanted to do to him, which she'd experienced in great detail in her dreams last night. In her dreams, he'd talked dirty to her as he'd pleasured her, and she'd given that pleasure right back to him. It had only been a dream, but she could still feel his hard length in her hand and sliding through her lips, could still hear the filthy things she'd said that made her cheeks burn just thinking about it.

Lord have mercy.

She was as hot and flustered as she'd been when she'd woken up this morning. She glanced at the clock. Dash wasn't supposed to call for another forty minutes. Giving in to her newfound curiosity, she picked up the remote, trying to remember the name of the movie Brindle and Lindsay gushed about a few weeks ago. Brindle had said the sex scenes were so hot, she and Trace had watched them together several times.

She grabbed her phone and texted Brindle. *What was the name of the movie you told me about with the girl who gets abducted and falls for the guy?*

Her phone rang, and Brindle's name flashed on the screen. She answered it, but before she could say hello, Brindle said, "You want to watch *365 Days?*"

Amber scrambled for an excuse. "One of my book club friends was asking if I knew any good billionaire romance movies, and you seemed to like it."

"One of your *book club* friends? *Really?* Because I'd think they'd all be in the know about that particular movie, especially since it was a foreign book first, and when the movie came out here, bookstagrammers posted about it for weeks in anticipation of the English books."

Shoot. "I guess not." Amber fidgeted with the edge of her sleeping shorts.

"I heard your *friend* is out of town. Are you feeling a little lonely? Looking for some visual inspiration to get you through the nights while he's gone?"

Amber had spent a lifetime listening to her sisters and friends rave about guys and the way they made them feel. Part of her wanted to claim her turn, to gush about Dash and how wonderful he was. To rave about the letter he'd written her, the gift he'd given her, and the incredible way he made her feel special. But a bigger part of her wanted to treasure those things and keep them all to herself. She didn't even know what it was between them yet or where it would lead. But she wanted to find out.

"*No*, I am not," Amber answered.

"If you say so. You know I'm cool with Dash getting all up in your *end zone*, right?"

"Ohmygod…" Another call rang through, and Dash's name flashed on the screen. Her pulse skyrocketed. "Thanks for the name of the movie. I've got to go. I have another call."

"From the sound of your voice, I'm guessing it's Dash?" When Amber didn't answer quick enough, Brindle's all-knowing voice came through the line. "Girl, forget the movie. Let *him* ease your loneliness. Have fun!"

Amber turned off the television and switched over to Dash's call. "Hi."

"Hey. I hope it's okay that I'm calling early. Are you busy?"

The sound of his deep voice made her forget all about the movie. "No. I'm glad you called. How was dinner? The few times I spoke with Shea, she seemed really nice."

"Shea's the best. A little pushy, but that's her job. And dinner would have been better if you were there."

"You say the nicest things."

"I'm just being honest. How was your day?"

"It was good. Work was busy, and I chose a winner to decorate the front window for November, which is always fun."

"You let other people decorate your front window?"

"Some months I do. I like letting the community be part of the bookstore, and it's fun to see how excited they get when they win. They put a lot of effort into the display. It's become a coveted contest. Believe it or not, I get hundreds of entries."

"That's amazing, but it's not surprising. Your shop has a really great vibe, and you're so personable, sending out cards to your customers. It sounds like they like giving back to you."

"I'm glad you think so. I want people to feel like they're stopping in to see an old friend, even if they don't know me that well. But I do the window display every October. It's my favorite month of the year."

"The display is gorgeous. Why is it your favorite month?"

She settled back against the pillows. "Because the sky is blue, but the air is crisper than any other time of year. Except winter, but winter skies are whiter. I love fall flowers and seeing the leaves change colors. Autumn is like Mother Nature's gift, and knowing that soon the branches will be bare and the blue skies will fade to white makes them even more special." She waited for him to respond, but silence stretched between them. "Sorry, did that sound weird?"

"Not at all. I was just thinking about how long it's been since I've even noticed those things and how much I'd like to be looking at them with you."

"I wish you were here, too." Her mind took that thought and braided it into a sexy scene in her head. "How long *has* it been?"

"Honestly? I'm not sure I ever noticed the sky or the leaves the way you do. Football is a fall and winter game, but off-season conditioning starts in the spring, and there's summer training camp. I've been playing since I was a kid. Between that and helping take care of our family after our old man left, there wasn't much time to stop and smell the roses."

"Can I ask you something about your childhood?"

"Sure."

"You said you practically raised your brothers and sisters, but if you were only thirteen when your father left, then your sisters were really young. How did you manage?"

"I don't know. When you're in that situation, you just do everything you can. Our neighbor got the girls off the bus and kept them until I got home, and when I had practice, either our neighbor would watch them, or I'd take them with me and they'd play on the sidelines. I made sure they ate and did their homework, that kind of thing. You know, I've never had anyone I wanted to share this with. Sin and the guys I grew up with know, but as an adult, I've never talked about it."

"I'm sorry. You don't have to tell me anything else. I didn't mean to pry."

"No, it's okay. I want you to know who I am beyond what you see on social media or in magazines."

"I'm getting a pretty good picture of who you are. It sounds like you would have done anything to help your mom."

"You've got that right. She's had a tough life, and she didn't deserve what my father did to her. My mom went into the foster system when she was eight after her mother was arrested for drug possession. Her mother spent a couple of years in prison and overdosed a few months after she got out. My mom went back into the system until she aged out. She had no other family. She's overcome a lot. Nothing means more to her than family, and she instilled that in us."

"Knowing that makes what your father did even more tragic. So the grandmother you told me about is your father's mom?"

"Yes. But his parents adore my mom, and they wanted to help, but she was too proud to take their money. Of course, every time we saw my grandparents, Grandpa George would slip me a few twenties, and I'd use them when my mom would send me to the store instead of using her credit card. But she never knew."

"At thirteen my biggest worry, besides epilepsy, was what I wanted to read on any given day. You had a lot of responsibility on your shoulders."

"I didn't see it like that. The person who should have taken care of us split. I was pissed at my father for leaving and for hurting everyone. Anger won out over hurt because I saw the damage his leaving caused. I guess I was partly driven by a need to show him that he didn't break us."

Her heart filled up and ached for him. "It sounds like his leaving really shaped who you are. That's probably why you pushed yourself so hard and have been so successful."

"It shaped all of us in different ways. My mom got stronger. Hawk had gotten his first camera earlier that year, and I'm convinced that as talented as he is, there's more to his success than that. I think it's easier to see the world through a lens than it is to face it head-on. And I told you what Damon was like."

And how you cleaned up his messes. "How do you think it affected your sisters?"

"They were so little. That might have been the worst part of his leaving, seeing how hurt and confused they were. Dawn cried an awful lot the first few weeks, and Andi turned it all inward, she basically went silent."

"I'm such a Daddy's girl, I can't imagine how sad they must have been."

"Sad, yes, but after Dawn's tears came anger. I did everything I could to convince her not to hate our father despite how I felt about him. I still held out hope that he'd come back for the girls' sake."

"That must have been difficult, given how angry you were."

"It wasn't easy, and trust me, I had my moments when anger won out. But it didn't end up mattering. About a year after he left, Dawn changed. I'll never forget when it happened. I was sitting out on the back steps with my buddy Joey, and Dawn came out the back door and stood in front of us with her little hands on her hips and said, 'Dad's not coming back.' I told her I knew that and I was sorry, and she said, 'It's okay. It's his loss. The idiot.' Then she went inside to play, and from then on, she's been the girl you see on television."

"Wow. I guess she processed it and made up her mind."

"She did. I'm still worried about Andi, though. She's afraid to step away from the safety of Port Hudson, and it limits her." His voice was thick with worry.

"There's nothing wrong with wanting to stay where she feels safe. That's what I do."

"Your situations are different. You're doing what you've always wanted. Andi wants to be a marine biologist, and she could go far in the field, but not if she stays there."

"It sounds to me like you're still taking care of everyone."

He laughed. "I think my sisters would call it *annoying* them, not taking care of them."

"Maybe, but if it's anything like how I feel about Sable watching out for me, I'm sure they appreciate it. It must have been hard to leave them when you went to college."

"It was the hardest thing I'd ever done, but I got a full ride, and I knew if I made it into the pros, my family would never have to worry about a thing."

"And that right there is one of the things I admire most about you."

"My *money?*"

"No, you goof. Your big heart. You think of everyone else before yourself. You were a kid caring for a family. And the other night, you said you were falling apart, too. Who was taking care of *you*, making sure you felt loved and were okay?"

"My mom and my grandparents. You had midnight walks with your dad. I had midnight chats over hot chocolate with my mom in our kitchen."

"Aw. I *love* that. It makes me happy knowing you had that time with her. You know what? I think you're right. I would have liked teenage Dash a whole lot."

"You would have been all over me. Especially when I first hit my growth spurt and I was skinny as a rail. That was *hot.*"

"You were probably adorable. I bet you had tons of girl-friends."

"Who had time for girlfriends? I think my longest high school girlfriend lasted about three weeks and involved lots of back-seat make-out sessions. How about you?"

"I've never had a girlfriend," she teased.

"Hold on. I have to scratch *threesome with Amber* off my bucket list."

"I've never even made out in a back seat, so use that infor-mation to scratch off whatever else shouldn't be on our list."

"What?" he exclaimed. "My girl has never been groped in the back of a horny kid's parents' car?"

"Nope, and I haven't made out under the bleachers, which apparently *is* a thing, or at a creek party, a barn dance, or JJ's Pub, all of which I think nearly every female in this town has done. I've also never stargazed with a guy, making wishes and spilling secrets. I missed all of those rites of passages, but I *have* kissed a boy on the Ferris wheel and in a corn maze."

"Are you sure under the bleachers is really a thing?"

"*Yes.* It's a little gross, right?"

"I'm not sure, but I know what we're doing when I get back to town."

She couldn't stop smiling. "Look at you, making all my teenage dreams come true."

"Maybe you can make one of my adult fantasies come true."

"I'm *not* having a threesome with you."

He chuckled. "Don't worry, sweetheart, that's not my fantasy. I have no interest in sharing you. In fact, I'm a little jealous of those Ferris wheel and corn maze kisses. Who were the lucky guys?"

She liked knowing he was jealous. "There was only one guy."

"Who was it?"

"I can't tell you *that*. I've never told anyone other than Pepper about those kisses."

"I need to meet this secret-keeping sister of yours, but I think I understand. Was he my wild thing's *first*?" His voice was low and seductive.

She lay on the bed. "No. I didn't do that until I was in college."

"We're in trouble now, Amber."

"Why?"

"I think I just fell a little harder for you. *Yup.* I feel it right here in my chest."

She buried her face in the pillow to keep a happy noise from slipping out.

"Are you still there?" he asked cautiously.

She rolled onto her back. "Mm-hm."

"Can I ask you something personal?"

"I just told you one of my most coveted secrets, didn't I?"

"And I'm glad you trust me enough to share it with me." His warmth slithered through the phone like an embrace. "I'm just wondering if you waited because it never felt right, or because of what you told me the other night about how boys kept their distance because of your epilepsy?"

She closed her eyes as the tenderness in his voice drew out her answer. "Both, I guess. I was also scared of it."

"Then we have that in common. I only did it in my senior year of high school because I was afraid of being the only Virginia State football player who was still a virgin."

"Really?" She was surprised he'd admitted that.

"Absolutely. There's a lot of pressure that goes along with being a cool guy."

His honesty was like a drug, luring her in.

"Any guy who tells you he wasn't nervous the first few times is lying. Hell, I was nervous last night."

"No way."

"Sure, I was. You're special, I didn't want to mess things up. I wanted to be the best kiss, best touch, best everything for you."

She closed her eyes, letting his confession soak in. "You definitely were."

"Yeah, I knew I'd ruin you for any other man, but I didn't want to sound too cocky."

They both laughed.

"I bet you have lots of other secret kissing stories from high school, don't you?"

"Not really. Just a couple of stories, but they aren't secrets."

"Why was your first kiss a secret?"

She rolled onto her side. "I don't know. It just is. He's someone I still know, and it was a private, special kiss."

"Ah, that's the romantic in you. I sure do like that. I'd give anything to have known you then, to have taken you to barn dances and fairs. I would have made your first time special, just the two of us in some private place that only you and I knew of. I would have set up candles, spread out blankets, and made love to you under the stars."

She sighed, shifting onto her back again. *I think I just fell harder for you, too.*

"Of course, as a teenager I would have lasted about a minute, so I might never have lived that down."

Laughter burst from her lips, and Reno lifted his head.

"You think that's funny, huh?"

"I'm sorry." She tried to stifle her laughter, but she pictured him as a lanky teen and couldn't hold it in. "I hope you're better at it now."

"Does that mean if I'm not, you're done with me?"

"For sure," she said through her giggles. "Although you *do* have a very gifted mouth."

He made a growling noise. "You haven't experienced the half of it. Remember what I said about clearing our schedules."

Her mind raced through all the dirty things they could do.

"Now we really do have trouble on our hands," he said gruffly. "You've reminded me of how sweet you tasted, and it's turning me on."

"Dash," she whispered, embarrassed.

"Am I alone in this? You didn't think about us today? You're not thinking about kissing me right now? Touching me?

Having my mouth on you?"

Her pulse spiked. She swallowed hard, mustering the courage to confess the truth. "You're not alone."

"Thank God, because I can't stop thinking about you, and I've never been like this with anyone. I want to see your beautiful face. I want to hold you in my arms and kiss you until we both lose our minds."

Me too. Her heart was beating so hard, she was sure he could hear it through the phone.

"FaceTime with me. Let me see you, sweetheart."

She held her breath, knowing where this was heading. She'd read some really hot phone sex scenes, and her sisters had told her stories that made her blush a red streak. She wasn't sure she could do it. But *oh*, how she wanted to.

"Come on, baby."

She opened her mouth to speak, and it took a second for "Okay" to come. A few seconds later, his handsome face appeared on the screen, his jaw peppered with stubble, his dark eyes gazing hungrily at her. His chest was bare, and she wished she could touch him.

"There's my beautiful girl."

Swept up in her desires, she could do little more than smile.

"You feel it too, don't you? A desperate need to be closer?"

She was breathing too hard. "Yes."

Reno must have sensed the change in her, because he lifted his head and laid his head beside hers.

"Hey, Reno, that's my spot." Dash's eyes never left Amber's. "Are you okay?"

She nodded.

"Nervous?"

She nodded again, embarrassed that she was that transparent, but also glad that he cared enough to notice.

"I want you to know something. I've never met anyone who I wanted to get serious with until you. I've never had a threesome, and I don't want to."

Relief washed over her. She hadn't even realized she was worried about that.

"I'm not a guy who video chats with women, partly because I've never fully trusted the women I've gone out with."

"Because everyone wants something from you?"

He nodded. "I think you and I are a lot alike. We both need a higher level of trust in order to open ourselves up to others in certain ways."

He saw her so clearly, she wondered how many other parts of her he was already taking note of. "What's the other reason?"

A smile played at the corners of his mouth. "I've never wanted to see anyone that badly. All of these feelings, this need to talk to you, to see you while I'm thousands of miles away, is new to me, too. Don't be nervous, sweetheart. Let's just talk. That's enough for me. *You're* enough for me."

Chapter Nine

DASH GOT UP at four o'clock in the morning to call his mother by seven her time, hoping to catch her before she left for work Friday morning. She was always doing a hundred things at once. He pictured her rushing around, her straight blond hair she'd worn parted on the side since he was a kid brushing the shoulders of one of her smart pantsuits.

"Hi, honey." Her words were carried on laughter. "How are you?"

"I'm good. What're you laughing at?"

"Oh, nothing." Nothing sounded like it was definitely something.

He heard a male voice in the background, and his muscles tensed, his sister's words coming back to him. *Professor Hottie Pants.* "Who was that?"

"Mitch Grayson. I told you we were seeing each other a few weeks ago, remember?"

"Yeah, I remember." He told himself not to make a big deal out of it, but a question came out before he could stop it. "Did he come over for breakfast?" *Please say yes.*

"Mm-hm. Yup. Sure did." She giggled.

Robin Pennington was *not* a giggler. Unless she was lying.

Dash silently chastised himself for feeling weird about his mother having a serious relationship. "That's nice. Does he treat you well?"

"Very well. Like a princess."

His mother was the farthest thing from a princess, but she sure as hell deserved to be treated like one. "Good. I'd like to meet him next time I'm in town."

"I was hoping you'd say that. Are you still coming before the fundraiser?"

"Yeah. I'll be there the Friday before." He knew he should let her go spend time with Mitch, but he was dying to tell her about Amber. "I met someone, too."

"Oh, *honey*. I want to hear all about her. What's her name? How did you meet her? Where does she live?"

He chuckled, loving her enthusiasm. "Her name is Amber Montgomery, and she grew up in Oak Falls, Virginia and lives in Meadowside. I think you may know her. She went to Boyer and spent a lot of time in the library."

"Amber...Amber...Was she in the LWW sisterhood? Dark hair, pretty, on the quiet side?"

"Yes, that's her."

"Oh, Dashy, she was one of my favorite girls," she said thoughtfully, the nickname tugging at his heartstrings. "We talked almost every day. It's all coming back to me. I remember she missed her family so much when she first came to Boyer, I worried she'd go home and never come back. But she stuck it out. How did you meet her? Through Sinny?"

"Yeah, at a party in a barn. She's really something, Mom. She's...She reminds me of home."

"I'm not sure that's a good thing. You had so much responsibility on your shoulders when you lived here."

There was no denying that, but nothing could ruin home. "It's a good thing, Mom. You showed me what family is."

"No, honey. You showed *me* what family is. You were the glue that held us together."

"I don't know about that, but either way, I don't regret any of those years, and Amber is all about family. She's wholesome and smart. She makes me laugh and *think* and *feel*. She brings out parts of me I had forgotten existed, and she's got this quiet strength and confidence that blows me away."

"It sounds like you're really taken with her."

"I am. I think about her all the time. I've only known her for a week. Is that nuts?"

"That's not nuts, honey. That's how you know it's real, when it bites you in the butt and you don't want to run away."

He chuckled. "I'm not running. I'm in LA for a couple of days, and I want to jump on the next flight out of here and get back to her."

"What does she do for a living? Will she be going with you on your tour?"

He hadn't considered that option. "She owns the bookstore where I'm starting the tour. I doubt she can take that much time off."

"A bookstore. She followed her dreams. I'm happy for her, and I'm happy for *you*, my sweet boy. You've been wrapped up in football for so long, I thought maybe you'd forgotten that there was more to life than winning a game and more to women than...you know."

"*Mom.* You know I'm not like that."

"Every young man is like that, even if you don't act on it all the time. It's hormones."

"Okay, we're *not* going there." He walked over to the balcony doors, looking out at the city, missing Amber. "I'd like to bring her with me when I come home so you can meet her."

"I would love that. Look at us, two solo flyers picking up copilots."

"Speaking of which, tell Mitch I'm sorry for taking up your morning and to expect the third degree when I get there."

They talked for a while longer, and after they ended the call, he sent a text to Amber. *I'm looking out over LA, but all I see is you.* Too keyed up to go back to sleep, he threw on a pair of shorts and headed out for a run.

AMBER GLANCED AT the notification on her phone as she rang up a customer, hoping it was another text from Dash. He'd texted a few times earlier in the day, and each text had been more romantic and playful than the last. He'd told her to check his Instagram feed, and she'd been on cloud nine all day after seeing a picture of the Hollywood sign against a dusky morning sky with the caption *I love morning runs in LA, but nothing compares to small-town starry nights.* Fictional heroes had nothing on him. But the notification was from her book club forum, about their upcoming meeting. Even though the club was online and discussions took place in the forum, they also held in-person meetings at different locations throughout the year. Amber had yet to attend one, but she tried to join via video chat. Their conversations always turned to their personal lives, and this month she'd actually have something fun to add to the conversation.

She put Dash's book and the other items Britney Gregson, a

pretty brunette who was a little younger than Amber, had purchased in the bag and handed it to her. "I hope you'll make it to the book signing next weekend."

"I wouldn't miss it for the world. I'm sure you've heard the buzz about his morning workouts at the park. I'm going to join them when he's back in town."

"Yes. I've heard he's quite the inspiration. Enjoy the books." Not only had Amber's mother spent most of breakfast going on about how much she and her friends were missing their morning exercises with Dash, but she'd also helped two other customers who had talked about joining the group and must have seen his post this morning as well, because they'd gossiped about his glamorous lifestyle—*Can you imagine jetting off to LA? I bet he flies on a private jet with champagne and pretty attendants.* Amber knew better. Dash had mentioned last night how exhausting the travel was. He admitted to flying first class, but only because it was easier to get on and off the plane with less fanfare. Maybe she should be jealous that so many women were into him, but it was hard to muster that emotion when everything he did showed her that, at least for now, he only had eyes for her.

Amber logged on to the book club forum to post about attending the virtual meeting as Phoenix came out of the stockroom with more copies of Dash's book. "Thanks, Phee. I was just going to ask you to do that." She pocketed her phone and went to help her. Reno pushed to his feet from his dog bed by the register and followed her.

"They're really flying off the shelves." Phoenix eyed Amber as they set out the books. "Are we going to pretend there were no sparks flying between you two the other night at Lyrics and Lattes?"

Phoenix hadn't worked since they'd gone to hear her play, and Amber had wondered if she'd bring it up. It was getting harder for her to hold in her happiness, when she really wanted to shout it from the rooftops. But as much as she trusted Phoenix, she was afraid that once she started, she might not be able to stop and might say more than she should. "Yes, pretending sounds perfect to me."

Phoenix lowered her voice. "Come on. I'm happy for you, and you know I won't gossip."

Amber's cell phone rang. "Saved by the bell."

Phoenix rolled her eyes as Amber pulled out her phone.

Pepper's name flashed on the screen. "It's my sister. I'm going to take it in my office."

As she hurried away, giggles rang out in the children's area, where a group of young mothers who had formed a moms' club that came in every Friday afternoon was picking out books with their toddlers. Her phone rang again as she slipped into her office and closed the door. "Hey, Pep. How are you?"

"I think a better question is, how are you? In the last few days, Mom called to tell me I needed to redesign your alarm necklace, Sable texted to say if you confided in me about anything having to do with Dash Pennington, I'd better let her know, and last night Brindle texted with an *Amber Alert* saying you wanted to watch *365 Days*, which I looked up. Supposedly the movie has all sorts of plot holes but amazing sex scenes."

As Amber processed what she'd said, one thing stood out. "You tell *Sable* my secrets? I know you're twins, but I've always trusted you."

"Can you feel me rolling my eyes at you? I would never tell her or anyone else the things you tell me in confidence. I promise."

"Good, because here's a secret. I'm going to kill Brindle and make it look like an accident. Why is she sending *you* an Amber Alert? She usually reserves those for Lindsay and Trixie." Brindle had coined the expression shortly after she and their friends had started trying to teach Amber how to flirt. It was basically a call to arms for anything guy-and-Amber related.

"Because she knows you'll talk to me about things you won't talk to them about."

Amber paced. "How does she know *that*?"

"Because nobody holds everything in, and everyone tells me their secrets. I'm the only trustworthy one of us."

"That's not true. I never divulge other people's secrets." Amber looked through the glass partition at the group of young mothers, dreaming of the day she could be part of a moms' club, too. "What do you know about Gracie? Are she and Reed trying to have babies yet?"

Pepper laughed. "You did *not* just ask me that."

Amber groaned. "Fine."

"Can we get back to your necklace? Is there a problem with it?"

"Mom didn't tell you why she asked you to redesign it?"

"No. She said you might need one that's less sensitive, but that could be a problem, because Reno has to be able to push it."

She remembered what her mother had said about Dash shutting down gossip and was surprised, and grateful, that her mother had kept the details to herself.

"Are you sitting down?"

"Should I?"

"I think so." Amber told her about when she'd first met Dash and how they'd come together, including the ambulance fiasco.

"Oh, Amber. I'm so sorry you went through that, but it sounds like Dash handled it well. I've never heard of anyone successfully shutting down gossip in our town."

Amber sat behind her desk. "I know, but all the gossipers have a thing for Dash, so…"

"It sounds like you do, too."

"I *do*, Pep." She told her everything she'd learned about Dash and his family and all that had transpired over the past couple of days. "There was this moment when I was sure he was going to try to convince me to get dirty with him over FaceTime. I was *so* nervous, even Reno sensed it."

"Oh my gosh, *Amber*. I would have been nervous, too. Did you go through with it?"

"No, and don't judge me, but part of me *wanted* to."

"What? This guy has *really* gotten to you. Why didn't you go through with it?"

"Because Dash noticed that I was nervous and asked if I was okay. I was embarrassed that he'd noticed, but then I remembered that he'd researched epilepsy, and I realized he was looking after me. You know what he said?" She didn't give Pepper a chance to answer. "He said talking was enough. That *I* was enough." She got choked up thinking about it.

"Oh, Amb. I think I'm falling for this guy now."

"*Please.* You'd never date a sports guy."

"A guy like Dash might be able to change my mind about that."

"Hands off, Sis. He's *mine*."

"You greedy little thing," Pepper teased. "I have to be honest. When you first started telling me about him, I was a little worried that you were falling under his celebrity spell like everyone else. But jerks don't put their siblings ahead of themselves or write handwritten letters, and they definitely don't research medical conditions of a woman they've known for ten minutes." She sighed. "But he said that to you? Amber, he sounds really special."

"He is, but it's new and definitely risky. He's outgoing and charismatic, and women flock after him, and I'm *me*."

"You're outgoing and charismatic, too. You're just not loud about it. And guys are always checking you out, but you won't give them the time of day."

Amber didn't argue, because like her other siblings, Pepper would always be one of her biggest fans, just like she was for them. "Maybe so, but there's no denying that we're different. He's an ex-football star, a bestselling author, and a motivational speaker who travels all the time, and I'm a bookish girl who leaves Virginia only under duress."

"It doesn't have to be that way. With the right person, you might enjoy traveling."

"Maybe, but probably not often, like he travels. He's in LA right now, and he said it's exhausting. I can't do exhausting—you know that. It messes with my epilepsy."

"You haven't had a seizure in years."

"Yes, but we know the things that can trigger them, and exhaustion is high on the list. I'm not letting any of that stop me from being with him. I'm just acknowledging that those hurdles exist, because you understand my worries."

"I do, and I'm glad you're not letting them hold you back because it sounds like even with your differences, your core values are well aligned. If you're that into him, why didn't you just tell Brindle? Sable, I understand. She'll threaten him within an inch of his life, but the most Brindle will do is cheer you on."

"I'll tell her. But Brindle just wants me to be happy. All she sees is a chance for me to have a good time, while you analyze everything. You see the good, the bad, and the red flags, and you give it to me straight. I need that."

"So I'm the buzzkill?" Pepper laughed.

"No. You're a realist who taught me to be careful with my heart, and I love who you are. Besides, you'll always be the sister with the best hidden figure."

"And you'll always be the sister with the best butt," Pepper countered. One silly evening long ago, the girls had decided who had the best assets among their siblings. In addition to Pepper's figure and Amber's butt, Grace had the best legs, Morgyn had the best lips, eyes, and hips, Brindle had the best boobs, and Axsel had it *all* going on.

There was a knock on her office door, and Phoenix peeked in. "Sorry to interrupt, but you just got a delivery." She set a box on the desk and headed back into the store.

"Thanks," Amber said as Phoenix closed the door behind her. "Pep, I have to put you on speaker." She put her on speakerphone and began opening the box. "What were we talking about?"

"How great your butt is."

"Ha ha." Amber snagged the card with the *Just Desserts* logo on it that was taped to a Styrofoam container inside the box and quickly read it. *Looking forward to working through those rewrites together. Dash.* "Dash sent me a package. His sister is the host of *Just Desserts*, and he must have had her send it."

"This guy is seriously into you."

"I know!" She was giddy with delight as she removed the Styrofoam top and the frozen cold packs inside, letting out a little squeal as she placed the expertly wrapped cake on her desk.

"He sent me a tiramisu crepe cake!"

"Okay, that's it. I'm getting started on a clone machine *today*."

Amber sat back in her chair, grinning from ear to ear. Even her brilliant scientist sister couldn't clone the very best parts of the man who was stealing her heart one sweet moment at a time.

Chapter Ten

THE SEVEN-HOUR flight did nothing to calm Dash's excitement over seeing Amber. He'd never thought of himself as a cheesy guy, but as he walked into Story Time bookstore Saturday evening, just the sight of her made him want to queue up eighties music, see her spin around with a beaming smile—maybe even drop a book from her fingertips—and run into his arms.

After only *two* nights away.

He was definitely losing it.

Amber was a sight for sore eyes in a red floral dress and cream-colored cowgirl boots, but she was busy talking with a customer. Dash tucked away his silly romantic notions and meandered farther into the store. Reno was lying on his dog bed by the register. Phoenix was in the children's section with a young mother and toddler, and there was a handful of other customers milling about.

Amber looked over and did a double take, the smile on her beautiful face widening. His heart thudded faster as "Dash" fell from her lips, breathless and excited. He winked, unable to stop his own excitement from shining through, sure he looked like a ridiculous overgrown toddler staring at his favorite candy.

"*I...*" She held up her index finger and returned her attention to the customer for only a few seconds before turning around, and as if she'd read his thoughts, she took a few fast steps, the beginning of a *run*, then slowed, glancing nervously around her.

She was so damn cute he wanted to haul her into his arms and eat her up, but her pink cheeks held him back. "Good evening, Ms. Montgomery. It's a pleasure to see you again."

"Hi. It's nice to see you, too." Her eyes danced with desire, the air between them crackling so hot, he was surprised the whole store didn't go up in flames. Her chest rose with her heavy breaths as she struggled to restrain herself. "How was your flight?"

"Too long." He leaned closer, breathing in her familiar feminine scent, his hands itching to touch her as he lowered his voice for her ears only. "I need to kiss you."

"*Oh!*" Her delight was unmistakable. "Yes, we just got that order in," she said loudly. "Why don't you come into my office, and I'll show it to you?"

That's it, sweetheart. Lead the way.

Dash followed her as she hurried toward her office, catching the knowing glance Phoenix tossed their way as he closed the door behind them. Amber ran to the glass partition, lowering her blinds, and had barely let go of the chord when he swept her into his arms, taking her glorious mouth with fierce possession, igniting the fire that had been burning for days. They'd talked and flirted for hours the last two nights. The more they talked, the more of her sweet self she revealed, and the deeper he fell. He would have kept her on the line all night just to hear her voice and see her sweet face if he hadn't been worried about her getting too exhausted. He'd spent every second since aching for these kisses.

He pulled back only long enough to take off her seizure-alert necklace and put it on the desk. Their mouths crashed together, and they both intensified their efforts. Her sexy sounds wound through him, tugging at his heart and his cock. Their late-night calls hadn't been sexual but had felt even more intimate, made him crave more of her. *All* of her. The way she kissed him with her entire body, rubbing and grinding against him, made it impossible to hold back. His hands were everywhere at once, groping her ass, caressing her back, in her hair. *God*, he loved her hair. He tangled both hands in it and tore his mouth away, gazing into her lustful eyes. "How can I miss you this much?"

She blinked rapidly, clinging to him and shaking her head, as if she couldn't make sense of it, either. She tugged his mouth back to hers, and the *why*s and *how*s of his missing her ceased to matter. He missed *everything* about her. Her smell, her touch, the way she clawed at him now, like she couldn't get enough. He backed her up against the wall, their mouths fused together, feasting hungrily, and ground against her, groping her breast through her thin dress. Her nipple pebbled against his palm, and a growl crawled up his throat. She must have loved that sound, because she arched into his hand. He was so damn hard, he felt like a volcano ready to blow and quickly realized he had no endgame. They were in her office. It wasn't like he could take her on the desk. Not his sweet Amber. But holy hell, he wasn't about to stop. Not yet. He needed this—*her*—and if her sinful noises and the rocking of her hips were any indications, she needed him just as desperately.

He wasn't usually this greedy, but he was driven by more than lust. He was driven by the power of *them*. He moved his hand down her leg, slipping under the hem of her dress, and caressed her thigh. "Tell me to stop" came out like a demand against her lips.

Her doe eyes filled with confidence. "I don't want you to stop."

Seeing his sweet girl open up to him here of all places sent his emotions surging. He kissed her rougher, greedier, and she was right there with him, opening her legs for him. He pushed his hand into her panties, his fingers sliding through her wetness, and God, he wanted to drop to his knees and devour her. He teased her, earning needy moans that made his entire body throb. His thumb circled her clit, and her head fell back. Her eyes were closed, her skin flushed. He slicked his tongue along her lower lip, applying pressure to the bundle of nerves that made her breathing hitch. "I hope you've cleared your schedule for me, because I cannot *wait* to get you naked and love every inch of you."

Her eyes opened, fire blazing in them as he pushed his fingers into her tight heat, and a long, lustful moan escaped her lips. He captured it with a hard kiss, working her faster, earning more sexy noises that seared through him like lightning. Her fingernails dug into his arms, her muscles flexing. He nudged her legs open wider with his knee, grabbing her ass with his free hand, using the angle to hit the spot that made her lose control. Her sex pulsed around his fingers, her hips bucking wildly. He swallowed her needful sounds, as lost in her pleasure as she was.

She clung to him, trembling as she came down from the high, and he gathered her in his arms. "You're going to get us both in trouble."

"Me?" She turned her radiant smile up at him. "You're the bad influence. I've never done *anything* like this. There are

customers out there, and I'm here…"

"Getting off with your guy?"

Her cheeks flamed, and she buried her face in his chest as a strange scratching sound filtered into his ears. "What is that noise?"

She tilted her head, listening. Panic sprang to her eyes. "Oh *no*. It's Reno." She hurried around him and opened her door. Reno trotted in, and she closed the door, leaning her back against it, panting out, "I can't believe I did that. I never leave him."

Dash closed the distance between them. "I was right here with you. You weren't alone."

"I know, but…" She swallowed hard.

"It scares you to be without him?" Seeing the answer in her eyes, he drew her into his arms. "I'll make sure we don't leave him again. I promise."

"*I'll* make sure. I was so excited to see you, I wasn't thinking."

"Neither of us was." He kissed her softly. "Some people would see that as a good thing, remarkable even."

"It is. But forgetting Reno makes it a little scary."

"I know you like to be in control. What can I do?"

She wrinkled her nose. "Be less *you*, so I don't want you as much."

He tightened his hold on her with a tender look in his eyes. "Not happening, sweetheart. But I will make a concerted effort not to drive you wild unless Reno is nearby and we're someplace where you feel *very* safe. Deal?"

Relief rose in her eyes. "Deal."

"That's my girl. Did you clear the rest of your weekend for me like I asked you to?"

"Maybe," she said coyly. "But don't you have a walking date with your harem in the morning anyway?"

"Nobody comes before you. We're not resuming our walks until Monday. I called your mom on the way over and asked her to spread the word. I know you have to get back to work, so just tell me you'll go out with me to JJ's tonight, and I'll get out of your hair."

"JJ's? That place is a meat market on Saturday nights."

"Only if you're looking for it. Otherwise, I hear it's the hottest dance club around." He cocked a brow. "Are you looking for more meat? You haven't even sampled mine yet."

Her cheeks flamed. "*What?* No. I like your meat. I mean, your meat is enough. I mean—"

He put her out of her misery with a long, slow kiss. "I know what you mean. But I have news for you, baby. Anywhere you show your pretty face would turn it into a meat market. I saw the way guys were checking you out when we were at the jam session. And if it's me you're worried about, don't think for a minute that anyone else will get their hands on my meat."

"You're…" She laughed softly, but amusement quickly gave way to a more serious expression. "Everyone will know about us, and they'll talk."

"I know you don't like drama, but you're my girl, and I don't want to hide that from the people you care about. I know Sable is playing there tonight, and from what I've been told, your sisters and friends hang out there. But the people here have been kind to us, haven't they? They've kept gossip to a minimum. It's good for them to get used to seeing us together this week, so when I leave for my tour, you're not stuck dealing with the worst of it alone."

Her gaze softened. "I can't believe you thought of that."

"We're in this together. What kind of guy would I be if I didn't think ahead to save you from the gossipmongers? Besides, I feel like the luckiest guy around. Is there anything wrong with wanting those leering cowboys to know you're mine?"

"No." She wound her arms around his neck. "But you really suck at *not* making me want you."

"I'll take that as a *win*." He lowered his lips to hers in a tender kiss. When their lips parted, she was looking at him longingly again. He squeezed her ass and raised his brows. "Keep looking at me like that, and we're never leaving this office, much less going anywhere else tonight. Except maybe over there to christen your desk."

AS AMBER HAD expected, JJ's Pub was packed. Sable's band played on the stage at the far end of the room, competing with cheers from around the mechanical bull in the next room and the din of overzealous cowboys and flirtatious country girls. Amber should be used to the vibe of lost inhibitions that practically seeped from the walls. Trixie's brother Justus—JJ— owned the pub, and her friends and sisters had dragged her there enough times throughout the years. But there were some things she might never get used to, like being on the arm of the most handsome man in there. Everyone was looking at them, and Amber was seriously second-guessing the cream-colored minidress she'd worn in an effort to look special for Dash. It was cute, with a flouncy skirt and lantern sleeves, but the lace-up bodice gave it an ultra-sexy flair, unlike anything she was used to wearing.

She reached down to pet Reno, remembering too late that she hadn't brought him. She didn't need him at the crowded pub when she had Dash, although she was still shocked that she hadn't noticed Reno's absence earlier, in her office. Then again, her brain had short-circuited the minute Dash had kissed her. Phoenix had teased her about locking out her guardian and *glowing* after Dash had left. Amber hadn't doubted it, because her body had hummed for the rest of the day, right up until the cold shower she'd taken to get ready for their date.

Dash put his arm around her. "Does it feel weird to be without Reno?"

She loved how he noticed every little thing. "A little."

"You can pet me anytime." He leaned in and kissed her neck.

Now, there was a mouthwatering thought.

As they wove through the crowd toward the bar, Dash had to move behind her to fit through the tight spaces. JJ was bartending. He looked over as they approached and whistled. "Damn, Amber, you're lookin' hot tonight. I missed our dance at the jam session."

"Sorry. I left early." She and JJ were the same age. They'd been friends forever, and they usually grabbed a dance or two at the jam sessions, but she'd been so rattled by Dash, she hadn't even given it a thought when she'd left that night.

"Next time." JJ winked. "The usual? Tiki spritz?"

"Yes, please." As she turned to introduce Dash, he put his arm around her, offering his free hand to JJ.

"Dash Pennington, it's nice to meet you."

"You too." JJ shook his hand, eyeing Amber curiously. "I heard you were in town, but I hadn't heard that you snagged a date with the hottest girl around."

Amber rolled her eyes.

"We've been flying under the radar." Dash pulled her in for a kiss, keeping her snug against his side, and flashed a cocky grin to JJ. "You'll be seeing a lot more of us around town."

"A'righty, then. What can I get you to drink?"

JJ served their drinks, and as they walked away from the bar, Dash said, "That's him, isn't it?"

"Who?"

He pulled her closer, speaking directly into her ear. "Your Ferris wheel kiss."

"How can you *possibly* know that?"

"Because I know you." He pressed a kiss beside her ear. "He implied that your missed dance wasn't a first, which means you trust him. You rolled your eyes instead of blushing at his comment about your looks, which means you're *very* comfortable with him. That could be from growing up together, but my guess is it's from something bigger than that. And when I introduced myself, he looked at you like he was a little disappointed that you hadn't told him yourself, which means *he* trusts *you*. And I'd bet my paycheck that he's still watching us."

Amber glanced over her shoulder, and sure enough, JJ was looking right at them. "That's crazy that you could tell all of that from one quick conversation. You missed your calling. You should have been a detective or a psychic."

"I'm at the top of my game in every way these days, and that's because of *you*, sweetheart. You make me want to be the best man I can be, more like my old self. You should have seen me at my speaking gig yesterday. I nailed it." He lowered his face beside hers, his voice low and seductive. "I can't wait to see how you inspire me in the bedroom."

And just like that she caught fire again. The man was a

walking aphrodisiac.

"Come on, sexy. Let's see if we can find a table."

The endearments he used sounded so genuine, they made her feel even more like *his girl* and *sexy*. They headed into the crowd, nearly bumping into Brindle and Morgyn. Brindle was all dolled up, with smoky eyes, soft-pink lips, a body-hugging black top that showed off her cleavage, skintight jeans, and knee-high leather boots. She's the only woman Amber knew who could have a baby and look ten times hotter afterward. Morgyn had her own brand of sexy, in a magenta dress with sprays of color, a gray fitted denim jacket with wide lapels and long fringe hanging from the sleeves, and cowgirl boots that she'd embellished with sparkling gems. She wore several necklaces, and her blond hair hung in messy waves over her shoulders. Amber had always envied how comfortable her sisters were in their own skin.

"Hey, you two. We heard you were going to be here, and we got a big table." Brindle hugged Amber and whispered, *"Just friends my butt!"*

Amber gave her a please-don't-embarrass-me look as Morgyn moved in for a hug and said, "He's even cuter with you on his arm."

Amber had a feeling that being hot and bothered was the least of her problems. With her sisters tag teaming her, God only knew what she was in for. "Dash, you know Brindle and Morgyn."

"Yes. It's nice to see you again."

"You too," Morgyn said. "Graham's looking forward to seeing you again."

"Is he here? I'd love to catch up with him."

"He *is*. Why don't you go say hi and we'll be over in a few minutes?" Brindle said encouragingly, making Amber one hundred percent certain she was in for an interrogation. "He's at the table with Trace and Sin." She pointed through the crowd to a table where the guys were talking.

Dash took Amber's hand, drawing her into a kiss. "Want me to take your drink to the table?"

What she wanted was to go with him, but she knew Brindle wouldn't be put off that easily. "Sure." She handed him her glass.

He gave her a quick kiss and nodded to her sisters. "Have fun, ladies."

As he walked away, Brindle and Morgyn flanked her, dragging her toward the dance floor.

"You look like he's already buttered your biscuit tonight," Brindle said excitedly.

"Shh." Amber looked around to see if anyone heard her.

"Nobody's listening." Brindle pulled her deeper into the crowd. "You're the one who looks all dreamy-eyed and is wearing the fuck-me dress we bought last year."

"Brindle!" Amber was now *seriously* questioning coming to JJ's. Brindle had always been some kind of sexual psychic, sensing people's sexual connections even before they did.

Morgyn stepped in front of them and began dancing to one of Surge's hit country-pop songs. "She means that you look beautiful and happy, like Dash is taking good care of you."

"Isn't that what I said?" Brindle ran her eyes down Amber. *"And* that you dressed to get laid, but hey, I'm all for that. Come on, shake that bootie for your man."

Amber fell into step with them. "I'm not dressed to get laid. I'm dressed to..." Her sisters eyed each other knowingly. "Okay, *fine.* I want him to think I'm sexy. So what?"

Brindle and Morgyn squealed and hugged her.

"Stop." Amber playfully shoved them away. "Can we just dance?"

"Yes, but you know how you always say you wear dresses because they're comfortable?" Brindle didn't wait for an answer. "After tonight, you'll know the *real* benefit of wearing a dress. We'll have to start calling you *Easy-Access Amber.*"

"Brindle!" Amber swatted her, and they fell into fits of laughter.

As they danced, Brindle peppered her with intrusive questions, which Morgyn tried to ease by twisting Brindle's words. It had been this way for as long as Amber could remember, Brindle pushing while Morgyn softened the blows. Before long, they were cracking up. Amber didn't know how it was possible that her parents had raised seven very different children, or how her sisters could take her from one extreme to another so quickly, but she wouldn't trade them for anything in the world.

"Tons of women are checking out your man, but Dash hasn't taken his eyes off *you.*" Brindle danced closer. "Let's sex it up for him. Show him your moves."

Amber glanced at the table where Dash was sitting, and their eyes connected with the heat of a thousand flames. Based on the way he was looking at her, she didn't think she needed to *sex up* her dancing. Or maybe she did, and it would turn him on even more. She wasn't sure *she* could handle that any better than she could handle staying away from him any longer.

"Sorry, you guys, but I'm going to the table." She weaved through the crowd with her sisters on her heels, and Dash's gorgeous eyes remained trained on her, his words whispering through her mind, *You're enough for me.*

He stood and reached for her hand, drawing her into his

arms. "You were the sexiest girl out there."

Thrills skittered through her as they took their seats.

"Yeah, she was," Morgyn said as she sat next to Graham.

"And she didn't even have to sex it up for you," Brindle said, making Amber blush.

Trace pulled Brindle down beside him. "Get over here, Mustang, and stop making your sister blush."

Dash put his arm around Amber and gazed into her eyes. "That adorable blush is one of the first things that drew me in."

"Which I followed up by immediately running away from you. It wasn't exactly a great first impression."

"That was actually pretty cute and quite memorable. I've never seen a woman walk *away* from this guy before." Sin hiked a thumb at Dash.

"She's the cutest." Dash kissed her. "But for the record, she wasn't walking away. She was throwing down a challenge."

"Talk about grabbing someone's attention. That's almost as good as getting water dumped on you while you're taking a piss," Graham said. "And then being told by your future wife that she thought you and your brother were lovers."

They all laughed.

"In my defense, I didn't know you were standing there when I dumped the water out of my boot," Morgyn insisted. "And as far as you and Zev go, you winked at him like you were a couple."

"You are a little *too* pretty," Trace teased Graham.

"*Yes*, I am, *but* the good looks got the girl." Graham kissed Morgyn. "I should thank you, Jericho. As I recall, the reason I got time alone with Morgyn at that music festival was because Brindle left to see your ugly ass."

Brindle picked up Trace's drink and sipped it, eyeing Graham over the glass. "You obviously haven't seen his ass up close and personal."

Graham waggled his brows. "Or maybe I have."

They joked around and told funny stories, and Dash was right in the thick of it, sharing his own humorous tales. His laughter was hearty and carefree, and even though Amber noticed women checking him out, his attention never left their table. He kept his arm around her or held her hand the whole time, just as he had when they were at Lyrics and Lattes, listening to Phoenix play. Only this time, he pulled her close, whispering in her ear or kissing her. JJ's was another place where she'd always been on the sidelines, watching her sisters have fun with their dates or her friends pick up guys, feeling more than a little uncomfortable. But right now, holding hands with the sexiest, most thoughtful guy she'd ever met, she felt like she finally fit in, and it was the greatest feeling in the world.

Dash leaned closer and whispered, "I'll be right back, sexy girl."

He kissed her cheek, and as she watched him walk away, she corrected her last thought. This was the *second* greatest feeling she'd ever had, because when she and Dash were alone and intimate, they reached a whole different plane of greatness.

"*Hello.*" Morgyn waved her hand in front of Amber's face, startling her from her thoughts.

"Sorry, Morg. What were you saying?"

"That I really like Dash, even more than I did when we met at the jam session. He's funny and sweet, and I love that he can't take his eyes off you."

"Or his hands." Brindle waggled her brows.

Amber felt her cheeks heat. "He's pretty great, isn't he?"

"He's one of the best," Sin said. "He's always kept a pretty tight rein on his reputation because of his family, so you're not going to see scandals popping up about him. And he's crazy about you. When he told me that he turned down a spot on *The Tonight Show* with *Jimmy Fallon*, I knew he was getting serious about you."

"What do you mean he turned it down?" Amber asked.

"When he was in LA, Shea got him a spot on the show," Sin explained. "But he would have had to fly to New York and then come back here later in the week after they taped it."

"He didn't mention that. I hope he didn't really give up that opportunity because of me."

"You're the only woman on the planet who would say that," Brindle said. "If Trace did that for me, I'd be all over him with the hottest kind of gratitude."

"But that's huge, Brin. I don't want him giving up a once-in-a-lifetime opportunity for me. Couples are supposed to support each other, to help each other be the best they can be. It sounds like I'm holding him back."

"No, you're not, trust me," Sin said emphatically. "But Sable might be."

They all followed his gaze to Sable and Dash, talking by the stage.

"Does she have her claws out?" Morgyn asked.

Amber hoped Sable wouldn't scare him off. She'd been supportive of them, even on a temporary basis. As if Dash felt them watching, he looked over, flashing that overzealous smile that made Amber's chest flutter, and he gave her a thumbs-up.

"Either Sable has him fooled." Trace took off his cowboy hat, raked a hand through his hair, and set it back on his head. "Or she's playing nice. My money is on having him fooled."

Sable went back to the stage, and Dash headed across the

room toward them, those dark eyes shimmering with something devilish, causing Amber's pulse to quicken.

Morgyn said, "That is not the look of a man who was just told to back off."

"Why are you all looking at me like that?" Dash asked as he approached the table.

"We're wondering how you escaped the wrath of our sister," Brindle answered.

"Sable?" Dash scoffed. "She's a tough one, but we're cool." He sat beside Amber and took her hand. "You didn't think Sable could scare me off, did you?"

"Not really." She couldn't stop thinking about what Sin had said. "But maybe I need to. Did you really give up a chance to be on *The Tonight Show* just to see me?"

His brows slanted, and he looked at Sin, who said, "Sorry, man. I didn't know it was a secret."

"It wasn't." Dash squeezed Amber's hand. "It just wasn't worth mentioning."

"Of course it was," she said. "You shouldn't have given up a once-in-a-lifetime opportunity just to see me."

"You've got it backward, sweetheart. I didn't give up my once-in-a-lifetime opportunity." Dash lifted their joined hands and kissed the back of hers. "I seized it."

Amber felt her insides turn to mush as her sisters said, *"Aw."*

"Dude, you're setting that bar kind of high for the rest of us," Trace said, and clinked glasses with Sin and Graham.

"What can I say? My girl is worth it." He turned a sexy grin on Amber. "Now, stop looking for trouble where there is none and dance with me."

He lifted her to her feet as Sable's voice boomed through the microphone. "This next song is a special request from a certain charmer who's got the ladies in this town all aflutter to his one and only *very* special girl."

"That's you, sweetheart." Dash leaned in to kiss her smiling lips.

"What did you do?"

Without answering, he led her to the dance floor, and Sable's band began playing "Wild Thing." Amber froze, but Dash pulled her into his arms. "You're not getting away that easily."

Her sisters and their husbands cheered, and Brindle hollered, "It's always the quiet ones! Go, Amber!"

People began clapping to the beat, stepping back to give them the dance floor as Dash twirled her around and hauled her into his arms again, singing with that infectious grin and sexy sparks shimmering in his eyes. Amber didn't think it was possible to like him more than she already did, but boy was she wrong.

They were literally the center of attention as he twirled her again. Laughter bubbled out as he clapped his hand over his heart, singing about how she made his heart sing. He threw a fist in the air to the beat as the song started over and her sister belted out the lyrics. Then he pulled her in close, holding her tight as they swayed to the music.

"I can't believe you had her play this song. I'm so *not* a wild thing."

"You're *my* wild thing, baby."

"I'm so different with you. I don't even understand it. You make me feel so many things, and right now I feel like the belle of the ball." She stole a glance at all the people clapping and cheering around them, and the truth came out hushed and rushed. "I've never even been on a date here."

"That's because you were waiting for me."

Her insides turned to mush. She wanted to say she thought he was right, but she was too swept up in him to speak, and as he lowered his lips to hers and said, "Now you can say you've made out at JJ's," her full heart won out over her burning cheeks, and she kissed him back like they were the only two people in the room.

DASH DIDN'T THINK anything could feel bigger than winning MVP, but *nothing* compared to dancing with Amber in *her* world and feeling her let go of her insecurities. He'd wanted tonight to be special, but as couples joined them on the dance floor and he and Amber danced slowly to their own private beat, he realized that he hadn't even known how special it could be. It wasn't just bigger or better than anything he'd ever experienced. It was indescribable, and he wanted a hell of a lot more of it. A hell of a lot more of her.

"I love this," she said sweetly.

"Me too."

"I thought I wasn't meant for this type of life."

"I told you, you were just waiting for me."

He kissed her, and as their lips parted, she said, "Take me home."

They said a quick goodbye to her sisters and their friends and hurried to his car, kissing and laughing, falling into each other's arms against the passenger door. Neither wanted to stop, but he remembered her necklace, and there was no way he'd trip that alarm again. It took everything he had to finally break away, and the short drive to her place was torturous. They stumbled inside, and he kicked the door closed behind them as they stripped off their jackets. Reno trotted over to greet them.

"Do you have to let him out?" Dash asked between kisses.

"*No.* The doggy door is electronic. He comes and goes as he pleases."

"Lucky dog." He lowered his lips to hers and lifted her into his arms without breaking the connection as he carried her into the bedroom.

As he set her on her feet, he caught a glimpse of white furniture, a floral comforter, and sheer soft-pink curtains. Supremely feminine, just like her.

He toed off his shoes and knelt to take off her boots and the pretty pink socks she had on beneath them, reminding him to take off his socks, before rising to his feet.

"This has to go." He removed her necklace, noticing a holder adhered to the nightstand beside her book club novel. He clipped the necklace into place and drew her into his arms. "Is that so Reno can push the button at night if he needs to?"

She nodded, sending a rush of emotions through him. He hated the idea that she could have a seizure at all, much less when he wasn't around. Tucking those protective urges down deep, he took her in a slow, sensual kiss as he untied the bow between her breasts, loosening the laces on the bodice. She pulled up on his shirt, and he quickly unbuttoned it, tossing it to the floor, *loving* the hunger in her eyes as they slid over his bare chest.

"*Mm-mm.* When you look at me like that…" He kissed the freckles on her shoulder, dragging her sleeves down her arms. Her dress slid off her body, puddling at her feet, leaving her bare, save for a pretty lace bra and matching panties. Moonlight streamed in through the curtains as he skimmed his hands down her sides, feeling goose bumps rise to his touch. He brushed his lips over hers, whispering, "You are so damn sexy."

He set his wallet on the nightstand, stepped out of his jeans and boxer briefs, and trailed his lips down her neck, dusting kisses over her warm flesh as he moved behind her. He gathered her hair over one shoulder, kissing across her back as he took off her bra and dropped it at her feet. He palmed her breasts from behind, taking her nipples between his fingers and thumbs, and sealed his mouth over her neck, sucking hard enough to earn a sultry moan and a rock of her hips. He continued sucking and kissing, teasing her nipples until she was panting for more. His hands moved along her stomach as he kissed down her spine. He hooked his thumbs into the hips of her panties, dragging them down her legs, and helped her step out of them. She was *glorious* with her feminine curves and porcelain skin. He took his time loving his way up the backs of her legs, kissing behind her knees, earning sharp gasps of pleasure. He moved higher, caressing her ass as he slid one hand between her legs, teasing her wetness and lavishing the soft globes of her ass with openmouthed kisses. She moaned, rocking her hips as he dipped his fingers inside her.

"Ohhh…"

"Mm. My girl likes that." He took his time, teasing and kissing, taking her right up to the edge, her muscles tightening, body trembling.

"Dash," she pleaded.

"I've got you, baby." He kissed his way up her back, pressing his hard length against her ass, earning more sultry, needful sounds. He felt her heart beating through her back, and it only made his beat harder. He remained behind her as he slid his shaft between her legs, the length of it against her sex, using one hand on her clit, the other on her breast. "Squeeze your legs together, baby." She did, and he thrust along her wetness. "Come on my cock before I make love to you."

"Oh my…" She whimpered.

He grazed his teeth along her shoulder. "You don't want to?"

"I want to *too* much."

He wanted to say there was no such thing as too much, but he knew she worried about losing control. "Do you need me to stop?"

"Don't you *dare*." She grabbed both his wrists, keeping his hands on her.

He grinned against her neck. "That's my wild thing." He thrust his hips, pushing his length along her sex, feeling her muscles clench, her breathing quicken. She reached behind her, grabbing his hips as he worked her clit faster, squeezing and rolling one nipple between his finger and thumb. She grabbed his arm, her head falling back against his shoulder.

"That's it, sweetheart, let go. I've got you."

He thrust faster, sinking his teeth into her shoulder. She went up on her toes.

"Squeeze my cock with your thighs." She squeezed her shaky legs together. *Tight.* "Oh *yeah*, baby. That's it."

"Dash…*Dash!*" flew from her lips.

She thrust and moaned, crying out as her orgasm consumed her. He felt her legs give out and wrapped an arm around her, continuing his ministrations as she rode his length. Desire swelled inside him, and he fought the urge to bend her over the bed and drive into her. But he wanted, *needed* to see her face, to hold her and be as close as they could be. To make her *his*. When she went soft and quivery in his arms, he turned her around and kissed her breathless.

Her eyes were hazy and lustful. "You set off a *bomb* inside me."

"Then it's time for an encore."

He lowered them to the bed, reveling in the feel of her softness beneath him as their mouths came together. He kissed her greedily at first, bodies grinding, both of them moaning, pleading for more. She kissed with her entire being, hungry and urgent, clawing at his arms like she wanted to climb into their bubble of intimacy and never come out. And man, he wanted that, too. The longer they kissed, the more lost he became. She was an intoxicating mix of sweet innocence and ravenous vixen. He didn't want to stop kissing her, but he needed *more*, to feel the very heart of her wrapped around him, to disappear into *them*. Need pounded inside him, burning and aching until he had no choice but to tear his mouth away.

"I need *you*, baby." The need to taste her again engulfed him, and he kissed her deeply and possessively, wishing a condom would magically appear on his cock so he didn't have to stop. But magic was for fairy tales, and they were as real as the blood surging through his veins.

He reluctantly pulled away, uttering a curse that made her giggle, as he reached for his wallet. He pulled out a condom and went up on his knees to sheathe himself. She watched his every move, lustfully licking her lips. Fucking hell. He wanted her mouth on him as desperately as he wanted to be buried deep inside her. She was a festival of sexiness, and he didn't want to miss out on any of it. But that would have to wait, because if he didn't make love to her soon, he was going to lose his frigging mind.

He'd wanted this moment since their very first kiss, and he

thought of all the things he wanted to say to her so she would know that this was as special for him as it was for her. But as he came down over her, the combination of trust and passion in her eyes brought his emotions rushing to the surface, stealing his ability to speak.

She rose up, meeting him in a slow, sensual kiss as their bodies came together so mind-numbingly perfect, they both stilled. Silent seconds pounded between them like drums announcing the overwhelming sensations gripping them as they gazed into each other's eyes, their emotions winding around them like chains he never wanted to break. Giving in to the powerful draw, their mouths connected, and their bodies took over. Their kisses turned feverish, their tongues crashing hard and slick. She pulled her knees up, and he clutched her bottom, angling her up as he drove in deeper. Her inner muscles squeezed so exquisitely with every thrust, he struggled for control. *Fuuck.* She had the power to destroy him and make him whole at once. He hadn't even known that was possible.

She clawed at his back, the scratch of her nails a scintillating mix of pleasure and pain, spurring him on. He quickened his efforts, and her head tipped back with a gasp, followed by a moan. He claimed her neck with his mouth, every suck bringing another gasp, an urgent plea—*"Don't stop...Harder...Yes!"* He lifted her knee beside his hip, loving her harder, faster, their slick bodies pounding out an erotic rhythm. Her eyes slammed shut, and his name flew from her lips, full of anguished pleasure. Her nails dug deeper into his flesh, sending heat searing down his spine, stealing the last of his restraint, catapulting him into a world so full of ecstasy and Amber, he never wanted to leave.

Chapter Eleven

SUNLIGHT STREAMED IN through Amber's bedroom curtains, splashing light over her closed eyes. She lay still, soaking in the warmth of Dash's body curled around her, the tickle of the hair on his chest and legs against her skin. One of his arms was beneath her head, the other wrapped around her middle, his hand cupping her bare breast. Heat slid through her core with the awareness, bringing even more delicious sensations into focus, like his hard heat against her bottom and his warm breath skating over her neck and cheek. She'd never woken up with a man in her bed before, and it brought a wave of nervousness. Not that she didn't want him there. Just the opposite. She didn't want him to leave. But she had to pee, which meant walking to the bathroom *naked*.

Her pulse quickened. She probably shouldn't be nervous after everything they'd done last night. After all, he'd made it his mission to discover all the places she liked to be kissed and touched, and he'd been *very* thorough. How many times had they made love? Two? Three? The night was a blur of indescribable pleasure. But that was in the *dark*.

"Good morning, wild thing."

She'd sure lived up to that nickname last night. She'd never been the least bit wild before, but he made her feel safe and special, and she liked being wild with him. "Morning."

He kissed her shoulder, hugging her with every hard inch of his body. Her body bloomed with desire, despite being a little sore from using muscles she hadn't even realized she had.

He shifted her onto her back, his arousal brushing enticingly against her hip. He was grinning like the big bad wolf, his hungry eyes moving slowly over her face. She cringed inwardly, imagining her eye makeup smeared and her hair as tangled as a rat's nest, while he looked like he'd walked off the pages of *Men's Health* magazine with his slightly tousled hair, sexy stubble, and a refreshing glow to his bronzed skin.

He caressed her cheek, his gaze warming. "How is it possible that you wake up this beautiful?"

She rolled her eyes. "How is it possible that you can lie with a straight face?"

"Lie?" He tickled her ribs, and she squealed, trying to wriggle away, but she was trapped by half his body.

"Stop," she said through her laughter. "I have to pee."

He nipped at her neck, his fingers perched to tickle. "Take it back, or you'll turn this mattress into a waterbed."

"I take it back" flew from her lips, and he kissed her, both of them laughing. His chest brushed hers, sending tingling sensations to all her best parts.

"You *are* beautiful, Amber, morning, noon, and night." His expression turned serious. "My father lied to all of us for a long time before he left. I'll never do that to you. Okay?"

"Okay," she said softly, thinking about how hurt he must have been by his father's lies.

He kissed her again. "Good. Go use the bathroom, and hurry back so I can ravage you."

She shivered with delight and sat up, holding the sheet over her. She swung her legs over the edge of the bed. Her nerves prickled again as she looked at their clothes strewn across the floor. She couldn't even reach his shirt to put it on.

As if he'd read her thoughts, he said, "Sweetheart, you don't need to hide your gorgeous body. I know every inch of it intimately."

Embarrassment heated her cheeks. "You might be used to waking up with naked women, but I'm not used to waking up with a man in my bed, naked or otherwise."

He moved beside her, semi-aroused, and so comfortable in his own skin she was a little jealous. "I'm not used to waking up with women. I've never been into slumber parties. That's not to say I've been a saint, but I've been careful with my reputation. I wouldn't want my mom or my sisters to have to combat rumors about their womanizing son and brother."

"Then why did you ask me to clear my schedule for today?" As the words left her lips, she already knew the answer. It was the same reason she'd not only let last night happen but had wanted it to.

"Because, as I've said since we first met, everything is different with you. I want *more* time with you, not less. We only have this week together before I leave for my book tour, and I don't want to waste a second of it."

A nugget of sadness burrowed deep inside her. She hated the idea of him leaving, but it was inevitable. She didn't want to waste a second of their time together either, or miss a moment of the way he made her feel. She stood with the sheet pressed to her chest and glanced over her shoulder at him. He was looking at her like she was his *everything*, making her want to let down her guard as she'd done last night. She wasn't naive. She knew things might change next week, that this time together might be all they would ever have, and that bothered her. But he was loving, supportive, and funny, even if a little pushier than what she was used to, and she really, *really* liked him. He made her feel special and safe and, she realized, much more comfortable in her own skin, too. She didn't want to pass up a chance at this beautiful happiness, even if short-lived. If this was all that was in the cards for them, she wanted to experience all of it. To soak it in and revel in it for as long as it lasted. And she did so knowing her sisters would be there to help her through her heartache.

Gathering all of her courage, she dropped the sheet and walked naked toward the bathroom.

He whistled. "*Damn*, baby. Best ass is right."

She spun around, jaw gaping. "Who told you that?"

"I plead the Fifth."

"*Ugh*. Brindle!"

"Don't be mad," he called after her as she stalked into the bathroom. "It's a compliment!"

After using the bathroom, she brushed her teeth and quickly ran a comb through her hair, noticing love bites on her neck and body. She skimmed her fingers over them, memories sizzling inside her. She really *had* become his wild thing. She set down the comb, breathing deeply as she gathered her courage again. It was one thing to show her bare ass and another to walk out there giving him the full monty.

She pulled open the door, and her knees weakened at the sight of him lounging against the headboard, reading her book club novel. One long leg stretched out in front of him, the other bent at the knee, flat on the mattress. His formidable cock lay soft just above his thigh. Her body ignited, and then she noticed Reno lying at his feet, happy as a clam, as if Dash belonged there. Lord help her, because she wanted to jump on board the Dash-belonging-there train, too.

Dash lowered the book, their eyes connecting for a hot second before he dragged his gaze down the length of her. Her nipples pebbled, and he was just as visibly aroused. He crooked his finger, beckoning her to the bed.

He made a clicking sound with his mouth, nudging Reno, and Reno jumped off the bed as Amber climbed on. "You're reading my book."

In one quick move, Dash shifted her beneath him, his cock rubbing against her center, creating delicious friction. "I read it while you were sleeping this morning, too."

"How long were you waiting for me to wake up?"

"A couple of hours. I'm an early riser, up by six most days."

It was nearly *nine.* "You should have woken me up."

"You needed to rest so we can test out my rewrites." He kissed along her jaw. "I plan on wearing you out again." He kissed her neck. "And again." He kissed her lips. "And again." He gazed down at her, desire burning in his eyes. "And that's just before lunch. Then we have to get cleaned up, because we have something very important to take care of."

"What?" came out breathless and needy.

He brushed his lips along her cheek, whispering, "Making your teenage dreams come true."

THIS WAS A day of firsts for Amber. As promised, or *warned,* Dash ravaged her senseless, completely wearing her out. She nodded off in his arms, and they didn't crawl out of bed until just before noon. It had taken some convincing for her to shower with him. She'd never showered with a man before. But *wow*, what a man he was. She would *never* think of showers the same way again. In fact, she couldn't wait to get dirty just so they'd have a reason to take another one.

It was nearly two o'clock when they finally left the house. Dash said he had a big day planned for them, but he refused to tell her where they were going. They left Reno at home and headed over to Sin's so Dash could get clean clothes.

Sin's truck was parked in the driveway, and as they walked up to the front door, her nerves prickled. Dash squeezed her hand. "Your hand is sweating. What's wrong?"

"I've never done a walk of shame, but this has that feel to it, doesn't it? You showing up at Sin's wearing the same clothes you wore the night before is like announcing to the world that we just had *sex*." She whispered *sex*.

He hauled her into his arms. "We had *sex*?"

She rolled her eyes. "I'm just not used to having my personal life on display." As she said it, she realized she'd never really had much of a personal life to protect until now.

"It's just Sin, not the gossiping grandmothers." He touched his forehead to hers. "You know, sweet thing, according to your sisters' husbands, the sparks between us could have caused a wildfire last night, and that was just while I was watching you on the dance floor."

"You're right. I'm just being silly."

"No, you're getting used to something new. But unless you plan to keep me chained to your bed, people are going to know we can't keep our hands off each other."

She pictured Dash in all his naked glory chained to her bed, and her insides caught fire. *Now, there's a tasty option.* "I wonder where we can get chains."

"Now you're thinking." He kissed her, and they headed inside. "Next stop, the hardware store."

After a little teasing from Sin about Dash missing his curfew, Dash changed his clothes, and they headed out again. He drove straight to the high school, parking in the empty lot. "What are we doing here?" Amber asked as she climbed out of the car.

"Teenage dream fulfillment. Come on." He took her hand, leading her toward the bleachers by the football field.

Excitement bubbled up inside her. "Are we going to make out under the bleachers?"

"Damn right we are." He tugged her in for a smooch, and then they ran toward the bleachers hand in hand.

As he led her under the bleachers, she felt like a naughty kid breaking the rules, which cranked up the excitement. Dash drew her into his arms. "Is my good girl ready to get bad?"

"Heck *yeah*." She was ridiculously giddy at the prospect.

His lips came down over hers, and as their tongues explored, one arm crushing her to him, his other hand threading into her hair—*oh*, how she loved that—it felt like they were discovering each other for the very first time. She didn't know if it was the naughtiness of breaking rules or the man who made her feel safe and special, turning their already magical kisses into earth-shattering steaminess, but whatever it was, she never wanted it to end. He kissed her more demandingly, *taking* and giving, then taking much more, sending desire whipping through her like a rolling storm building, intensifying with every swipe of his tongue. The force of their kisses sent her stumbling back against the metal stand, and she was glad for the leverage, using it to go up on her toes to fist her hands in his hair, pressing her whole body against his exquisitely hard frame, wishing she could feel the heat of their passion flesh to flesh. Their hands moved greedily over their bodies and the rest of the world spun away, a single thought clinging to her—that the raw, unbridled passion they shared was more powerful than she ever thought she'd find. How was it possible that they'd known each other for only a little more than a week, when she knew in her heart that he'd been right when he'd said she'd been waiting for him her whole life?

Their lips parted on a series of kisses, both of them breathing hard, clinging to each other like they needed the other to survive.

"Jesus," he panted out. "I want to kiss you forever."

"Then do it." She pulled his mouth back to hers.

They lost themselves in a mesmerizing rhythm of slow and sensual, then urgent and demanding, all-consuming kisses. Time ceased to exist. When they finally made their way back to the car, they were utterly *drunk* on each other.

Dash started the engine and reached for Amber's hand. "What's going on in your beautiful mind?"

"I think you really have ruined me for any other man."

"My evil plan is working. Buckle up, hot stuff, we're just getting started."

"I STILL CAN'T believe Brindle and Morgyn told you that I've never made out in a movie theater." Amber popped a fry into her mouth. "I think I'll have to thank them."

Dash kissed her smiling lips.

They'd gone to the movies and sat in the back of the nearly empty theater. After kissing until they were both hanging on to their sanity by a thread, he'd pushed her boundaries and had given her the orgasm she'd so desperately needed. Which had done nothing to diminish the wood he'd been sporting, but seeing his careful girl set herself free was worth it. She wasn't the only one setting herself free today. These were firsts for him, too. He couldn't remember the last time he'd actually enjoyed life as much as he had these last few days with Amber. Now they were finishing dinner at the Stardust Café.

She snagged another fry, looking gorgeous and sweet in a buttercup-yellow sweater that brought out the flecks of gold in her eyes. "What else did the *blond birdies* tell you?"

"You'll see. I don't want to ruin the surprise."

She eyed him curiously. "I need to get to know your brothers and sisters so I can learn *your* secrets. Tell me something I don't know about you."

He finished his milkshake and set down the empty glass. "Today was the first time I've made out under the bleachers or in a theater."

"No way."

"It's true. I told you my life was busy when I was a kid, and I was the guy on the field, not under the bleachers." He stole a kiss. "You're also the first woman I've ever been crazy about."

She blushed. "That's hard to believe. You're so warm and expressive. I know you said you've had a hard time trusting women, and I believe you, but still."

He took her hand, gazing into her trusting eyes, wanting to share all of himself with her and explain why it was hard for him to trust women. But a café was hardly the place for that conversation. "That's because you bring out the best parts of me, and you get to see things in me that others don't. I think the same of you. You're the brightest star in a night sky, and I have *no* idea how you've gotten this far without a ring on your finger and a baby in your arms."

She shook her head, like she didn't believe him, and a tease rose in her eyes. "You know why."

"I do?"

She lowered her voice. "Because I was waiting for you."

He was *dead*. Slayed through the heart with a fricking arrow. "That's right, sweetheart, and don't you forget it." He pulled her into a kiss, choking back the emotions trampling through him. "Want to know another secret?"

"I want to know them *all*."

"A guy has to keep an air of mystery about him. But I'll share this one if you promise not to tell anyone."

She made an X over her heart.

He leaned in, speaking in a hushed tone. "Football wasn't my first career choice."

"Really? In the interviews I read, you said you'd wanted to play since you were a kid. That you were born to do it."

"I was born to do it. Not many wide receivers are given MVP awards, and I love the game and the camaraderie with my teammates. But being born with a good genetic foundation that you hone and perfect to do something you enjoy is different from following your dreams. I gave the public what they wanted to hear."

"You just got even more interesting, Pennington. What did you really want to do?"

"The kind of thing I'm doing with the ladies around here in the mornings but on a bigger level, like a boot camp. I loved setting up those obstacle courses I told you about for my brothers and sisters and coming up with creative ways to get them motivated and moving. But reality set in pretty quickly, and by the time I was fifteen, coaches were all over me about my athleticism and football. As I said, I loved football, so when I realized I could use those skills to help my family, it wasn't a hardship. I just split my focus. When I went to college, I studied kinesiology, the psychological and physiological principles of movement, which fed that passion, and focused on football to help my family. It was the right choice. My family is set for life, I enjoyed my career, and I made the best friends a guy could ask for."

She had that dreamy expression again. "I love knowing this secret."

"I've never told anyone, but I want you to know the real me. Inside and out."

"I think we're doing a pretty good job of getting to know each other inside and out."

He chuckled. "We sure are, and now you know some of my secrets."

"Yes, but *please* tell me there's a follow-up secret."

"What do you mean?"

"I know you retired to work on your motivational speaking and launch your book, which is great, but when do you plan to follow your heart and start a boot camp?"

"I have no idea about the boot camp, but I'm going to follow my heart right now. I think it's time for your next surprise." He took her hand as he rose to his feet, bringing her up with him. "A gaggle of grannies told me about the infamous *Let it Out* wall."

Her eyes lit up as he led her to the graffiti wall in the back of the café, which was covered with initials in hearts and other scribblings about couples and matters of the heart. He snagged one of the permanent markers from a bucket on a table by the wall.

"I recently learned that a certain beautiful girl's name is missing from this epic monument of coupledom, and if I want to stake my claim on her, I'd damn well better do it right."

She grinned from ear to ear as he found a spot on the wall and wrote their initials in a heart. He drew an arrow shooting through the lower left and emerging from the upper right of the heart, then drew three stars around the arrowhead.

"Those same grannies told me I was shooting for the stars." He tossed the marker into the bucket and hooked his arm over her shoulder, heading for the door. "There's no getting away from me now, Amber Montgomery. We're up there for all the world to see."

"Be careful what you wish for." She sounded like she was warning herself rather than him.

Trust me, sweetheart. "I have yet to make a wish that hasn't come true."

He pulled open the door, and as she walked through, she said, "In case you've forgotten, you're leaving next weekend."

"Yes, and you've given me a thousand reasons to come back." The sun was just beginning to set as they headed to the car. He opened the door and patted her ass. "Get in, pretty thing. It's time for your next surprise."

"There's *more*?"

"You're my girl. There's *always* going to be more."

Fifteen minutes later he parked at Jericho Ridge, which he'd learned from the guys last night was home to all the greatest parties in Oak Falls.

"How do you even know about this place?" Amber asked as

they got out of the car.

"I'm a resourceful guy." He opened the trunk and pulled out a cooler, a blanket, and a bag full of supplies.

"Wow, you sure are. Want me to carry something?"

"I've got it, but we'd better get down there. We have a creek party to attend."

"Oh, *Dash*. That's a sweet thought, but there's no party tonight," she said apologetically. "You'd hear the music and see the bonfire."

"Damn." He feigned disappointment. "We can still make the best of it."

The scent of pine and damp earth hung in the air as they made their way down to the creek, and he said, "This is a beautiful rite-of-passage spot."

"It is pretty. Reed and Grace shared their first kiss in that creek after being apart for a decade."

"I bet a lot of people shared their first kisses down here." He spread out the blanket. "What did you think of the creek parties?"

"I rarely went to them. Parties intimidated me when I was young." She looked out at the water, talking with her back to him. "I was afraid there would be too much commotion, and when there were parties at people's houses, I worried about strobe lights because they're a trigger for my seizures."

He finished setting out the rest of her surprise, filling two wineglasses with sparkling cider. He streamed music from his phone, which was connected to a small set of speakers, and went to her. "I wish I could have been with you then. You wouldn't have been intimidated if you'd had me by your side."

"I wish you were, too." She turned, surprise rising in her eyes as she took in the crackling fire and the lanterns he'd hung in the trees and set around the blanket.

"Welcome to your private creek party." He handed her a wineglass. "It's cider, not alcohol."

"You *knew* there was no party?"

"Actually, I had planned a party with your family and friends, and I had even invited Nana and Hellie and the ladies. But once we got to Sin's and you said what you did about not wanting your private life on display, I realized I'd made a mistake. You wanted the rite of passage, but you don't need spectators." He loved that about her. She was so much *more* than the quiet, careful woman she appeared to be. "So I texted Brindle, Nana, and Sin, since I couldn't tell Sin in front of you, and I asked them to get the word out that the party was canceled."

She blinked several times, like she was trying not to cry. "You set it up *and* canceled it? You must think I'm nuts."

"No, sweetheart. You're the sanest person I know, and I am honored to be part of your rites of passage." He held up his glass. "To making out at a creek party."

"To the best creek party *ever.*"

They clinked glasses as "Wanted" by Hunter Hayes came on. "Sounds like our song."

She smiled, lowering her eyes, reeling him in deeper with her sweet innocence. He set their drinks on the ground and drew her into his arms for their dance. Moonlight glittered in her eyes as he twirled her by the rippling creek, singing about wanting to make her feel wanted and the world making sense when she was in it. The words were as true as the deeper emotions blooming inside him.

They danced to several songs, kissing and talking and laughing more than Dash had ever laughed on a date. As the night wore on, they sat on the blanket sharing funny stories about football, her bookstore, and their families, and they walked along the creek hand in hand. Amber grew quiet, her expression thoughtful.

"What're you thinking about?"

"*Life.*" She tucked her hair behind her ear. "This may sound silly, because you have this big life, full of travel and meeting new people. But I never thought I'd have a day like this or feel this way about anyone. I sort of thought it might be just me and Reno forever."

"Why would you think that?"

"Because I run a bookstore in a tiny town, and other than college, visiting my cousins, or an occasional wedding, I almost never leave Oak Falls. I don't do online dating or even enjoy going to bars. Or at least I never did, until we went together last night. That was unforgettable."

"I'm glad to hear that because it's exactly how I feel."

"You've probably had a million unforgettable nights, and I'm glad that you have, but for me, it was one in a million. This whole day, and all of the time we've spent together, even our phone calls have been off-the-charts wonderful. I love peeling back your layers and discovering all your hidden parts, and my own, which is really unexpected. You're so much more than I thought you were. You make me *feel* things I was afraid to feel and *want* things I never imagined myself wanting. With you I'm not afraid to be curious. I can't believe I ever thought you were just an attention hog who was only interested in fast women and one-night stands."

He cocked a brow. "An attention hog?"

She shrugged with a little laugh. "Sorry."

"I do love *your* attention." He kissed her. "I know you think

I've had a *big* life, and in many ways I have. But as far as meeting people or getting close to them goes…" He shook his head. "There's a downside to having a big life. You know how I told you that I've had a hard time trusting women?"

"Yes," she said curiously.

"There's a reason. I've never told anyone this except for Hawk. My mother doesn't even know, but as I said before, I want you to know all of me. The good and the bad."

"Should I worry about what you're about to reveal?"

"It's definitely not one of my best moments, but I want you to know. I was never the kind of guy who slept with every woman who offered, but I had more than my fair share of hookups. About three years into my career, a girl I'd hooked up with claimed to be pregnant with my child and threatened to go to the press. I knew in my gut that it wasn't my kid. Don't ask me how. It was just one of those feelings I would have bet my life on. I'd never had sex without a condom and never had one break. But things happen, and after what my father did, I wouldn't have left a child behind, regardless of how it came to be. If the kid was mine, I would have done the right thing. Anyway, she refused to take a paternity test until the baby was born, which was enough of a red flag for me to know I was right. But right or wrong didn't matter because the decision I was facing had little to do with the truth. If I let her go to the press, my reputation would be scrutinized and my family would have to deal with that. From then on, I would either be the guy who had knocked up a one-night stand, or the guy who was falsely accused of knocking her up. My mother had been through enough hell with my father. I didn't want to add to it."

"I didn't read anything about that online."

"That's because I paid the woman off and got a gag order.

As I thought, the baby wasn't mine. All she wanted was the money, and she didn't care if she ruined my reputation or hurt my family in order to get it."

"That's awful. What kind of person would do that?"

"I can't answer that without using foul language. Needless to say, I've been much more careful and much less trusting. I didn't have anything to do with women for a *long* time, but…" He shrugged. "Eventually that changed, but it was different, few and far between. The women I got together with were mostly friends of my buddies or friends of their girlfriends, people they trusted, which made it easier for me to trust them enough to scratch that itch, so to speak. But it wasn't real, unconditional trust. Not like I trust you, or Sin, or my other buddies. It was just enough trust to feed an urge, which I'm sure sounds horrible to someone as careful as you, but I want to be honest with you."

She stopped walking and gazed up at him with more compassion than he probably deserved. "I'm sorry you went through that. It must have been stressful."

"It was." He felt the burden of his secret lifting from his shoulders. "While she was pregnant, all I could think about was what if it was my kid? Then I'd get pissed off at myself for being in that position with a woman I didn't care about, and in the next minute I was angry at her because I was sure she was lying. Part of the reason I never told my buddies was because I knew they'd never pay someone off to keep them quiet. They'd stand proudly in front of the media and deny it. But I just kept thinking about my mom. It's one thing to know your son is out there doing what single people do, but to have it all over rag magazines and the internet, portrayed in some kind of devious light, was a whole different ball game."

"It sounds like you did the right thing. But you said it would sound bad to someone as *careful* as me. I wonder if I've been careful because of circumstances, or if it's who I am."

"Baby, I don't know how many guys you've been with, and it doesn't matter. I'm sure they meant *something* to you. That's what I meant by careful. You don't strike me as the kind of girl who's been into meaningless hookups."

"I see. I've only been intimate with a couple of guys, and while you're right, I don't think I'd ever be into meaningless hookups, I do wonder if I would have been with more guys if I didn't have epilepsy. Those early seizures I told you about didn't just shape my life. They gave me insecurities. I'm not embarrassed about having epilepsy, but I'd be lying if I said I didn't think about it when I was with a guy. When I first had sex, I was terrified of having a seizure while we were doing it, and that fear never really went away until you came along. You're the first person I've ever been intimate with and *not* thought about it. But when we're together like that, I can't hold on to a single thought." Her voice softened. "I've always been curious about sex, but even in college I was never all that interested in it, which can be a side effect of epilepsy medication. But when I started researching you, every time I saw your picture, my body kicked into overdrive. Then I met you, and I think it's pretty clear that it wasn't my medication killing my sex drive. I just hadn't met the right man."

"You really were waiting for me." He wrapped her in his arms and kissed her. "I'm sorry that you missed out on those experiences."

"I didn't tell you so you could feel bad for me. Everyone thinks I'm good—innocent and pure—and I'm really not. I might not flaunt my sexuality like Brindle or Sable, but with you I'm discovering how much I enjoy it."

"I love discovering it with you, but you're wrong about one thing. You are pure and good, because purity and goodness speak to the heart of a person, not their sexual history or their hidden desires."

"I have a lot of desires," she whispered.

"I suppose for you I can set aside my own prudish values and try to conquer any fantasies you might have."

"That's very gracious of you."

"A gracious attention hog." They laughed, and he slipped his arm around her and kissed her temple as they began walking again. "See, sweetheart? We were meant to be."

She rested her head on his shoulder as they wandered along the grass. Dash had never slowed down enough to think about perfect moments or dreams of the future. But there he was, feeling like life was pretty damn perfect and having thoughts of bringing Amber home to meet his family and seeing her beautiful face light up on Christmas morning.

When they came to the edge of the woods, she pointed to a bunch of acorns scattered along the ground. "Look. It's a sign."

Dash picked one up. "This one is going in *our* acorn jar as the start of something wonderful." He pocketed the acorn, gathering her close again.

"I love that idea." She wound her arms around him. "We need to write down a memory to keep with it. I know what I'll write: *The best day of my life.*"

"And on the other side, I'm going to write, *The night I never wanted to end.*"

He lowered his lips to hers. She tasted like sweet afternoons and sinful nights, and he wanted to share every one of them with her until he had to leave town.

As their lips parted, she said, "It doesn't have to end. You could stay at my place again."

She said it cautiously, as if he might actually turn her down, which endeared her to him even more. He loved her quiet strength and the way she was letting herself ask for what she wanted. But he had to tease her, because *embarrassed Amber* was excruciatingly sexy. "So, you like having *a lot of man* in your bed."

He was sure she'd look away, blushing a red streak, but she didn't even flinch, didn't miss a beat, as she said, "And in my shower."

Her confession stoked the fire that had been burning inside him all day, and he crushed her to him, kissing her smiling lips. "I'll need to get clothes from Sin's place. You know, to avoid the walk of shame and keep my reputation intact. In fact, why don't I get all of my things? We both know I'm going to end up in your bed every night until I leave town anyway."

Now her gaze fell to his chest, and she breathed a little harder, as if she were considering it. But when she lifted her face, she was almost smirking. "I just threw you the ball. I didn't say you could make a touchdown."

"You know that was my job, right? To literally catch the ball in the end zone or run it in for a touchdown."

"Well, we're not doing the *end zone*. We're doing the *middle zone*."

She was so damn cute, he had to laugh. "I'll do whatever zone you want, but I prefer the erogenous zone." Her cheeks bloomed red. "Sweetheart, one night with you is better than a touchdown. But if you keep spouting football metaphors, I may never leave your side."

Relief rose in her eyes. "Do you think Sin will mind?"

"If I never leave your side? Sin can get his own girlfriend," he teased, earning a sweet laugh. "I'll still see him at the community center. I'm helping him out with clinics all week. He's happy for us." He kissed her softly. "And there's no place I'd rather be than lying in your bed with you safe in my arms."

Chapter Twelve

IT WAS OFFICIAL. Amber and Dash sucked at avoiding walks of shame. She'd fallen asleep with his naked body cocooning hers every night since they'd gone to JJ's and had enjoyed four glorious mornings waking up to his heart beating against her back, his strong arms holding her like he would never let her go, and *Good morning, sleepyhead* or *beautiful* or *wild thing*, whispered in her ear. Dash had woken with the sun the other days, but this morning she'd been up at the break of dawn, unable to stop her mind from racing, and he was still fast asleep. She wondered what that meant. She'd noticed that he never slowed down. Had they worn him out last night? They had gotten a little wilder than usual. That thrilling thought brought a shiver of delight. She could see the headlines in gossip magazines across America—UNASSUMING BOOKSTORE OWNER WEARS OUT HOT JOCK. She giggled to herself but stopped as reality traipsed in. They had only four more mornings together until he had to leave for his book tour.

She ached at the thought of not seeing him every day. The last few days had been nothing short of amazing. Dash had convinced her to go with him to meet Sin at JJ's Monday night to watch the Giants play, and they'd had a blast. She'd cheered on his team as loudly as he had, and they'd even squeezed in a few dances. They'd had breakfast with her family yesterday, and she'd watched him coach the clinic yesterday afternoon. Tonight they were having dinner with Morgyn and Graham at their place. Amber knew she should protect her heart, but she couldn't, no matter how scary it was. Everything Dash did made her fall harder for him. When she'd watched him coaching, he'd known every kid by name. He was a natural motivator, cheering them on and building them up, and the kids adored him. But the most extraordinary moments were when he pulled kids aside to help them individually. It was easy to see his interest in helping them feel good about themselves was genuine. She'd watched with awe as he'd bolstered the shy kids' confidence and had encouraged the young natural-born leaders to use their skills to help others.

He was doing the same for her. In fact, he made her feel so safe and confident, she was pretty sure she was turning into a sex maniac. They'd had more sex in the last four nights than she'd had in her entire pre-Dash life. Not just run-of-the-mill sex, but the type of rip-off-your-clothes-can't-make-it-to-the-bedroom sex she'd thought existed only in movies and novels. All it took was thinking about his mouth on hers, or even better, his mouth on her *body* or his big, rough hands groping and teasing or tangling in her hair. And Lord have mercy when she thought about his insanely talented trouser snake finding her G-spot like a heat-seeking missile. That turned her into an addict willing to sell her soul for her next hit.

She didn't know how news of Dash staying with her had spread so fast, but by Tuesday evening she'd heard from not only her girlfriends and parents but also all *six* of her siblings. Even a few friends from out of town, who were clued in by

Grace and Trixie, had called. Everyone was a bit shocked, but they were mostly happy for her. She hadn't even known she was capable of wanting someone so badly that she wouldn't care if the entire town was abuzz with the news of her *shacking up* with Dash Pennington. But *no* part of her wanted to pull back the reins.

It turned out that gossip was good for business. Dash's books were selling so fast, she had to place a rush order to have more delivered before the signing. She knew people were interested in his book signing, but there was no denying that some customers were coming in to buy books just to get the scoop on the two of them. Their relationship wasn't just affecting the people in town. Amber had noticed a funny thing happening to *her*, too. She was no longer embarrassed about people knowing that they were intimate. She was proud to be with Dash, and she didn't care that most of those gossipers saw him as only a hot ex-professional football player. She knew the *real* Dash Pennington. The man whose heart was bigger than the moon, who treasured family, and cared about the women and children he was helping in Oak Falls. The man who had already taken root in *her* heart.

Dash's cock twitched, growing harder against her bottom, sending her body into withdrawal. She didn't know what he was dreaming about, but she sure hoped it was *her*. She contemplated taking him inside her while he was sleeping. She'd never been a take-charge lover, or even been able to keep eye contact during sex. She'd always thought she was lacking in that department, but Dash had showed her otherwise, proving that she simply hadn't felt safe enough, or close enough, to any man before him to want to do those things. She loved the journey of self-discovery she was on with him, and as she turned in his arms and kissed her way down his chest, the appreciative noises he made told her he was enjoying it, too.

He ran his fingers through her hair. "Morning, beautiful."

"Morning." She slicked her tongue over his nipple and sucked it into her mouth.

He gritted out a curse. "You *know* what your mouth does to me." He fisted his hands in her hair, sending stings of pleasure skating down her core.

"I sure do." She grazed her teeth over his nipple, earning a heady groan.

She'd learned a few things during their sexy nights, like how much it turned him on when they watched each other and how his excitement made her feel wild and sexy, untethering parts of herself only *he* brought out. She watched him watching her as she trailed kisses down his stomach, the flames in his eyes emboldening her. She lingered on his abs, sliding her tongue along the ridges and lavishing his stomach with openmouthed kisses. She kept her eyes trained on his as she slithered down his body, taunting him with kisses around his erection without touching it. His eager arousal twitched with every press of her lips. She'd never considered that particular body part to be attractive, but everything about Dash was beautiful. She knew she felt that way because of their connection, which was becoming deeper and truer than anything she'd ever known.

When his breathing became ragged, she dragged her tongue along his length, and a low growl escaped through his clenched teeth. She turned up the heat, holding his gaze as she licked his length until it was slick, moaning with desire as she fisted his cock, giving it a few tight strokes.

"*God*, baby. You're driving me insane."

"Who, *me?*" She licked around the broad head, earning

more hungry sounds.

"If this is what getting up with the sun does to you, I'm setting an alarm."

Loving that idea, she continued taunting him, until his entire body flexed with restraint, and he gritted his teeth so tight, she feared he'd crack them. She felt him swell in her grasp and lowered her mouth over his rigid length, working him with her hand and mouth, tight and slow, his greedy sounds heightening her arousal. She hadn't realized how sensual oral sex could be. She *savored* the feel of his muscles tensing, the sight of his eyes igniting with passion. Each of his reactions earned one of its own from her, until desire surged through her like a raging river.

His hips rocked, and she was so lost in him, her hips were rocking, too. The primal look in his eyes had her quickening her efforts.

"Fuck...Baby." His warning was clear.

His fingers tightened in her hair, his eyes driving that warning deeper, but she had no interest in heeding it. She wanted to feel all of him, to release the inner beast he was holding back. She held his gaze with a challenge, working him into a cursing, hair-pulling frenzy, until he finally, *gloriously*, lost his battle for control. He rose off the pillows, her name shooting from his lips, and she took everything he had to give.

When he fell to the mattress, she slicked her tongue along his length and he shuddered, panting out, "Get up here." He hauled her up beside him, crushing his mouth to hers, taking her breath as his own. "We are never leaving this bedroom."

She giggled. "I think your morning fan club might have something to say about that."

He rolled her onto her back, pinning her hands beside her

head. "Do I sense a hint of jealousy over my exercise ladies?"

"You mean your breakfast dates?" she teased. Not only did the women he exercised with drag him to the diner for breakfast every morning after they were done working out, but Nana had also wrangled him into helping her husband, Pete, whom everyone called Poppi, repair their barn. Dash didn't seem to mind, as Nana spoiled him daily with homemade goodies.

"Hey, if that's what it takes to keep them on a healthy path." He kissed the tip of her nose and whispered, "Jealous?"

"After what we just did, I hope I don't have a reason to be jealous."

The humor in his eyes morphed to warmer, deeper emotions. "Sweetheart, you haven't had a reason to be jealous since I first saw you across the barn." His mouth came coaxingly down over hers in a penetrating kiss that had her writhing for more. He read her body perfectly, his hands and mouth traveling south, paying homage to every inch of her for a luxuriously long time, leaving her too spent and sated to move.

As his handsome face came back into focus, she whispered, "Am I still breathing?"

"I don't know. I'd better do mouth-to-mouth, just in case."

He kissed her until she was dizzy with desire, and he went hard against her, awakening her body anew. He grabbed a condom from the nightstand drawer and pushed to his feet, naked and aroused, leaving her confused.

She stood, reaching for his hand. "Where are you going? I thought we were going to…"

"Oh, we *are*." He tossed her over his shoulder.

She shrieked. "What are you doing?"

"Taking my fair maiden where she likes it most."

He carried her to the bathroom and turned on the shower,

putting the condom on the shelf beside the shampoo. When he lowered her to her feet, he reclaimed her mouth with a fierceness that had her trying to climb him like a tree. They stepped into the shower in a tangle of kisses and gropes, but he slowed them down to an intensely passionate devouring. His hands moved roughly over her wet flesh, dragging needful moans from both of them. He kissed her so thoroughly, her knees weakened, but he was there to catch her, tightening one arm around her waist and backing her up against the wall, their bodies sliding and grinding against each other.

"I don't want to ever stop kissing you," he said between hard, possessive kisses.

He kissed her slower and sweeter than *ever* before, drawing out her need. She was trembling with desire as he broke away to sheathe his length. Then his mouth was on hers, kissing her harder, more urgently. He lifted her into his arms, lowering her onto his shaft as slowly as he'd kissed her, magnifying every sensation. Neither said a word, but their emotions were as loud as the pounding of their hearts. Their mouths came together desperate and hungry, and they found their rhythm. The feel of his thickness moving inside her achingly deep sent pleasure radiating outward from her core, shooting all the way to the tips of her fingers and the very soles of her feet. She clung to his shoulders, his arms, wherever she could find purchase, quickening their pace. He was right there with her, eating at her mouth, clutching her tightly as their bodies pounded out a frantic beat, the tease of an orgasm swelling and pulsing until she could taste it. She dug her fingernails into his skin, as it crashed over her, her body clenching, hips thrusting in sweet agony.

She cried out his name, and he sealed his teeth over the curve of her neck, sending her soaring to the peak, her body burning, aching, throbbing as he followed her over the edge in his own magnificent release. His muscles bulged and flexed. She felt his pleasure as her own, filling every iota of her being as they rode the waves of their passion. Their mouths came together, breathing air into each other's lungs—and though she'd never been in love, she swore they were breathing love into their hearts—as they floated down from their high.

Her back met the tiled wall ever so gently, and his head tipped back, his eyes at half-mast. "First you suck me in with your sweetness." He nipped at her lower lip. "Then you hook me with your secret seductress side." He gazed deeply into her eyes with a tortured expression. "How am I ever going to leave you at the end of the week?"

As he came in for another kiss, she wondered how she'd ever let him go.

Chapter Thirteen

DASH TOSSED THE footballs into the bin as he and Sin put away the equipment after the last clinic late Thursday afternoon. His mind was miles away, on a certain brunette that had him tied in knots over leaving in a few days. He wanted to bring her with him, which he knew was ridiculous. It was a book tour, not a vacation, and she had a business to run. But hell if he didn't want her with him every second. He'd finally called Hawk and Damon and clued them in about her earlier that morning, and he was sure he'd sounded like a lovesick fool the way he'd rambled on.

Sin locked the equipment room, and they headed for the exit. "How's that whole slowing-down thing working out for you?"

It had been a fantastic week of football, getting to know Amber's family and falling into each other's arms at the end of every day.

"I'm loving it. I've got a great girl, I get to hang out with one of my best buddies, and I fucking love this town. I've never met such fun, quirky people. You're going to check in on my ladies while I'm gone, right? Make sure they don't get injured. Nana and Hellie try to push themselves. I swear they think they're thirty years old."

"I like how you call them your *ladies*. You know I'll keep an eye on them, but it's you they want to hear from. The whole town is talking about the big man and his motivational skills, which I think is code for how much they love watching you work out."

"Hey, man. Whatever it takes to keep 'em healthy, right? Don't worry. I've got them covered. I put together exercise schedules with pictures of certain exercises and daily goals for them to check off. That should keep them motivated. I just don't want them overdoing it. This morning at breakfast I showed them how to video chat on their phones, and we made a schedule for video check-ins while I'm gone."

"No wonder they love you. I grabbed a late breakfast at the Stardust this morning, and Winona offered me a *Pennington Playmaker*." Sin shook his head. "I've lived here for a few years now. Where's my namesake meal?"

The Pennington Playmaker featured hot cross buns, eggs, bacon, and sausage. Winona Hanson ran the Stardust Café and had presented the new menu option to Dash that morning when he'd had breakfast with Nana and Hellie.

"Winona's a trip. I'll put in a good word for you. The *Sinful Sunday Brunch* has a nice ring to it."

"I wonder how Amber will feel about every woman in town having their hands on your hot cross buns."

They both laughed.

"When I texted her about it this morning, she said Nana and Hellie probably put Winona up to it. That they were secretly finding ways to keep the weight on so I'd continue exercising with them."

"She might be onto something." Sin pushed through the

doors, and they headed for the parking lot. "You said Nana's been plying you with sweets."

"It's not just Nana. All the grannies come over to her house when I'm working on the barn. They park themselves in the grass, offering me treats, and complimenting our workmanship. But I'm onto them. They're just trying to get the dirt on me and Amber."

Sin stopped by his truck, giving Dash a serious look. "Everyone's curious about that."

"Even you? I told you I'm into Amber."

"I know you are, and you seem a thousand times happier than I've ever seen you. I meant everyone else. I'm more worried about your inability to slow down. You came here to chill and immediately got roped into leading an exercise group, daily breakfasts with your granny fans, and working on a barn. Not to mention the work you're doing with me and your relationship with Amber. You've had no downtime, and you're about to leave for a grueling month on the road."

"I like having breakfast with the grannies. They remind me of my grandmother. And you know I like working with my hands. Poppi's a great guy. He remembers when we played for Virginia, and we talk about all the old games." Dash shrugged. "I guess I didn't need downtime as much as I needed a change." He pulled out his keys, thinking about what he'd said. "Actually, I think I just needed Amber. Man, she lights me up inside. I could do twice as much work as long as I knew I'd see her every day. Can you keep something under your hat?"

"Of course."

"I'm toying with the idea of putting together training programs with online access like Chris Hemsworth's Centr program, or maybe something bigger with in-person boot camps. I don't know yet."

"Jesus, man. What about your motivational speaking gigs?"

"What about 'em? I told Shea I was cutting back. After the book tour I'll only be doing a handful a year, and we both know I can't sit on my ass and do nothing. What do you think about the idea?"

"I think anything you touch turns to gold. Just don't get burnt out."

Dash scoffed. "Remember who you're talking to."

"Yeah, I know. The guy who was up before sunrise throughout college, never missed a class or a practice, and still found time to call home and harass his siblings so they stayed on the right track."

"Just call me Superman." Dash puffed out his chest with an arrogant grin. "I've got to fly. I have big plans tonight and need to do a little prep work." Today was Hellie's anniversary, and Dash had a surprise planned for her and for Amber. He was picking Amber up at five, but he'd kept her in the dark about his plans.

"I don't want to know about your manscaping. But I would like to know why the hell you're leaving your stuff at my place when you spend every night with Amber."

"Because she's the quarterback in this game. She calls the plays. If it were up to me, I'd have moved my stuff to her place the day I came back from LA." But Amber needed control, and he'd do whatever it took to help her feel safe. "Do you mind?"

"Of course not. I see your sorry ass every day. I like having the break at night." Sin chuckled as he climbed into his truck. "But, dude, you are so far gone for her."

"You know it." And he wouldn't have it any other way.

DASH WALKED INTO the bookstore at five o'clock sharp to pick up Amber and found her leaning on the counter by the register writing something. Phoenix and another girl were stocking shelves. He put his finger in front of his lips, shushing them, as he snuck up behind Amber and wound his arms around her, kissing her neck.

"Better be careful doing that," she whispered. "My boy-friend gets vicious when he's jealous."

"Where is the bastard? I'll take him down." He loved how relaxed she'd become with him in public. "Is that birthday card for me?"

She turned with panic in her eyes. "Is it your birthday?"

"No, but I'd like to get a card in the mail from the prettiest girl in Oak Falls."

"Don't do that to me. I thought I missed it. This card is for Mr. Sanderson, who's turning seventy-eight next week. I send him a card every year, but it's been such a madhouse this week, I forgot to send him a card when I sent out the others on Monday."

"Do you send cards weekly?"

"Sometimes. I got a little sidetracked with a certain pushy ex-ball player the night I usually send them out and didn't get through the list."

"But I bet it was worth it." He kissed her. "And I think good old Mr. Sanderson would forgive you if it was late. We can drop it in the mailbox on the way out. Are you about ready to go? We don't have much time."

"I just need to grab my purse. Are you finally going to tell me where we're going? Can we bring Reno?"

"We're going on a secret mission, and yes, I brought provisions for my buddy." He winked at Reno as he came to Amber's side.

"A secret mission sounds fun. I'll be right back." She petted Reno's head. "Go visit."

Reno's tail wagged, and he made a beeline for Dash. Dash loved him up, and a few minutes later they headed out. Amber dropped the card in the mailbox, and then they climbed into his car. As he pulled away from the curb, Amber said, "Shea doesn't mess around with your PR. I set up Google alerts for your book tour, and I usually get a few each week, but the internet has been on fire all day. We've been getting calls about the signing from people who live an hour or two away. I'm a little worried that we'll run out of books."

He shrugged. "If we do, we do."

"How can you be so nonchalant about it? I'm a nervous wreck. I didn't realize how big a deal this was going to be. Lindsay came by to go over my plan. You met her at the jam session, remember? Nana's granddaughter? Pretty blonde."

"I remember her. When you ran away, she made a remark about flirting lessons."

"That would be her, and we're *not* going to discuss that. She's an event planner, and she told me about an engagement party she handled for a college football player in Maryland. It sounded like a wild crowd. I knew you were a big deal to people who like football, but I guess I didn't realize how big that crowd is. Lindsay thinks I'll be fine with a few modifications to the setup, so that's good. But I'm still nervous about it."

"There's nothing to be nervous about. People will line up, I'll sign books, Hawk will take pictures, and then it'll be over and we'll all go to dinner."

She looked at him like he'd lost his mind as he drove through town toward Hemlock Park. "Have you ever been to a book signing?"

"No, but we're talking about readers, not football fans who paint their faces and show up drunk from tailgating."

"If *only*. We're talking about a whole different group here, and I didn't really think it through until today. We're talking about *your* fans. The men and women who appreciate you on the field or when you give motivational talks. And we're expecting general readers who might be interested in hearing what you have to say, but we're also talking about *fangirls* who may or may not read but would do anything to get in front of you. That's the group that worries me. They can get loud and aggressive, and God forbid someone butts in line."

"You're really worried about that?"

"I'd be stupid if I weren't. When my phone started blowing up today, I realized that, and Lindsay's right. I'm going to have to rearrange things differently than I had planned to make more room for people who are waiting in line. This afternoon I went to the other businesses on the street and apologized ahead of time in case we get so many people the line goes all the way down the sidewalk and blocks their doorways."

He hadn't realized a book signing took so much preparation. He pulled off the road by the far end of the park and cut the engine, meeting her worried eyes as he took her hand. "Shea will be there to help keep things under control, and you know I won't let anything get out of hand. Hawk will be there, too, and I'll clue him in on your worries. I can ask Sin to help, too."

"There's no need to ask Sin, and Hawk is a photographer. He doesn't need to worry about this."

"He's my brother *first*. He'll worry about what I ask him to worry about, which is keeping things calm and organized for you."

"*You* are the sweetest. I love that you want to fix this for me, but that's not your job or Hawk's, or even Shea's. It's *mine*. There's a lot of pressure, but I'm just venting, letting you know what to expect and that I have fifteen balls in the air at the moment. This is the kickoff to your tour, and I want everything to be perfect. But don't worry. I've hosted signings before. Not big ones like yours, but I can handle it." She leaned across the console and kissed him. "Now, do you want to tell me what kind of secret mission we're on at the park?"

"We're going to give Hellie the anniversary she deserves." He reached over the back of the seat for the bag he'd brought and pulled out two black knit hats, handing one to her. "Put this on."

"Why?"

He pulled on his hat, and then he took hers, and as he put it on her, he said, "Because we have to be stealthy, like ninjas, if we're going to pull this off." He pressed his lips to hers. "Besides, you look adorable in that hat. Now take off your sweater."

"How is taking off my sweater for *Hellie?*" Her cheeks pinked up, but a tease shimmered in her eyes. "Why do I have to wear a hat if you really just want to fool around? I'm not sure I want to be a ninja if they skip the foreplay and use their friends as excuses."

"This ninja would never skip foreplay with you, wild thing." He waggled his brows. "Come on, now, take it off."

"We're parked on the side of the road. I'm *not* taking off my sweater." She looked around nervously.

"Do you really think I'd ask you to fool around out here? The last thing I want is other guys checking out your naked body. I was with you when you got dressed this morning, remember? I know you have a silk camisole thingy under there." He remembered quite explicitly, because when he'd seen her in that and skimpy pink lace panties, he'd chased her around the bedroom trying to get her naked again, and they'd fallen to the mattress in fits of laughter.

He pulled out the black sweater he'd bought her and tossed it to her. "If you're going to be stealth, you have to dress the part. Take that pretty pink sweater off, baby. Time is slipping by."

She finally relented, putting on the black sweater, and they climbed out of the car. While she got Reno out of the back, Dash opened the trunk and began setting out boxes of supplies on the grass.

Amber watched in confusion. "What is all this?"

"Solar lights. I brought string lights to wrap around the columns of the gazebo and ground lights to light the path from the gazebo to the entrance of the trail she takes through the woods when she comes to the park. We'll hang solar lanterns in the trees to light her way through the woods. I've been charging them in Sin's backyard since I first met Hellie, when she told me about Edgar and how she came here every year on their anniversary. I also brought these to hang around the gazebo." He pulled out a string of heart-shaped solar lights. "I enlisted Nana and her friends to make paper hearts and write something about Edgar and Hellie on them." He opened a box and showed her the pink and white paper hearts, picking out one by the red ribbon Nana had tied to it. "I thought we could hang them around the railing of the gazebo. And lastly, I stopped by the

Stardust Café and got one hamburger, no ketchup, and a bottle of Coke with two straws, which was all Edgar could afford on their first date. It'll be cold when she gets here, but that's how they ate it that night."

She looked awestruck. "I can't believe you did all of this. Hellie is going to be so surprised. How did you come up with the idea?"

"My grandfather does things like this for my grandmother sometimes, and after my dad left, my grandfather and I did it for my mom when she needed a pick-me-up. And I did it for my sisters when they were having a hard time or when guys were being jerks." He tugged her into his arms. "Are you disappointed that the mission wasn't just for us?"

She gazed up at him with disbelief. "How could I be disappointed in a man who thinks of everyone else before himself? You *know* how much the people here mean to me. I'm thrilled for Hellie. You've known her for less than two weeks, and you're about to make this her most memorable anniversary since she lost her husband. I think you are officially the most romantic man I've ever known."

"I don't know about the most romantic, but I sure as hell am the luckiest."

THE GAZEBO SPARKLED like a holiday bandstand against the evening sky with string lights wrapped around the columns and heart-shaped lights dangling from the rafters. Amber and Dash tied the last of the paper hearts to the railings. It was a magical sight with the path of lights in the grass leading from the gazebo to the trail that Hellie frequented through the woods, where lanterns dangled like giant fireflies swaying from branches deep into the distance. They'd set the bag from the diner and the Coke with two straws on the bench. Dash had failed to tell Amber that he'd also brought a single rose just because he thought Hellie should have one. Amber's heart was so full as she watched him, with his black sweater and ninja hat, gathering boxes and putting one inside the other. She had a feeling there was nothing he couldn't do. Or maybe *wouldn't* do was a better way to think of it, because if she'd learned one thing about Dash Pennington, it was that he always led with his heart, and it sure seemed like when he set his heart on something, he made it happen.

"We finished just in time."

He set the boxes down and turned a sexy smile on her, closing the distance between them. "We're not quite done." He handed her a pen and a paper heart, keeping one for himself. "She'll be here soon, so if you want to leave a note, do it quick."

He'd thought of *everything*. How had she ever worried that he was too much man for her? She couldn't imagine another man holding a candle to him. As she leaned on the bench to write Hellie's note—*Dear Hellie, I believe you can see the truest love in a person's eyes, and I saw it every time Edgar looked at you. Happy anniversary, love, Amber*—she glanced at Dash, hanging his paper heart. Edgar Camden had nothing on him.

"Ready?" Dash reached for her paper heart. As he tied it to the railing, she read what he'd written on his. *You look marvelous, m'lady.*

"That's a funny thing to write."

"That's what Edgar said to her every time they went on a date, right up until their very last one."

"How do you know that?"

"When I walked her home from breakfast, I asked her what things she missed most about him, and that was one of them."

You walked Hellie home from breakfast? He was surprising Amber at every turn, but one thing was for sure. There weren't enough words in the English language to describe his thoughtfulness. "You forgot to sign your name."

"I didn't want to. When I was a little boy, my grandfather told me never to give gifts looking for thank-yous. He says making someone happy should be enough, and it is. I like the idea of Hellie knowing she was on people's minds but not knowing who was behind all this." He grabbed the large box containing all the smaller boxes in one hand and took her hand. "We've got to get out of here. She'll be here any minute. Are you up to a quick run?"

"Absolutely. Come, Reno."

They ran up a hill and out of sight behind a row of bushes. Dash reached into the bushes and pulled out a duffel bag. "Hellie can't hear us talking up here."

"You really are good at this ninja stuff. What's in the bag?"

He pulled out a blanket and began spreading it out beside the bushes. "I figured you'd want a front-row seat when she arrives." They sat down, and Reno settled in beside the blanket, resting his chin between his paws. Dash put his arm around Amber and kissed her temple. "After that, we'll be busy stargazing, making wishes, and spilling secrets."

Happiness bubbled up inside her. "You remembered."

"Why does it surprise you every time I remember something you said?"

"Because it was nonsense. High school stuff."

"Nothing you say is ever nonsense." He leaned in for a kiss

as Hellie came out of the woods.

"Look." Amber pointed down the hill to Hellie standing at the edge of the woods wearing a long, flowing dress and a colorful cardigan, with a shiny blue scarf draped over her shoulders. Her silver braids were twisted into a knot on the top of her head, and she had one hand pressed over her heart as she took in the lights on the ground and gazebo.

Amber could barely contain her excitement as Hellie stepped tentatively down the lighted path, looking all around her. "I bet she thinks it was decorated for someone else."

"That's what the hearts are for, so she knows without a doubt it was meant for her."

They watched as she climbed the gazebo steps and walked around, her fingers trailing along the railing as she looked up at the heart-shaped lights. She read one of the paper hearts and looked around again, as if she couldn't believe it was all for her.

"I have goose bumps," Amber whispered.

Hellie went to the bench, looking at the food they'd left; then she began reading more of the hearts.

"Can you imagine loving someone so much that you cling to every little thing they did and said?" As she said it, she realized she'd been doing that with Dash.

"I think I can."

His words were drenched with emotions, sending her nerves into a wild flurry. She wanted to see his face, but she was afraid to look, afraid of what seeing such raw emotions might do to her, so she kept her eyes trained on Hellie. "I'm glad you thought of doing this. Seeing her so happy is a beautiful sight."

"You sure are." Dash's voice was low and husky.

She stole a glance and found him watching *her*, his emotions as real as the butterflies swarming inside her. "Why are you watching me instead of Hellie after all the effort you put into this?"

"Because seeing you happy for someone else is ten times as beautiful as anything I've ever seen. I love when you get dreamy-eyed, like you were when your friends got engaged at the barn. Getting to see that look twice in two weeks? *That's* beyond beautiful."

"You're too much. What are you hiding?"

"What makes you think I'm hiding anything?"

"You're too perfect."

"I'm far from perfect. Remember the toddler smile?" He grinned, pointing to his smile.

"Your smile is *not* a flaw."

"You want to hear my flaws? I've spent more than a decade so entrenched in my career, I barely saw my family for weeks at a time. And what do I have to show for it? Money? A little notoriety? Who cares about any of that? I already told you what I was like for the first few years of my career. Did I mention that I feel like a bit of a fraud? I wrote a book that I believed in when I was writing it, telling people to work their asses off to achieve their goals. But until recently, I didn't even have a clue what my next step was going to be, much less what goal I had for the next fifty years of my life. I knew I was missing something, but I'm only now realizing what that was." He gazed deeply into her eyes. "It was *you*, Amber, and moments like these, nights like the ones we've shared."

Me too, her heart whispered back.

"But it's even deeper than that. I never imagined trusting anyone enough to want to share *all* of myself, to admit my faults and fears and be comfortable just being the guy who grew up in Port Hudson and loves his family. The guy who enjoys getting together with the people here and walking with older ladies. Not the football player, motivational speaker, or bestselling author. With you, all of that is as natural as it was instantaneous. Maybe I'm a fool, but if I am, I never want to be smart again. I finally feel like I'm becoming the man I was always meant to be, and that's because of you."

Her heart turned over in her chest. "I feel the same way about you, that I can just be myself all the time, but it's kind of scary. I'm falling for a guy with a *big* life, and I don't even know what will happen after you leave town."

"I'll come back—that's what'll happen—and we'll figure it out from there, because I'm falling for an amazing woman who lives a big life in a small town, and I want to be the guy who never stops giving her reasons to look at me the way she is right now." He leaned closer, his breath whispering over her lips. "Don't be scared. I won't let you down."

He sealed his promise with a kiss so sweet and tender, she wanted to disappear into it.

"I know the timing of the tour sucks, and these next few weeks will be trying when we're apart, but we'll talk every night."

"It's okay. If it weren't for your tour, we might never have met."

"That's our silver lining. I don't know exactly what my future schedule looks like. I've got ongoing sponsorships and speaking engagements, and I'm toying with some other ideas, but I know I want to figure it out *with* you, not without you. I'm flying back to New York in two weekends to see my family and attend the fundraiser I told you about. I want you to come with me."

"To the fundraiser?"

"And to meet my family if you can take the time off. I thought we'd spend Friday evening with them in Port Hudson, then drive to the city and stay at my place. Saturday we'll hang out in the city and go sightseeing before the fundraiser. My buddies will be at the event, and I really want you to meet them. I'll have to leave Sunday for Monday's signing on the West Coast, but we'll have most of the weekend together, and then there'll only be two weeks left of the tour."

Excitement bubbled up inside her, and her mind raced from meeting his family through schedules for the bookstore, zipping right back to—*You want me to meet your family!*—immediately followed by worries over what to wear to the fundraiser. "That sounds wonderful. I can arrange the time off."

"Yeah?" His smile expanded to heart-melting proportions.

She nodded eagerly. "I'd love to meet your family. I have no idea what to wear to a fundraiser, but I'll figure it out. Is it formal?"

"It's pretty formal and themed. Casino night, old-Hollywood style. But don't stress over it. You'll be the most beautiful woman there, no matter what you wear. We can shop for a dress in the city if you want."

Her giddiness bubbled out. "Are you kidding? I can't wait until the last minute. I'm already a nervous wreck. I'll find a dress—don't worry."

"Why are you nervous?"

"I'm leaving Oak Falls, meeting your family and friends, and attending a formal event. This'll be the most exciting thing I've done in years."

He hauled her into a hard kiss. "This is going to be *great*. You'll love my family. You know my mom, and my brothers are the best. My sisters will adore you and tease the hell out of me, and…" He took her in another toe-curling kiss, the air around them electrically charged. "I'm so frickin' happy."

They kissed again, both of them laughing.

"It's going to be our greatest weekend yet. Or at least I hope so. We'll be meeting my mom's boyfriend, which is a little weird for me, but that won't even matter. I'm so freaking happy you're coming with me."

"Me too! And after everything you told me about your mom, I'm glad she has someone in her life."

"Yeah, I am too. It's just weird thinking about my mom and a guy in the new stages of a relationship, like us."

"Try catching your parents making out behind the barn at a jam session. *That's* awkward."

He laughed. "I knew I liked your parents. I'll arrange your flight and meet you at the airport."

"I'd rather drive, if you don't mind. I've only flown twice before, and there was so little room at my feet for Reno, I felt bad for him. Some other passengers also gave me uncomfortable looks because of him, and that made me anxious. I don't have to bring Reno to the event, but I need to have him with me when I travel. Driving would be less stressful for me."

"That's fine, and if you'd be more comfortable if he's with you, we can bring him to the event. Whatever you need, we'll make it happen. You've just made my night."

"And you've not only made my night, but you made Hellie's, too. Look." She nodded toward Hellie sitting on the bench with a pile of paper hearts beside her and another in her lap, reading one in her hand.

Happiness vibrated around them as they enjoyed their perfect evening. A long while later, when Hellie made her way back toward the woods, her arms full of paper hearts, Dash and

Amber lay on the blanket, gazing up at the starry sky, hands joined between them, hearts full of hope.

"I don't think I've ever taken the time to look up at the stars."

Amber could only see his profile as he stared up at the sky. Did he know she was falling harder for him even now? That she was going to miss him like crazy and count down the hours until they talked each night?

She looked up at the sky, thinking about him. He'd shared so much of himself, but she wanted to know more about where he thought he might be heading. "If you could sum up what you want in life in one or two sentences, how would you say it?"

He didn't answer for a long moment, and she didn't rush him, because she was mulling over her own answer. Their fingers were laced between them, and his thumb began brushing over her finger in a soothing rhythm.

"I've lived in a boiling pot of never-ending excitement and pressure, so I guess I'd like a lot less of that and a lot more of this." He squeezed her hand. "Maybe a trip to Maui, lying in the hot sand with my wild thing in a bikini." He pushed up on his elbow, smiling down at her. "How about it, sweetheart? Are you up for Maui after the book tour?"

"I don't know. That's an awfully long flight. Maybe you can send me pictures."

"What fun would that be?" He leaned in for a kiss and tickled her ribs.

She squirmed. "Virginia Beach *is* right around the corner."

"Virginia Beach?" He tickled her again, making her squeal with delight. "You deserve to see the world with your toddler-grinning guy." He gave her another quick kiss, running his fingers through her hair. "To see the stars from special places."

"But I like my safe little world."

"I know you do. I like it, too." He settled onto his back again. "Ready for another secret?"

"Always."

"I've never wished upon a star with someone special, either."

She turned her face to the side so she could see him and found him looking at her again, emotions brimming in his eyes. "I love that this is a first for both of us."

"Me too. I don't need to ask what you're going to wish for."

"Why is that?" she asked.

"Because I already know." He gazed deeply into her eyes, so steady and sure, she couldn't have looked away if she'd wanted to. "A man who thinks of you first thing in the morning and last thing at night, a magical proposal that tops your friends', and a lifetime of looking deep enough into every moment to see the seeds of all of the wonderful things to come."

She could do little more than stare at him.

He looked up at the sky again. "And if all that comes with a sexy, muscle-bound retired football player who grins like a toddler and has filthy fantasies about you, well, you'd be set for life, wouldn't you?"

She laughed. "And you're going to wish for the dirty fantasies, aren't you?"

"You know it. Close your eyes, baby. It's time to make our filthy fantasies—I mean *romantic wishes*—come true."

She closed her eyes, and as their hands joined between them, she knew that even if she never got all those future wishes, she'd be happy with a lifetime of this.

Chapter Fourteen

"I'LL BE RIGHT back." Amber popped to her feet for the fourth time in what felt like as many minutes early Saturday morning.

Dash grabbed the back of his T-shirt she was wearing, the one he'd worn last night when they'd had dinner with her family, and tugged her back down to the bed, wrapping his arms around her from behind. "What could you *possibly* need to do now?"

"I want to grab the large glass jar from the kitchen for the gift card raffle." She'd come up with a great idea to have everyone who showed up for the signing enter to win a gift card by signing up for her newsletter.

"And why do you need to rush out of bed to do that? The signing isn't until ten and it's not even six yet."

"So I don't forget."

"Babe, between your excitement over meeting my family, worrying over finding a dress for the fundraiser, and today's book signing, you've barely slept the last two nights." He was worried about her. Last night when they'd made love, she'd gotten teary-eyed, and when he'd asked about it, she'd brushed him off. He'd let it go, but he had a feeling all of this nervous energy might be partially due to his leaving. God knew he wasn't thrilled about it.

"Can you blame a girl for being excited?"

"No. I'm glad you're excited, but don't jump out of bed. Stay with me. I promise to remember the glass jar." He lowered her down to her back and moved over her. "You've gone over the details for today with a fine-tooth comb. There is nothing left to do but show up and sell books while I sign. What's really going on?"

"I'm just nervous about your signing. This is a *huge* day for you. One you'll remember forever, and tell your kids and your grandkids about. It's your *debut*. The kickoff to your author life." She was talking a mile a minute, her heart racing against his chest. "The pictures Hawk takes will be all over the internet, and I want everything to be perfect for you, for Shea, for Story Time."

He held her gaze, caressing her cheek. "Are you sure you're not feeling funny about me leaving tomorrow?"

"Mm-hm." Her eyes drifted away from his, focusing on his mouth instead. "I'll miss you, but we'll talk on the phone and it's only a couple of weeks. It's not a big deal. I'll be busy at the store and with the book club. I need to finish reading the book for it, and the Halloween bash is coming up, so I need to figure out a costume…"

She was so cute when she was nervous, he was tempted to let her keep rambling.

"I'm going to hate being away from you, sleeping in hotels without you," he said, bringing her eyes back to his. "All the while knowing the cowboys around here will probably be trying to get you to ride off into the sunset with them." That earned him a soft laugh. "I'll even miss my buddy sneaking up on the bed after we're asleep." He glanced at Reno stretched across the foot of the bed. "But I'll miss *this* the most, getting to hold you, read your thoughts through your beautiful eyes. I think you're worried about me leaving, but if I'm totally off base and you're cool with being apart, then I guess I'm just reading you wrong." He started to move off her.

"Wait." She grabbed his arms. "I *am* nervous about you leaving. I'm going to miss you a lot, and I don't know what to do with those feelings. I got used to you being here and seeing you every day. I've never had to deal with this before, except with my sisters and Axsel, but that's different. And now I'm rambling, and getting all worked up, and you're not even gone yet. I can't think about it or I'll be a mess at the signing, and keeping myself busy is the only way I can stop thinking about it."

"I know a much better way to keep your mind busy." He lowered his lips to hers, tangling his fingers in her hair, desperate to heal her sadness, to fill the void he knew he'd leave behind. And if he was lucky, there might even be a little bit of them left to fill the emptiness he'd carry with him when he was gone.

AFTER A MORNING spent lavishing each other and an incredibly sensuous shower, they were both riding high when they arrived at the bookstore two hours early. He watched her hustling around the shop, gorgeous in a pretty paisley dress that hugged her waist and skimmed her thighs, the mix of golds and greens bringing out her eyes, and knew he could spend morning, noon, and night loving her, and he'd never get his fill.

"Babe, where do you want the glass jar for the raffle?"

"On the table by the front door, which reminds me. I have to print the entry forms. I'll be right back." She headed into her office.

Dash set the glass jar on the table by the door just as the flowers he'd ordered arrived. The delivery man wheeled in a cart with two large bouquets of Amber's favorite flowers and an empty mason jar with a pink ribbon around it. Dash put one bouquet by the register and the other near the table where he'd be signing books.

After the delivery man left, he locked the door and brought the mason jar into Amber's office. "Hey, babe?"

"I was just thinking about the setup. Do you think there's enough space around your signing table?" She turned from where she stood by the printer. "Where'd you get that?"

"I knocked out a guy who was delivering flowers and took it from him." He set the jar on her desk.

"You knocked him out, huh?"

"Yup. We needed someplace to keep this." He reached into his pocket for the acorn they'd picked up when they were at the creek and dropped it in the jar.

"Dash," she said with a hint of disbelief. "You saved it."

"Of course I did. It's the start of our many wonderful things." He gathered her in his arms and kissed her. "As I recall, we have notes to write, and the guy I decked didn't have any paper."

"I think I can cover that." She grabbed a pink notepad from the desk drawer and cut out two hearts, handing one to him.

"I like your style, wild thing." They wrote their notes, folded them in half, and as they put them in the jar, his phone rang.

He pulled it out of his pocket and saw Dawn's name on a FaceTime call. "It's my sister."

She grabbed the papers from the printer. "Talk to her. I'm going to put the entry forms up front."

He pushed the green icon to answer the call and followed Amber out of the office. She said, "Oh, Dash! They're beautiful!" as both of his sisters' faces appeared on the screen.

"Look at that, Andi. We got the toddler grin," Dawn teased.

"Who was that? Shea?" Andi asked.

Dash watched Amber setting up the raffle table. "No. Shea and Hawk should be here in a little while. That was the most beautiful girl in Oak Falls, the one and only Amber Montgomery."

Amber looked up, pink cheeked.

"That sounds like she's someone special," Andi said.

"I knew that cake meant something!" Dawn exclaimed.

Dash held Amber's gaze, closing the distance between them. "Yeah, it meant something, all right."

"*Hello?* Dash! We're over here," Andi teased.

He looked at the phone as he reached for Amber's hand, drawing her into the camera frame. "Sorry. Dawn, Andi, this is Amber. Amber, these are my sisters."

"Hi, Amber," they said in unison, beaming curiously.

"Hi. Dash has told me so much about you guys."

"Well, it's good to know he didn't leave us *all* in the dark." Dawn gave Dash her best scowl, which always made him laugh.

"Chill out, Sis." He put his arm around Amber and kissed her temple. "You're meeting her now."

"I almost forgot," Amber exclaimed. "Dawn, thank you for the tiramisu crepe cake. It was delicious. I'm a huge fan of your show."

Andi's brows knitted. "You made her a crepe cake? You've never made me that crepe cake."

"You get everything else I make," Dawn said.

"Yeah, leftovers from the show," Andi complained.

"*Pfft.*" Dawn rolled her eyes. "You want a crepe cake? I'll make you a crepe cake, but you have to set me up with Sutton's boss." Sutton worked for Clay Braden's younger brother Flynn.

Andi's jaw dropped. "I will *not* set—"

"Hey!" Dash snapped, silencing them. "Did you call to talk to me or to bitch at each other?"

"Sorry," Andi said with genuine regret, while Dawn gave him a smug look.

He narrowed his eyes at Dawn. "You're not going out with Flynn. That would be a nightmare waiting to happen when you got bored of him after two dates."

"What*ever*." Dawn rolled her eyes. "Clay's looking awfully good this season."

"*Dawn,*" he warned.

"I'm kidding. We called to say good luck at your signing, but now that we know about Amber, how about you go sign some books and let us get to know her?" Dawn motioned with her hands, shooing Dash away.

"How long have you two been going out?" Andi asked.

Before Amber or Dash could respond, Dawn said, "Did he win you over with his toddler grin?"

"I love his grin," Amber said.

"You have to say that because he's standing there," Dawn said. "We all know it's too toothy."

"Man, you are harsh." Dash shook his head. "Listen, Amber's coming home with me before the fundraiser in a couple of weeks. You can grill her then."

"She *is?*" Dawn's excitement radiated through the screen. "I cannot wait to meet you in person!"

"Me too," Andi exclaimed. "You guys must be pretty serious. Dash has never brought a girl home before."

"That's because he hasn't had any girlfriends. You *know* that." Dawn narrowed her eyes. "Wait. Have you had secret girlfriends?"

Jesus. "Of course not. We need to go. We have to get ready for the signing."

"Fine," Dawn relented. "For what it's worth, you probably found the only woman on earth who's prettier than you are. She just might be too pretty for you."

Amber blushed.

"I agree with you," Dash said. "But if I keep giving Amber your cakes, she might just stick around."

"Good luck today. Give Hawk a hug for me," Andi said thoughtfully. "Amber, I'm looking forward to getting to know you better."

"Me too," Amber said. "You guys sound fun, like my sisters."

"How many sisters do you have?" Andi asked.

"Do you have any hot brothers?" Dawn asked.

"Five sisters and one very hot, very gay brother," Amber said. "He tried to pick up Dash the first night we met."

"So you're saying he's hot, gay, and has bad taste?" Dawn flashed a teasing smirk.

Dash uttered a curse. "We're going now. Love you guys. Thanks for calling."

"Love you," they both said. "Bye, Amber."

He ended the call and pocketed the phone. "Sorry about that."

"Why? I'm excited to meet them in person. They obviously adore you." She went up on her toes and kissed him. "And *you* must be crazy about *me* to buy me flowers and remember our acorn jar. Thank you."

"Sweetheart, if anyone deserves thanks, it's you. For hosting my signing and for reminding me what life should be about."

"You mean like *kissing*?" She rose on her toes, kissing him again.

"Like kissing *you*." He dipped her over his arm and kissed the hell out of her.

Someone banged on the front door, startling them apart. Shea waved through the glass, her long blond hair falling loose over the shoulders of her tailored navy pantsuit. Hawk stood beside her smirking, as trendy as ever in plumb-colored jeans, a white dress shirt, and suspenders. His thick brown hair was slicked back, and his bearded face was hidden behind his camera.

"It's Shea and Hawk."

"That's embarrassing," Amber said softly.

"No, it's not. Come on, you'll love them, too." He took her hand and went to let them in. "Hi." Dash leaned down and kissed Shea's cheek as she walked in. "Shea, this is Amber Montgomery. Amber, this is Shea Steele." Dash pulled Hawk into a manly embrace as Shea said hello to Amber and Reno and gushed about how much she liked Amber's store. "How are you doing, man?"

"Great. I'll be rich in no time. I'm selling those pictures to the tabloids." Hawk chuckled.

"No, you won't," Shea warned, then turned a warmer expression on Amber. "He's already signed his life away. Pictures from the signing are fair game, but if pictures of Dash's personal life get leaked to the wrong outlets, I'll own his ass."

Hawk cocked a grin. "Hey, I might leak them just to make that happen."

Shea rolled her eyes.

"Hawk, this is Amber, and her service dog, Reno." Dash had already filled his brother in on Amber's medical condition.

"It's nice to meet you," Amber said. "I see you share your brother's charm."

Hawk scoffed. "I'm much more charming than Dashell."

Amber's eyes lit up with amusement. "Dashell?"

"Thanks a lot, man. Way to bring down my street cred." Dash shook his head. "It's our mother's maiden name."

"I like it. It's pretty." Amber glanced challengingly at Hawk. "It takes a whole lotta man to pull off a pretty name."

Dash puffed out his chest, snickering at Hawk.

"Now you've done it," Shea teased. "They'll be one-upping each other all day."

"Nah. This is Dash's day. It would be rude to outshine him. It's no wonder my brother has been blowing up my phone about meeting the woman of his dreams. It's a pleasure to meet you." Hawk leaned in to hug her.

"You, too," Amber said sweetly. "Dash has told me great things about you."

"All lies," Dash teased.

Shea crossed her arms, staring at Dash. "Why am I just hearing about you meeting the woman of your dreams?"

"Because you'd tell me not to mix business with pleasure. I figured that was why you thought Amber wasn't my type."

"That wasn't why, although it is a good reason," Shea said. "When I spoke to Amber on the phone, she was sweet and soft-spoken and fairly reluctant to host a signing for a sports figure.

Remember, Amber? You said you weren't sure he was a good match for your low-key bookstore. Naturally, I didn't think he was your type." She looked at Dash. "You aren't exactly quiet, and you're always looking for the next mountain to climb. I half expect you to come out of retirement after the signing and get back to playing ball."

"That's *not* happening." Dash exchanged a knowing glance with Hawk.

"To be honest, I didn't think he was my type, either." Amber gave Dash that bashful, adorable glance he loved.

Hawk barked out a laugh. "You mean his toddler smile didn't set your heart on fire?"

"It took a hell of a lot more than my smile to get on her radar." Dash hugged Amber against his side, earning a sexy blush.

"That's a relief," Shea said. "I was worried I was losing my touch."

Hawk looked coyly at Shea. "Let me buy you a drink when we're done here, and I'll check out your *touch* and give you an expert opinion on it."

Before Shea could get a word out, the bells above the door chimed, and Amber's mother, sisters, and Lindsay flew into the store with Phoenix and two other young girls. Marilynn was carrying a large tray of cookies. Morgyn and Brindle held fistfuls of balloons. Lindsay's hands were empty, but she was surveying the signing area, and Sable waved a bottle of champagne over her head, exclaiming, "The cavalry is here!"

Phoenix locked the door behind them. "I didn't know you'd called in more help."

"She didn't," Brindle said. "But did you see the *line* out there? It's already almost to the end of the block. It's a good thing we're here."

"*What?* Already?" Panic stretched over Amber's face, and she reached down to pet Reno. "We don't open for another forty minutes."

"Why do you have balloons?" Dash asked.

"For the signs Amber said she was putting out front," Morgyn answered. "Lindsay thought they were a good idea."

"Where are the signs? We can set them up," Lindsay suggested. "We need to get a jump on things anyway, to manage the line."

"I need to hire you," Shea said.

Amber cringed. "I can't believe I forgot to put the signs out."

"Are you kidding?" Morgyn put her arm around Amber. "You *just* agreed to meet Dash's family, you're going to a black-tie fundraiser in New York City, *and* you're about to host the biggest signing you ever had. It's a wonder you can think at all."

Lindsay's index finger shot up in the air. "Have no fear. Your troops are here!"

"I'll get the signs," Phoenix called out, and Lindsay followed her toward the stockroom.

Marilynn rested the tray of cookies on the edge of a table. "I thought I'd hand out cookies to keep people from getting antsy while they waited. I have more in the car, but if that line is any indication of what you're in for, I'm not sure I brought enough."

"That's okay." Amber's gaze darted nervously over the cookies. "Cookies mean dirty fingers on book jackets, but I have napkins in the kitchen. I'll get them."

"I'll get them," Brindle offered, and hurried off toward the back.

"I can't believe there's already a line," Amber said.

"Take a breath, wild thing," Sable teased. "I brought a little something for later, so you and Dash can celebrate." She handed Amber the champagne. "I know you won't drink much, but you can get Dash loaded and take advantage of him. *Win-win.*"

"Thanks, but I can't think about that right now." Amber set the bottle on the table and looked at Dash. "What if we don't have enough books?"

"Whatever we have will have to be enough," Dash reassured her.

"I hate to disappoint customers, but you're right." Amber breathed deeply and squared her shoulders, morphing from panicked hostess to professional business owner right before his eyes. With one hand brushing Reno's head, she made quick work of introducing everyone and began directing activities.

Dash watched in awe as she took apart her perfectly planned itinerary and checklist, divvying and delegating responsibilities so her sisters and mother each had a job. She looked completely in control, but he sensed that beneath that unflappable facade she was as nervous as a mouse in a snake pit. Not because she couldn't handle a signing, but because bringing new players into a game at the last minute was nerve-racking for anyone, and she'd put an incredible amount of pressure on herself to make today perfect for him.

Shortly before the start of the signing, Hawk sidled up to him. He'd taken pictures of the whole process, including the line outside, which Brindle had just reported was wrapping nearly around the entire block.

Hawk lifted his camera, taking a picture of Amber talking with Shea. "Amber's really something. No wonder you're bringing her home to meet everyone. But you'd better keep her close at that fundraiser. I know you don't worry about competition, but she's got something special, and you know how some of those guys can be."

Special didn't begin to touch on how remarkable she was. "I'm not worried." Amber glanced over, and their eyes caught with the same summer lightning they always did, luminous and scorching. "I'm going to miss the hell out of her when I'm gone."

"Good. Maybe you'll actually give yourself a break and slow down after the tour. Shea's right to wonder what your next big adventure will be. You suck at slowing down."

"I've never had a reason to before. Do me a favor? Take a few pictures of me and Amber?"

"I'd love to. I took some great candid shots of you two. The way you look at her, *man*." Hawk shook his head. "It's really something."

"It's not half as great as the way she looks at me."

After Hawk took their pictures, Shea called out, "Three minutes!" sparking a flurry of activity and conversation.

Nervousness crackled in the air as Dash drew Amber into his arms.

"It's almost time," she said anxiously.

He took her face between his hands, gazing deeply into the eyes of the woman he'd come to love. The realization hit him like a gale-force wind, whipping through him, bringing fullness to his chest and a thickness to his throat.

"Dash, we need to hurry," Amber urged, jerking him from his thoughts.

He stuffed those raging emotions down deep until he could process them and figure out how to tell her in a way that was as magical as she deserved.

Filled with a joy like he'd never known, he said, "I am so glad you hesitated to host my signing so it had to start here. It means the world to me that we're doing this together. I'm always in awe of you, but watching you orchestrate all of this was pretty damn amazing. Thank you for making it such a special day for us."

She fanned her face. "You're going to make me cry."

He hugged her tight. "I don't want to make you cry. I just really appreciate all of your efforts."

"Thank you. I'm *so* excited for you. I hope nothing goes wrong."

"Listen, sweetheart. If I learned one thing during my football career, it's that games rarely go off without a hitch. If we run out of books or fans get out of hand, I want you to know that it doesn't change the incredible day you've given me. Do you understand?"

She nodded.

"Are you ready for the Oak Falls episode of *Fan Girls Gone Wild*?"

She laughed. "As ready as I'll ever be. How about you?"

"With you by my side, I'm ready for anything."

He kissed her again, and as Shea ushered him to the signing table, he watched Amber push past her worries and warmly, gracefully welcome into her quiet bookstore a horde of loud, excited women who were making a beeline straight to him.

Two hours passed with an endless flow of men, women, and children getting signed books, taking photographs with Dash, and checking out the bookstore. Shea stayed by the table, managing the signing and ushering fans along who tried to take up residence beside Dash, while Amber and Lindsay helped customers and answered questions, and Hawk moved seamlessly through the crowd taking pictures. It was a good thing Amber's family had shown up to help, because Amber and her staff hadn't had a second to spare. Marilynn and Brindle were reading to children whose parents were waiting in line, while Morgyn helped Phoenix at the register, and Sable took on the role of bouncer, keeping people in line and heading off trouble.

Dash was thrilled that the signing was going smoothly, and Amber was gaining so much business. He wasn't surprised to see Nana and her friends, Poppi, Cade, Sin, Trace, Graham, and practically the whole rest of the town come through the line. The community support was endless, though Dash was under no misconception that it was all for him. He knew they were there to support Amber. He was just a sidebar.

A teenager stepped up to the table as Amber arrived with another stack of books and Reno on her heels, nervous energy still zinging around her. Dash caught her attention as she set the books on the table and winked, wishing he could tug her onto his lap for a kiss. She flashed a sexy smile as she was pulled away by a customer, and the boy handed Dash a book and asked him to sign it to Mike.

He autographed it and handed it back. "Here you go, Mike. I hope you enjoy the book and find some inspiration in it."

"I know I will. Can I get a picture with you to show my dad?" He pulled out his cell phone.

"Sure." Dash went to stand with him for a selfie.

Mike held up his phone, and Dash leaned into the picture as Reno began whimpering and barked. Dash whipped his head around just in time to see Amber staring vacantly into space as she fell toward the woman beside her. He bolted across the store as a collective gasp rang out. Fear and heartache clashing, he took Amber from the woman's arms. His chest seized as he lowered her rigid body toward the floor just as she began convulsing.

"Please stand back!" His heart thundered as he rolled Amber onto her side and her sisters ushered people away, explaining that Amber was having an epileptic seizure.

Reno circled her, whimpering, trying to get to the button on her necklace.

"It's okay, buddy. I've got her." Dash kept his hand beneath Amber's face so she didn't hurt herself. She made stilted sounds as her body jerked uncontrollably. "You're okay, baby. I'm right here." He tried to remember what else to do. *Keep her from choking. Time the seizure.* "Time! Someone watch the time."

"I'm already on it." Marilynn crouched beside him with her phone in her hand, perfectly calm. "Are *you* okay, honey?"

"Yes. *No.* I mean, *yes*, but I feel helpless. My poor girl." Spittle seeped out of the corner of Amber's mouth, and Dash noticed a streak of urine sliding over her leg, puddling beneath her, his heart breaking. "Marilynn, protect her face." She put her hand beneath Amber's cheek, and Dash tore open his dress shirt, sending the buttons flying, and draped it over Amber's lower half. Memories of what Amber had said about her teenage seizure slammed into him just as she went limp, eyes closed. "It's okay, baby. Just breathe, sweetheart." Amber jerked a couple of times, and then she stilled again, eyes closed, head back, mouth agape. Dash realized she was in the end stage, or postictal phase, during which her body returned to baseline.

"Two and a half minutes," Marilynn said. "She's okay."

Thank God. A seizure that lasted more than five minutes usually meant trouble. He sank to his ass, stretching his legs around Amber, drawing her back up against his chest, cradling her sleeping body against him. He wiped the drool from her cheek with his hand and brushed a kiss to her forehead. "I've got you, baby. You're okay."

"You're doing great, Dash," Marilynn said.

"Me?" he panted out, confused.

"I know how hard it is to see someone you love have a seizure." Marilynn glanced around them and smiled. "I think some of these women would probably like to thank you for taking your shirt off."

He looked down and realized his chest was bare, his lungs constricting as his shirt came into view, covering where she'd wet herself, and he processed the last few minutes. He looked up. Sable stood with her back to them, her arms out to the sides, shielding Amber from the crowd with her body, a sea of empathetic and scared faces staring back at him, bringing reality into focus. Shea stood beneath Hawk's protective arm, her hand on her chest, tears in her eyes. *Fuck.* He'd forgotten about the signing and all the people.

None of that mattered.

The only thing that mattered was the woman he loved, slowly regaining consciousness in his arms.

AMBER WAS TRAPPED in a dense fog, disoriented, sounds hovering just out of reach, too unclear for her to make sense of them. She was tired. *So tired.* She struggled to get to the surface, but bone-deep fatigue kept sucking her back into its depths. Something rough and warm moved over her face. She wanted to chase that touch, but noises, *voices* clattered in the background, throwing her off.

"You're okay, baby. I've got you."

The familiar deep voice, full of anguish and warmer emotions, tugged at her, dragging her toward the surface. She fought the fatigue, forcing her eyes open, but her eyelids were too heavy, and they fluttered closed. She tried once more, squinting against the harsh light as Dash's worried eyes came into focus. Where were they? Why was her butt wet?

"Dash?" she managed, a shaky whisper.

"I'm here, sweetheart. You had a seizure, but you're okay. Your mom is here, and your sisters."

Her mother's face came into focus. "I'm right here, lovey."

"Where are we?"

"At the bookstore," Dash said. "Your sisters are taking everyone outside."

Panic bloomed in her chest as her memory kicked in, and she tried to sit up. "The signing."

Dash gently pulled her back against him. "It's over."

"No!" She pushed from his chest, sitting up, swaying unsteadily.

He put his arm around her, holding her in place. "It's fine. We only had one hour left."

"*No*. It's *not* fine," she said groggily, trying to force the confusion from her brain. "Those people waited for you." She felt like she was swimming against a tide. "*Mom?*"

"I'm right here," her mother said.

"You can't let this happen." Amber tried to push to her feet but only made it to her knees as cold wetness hit her butt and a shirt tumbled from her lap. It took a moment for her to put the pieces together. Embarrassment swelled inside her, throbbing like a pain she couldn't shake, but she couldn't—*wouldn't*—let that take over as she had as a teenager. Adrenaline surged inside her. "You're finishing the signing."

"I'm *not* leaving your side, baby."

"I'm leaving *yours*." Amber swallowed hard.

Confusion riddled Dash's face. "What are you talking about?"

She looked around, fighting the need to close her eyes. "Where's Sable? I need a ride home."

"*I'll* take you," Dash insisted, his arms tightening around her.

"I'm right here." Sable moved into view, her hands on her hips. "I told him you would want him to finish the signing, but I don't think he heard me. Lindsay said she'll help Shea and make sure everything runs smoothly."

Lindsay stepped beside her. "I won't let you down, Amber."

"*Jesus,*" Dash gritted out. "She *just* had a seizure. Who gives a damn about the signing?"

"*I* do!" Amber snapped. "You can't let *my* medical condition get in *your* way." Every word took too much energy, but she had to make him understand. "You worked hard to get here." Tears brimmed in her eyes. "It's bad enough that I peed myself. Please, for *me*, see this through."

His jaw clenched, his muscles flexing and bulging, as if he were about to explode. His fingers dug into her skin. "I *love* you" roared out, ferocious and angry. "How can you ask me to choose a signing over taking care of *you*?"

Her breath rushed from her lungs, and she was sure she'd mistaken his words.

He grabbed her face with both hands. "I *love* you. Do you hear me? I will *not* sit on my ass and sign books when I should be with you."

"Oh, fuck. The baller is about to get his ass handed to him," Sable said snarkily. "All in the name of *love*."

"You *love* me?" Amber choked out, his words circling her foggy head.

A tethered smile curved his lips. "With everything I have and everything I am."

Tears slipped down Amber's cheeks. She wanted to profess her love, too, but she couldn't. She knew what she *had* to do, and she didn't have the energy for both. "If you love me, you'll do this for me."

"Get with the program, Pennington." Sable crossed her arms. "You have to sign the damn books or you'll invalidate all of her hard work. I'll take good care of her."

Dash looked unconvinced.

Her mother put her hand on his arm. "I know how hard this is, but she's right. She knows you'd rather be with her. Sable and I will take care of her. I promise."

Dash looked at Amber, the muscles in his jaw bunching, tension written in the harsh lines on his forehead and around his mouth, his heart hammering against her body. "You want me to sign books? *Shirtless?*"

"I've got a dress shirt in my bag," Hawk called over.

Amber managed a smile. "Please say okay so I can go home, get cleaned up, and lie down."

He touched his forehead to hers, holding her so tight his love seeped beneath her skin. "I *hate* this with every fiber of my being, but I'll do it for you." He breathed heavily. "*Damn it*, Amber. I'm pampering you tonight, and you're going to suffer through it."

God, she loved him. "I wouldn't have it any other way."

Chapter Fifteen

DASH THREW THE car into park in Amber's driveway and cut the engine after the worst fucking test of fortitude he'd ever endured. The signing had lasted for two and a half more hours instead of one because he'd had to go up against *Amber's Angels*—Lindsay, Brindle, Morgyn, and Phoenix—who were tougher than any defensive line he'd ever faced. They'd insisted that Amber would never end a signing until all the customers had gotten autographs. When they ran out of his books, he'd signed other items they'd bought from the store, like tote bags and journals. It had been excruciating being away from Amber, made worse because Amber's fall, and visions of her lying on the floor convulsing, replayed in a loop in his head like a bad movie. Not to mention the guilt hammering him because he was at fault for her exhaustion. How the hell was he supposed to leave her tomorrow knowing that could happen again and he wouldn't be there for her?

He grabbed the box of food Patty Ann, who ran the Catch Up Diner next door to Amber's bookstore, had sent home for her and rushed up to the house. He threw open the front door and stalked inside. Marilynn jumped to her feet from the couch, and Sable, standing by the fireplace, casually pocketed her phone.

"How is she?" he asked at the same time Marilynn said, "She's sleeping."

"She's *fine*, but you look like you need some Xanax." Sable sauntered over, eyeing Hawk's mustard-yellow shirt Dash was wearing with amusement as she took the box of food from him. "Gotta love the ladies at the diner."

"She said those are all of Amber's favorite comfort foods." And she'd taken way too fucking long explaining each dish to him before he left. As word of Amber's seizure had traveled, it seemed like everyone in the whole damn town had come back to check on her. His girl was more than loved by the community. She was *revered*, and he was learning even more about what the word *safe* really meant for her. He was also learning just how strong Amber was and how weak love could make a person. Even in her groggy state, she'd been stronger than him, able to leave his side when he'd have clawed people's eyes out to stay with her.

"She'll sleep for a while," Marilynn said. "Come into the kitchen so we can talk."

"I need to see her" came out as desperate as he felt.

Sable eyed him skeptically. "You can't wake her up with that look on your face. You look twisted, riddled with pain or guilt."

"*Sable,*" Marilynn chided.

"It's okay. She's right. I'm all those things. How else should I feel? Amber had a seizure, and it's all my fault. I read up on epilepsy when I first found out she had it. I *knew* stress and exhaustion could increase the chance of a seizure, and I *still* kept her up too late all week." The words rushed out like rabid animals he'd been holding in since she'd left, their jagged teeth gnawing at him, leaving raw, gaping wounds he knew might never heal. "I was selfish, too wrapped up in how phenomenal it was being with her to think of the ramifications. I should have made sure she got enough rest."

"Nonsense, sweetheart." Marilynn took him by the arm, and they followed Sable into the kitchen. "You have brought joy and love into Amber's life, and those things are too exciting to put away at the end of the day, especially when they're new."

"She means it's okay to hump like bunnies." Sable began unpacking the food.

"Sable, *please*," Marilynn implored her.

"I'm just spelling it out for him." Sable plucked a french fry out of a container and popped it into her mouth. "Amber won't want to eat until tomorrow. Have you eaten? Do you want some?"

Dash shook his head, pacing the kitchen.

As Marilynn helped Sable put the food away, she said, "While I would not put it as crudely as my daughter did, Sable is right. Amber has lived with this for a very long time. She knows her limits, and she is perfectly capable of slowing herself down."

Sable scoffed. "If you say so. These two could put a forest fire to shame."

Dash felt a smile tugging at his lips. He couldn't deny it. They couldn't have pried themselves apart the past several nights if their lives had depended on it.

"Well, good for them." Marilynn winked at Dash. "It's about time Amber let her hair down."

"That's not all she's lettin'—"

Marilynn silenced Sable with a glare.

Dash continued pacing. "I need to know a few things."

"Anything, honey." Marilynn put the container she was holding on the counter, giving him her full attention.

He had so many questions, but the two that had been plaguing him rolled out. "What if we hadn't been there? What if she'd fallen against the bookshelves and hurt herself?"

"Phoenix and the other girls know what to do for her," Marilynn answered. "And if she'd been alone, Reno would have pressed that button and emergency services would have been there for her, as would her father and I."

He shook his head, his chest constricting. *That's not enough.* Would anything be enough? "Should I have done anything differently?"

"No. You were calm, and you handled it perfectly," Marilynn reassured him. "You kept her from hurting herself, and you remembered to time the seizure. Those are the most important things."

He glanced at Sable, knowing she wouldn't cushion a blow.

"You did good, Pennington. But you *can't* argue with her." Sable leaned against the counter and crossed her arms. "I know you want to protect her. We all do. But she's not defenseless." Regret rose in her eyes. "Take it from someone who learned that lesson the hard way. If you truly love her—"

"I *do.* I didn't intend to tell her the way it happened. I wanted to make it special, better than anything she's ever dreamed of, but it just came out."

"That's how you know it's real, honey," Marilynn said.

"It was definitely memorable." Sable's expression turned serious again. "But as I was saying, if you love her, you'll listen to her when she tells you what she needs. The minute she thinks she's holding you back is the moment you'll lose her forever, so you might want to choose your fights more carefully in the future."

He felt sick at the thought of losing her. "I'm not great at thinking before I speak, especially when it comes to Amber. I'll have to work on that."

"You'll learn," Marilynn said. "It's hard to put your head before your heart, but in this case it's important."

"I know. I'll try. What else should I know? Should we get in touch with Amber's doctor? How long should I let her sleep? What can I do to help her tonight?"

"I spoke to her doctor and made an appointment for Monday so he can check her out," Marilynn answered. "It's been years since she's had a seizure, and breakthrough seizures, which is what they call seizures that occur after a sustained period without them, aren't all that uncommon, but he wants to run some tests and check her out in case her meds need to be tweaked. As far as tonight goes, let her sleep. She will probably be sore and a little foggy. It takes a while for her body to recover. Just be your loving self. She'll let you know what she needs."

Sable smirked, earning an eye roll from Marilynn.

"I spoke to Phoenix earlier. She's covering the bookstore for tomorrow, so Amber won't need to go in. Do you want or need us to stick around?" Marilynn asked.

"No, but thank you for everything."

Marilynn hugged him. Then she touched his cheek the way his mother often did, and said, "I'm going to miss our morning chats while you're gone, but we'll take good care of our girl."

He wasn't sure he was going to leave, but he kept that to himself as he walked them to the door. After they left, he headed into the bedroom. Amber was lying on her side sleeping, her hair covering one cheek, a pillow tucked against her stomach and Reno stretched out against her back. She was wearing black leggings, his VSU sweatshirt she'd confiscated earlier in the week, and pink ruffled socks. He swore his heart tripled in size at the sight of her.

Reno's head popped up.

"*Shh.* It's okay, buddy. Go back to sleep." Dash toed off his shoes and climbed onto the bed beside her, lying nose to nose, the pillow between them. He put his arm around her, wishing with everything he had that he could take her epilepsy away, suffer it himself instead of her. He pressed a kiss to her forehead and closed his eyes, her nearness righting all of his disheveled pieces.

WAKEFULNESS TRICKLED IN slowly with Dash's familiar scent, his warm breath wisping over Amber's lips. The weight of his arm on her side brought a feeling of safety. The bedroom was dark, the house quiet. He was still there, and he *loved* her. *With everything I have and everything I am.* She'd been too foggy to trust her own memory when they'd left the bookstore, and she'd made her mother repeat his words so many times, Sable had finally offered to get them tattooed across her chest if it would stop Amber from asking again. Their mother had told her how well Dash had handled her seizure, and Sable, her overprotective, big-hearted sister who didn't believe in anything warm and fuzzy had said she'd felt Dash's fear, *but it wasn't the fear of a pussy*—Amber had cringed at her sister's raunchy word choice then, just as she did now—*it was the fear of a man who loved a woman so desperately, he couldn't fathom anything*

happening to her.

Dash's eyes opened, and he touched her face. "Hi, beautiful. How're you feeling?"

"Like I slept for a month and want to sleep for another. I'm a little sore and my head's still foggy. How long have I been asleep? And where are my pants?"

"Several hours." He glanced at the clock. "It's midnight. You got hot about an hour ago and took your pants off."

"I'm sorry for ruining your signing and embarrassing you."

"You couldn't *ever* embarrass me, and you didn't ruin the signing. We sold out of the books, and it *still* lasted an extra hour and a half because your enforcers made me stay and sign every book, bag, and notebook in the place."

My enforcers. She warmed all over. "I'm glad you did. But shouldn't you be at dinner with your brother and Shea?"

"Are you really asking me that? They're having dinner with your sisters and their husbands, and then they're flying out."

"You should—"

He silenced her with a kiss. "You banned me from coming home with you and insisted I finish the signing. You will *not* send me away."

"Okay, *bossy.*" She put her hand on his face, his whiskers tickling her fingers. A sliver of insecurity slipped in, and she hoped he wasn't having second thoughts about saying he loved her. He didn't sound like he was, but those were three big words. He could still care deeply about her but not have meant to say them. "How about you? How do you feel?"

"Like I watched the woman I love fight her way down the field without any protective gear, and I was shackled to the bench, unable to help."

Tears dampened her eyes, because she knew he was telling

the truth about loving her *and* feeling helpless.

"And like I never want to leave your side, but I know you won't allow that to happen." He tucked her hair behind her ear and pressed his warm, rough palm to her cheek. She put her hand over his, holding it there. "But mostly I'm glad you're okay and sorry for not taking better care of you, for wearing you out and making your life more stressful with the signing."

Emotions billowed inside her. She knew better than to let herself get run-down, and she wasn't about to let him take the blame for her inability to keep herself in check. "That blame's not yours to take, even if it feels like it is."

"I'm *owning* it, sweetheart, and learning from it. I will take much better care of you in the future."

A tear slipped down her cheek at his boundless love for her.

He brushed it away with his thumb, his brows knitting. "Why are you sad?"

"I'm not. I'm happy. You've seen all of me, and you're still here. If I'd known wetting myself would make you fall in love with me, I might have done it sooner."

He moved the pillow from between them and shifted closer, gently pulling her into a kiss. Threading his fingers into her hair, keeping her close, he whispered, "How am I going to leave you tomorrow?"

"Hopefully sexually satisfied." She was in no shape to have sex, but she loved teasing him.

He growled and kissed her so tenderly, she knew he was worried about hurting her.

"What are the rules about sex and seizures?"

"You probably shouldn't have sex with me while I'm having a seizure."

He laughed softly. "You're a regular comedian, aren't you,

sweet thing?"

"I get to see you smile when you laugh." Her pulse quickened as her heart poured out. "I love your smile, and I love you."

He closed his eyes, exhaling like he'd been holding it in all day, and his forehead fell forward, as if her confession had released the tension from his body. He opened his eyes, gazing deeply into hers as he said, "How can three little words change my entire world?"

Chapter Sixteen

DASH AWOKE WITH a start, a bead of sweat on his brow, his chest heaving. He'd been dreaming about yesterday, stuck in an endless cycle starting with the jolt of fear that had hit him when Amber's vacant stare had registered and she'd begun falling. But in the dream, the woman wasn't there to catch her, and he was running as fast as he could, but he wasn't fast enough and she'd hit the bookshelves and gone down—over and over again.

He wiped the sweat from his brow. The bedroom was empty, the dusk of dawn creeping in through the curtains. He jumped to his feet in his boxer briefs. "Amber?" The bathroom light was off. He headed out to the living room, his heart hammering. If she'd had another seizure, surely Reno would have barked. "Babe?"

He found her in the kitchen, leaning over a half-eaten cinnamon bun, licking icing off her fingers, wearing his sweatshirt and those ruffled socks he loved. Her color had returned, and her eyes glittered again, all greens and browns and flecks of golds, and her sweet smile hit him square in the center of his chest as relief swept through him.

Reno lifted his head from where he lay at her feet.

"*Sorry.* I was starved."

He slid an arm around her waist and kissed her cheek. "No worries. Starved is a good sign, right?"

"Yes. I feel much better, just sore. Sorry I was so out of it last night."

"Sweetheart, don't ever apologize for that. I'm glad you're feeling better."

"I can't believe how much food Patty Ann sent over. I want to hear all about the signing again. I'm sorry about missing out on dinner with Hawk and Shea. Have you talked to them? I need to apologize to them. Did you eat last night? This is *delicious.* Here, try it." She held up the cinnamon bun.

He knew her nervous ramblings when he heard them, but he didn't need to ask her reasons, because he felt it, too. He was leaving soon, and even though he'd see her again in a little less than two weeks to meet his family and go to the fundraiser, he wanted to blow off the tour and never leave her side. Eyeing the cinnamon bun, he said, "That alone is not nearly sweet enough."

He set the bun on the plate, scooped icing off with his finger, and painted her lower lip with it, taking her in a deep, sensual kiss. She was sweet heaven and gracious earth, white-hot desire and soul-deep love, and he was so fucking glad she was feeling better. He needed her more than he'd ever needed anything. Needed to fill up on her taste, revel in the feel of her, drown in the sweetness that *was* Amber Montgomery. Their lips parted on a sigh, and her eyes fluttered open, full of want and need, dredging up all the emotions he'd been trying to chain down.

He buried his hands in her hair, his lips against hers. "I want to stay."

"You can't do that to me," she said softly, almost pleadingly.

He gritted his teeth. "God, I'm going to miss you. It's only twelve days until New York, but *man*, I'm going to hate it."

"I know. Oh *no. Dash.*"

"What is it?" He pulled back at the pain in her voice.

"I can't drive to New York. I have to be seizure-free for six months to drive again."

"Okay. Can you fly? Will you fly?"

She nodded, looking uneasy. "Yes. I don't have a choice, and I'm going to hate being away from you."

"I'm sorry about having to fly. But I'll book you in first class so you have more room for Reno. Hell, I'll charter a private jet."

"You're so silly. I can fly coach."

"Not after what you told me about the last time you flew. You're flying first class." He kissed her hard. "And I'm getting you an on-call driver for the next six months."

"No, you are *not.*"

"You're right. You only need a driver while I'm on my book tour. After that I'm not leaving your side. We'll travel together for my speaking gigs and press events. They're usually only a day or two." He cocked a grin. "And we're not done talking about Maui."

"You're *crazy.*" She wound her arms around him, laughing softly. "I don't need special treatment. All I need is *you.*"

"You've got me for as long as you'll have me." His lips came down softly over hers, and she arched against him, making him hard. A growl slipped out as he drew back. "Are you too sore to…?"

"*No.* Just be gentle. I'm a little nervous about losing control."

She pulled his mouth toward hers, but he stopped short of

kissing her. "We don't have to do anything."

Her eyes darkened wickedly. "We'd *better* do *everything*."

They kissed tenderly at first, but careful quickly turned to devouring. His thoughts began to fracture, and he tried to pull back, to make sure she was okay, but she clung to him, kissing him harder, telling him she was fine in her own sexy way. He lifted her onto the counter, wedging himself between her legs, and drew his sweatshirt over her head. His eyes raked down her gorgeous body to her skimpy lace panties. She wore some form of lace every day—socks, bra, panties, shirts. He'd never had such a visceral reaction to fabric before, but every time he saw it on her, fire and desire coalesced, giving her the power to take him to his knees. "You're so feminine, you kill me."

He reclaimed her mouth, slow and deep, his hands traveling over her hips, pressing against her ass, holding her tight against his erection. She moaned into their kisses, rocking against him. He tore his mouth away, lowering it to her breast, teasing and sucking, earning one sinful sound after another.

"*Oh...yes,*" she said urgently. She pushed her hands into his hair, holding him there, mewling and arching. "Feels so good."

She yanked him up by his hair, bringing his mouth to hers, thrusting her tongue greedily into his mouth. He fucking loved her mouth. He needed *more*, needed to lay her out for his taking. He lifted her into his arms without breaking their kisses and carried her to the bedroom, the scratch and patter of Reno's paws on the hardwood trailing after them. He lowered her to the bed and stripped off her panties, visually devouring her as he tore off his briefs. His hand circled his cock, giving it a few tight tugs, loving the desire burning in her eyes, the wetness glistening between her legs as she watched him.

She sat up on the edge of the bed and reached for him. "Let

me love you."

He strode forward, his cock swelling in his hand as she licked her lips. She held his gaze as her delicate fingers circled his shaft. He was mesmerized by the love in her eyes as she loved him with her mouth, slow and so damn perfect, he struggled to keep from coming. Her eyes fluttered closed, and he tangled his fingers in her hair, thrusting slow and deep. Her eyes opened, holding him captive as she put her hands over his, moving them faster, giving him the green light for control. The trust and love that took was overwhelming. She loved him right up to the edge of madness, and he gritted out, "Christ, baby."

He withdrew and bent over, greedily crushing his mouth to hers, fucking it with his tongue as he'd done with his cock. Lust pooled like lava inside him, and he tore his mouth away. "You're going to come on my mouth so I can still taste you when I leave, and then I'm going to make love to you until we both forget our names."

"God, *yes*," she panted out.

He dropped to his knees and fulfilled that promise with hair-pulling fervor. She cried out his name, grinding against his mouth as he took his fill. When the last pulse of her climax moved through her, he kissed his way up her belly and breasts and took her in a long, slow kiss. She never pulled away when he tasted like her. She kissed him deeper, more possessively, like everything they did made him *hers* as much as it made her his. He reveled in her possession, wanting to drive his cock into her, to feel her tight heat wrapped around him with nothing in between.

One day...

"I don't want to stop kissing you, not even for a second." He reclaimed her mouth, fierce and demanding, working up the willpower to break away for a condom. She clung to him, rocking against his erection, moaning, feverishly returning his efforts. Kissing her was *everything*, a gateway drug to the rest of their nirvana. He forced himself to draw back before they both lost their minds and snagged a condom from the nightstand. He quickly sheathed himself and came down over her, aligning their bodies.

He cradled her beautiful face in his hands, the urgency he'd felt obliterated by his need to love her, *treasure* her, fill her up with so much of him she would never be lonely again. He held her trusting gaze as their bodies came together, deep and tight and so perfect, he felt her in his every pore.

Her brow wrinkled, eyes dampened, whispering his name so sweet, tender, and tinged with pain, he knew he'd hear it in his dreams. He stilled.

"Does it hurt?" The thought that he'd hurt her crushed him, and he started to pull out.

"No." She held him tighter, tears slipping from the corners of her eyes, tearing at his heart. "I didn't know it was possible to love someone this much."

Relief swamped him, and his heart roared out. "With us, anything is possible."

He lowered his mouth to hers, finding the rhythm that bound them together. They thrust and ground, arched and groped, passion burning between them. They moaned and pleaded, the sounds of their lovemaking echoing off the walls. Their kisses were torturously rough and agonizingly sweet at once. When Amber cried out his name, her body clenching tight and taunting around him, he reared up, thrusting deeper, feeling every fiber of his being intertwine with hers as the world careened on its axis.

They fell to the mattress spent and panting, and he gathered her in his arms. Her heart thundered against him, her breath coming in short, warm puffs against his slick skin.

"Are you okay, baby?"

"Uh-huh," she panted out. "So much for not losing control."

He touched his lips to hers. "That's just one more reason to love you."

"Because I lose control?"

"No. Because you can't *help* but lose control when we're together. Neither can I. But don't worry, sweetheart. I've got you." He held her tighter, kissing her softly. "I'll always have you."

"And I'll always have you." She snuggled closer. "Like in the shower as soon as I catch my breath."

He gazed into her eyes, heat stirring between them again. "You're going to make it even harder for me to leave, aren't you?"

"That's *my* evil plan." She fluttered her lashes innocently. "What was it you said to me? *Buckle up, hot stuff. We're just getting started.*"

THEIR TIME TOGETHER flew by too fast, but as Dash put his bags in the trunk of his rental car, Amber knew even if they'd had all day, it wouldn't have been enough. They'd spent much of the last three hours talking about how much they'd miss each other, going over Dash's travel schedule, working out time-zone differences, and making plans to call each night. She had no idea why she was getting so emotional over his leaving. She'd never needed a man to be happy, not even a man as wonderful as Dash. But she knew those twisted up feelings were driven by *want*, not *need*. Her parents had drilled the difference into her and her siblings' heads when they were young and they had little money to buy extras.

But now the difference between want and need didn't seem so cut-and-dried. She may not need Dash in the true sense of the word. She wouldn't *die* without him. But if the emptiness burrowing into the pit of her stomach was any indication of how she'd feel while they were apart, and if being with Dash soothed that ache, couldn't her wanting to be with him be considered a *need?*

Dash closed the trunk, and her throat thickened. Suddenly twelve days felt like a lifetime, which was absolutely ridiculous. She reached down to pet Reno, trying to push those feelings away as Dash embraced her.

His sexy dark eyes gleamed down at her. "You okay?"

"Of course. I can totally handle this."

He studied her face, like he wasn't buying it.

"Stop looking at me like that. I'll *be* fine. I can't help it if I'll miss you. Just kiss me and leave. The longer it takes, the worse it is."

"Kicking me out again, huh?" He kissed her, slow and sweet. "Sin's coming over tonight to post signs in your yard that say BACK OFF, COWBOYS. THIS WOMAN'S TAKEN."

God, she loved his sense of humor. "I'm not sure why you're worried about cowboys when you know Zac Efron is my hall pass."

He scowled. "Seriously? You'd hall pass all this"—he puffed out his chest and flexed his biceps—"for Efron?"

Sweet baby Jesus. She'd have to be crazy to do that. "I guess we'll see."

"I'm canceling the tour." He went for his phone.

She threw her arms around him, pressing a kiss to the center of his chest, knowing he really would cancel his tour to be with her. "I wouldn't hall pass you for anyone. Now, get out of here before you miss your flight."

"You really do enjoy kicking me out."

"Not as much as I enjoy dragging you into my bedroom."

"Canceling is sounding pretty damn good."

"I get to watch you on *Good Morning America* tomorrow. You're not canceling." She went up on her toes, and he lowered his lips toward hers in one of his incredible kisses, leaving her weak-kneed and tingling from head to toe.

He brushed a kiss to her forehead. "It's not too late for you to come with me."

"I wish I could, but we both know I can't."

"It doesn't hurt to try. I'll text you when I get to my place." He kissed her again. "And I'll miss you every second of every day."

"Me too." Tears stung her eyes, and she nudged him toward the car. "Now go before you make me cry."

He loved up Reno. "Take good care of our girl, buddy."

Amber petted Reno as Dash climbed into the car and started it up. He rolled down the window, reaching for her hand. "I better not find out Efron was here. I'd probably get hefty prison time for killing a celebrity."

Reading between the lines, she said, "I love you, too."

He pulled her in for one last kiss, winked, and waved as he drove away. *Twelve days. It's only twelve days.* When his car disappeared around the corner, Reno whined, and she reached down to pet him. "I know. It's going to be the longest twelve days of our lives."

Chapter Seventeen

"STOP BEING SO stubborn! He loves you. He just doesn't know how to tell you!" Amber shouted at Keira Knightley in *Pride and Prejudice*, which was playing on the television, just as she'd done the dozens of other times she'd watched it. It was one of her favorite movies.

Reno lifted his head from where he lay on the floor beside her.

"He's *not* wrong for her. Look at me and Dash."

Reno tilted his head at the mention of Dash's name.

A pang of longing washed over her. Her body hurt from her seizure, but she'd wanted to go to work this afternoon anyway to keep her mind off Dash *and* the seizure, both of which had thrown her for a loop, but Phoenix had threatened to quit if she showed up at the bookstore. So here she was, having a picnic on her living room floor, watching a movie she knew by heart. She surveyed the plethora of half-eaten foods from the diner surrounding her on the blanket. Dash had been gone for only two hours, and she'd tried to eat her way past missing him.

Comfort food wasn't nearly as comforting as having Dash's arms around her.

She scooped macaroni and cheese onto what was left of a

hamburger and shoved it into her mouth as a knock sounded on the front door. Before she could get up, the door flew open and Brindle, Sable, Morgyn, and Lindsay charged in.

Brindle shifted Emma in her arms and stopped in her tracks, her eyes nearly bugging out of her head. "*Whoa.* Houston, we have a problem."

"You keep eating like that, and Dash will have to roll you out of here." Lindsay sauntered over to the blanket.

"*Roll* her into the bedroom is more like it." Sable put her hand on her hip, her cowgirl hat perched on her head. "Something tells me he won't mind."

"Cut her some slack, you guys. Can't you see she's missing him? She's even wearing his sweatshirt." Morgyn hurried closer, bell bottoms swishing along the floor, bangles jangling on her wrists as she knelt beside the blanket and tossed her long blond hair over her shoulders, her expression softening. "Are you okay, Amb?"

"I'm fine." She didn't want anyone thinking she was lost without Dash, even if she felt like a piece of herself was missing. "I was just hungry. What are you guys doing here?"

"Hello?" Brindle said sarcastically. "You had a seizure yesterday, your boyfriend told you he *loves* you, and he left today. We were worried about you, and from the looks of things, we have reason to be."

Amber turned off the television. "I'm really okay."

"Did you hear that?" Sable raised her brows. "That was my bullshit meter going off."

"You guys have already done so much. You took care of me yesterday, and all of you took over the signing, and Morgyn and Brindle even went to dinner with Shea and Hawk."

"Dinner was hardly a hardship," Morgyn said. "We had

fun."

"Fun drooling over Hawk. That man is hotter than all get-out," Lindsay said.

"You're not kidding," Brindle agreed. "He and Shea nearly combusted at dinner."

"I'm glad you had fun." Amber leaned forward and hugged Morgyn. Then she pushed to her feet to hug the others.

Sable rolled her eyes. "Why are there always hugs?"

"Because I love you." Amber hugged her *tight*. "Dash said all of you guys were wonderful at the signing."

"Aren't we always?" Brindle said. "He did great, by the way. But he must have asked me a hundred times if I'd heard from Mom or Sable to see how you were."

"He was a wreck when he got here yesterday," Sable said. "He was worried he'd caused her seizure."

"He didn't cause it. You know that." Amber tried to ignore the smirks her sisters were exchanging, and reached for Emma. She was adorable in striped leggings and a long-sleeved shirt Sable had given her, which had BOYS DROOL, AUNTIES RULE across the front.

"Of course he didn't," Morgyn said.

"His goal post did." Lindsay laughed.

"Amber's not used to all those late-night touchdowns," Brindle added.

"Would you tell your mama to stop?" Amber said to Emma, and nuzzled against her cheek, earning drooly motorboat noises. Emma squealed, reaching her grabby hands toward the food. "Is she hungry? Can I give her something?"

"She's always hungry. That girl can eat her daddy under the table." Brindle tickled Emma's tummy, and Emma's giggles filled the air.

Lindsay nudged Amber. "I heard Daddy likes to eat Mommy under the table."

Everyone laughed.

"What can I say? My man is good on his knees," Brindle said with a laugh. "You can give Emmie some macaroni noodles, but I didn't bring a bib."

"It's a little scary how you can go from sexy talk to baby talk so easily." Amber sat with Emma on her lap and handed her a noodle. Eyes wide with delight, Emma shoved it into her mouth.

"Wait until you have kids," Brindle said. "You learn to fit your *sexy* in every which way you can. It's a good thing babies don't remember when they're this age, or our baby girl would have all sorts of naughty stories to tell."

"How about you keep those stories to yourself. I don't want to lose my appetite," Sable said, and she and Lindsay sat down on the blanket.

Brindle grabbed Amber's laptop from the end table and joined them, her fingers flying across the keyboard. "I promised Pepper and Grace I'd get them on a video call when we got here. Axsel had band practice, but he said he'll call you tomorrow."

"Don't forget to add Trixie and Jilly to the call," Lindsay said.

Brindle gave her a deadpan look. "Like I could forget them? They've been texting all morning." Trixie Jericho and Jillian Braden, Graham and Nick's younger sister, lived in Pleasant Hill, Maryland.

As Amber gave Emma more noodles, which Emma immediately fed to Reno, she looked around her at the women who had been there for all of her trials, tribulations, and celebrations, and she felt monumentally blessed. "It's been so long since I've had a seizure, I forgot how everyone huddled around me afterward. I'm really glad you're here."

"Oh, darlin', this is about much more than your typical seizure aftercare. Your man told you he *loved* you when you were bleary-eyed from a seizure." Lindsay rubbed her hands together. "We want all the juicy lovesick details."

"*After* we talk about your seizure." Pepper's voice came from the laptop as Brindle set it on the coffee table so they could all see it. Pepper might be Sable's twin, but she was as proper and careful as Sable was brash and risky.

Amber braced herself for an inquisition as Pepper, Grace, Trixie, and Jillian said hello to everyone and gushed over Emma. While Grace, Sable, Amber, and Axsel were brunettes like their mother, and Morgyn and Brindle were fair-haired like their father, Pepper was a beautiful mix of both.

"Amber, how are you feeling?" Grace asked, and a seriousness fell over the room.

"I feel okay—a little tired and a little sore, but that's to be expected." Amber gave Emma more noodles and kissed her head.

Pepper's brows knitted. "You've gone through so many changes the past couple of weeks. It's not surprising that you had a breakthrough seizure."

"Nobody gets much sleep when they're in a new relationship," Trixie said. "If you're not making out, you're thinking about making out or reliving things you've done or said together. Sleep is just not a priority."

There was a murmur of agreement.

"Plus, you had the signing to deal with." Jillian tucked her mahogany hair behind her ear, leaning closer to the screen.

"That's a lot for anyone."

"Are you worried about having more seizures?" Grace asked.

It took everything Amber had to admit the truth, because saying it aloud made it real. "*Yes.* It's been so long since I've had one, and I got used to not having them. The seizure really threw me off, and I hate that it happened at Dash's signing. And not just any signing, but his very *first* signing of his writing career. Do you have any idea what it's like to wake up from a seizure and not know what happened? To see everyone looking at you with a mixture of worry and fear? Or to realize that you've peed yourself in front of your boyfriend and a crowd of people? I swear I felt like I was thirteen years old again." It was as if she'd opened floodgates that had been held shut for too long, and she was powerless to stop the unexpected anger from coming out. "And don't get on my case about not being embarrassed about my medical condition. Who *wouldn't* be embarrassed if they'd wet themselves?" She scoffed. "*Seriously.* It's a good life rule not to be embarrassed about a medical condition, but when you're lying there with your boyfriend's shirt over your pee-soaked clothes, feeling like you've been run over by a truck, who has the energy to *try* not to be embarrassed? It just happens, like breathing. And now I can't drive, which means relying on Uber or one of you."

"We don't mind driving you," Brindle insisted.

"I know you don't, but that's not the point. It's all so annoying. I didn't even know I was so mad until just now. I'm sorry for dumping it on all of you."

"Please dump it on us. That's what we're here for. You have a right to be upset." Morgyn put her arm around her. "I'm sorry this happened again."

"The whole thing fucking sucks," Sable said vehemently. "If

epilepsy were a person, I'd beat the hell out of it."

"Me too," Brindle said, and everyone else agreed.

Amber struggled against the lump forming in her throat.

"Does having one breakthrough seizure mean you'll have more?" Trixie asked.

"It doesn't always mean that," Pepper answered before Amber could respond. "Amber, Mom said you're seeing the doctor tomorrow. Maybe your meds just need to be adjusted."

"They might, but even if they need adjusting, we all know that stress and lack of sleep is an issue for me. That's why I live my life the way I do. I'm usually in bed by ten, and I don't think I've fallen asleep before two in the morning since Dash and I got together."

"*Damn.* The man has stamina," Jillian said.

"Apparently so does Amber." Sable reached for Emma, who babbled as she went to her.

"No wonder Dash requested 'Wild Thing' last weekend at JJ's," Brindle added.

"The bottom line is that Amber deserves to be loved until she's too exhausted to move," Morgyn said reassuringly. "So this needs a solution."

"That's for sure," Grace agreed.

"I *know*," Amber said vehemently. "But the reason we're up late isn't just sex. Sometimes we just lie in each other's arms, whispering about whatever's on our minds." She laughed a little, thinking about those times. "Silly things sometimes, like how the color blue makes him shiver, and every time he sees the color peach, he thinks of me because I was wearing a peach sweater the first time we met. And how he has to put his left shoe on first for good luck, because before his first touch-football game when he was six, his grandfather told him to watch what the other boys were doing and to do it different and better. He meant his position on the football field, of course, but even little Dash was an overachiever. I *love* knowing those types of things about him and sharing that time together. When it's late like that, it feels like everything is still except the beat of our hearts. It's special, and it makes me feel closer to him. I don't want to fall asleep and miss *any* of it."

"That's *true* intimacy," Morgyn said. "Those are some of my favorite times with Graham, too."

"It's what I've always dreamed of having," Amber admitted. "It's finally my turn to go on dates and be with a great guy. Dash brought more than love and affection into my life. He brought the excitement I've spent my life avoiding, but with him, I want *more* of it. I *want* more nights at JJ's with everyone, where he holds my hand and takes me to the dance floor, embarrassing me and making me feel like a princess all at once. That's exhilarating, and I loved it. I want more walks and slow dances at the creek, collecting acorns and writing down our memories, and doing nice things together like what we did for Hellie at the park. I want it *all* with him."

"I totally get wanting to take his hand and let him lead you out of your comfort zone," Morgyn said encouragingly. "Graham showed me a whole world I'd been missing out on, and I'm happier than I ever imagined possible."

Brindle snagged a cinnamon bun. "How funny is it that I was the girl who wanted to see the world, and all it took was one trip away from Trace to realize that everything I wanted was right here in Oak Falls. Who would have ever thought I'd be married with a daughter and happy as a peach staying home most nights?"

"Or that I'd end up back in Oak Falls madly in love and

married to Reed?" Grace chimed in.

"I always knew Brindle would end up with Trace one way or another," Amber said. "And once I saw you and Reed together, I knew he was your soul mate. But I never thought I'd want to step out of my safe little nest for anyone or anything. Dash is even talking about going to Maui. *Maui!* Can you believe it? You guys know how freaked out I get by flying, but I want to be the girl who can jump on a plane with the guy I love and just *go*. I don't *want* to give up, or limit, my time with Dash."

"Then don't," Sable said.

"I don't think I have a choice if I don't want to risk having more seizures." Amber looked down at her lap, the truth cutting like a knife. She met the eyes of the women who she knew would give anything to fix this for her. "What my heart wants and what my body needs are two sides of a war that I can't win."

"Oh, Amber, don't say that." Pepper's compassionate gaze felt like an embrace.

"Have you talked to Dash about this?" Jillian asked.

"Not really. He's been wonderful, and I know if I told him my worries, he'd make sure I was asleep at a reasonable hour every night and change everything. Including his own wants and needs. But would any of you want to tell the hottest, sweetest, kindest guy on the planet—the man of your dreams—that you need to slow down and ruin his fun, or that you can't have sex with him if the urge hits late at night?"

"No, but this is different." Grace leaned closer to the screen. "You're not saying you don't want to be with him. You're suggesting you do what's best for your health. Is there a part of you that's afraid you might lose him over this? Even a small part? Because if that's the case, then that's an issue in and of itself."

"No, that's not it, Gracie. I *know* he loves me for who I am and he accepts *all* of me. I'm meeting his family in two weeks, for Pete's sake, and he's taking me to meet his friends at a big fundraiser in New York City. I mean, think about it. He told me he loved me right after my seizure, when I was literally lying in my own urine."

"That was pretty incredible," Lindsay said. "We could all feel his love for you."

"He was upset that he didn't get to make the first time he said he loved you a magical event," Sable said. "I'm not into all that touchy-feely stuff, but that got me."

Amber looked at her curiously. "He said that?"

"Sure did, when he got back from the signing looking like he hadn't taken a breath since you went down," Sable said.

"I love that he wanted it to be special for you," Morgyn said.

"I must be missing something," Jillian said. "If he's that crazy about you, why can't you tell him you might need to slow down? Isn't that what being a couple is all about? Compromise? Doing what's best for each other?"

"Yes, but I don't want to tell him because it would be a *lie*," Amber said. "If we cut our intimate time short, I'd probably lie awake wanting him anyway and negate the purpose of telling him in the first place. And as far as the rest goes, he's always on the go, and he enjoys doing things for others, like I do. I love that about him. I don't want to take any of it away from him or limit him. I want to be part of those things with him."

"He does seem to like doing things for others. Mom told me she's been walking with him and a bunch of women in the mornings," Pepper said. "She very proudly told me that she can do *two* pull-ups."

They all laughed.

"I'm sure that's more than I can do," Amber said. "Did she tell you that Dash made exercise schedules for the group, and he's making time to video chat with them while he's on the book tour?" There was a round of surprised murmurs. "*Now* do you see why I'd rather jump off a cliff than hold that man back?"

"Well, I can't help with that," Brindle said. "But I am an expert at fitting sex into busy lives. I think you should skip dinner and go to bed early sometimes. Sex always trumps food in our house."

"You don't even need to skip dinner. Just go to bed a couple of hours early when you want to fool around," Morgyn suggested. "Sometimes Graham and I go to bed at six."

"And you stay there until noon the next day," Lindsay said. "The entire town knows this about you two."

"You know, Amber," Pepper's serious tone drew everyone's attention. "Everything you just told us is enough to stress any of us out. Talk with your doctor about your concerns. I'm sure you're not his only patient who's gone through this."

"You're probably right. I'll talk to him and figure it out one way or another. And I think I will talk to Dash after his book tour is over. He doesn't need relationship stress on top of his chaotic schedule, and if they do tweak my medication, that'll give me time to adjust to it. That way we can enjoy the weekend with his family and the fundraiser, and then he can finish the last two weeks of the tour, and once he can breathe again, we'll figure it out."

Everyone agreed that sounded like a solid plan.

"Thanks, you guys. I feel a lot better getting it off my chest."

"I had no idea you and Dash were so serious," Grace said. "I'm really happy for you."

"Me too," Pepper said. "Meeting his family is a big deal."

"I know." Amber told them about her conversation with his sisters and how she remembered his mother from Boyer. "I'm sure it'll be fine, but between that and meeting his friends at the fundraiser, I'll admit that I'm a little nervous. I don't have any idea what to wear to either."

Jillian's hand shot up in the air. "Fashion afficionado to your rescue." She was a sought-after fashion designer and owned a high-end boutique. "I have several perfect meet-the-family dresses that you'd look gorgeous in, but tell me more about the fundraiser."

"It's hosted by Brett Bad's family to raise money for the Ronald McDonald House." Amber told them about the old-Hollywood themed casino night.

"I'm jealous. You'll get to see Sophie and Brett," Lindsay said. "I wish I could go to the fundraiser, but I have an event that weekend."

"Amber, you'll get to meet Harlow Bad," Grace said excitedly. Harlow was the actress playing the lead role in the movie based on their friend Charlotte Sterling's book, *Anything for Love*, for which Grace had written the script. Charlotte was Amber's LWW sister, and she was married to Graham and Nick's oldest brother, Beau. "You'll love Harlow. She's super sweet. She's been apologizing to the director for the last two weeks about taking that weekend off to go to the fundraiser."

Jillian scoffed. "At least one of the Bads cares about their career. If Johnny is supposed to go to the fundraiser, he'll probably cancel at the last minute." Harlow's brother Johnny was a bigger rock star than Axsel. He'd hired Jillian to design his wardrobe for an upcoming tour, and after she'd put off the release of her new clothing line, he'd canceled it.

"I think you mean at least *two* Bads care about their careers. Their brother Kane owns half of the East Coast," Grace pointed out.

Jillian sighed. "Okay, fine, *whatever*. Johnny Butthead aside, I have great old-Hollywood gowns. You should come to Maryland next weekend and check them out."

"Yes, *please*," Trixie pleaded. "I want to see you guys."

Amber let out a relieved sigh. "Thank you, Jilly. That sounds great. I'll get Phoenix to cover the bookstore."

"I'm going with you," Lindsay exclaimed.

"Me too," Brindle and Morgyn said.

"Have fun with that," Sable said.

After they made plans for next weekend, Grace told them about the filming of Charlotte's movie, and then they chatted about costumes for the Jerichos' Halloween barn bash next weekend. For the first time ever, Amber wasn't counting down the days to one of the barn bashes. Now that she had someone special in her life, she knew she'd spend the whole time thinking about how much more fun it would be if Dash were with her.

Lindsay leaned close to Amber and said, "You can be my date for the barn bash. I'll even let you call me Dash."

"We should come up with a schedule to keep Amber company so she doesn't miss Dash too much while he's gone," Morgyn suggested, and the others chimed in their agreement.

As they pulled out their phones and began making plans, penciling their evenings around Amber's schedule, noting the nights of her book club and the Meeting of the Female Minds,

Amber filled with gratitude. It didn't matter where they were in their lives or what they had going on. When one of them needed something, they were all there to help, and she knew it would always be that way. Her thoughts tiptoed back to Dash taking care of his family as a teenager, his sisters calling him the morning of the signing, and the love she'd seen between them. She felt like the luckiest girl in the world to have found a man who treasured his family as much as she treasured hers, and she couldn't wait to hear his voice in four and a half hours.

Not that she was counting down the minutes or anything…

DASH STEPPED FROM the elevator into his luxurious waterfront penthouse in the heart of Tribeca, a hip area in New York City that was *thankfully* overlooked by many tourists. That was only one of the reasons Dash had settled there. The slower pace of Tribeca and the aesthetics of the cobblestone streets reminded him of Port Hudson. He also found the trendy boutiques, restaurants, and old industrial buildings more appealing than the skyscrapers, neon billboards, and frantic pace of other areas in the city.

He dropped his bags by the door and rolled his shoulders back. The six-plus hour drive had sucked. Especially since he'd spent the first hour debating turning around and heading straight back to Amber. He carried the pile of mail that he'd picked up into the living room and set it on the glass coffee table, looking around the ridiculously spacious room, which at thirty-four feet wide was almost as big as Amber's entire house. He hadn't cared about the size of the living room when he'd bought the unit, but the breathtaking views of the Hudson River had definitely been a selling point, once again reminding him of home. He gazed out at the river, but now instead of carrying the comforts of home, it was a stark reminder of how far he was from Amber.

He pulled his phone out of his pocket to text her and saw that he'd missed two messages from her and one from Damon. He opened Amber's first as he walked over to the couch, and a picture of Amber with three of her sisters and Lindsay gathered around a laptop, on which her other two sisters and Trixie, the girl who had gotten engaged at the jam session, and another brunette were waving on a video call. Amber was wearing his VSU sweatshirt, her head tilted, hair adorably messy, and the entrancing smile he'd fallen so desperately in love with lighting him up from the inside out. He remembered how she'd given off a sweet girl-next-door vibe when he'd first seen her, and now that he knew her better—now that he loved her—he knew she was so much more than that. He read the second message from her. *We might be talking about you.* She'd added two kissing emojis.

"I bet you are." He took a selfie, grinning hard because it was impossible not to when he thought of Amber, and thumbed out, *I'm definitely thinking of you.* He added a peach emoji, then thought better of it in case she was still with her family, and deleted it. He typed, *Just got in. I'll call you in a few minutes.*

After sending the message to Amber, he read Damon's text. *Still doodling DP loves AM in your playbook?*

Dash responded with, *Hell yes. Still calling your right hand Natasha?*

He scanned the pile of mail, his eyes catching on a pink envelope as his phone vibrated with Damon's response. He quickly read the text. *No. I changed her name to Amber.* Dash gritted out a curse as another text from Damon rolled in. *I'm queueing up GMA tomorrow at the board meeting so everyone can see my famous brother. Good luck.*

He texted back, *Thanks. See you soon*, and set his phone down to pick up the pink envelope, instantly recognizing Amber's swirly handwriting. *You sneaky little minx.* He sat back and opened the card, filling with happiness at the picture of tiramisu with a smiley face on it, and I TIRA-MISS U written above it. He opened and read the card.

Dear Dash, it's Tuesday morning and we've just survived our first breakfast as a couple with my family. I've never brought a boyfriend to breakfast before, which made ours even more special. I can't stop thinking about the morning after we first met, when I found you sitting at my parents' kitchen table with baby Emma on your lap. I think every-one but me and Sable knew you and I would end up together, but I doubt they'd imagined we'd get this close this fast. Actually, I think you might have known that all along. Did you?

Dash had never had a doubt.

I already know I'll miss you like crazy when you're gone, and we still have several days together before you leave. If they're anything like the time we've already shared, I'll be twisted up like a crown of thorns when we say good-bye. But I don't want to think about that right now. We have more important things going on, like your book tour. Reno and I are sending you loads of luck. I can't wait to watch it all unfold. Have fun, and try not to forget the girl in Oak Falls whose heart you stole. Xox, Amber

Dash reread the letter. He couldn't believe she'd thought to send him a letter ahead of time. Tuesday seemed like a lifetime ago. He didn't even feel like the same man he'd been on Tuesday. In the days since, Amber had become an even bigger part of him. Their relationship had evolved, becoming more important than everything else.

He picked up his phone to call her on FaceTime. Her gorgeous face brightened the screen, filling some of the empty spots leaving her had created.

As he said, "Hi, sweetheart. I tira-miss you, too," he knew the evolution of Dash and Amber had only just begun.

Chapter Eighteen

AMBER GAZED OUT the airplane window at the late-afternoon, early-November skies, a chilly mix of whites and grays with a dappling of pinks and blues, bathing the city beneath in shadowy layers. The last twelve days had passed in a busy blur with what felt like the entire community stopping in to check on her, but at the same time, even though she and Dash texted as often as they could, the days seemed to take forever until she got to hear his voice at night. She'd seen her doctor, and she hadn't needed an adjustment to her medications after all. Sleep deprivation and stress had been the culprit of her breakthrough seizure. Her doctor had recommended several ways to alleviate stress, like yoga and meditation, and he'd given her sleep aids, but she hadn't needed them. With the exception of when she'd been stressed about the signing, insomnia hadn't been an issue. She'd simply had better things to do with Dash. She hadn't had another breakthrough seizure and had caught up on her sleep while he was gone. She was prepared for a couple of late nights, and she knew her doting boyfriend would not let her get too run-down.

The flight attendant stopped by Amber's seat. "We're going to be landing soon. Would you like to finish your juice before I take your glass?"

Amber had been too nervous about seeing Dash and meeting his family and friends to drink it. "No, thank you." She handed her the glass.

"You'll need to put your seat upright and fasten your seat belt."

"Okay, thank you." Amber could get used to the luxurious pampering of first class, which Dash had insisted on. It made flying much less stressful for her and Reno, who was lying in the spacious area at her feet. Or maybe her excitement about finally seeing Dash would have made any flight better.

He had surprised her in so many ways while they were apart. He'd left his copy of last month's book club novel on the nightstand, and it had notes and rewrites throughout the margins, which were *much* hotter than the original scenes. But what she'd loved even more than that were his notes about things the hero could have done differently or things he should have said. Not only had he really read the story, but unbeknownst to Amber, with her blond matchmaking sister's help, he'd created an account on the book club forum and had popped into the video chat during the discussion. She'd cried happy tears, and all the other girls had been jealous.

That was the first of many surprises. Like on Halloween, when she'd sent him a picture of her and Lindsay in costume. Amber had dressed as Sandy from *Grease*, and as promised, Lindsay had dressed as Dash, wearing a football jersey with his name on the back, a man's wig, and a wide smile. Dash had called Amber on FaceTime, decked out as Danny from *Grease*, and he'd stayed on the line all night, making her feel like he was at the barn bash with her. Everyone had gotten a kick out of it, most of all Amber.

He'd sent her selfies at every signing and press event. She'd been shocked he'd called her after they'd taped the Jimmy Kimmel show to introduce her to Jimmy. But he'd blown her away when she'd seen the show, and Jimmy had asked Dash about his personal life. Her whirlwind of a boyfriend had protected her privacy and said he was *officially off the market and madly in love.* She was pretty sure Dash thought about her twenty-four-seven, which was great, because she'd feel pretty stupid if she was alone in that.

After the plane touched down, it took all of her willpower not to run through the gate to find Dash. Her pulse was beating wildly. She'd never power walked so fast in her life, and the second she saw him standing there with a bouquet of flowers, that gorgeous smile lighting up his eyes, her willpower shattered. She sprinted to him with Reno by her side and launched herself into his arms, absolutely giddy as they kissed and laughed and kissed some more.

"I don't want to put you down, sweetheart. I've waited too long to hold you."

What was she supposed to say to that? She was in no hurry to leave his arms, either. So she lowered her lips to his, right there in the middle of the busy airport, pouring twelve days of missing him into their kiss. When he finally lowered her to her feet, he loved up Reno, who gave him a face full of sloppy dog kisses.

Dash hugged Reno. "I've missed you almost as much as I missed your mama." He pushed to his feet and tugged Amber in for another kiss. "How did you get even more beautiful since last night?"

Her cheeks burned. She'd surprised *him* last night and had fulfilled his dirty video-chat fantasy. "*Shh.* We're not going to talk about last night." She went up on her toes, pressing her lips to his. "Your sisters are going to tease me about having a toddler smile. I'm pretty sure I'll look like this all weekend."

"I love your smile. How do you feel? Are you tired? Was the flight okay?"

"I feel good, and you were right about first class. It's a good thing I'm not a world traveler, because I'd be broke."

"I just might make a world traveler of you yet, wild thing. But don't worry. I've got pretty deep pockets."

They retrieved her luggage and talked the whole way to Port Hudson. As they drove through town, Amber said, "I missed this place. I was so scared when I first came here. The day my parents dropped me off, I was sure I'd made the biggest mistake of my life."

He squeezed her hand. "You love your hometown so much. Why did you decide to go away to school?"

"Grace and Pepper convinced me. They said I needed to experience the real world. They'd never misguided me before, and in the long run, they were right. It's good that I have someplace to compare to home. But I got really homesick at first, and then my RA suggested I connect with the LWW sisterhood. That's where I met Charlotte Sterling and Aubrey Stewart. They were seniors when I was a freshman, but they were great. They introduced me to other LWW girls. We weren't all alike or anything like that, but there were enough bookworms who preferred low-key activities that I fit in, which was exactly what I needed. Being part of LWW made everything better."

"Wait a second. You know Aubrey Stewart and Charlotte Sterling?"

"Yes. Why? Do you know them? Aubrey's engaged to Graham's business partner, Knox Bentley, and Char is married to Graham's brother Beau."

"Yes, I know them. They grew up here. I don't know Char as well as I know Aubrey, but they were best friends. The Stewarts are my mom's neighbors. Mrs. Stewart is the one who watched my sisters, and Aubrey's older brothers, Troy and Joey, are two of my closest friends. Troy and I played together for the Giants." He glanced at her with amusement in his eyes. "I had a crush on Aubrey when I was about sixteen. She was a pretty little sass-mouthed tomboy."

"I can't believe you know them. Please tell me you didn't sleep with Aubrey because that could be awkward."

"I didn't. My crush lasted about as long as it took for her to tell off a guy two years older than her for checking her out, which was just long enough for me to realize two things. A, she'd never give me the time of day *and* B, I had a *type*, and it definitely wasn't tomboys." He reached over and squeezed her hand. "You can breathe now."

She let out a breath she hadn't realized she was holding, and they both laughed. They talked the rest of the way, and when they pulled up in front of his mother's modest two-story house, there were four vehicles in the driveway and two more parked at the curb. Her nerves flared to life.

Dash cut the engine and turned toward her, taking her hand. "Nervous?"

"A little." She looked down at her rust-colored sweater, skinny jeans, and suede ankle boots, wondering if she should have worn a dress.

He lifted her chin with a reassuring gaze. "I love you, and they'll love you, too. You've already gotten through the hard part. You've met everyone except Damon and my grandparents."

"Your grandparents are here?" *Oh boy. No pressure or anything.*

"Do you think I'd bring you home and not introduce you to the most important man in my life and the woman who taught me about acorns?" He pulled her in for a kiss and slid a hand to the nape of her neck, keeping her close. "I know one way to help you relax."

He pressed his lips to hers, kissing the nervousness right out of her and leaving her breathless. She sighed. "If I get nervous again, just drag me into a dark corner and do that."

"THAT WILL NOT be a problem." He gave her another quick kiss and came around to help her and Reno out of the car. He was relieved her flight had gone well. After learning her seizure had been caused by stress and sleep deprivation, he'd made a few modifications to their plans for tomorrow, so as not to wear her out.

She took Reno's leash and immediately reached down to pet him.

Dash put his hand on her back. "If it makes you feel any better, I'm nervous, too."

"Why? It's your family."

"I'm meeting my mother's boyfriend, *and* I don't know how I'm going to keep my hands off you all evening." He lowered his lips to hers, kissing her one last time.

"Are you going to smooch Amber all day, or let the rest of us meet her?" Dawn's voice startled them apart.

They looked up and saw her heading across the yard toward them, her golden hair flouncing over the shoulders of her forest-green sweater.

"Great first impression," Amber whispered.

Andi appeared in the doorway, "Mom, they're here!" and ran after Dawn.

Dash took Amber's face in his hands, relieved to see her smiling. "We're coming off twelve long, lonely days, and we have fourteen more to endure after Sunday, so buckle up, sweetheart. We're just getting started."

He kissed her softly as his mother hurried down the porch steps, pretty in jeans and a black-and-white sweater, holding the hand of a dark-haired man who had to be her boyfriend. Dash had expected to feel strange seeing his mother with a man, but even from that distance, he saw a difference in his mother. She looked happier, younger even, leaving no room for him to feel anything but happy for her.

"I see how tonight's gonna go," Dawn teased as she hugged Dash. "Between Mom and Mitch and you two, *I'm* going to need a cold shower."

Amber's cheeks pinked up.

"Ignore her. We're really glad you're here." Andi embraced Amber.

"I'm glad she's here," Dawn said, swapping places with Andi to hug Amber. "We're going to have so much fun tonight."

His animal-loving sisters looked longingly at Reno. Hawk had mentioned Amber's seizure to their family, and when they'd called Dash to check on her, he'd given them the rundown on Reno, too.

"This must be Reno," Andi said. "He's beautiful. I know we're not supposed to pet him, but I wish we could."

"It's okay. You can," Amber said. "Reno, visit."

Reno's tail wagged, and the girls loved him up as their mother came to Dash's side and hugged him, bringing with her the scents of home. "It's good to see you, honey."

"Hi, Mom." He reached for Amber's hand. "Mom, you remember Amber."

"Of course I do. It's lovely to see you again." She embraced Amber.

"You, too," Amber said. "Thanks for letting me join your family today."

"We're glad you could make it," his mother said. "When Dash told me he was seeing you, it brought back lots of good memories."

"Yeah, Mom's been acting like you're her long-lost daughter." Dawn leaned closer and lowered her voice. "She's jealous that you were an LWW girl."

"She tried to get us to join," Andi added. "But Dawn was too rowdy and despises writing anything longer than a tweet, and I'm not much for group activities. But I think Mom would have fit right in."

"Thanks, sweetie," his mother said. "I would have loved to have been part of that group. But before we get into *that* conversation, I want to introduce Amber and Dash to Mitch." His mother gazed warmly at the man beside her. "Mitch, this is my son Dash and his girlfriend, Amber."

Mitch extended his hand to Dash. "Your mother has told me a lot about you. It's a pleasure to meet you." He was a handsome man with a kind face and dark hair that was graying at the temples, like an older Clark Kent. His black-framed glasses and blue-and-white checked dress shirt buttoned all the way up gave him a professorial look.

Dash shook his hand. "I've heard a lot about you, too. I look forward to getting to know you."

"Likewise." Mitch smiled familiarly at Amber. "Amber Montgomery, it is a joy to see you again."

"Thank you, Professor. I miss our talks. What a small world."

"Indeed. Call me Mitch, please."

"Okay." Amber looked at Dash. "Prof—*Mitch*—was my favorite English teacher. I never wanted his classes to end."

"I guess that means you have Amber's stamp of approval." Dash took her hand as his mother and Mitch greeted Reno.

"That's faster than I got your mother's." Mitch reached for their mother's hand. "It took me about twenty coffee dates before she agreed to go on a real date with me."

Their mother looked adoringly at him. "That's because we'd become such good friends, and you were so supportive when I took on the teaching position, I didn't want to take a chance of ruining it."

"I, on the other hand, never had any doubt that we'd be great together."

"That's it," Dawn said. "I need a boyfriend."

As they all laughed, Dash spotted his grandmother coming down the porch steps. She'd worn her hair short and layered for as long as he could remember, and she exuded an air of ladylike elegance, which showed in her smart white blouse beneath a charcoal cardigan and dark slacks. Dash waved to her, and noticed Hawk standing by the side of the house, taking pictures of them. "There's Hawk and Grandma."

Hawk lowered his camera, waved, and went to take their grandmother's arm.

"Why don't we finish introducing Amber to the family," his

mother suggested. "Damon and Grandpa are out back, probably arguing over the barbecue."

"Reno, come," Amber said, and Reno trotted to her side as they made their way across the lawn.

"Can you train a guy like that for me?" Dawn asked.

"I bet my mother could," Amber said. "She trains service dogs, and she trained Reno."

Dawn smirked. "I need to get her number."

Dash shook his head.

"I got some great pictures," Hawk said as they met in the yard. "Great to see you again, Amber." He embraced her.

"You, too," Amber said. "I'm sorry we missed dinner with you and Shea after the signing."

"No worries," Hawk said. "I'm glad you were okay. Your sisters and their husbands were great company."

Dash put his hand on Amber's back. "Babe, this is my grandmother, Harriet. Grandma, this is my girlfriend, Amber."

Amber's expression softened. "I'm so happy to meet you. I understand we share a love of acorns."

"It's even more lovely to meet you now that I know that." His grandmother embraced her, eyeing Dash. "You didn't tell me she was a fan of acorns."

Dash hugged her. "Actually, Gram, if it weren't for acorns, I might never have gotten a first date with Amber."

"Really?" Andi asked.

"It's true. I thought Dash was very different from who he turned out to be." Amber reached for his hand, holding his gaze with no pink cheeks in sight. "The acorns might have opened the door, but it was his big ol' heart that won him the first date, and every date thereafter."

"Aw," his sisters said in unison.

He pulled her in for a hug. "I'm going to plant a forest full of oak trees just to keep her around. Did I tell you guys she sent me a card at every stop on my tour? Instead of dreading each new hotel, I had something to look forward to."

"I didn't want you to feel alone," Amber said softly.

Hawk nudged Dash. "If you let her get away, I'll be hot on her path."

"Yeah, like that's going to happen," Dash said as they went around the side of the house. The backyard still looked as it had when they were kids. The wooden playset with a rock-climbing wall and a fireman pole had seen better days, but the thick rope swing still hung like a massive snake from a branch, and the old metal shed anchored the far-left corner of the yard. Damon and their grandfather were tending the barbecue on the patio, their hearty laughter and the savory smell of their grandfather's famous ribs hung in the air. It was a damn good sight. "What kind of trouble are you all getting into back here?"

Damon looked over. His black Henley and scruff made his chiseled features look sharper, and his brown eyes—which were currently locked on Amber—even darker. He shifted a challenging smirk to Dash. "We were just making bets on how long it would take Amber to drop your ugly ass for me."

Their grandfather, a fairly large man in his early seventies, with snow-white hair, kind dark eyes, and the best business sense of anyone Dash had ever met, scoffed. "With the number of women you're juggling, *Big D*, I think you've got all you can handle." He looked at Dash and Amber, hiking a thumb at Damon. "Can you believe one woman actually calls him that?" His grandfather closed the distance between them, sporting his usual dress pants and a blue sweater, and pulled Dash into a manly embrace. "Good to see you, son."

"You too, Gramps. Thanks for having my back." He put his arm around Amber. "Amber, this is my grandfather, George, and my brother, Damon."

"It's nice to meet the romantic man who taught Dash how to light up people's lives," Amber said.

Before his grandfather could respond, Damon said, "What can I say? I'm a romantic guy," and rolled his shoulders back, flashing an arrogant grin.

Amber tilted her head, smiling sweetly. "Really? Who's the last person you set up romantic lights for?"

"Himself," Dawn said, sparking a litany of jokes.

"Does the bedroom count?" Damon smirked.

Amber glanced at Dash. "Yes, but what happens outside the bedroom counts more."

Everyone laughed.

"I can see you'll fit right in." Their grandfather embraced Amber.

Amber looked at Damon and said, "I'm sure you're romantic in your own way. No hard feelings?"

"It takes a lot more than that to hurt my feelings." Damon pulled her in for a hug, mouthing, *She's too hot for you*, to Dash.

Dash shook his head. "Dinner smells good."

"It'll be ready in about half an hour," his mother said. "I have a few things to finish up in the kitchen. Can I get you or Amber something to drink? Or a bowl of water for Reno?"

"I'm fine, Mom, thanks."

"None for me, thank you, but I would appreciate water for Reno. Would you like me to help?" Amber asked.

"No, sweetheart. Relax and enjoy yourself." His mother and grandmother headed inside.

Amber looked around. "So *this* is where the mayhem took

place."

"If by mayhem you mean ninja obstacle courses run by a drill sergeant, then yes," Hawk answered.

"You told her about that?" Damon asked.

"Yeah, why not?" Dash was sure they'd give her an earful.

"Did you tell her how you used to chase us up the rock wall, yelling"—Andi lowered her voice an octave—*"Go, go, go! You can't slow down until you can beat me!"*

"No, he did not." Amber looked imploringly at Dash. "That's a little harsh."

"That's not harsh, babe. That's just one example she picked out of a hat. More often they heard about how great they were doing. I had to motivate them."

"He always praised us." Dawn put her hands around her mouth and yelled, *"Great job! You're a backyard winner! Now be an Olympian!"*

Amber laughed.

"He was tough on them sometimes, but he made these kids what they are today," his grandfather said.

Dawn arched a brow. "Neurotic?"

"Come on, you guys." Dash raked a hand through his hair. "We had fun sometimes."

They all started talking at once.

"Fun is *not* the word I'd use," Hawk said.

"It was more like torture, with a dose of therapy," Andi agreed. "All I wanted to do was to be left alone."

"That's why I did it. You needed to get out of your own heads," Dash explained.

"My head has always been a great place to visit," Damon said.

"For a circus," Hawk teased.

Dawn crossed her arms, lifting her chin defiantly. "I bet I could beat you now, Dash."

"Hell, we all could," Damon said.

"Sounds to me like someone is throwing down a challenge," Mitch said.

They all exchanged grins and glances.

"Mom still has all the stuff in the shed," Andi reminded them.

Damon eyed Dash. "You up to it, old man?"

"Blowing you away?" Dash scoffed. "Hell yes."

"Game on!" Damon said, and took off with Dawn and Hawk for the shed. Dash touched Amber's hand. "Will you be okay for a few minutes?"

Andi took Amber's arm. "What are you talking about? She's joining us. Right, Amber?"

"I'm not very athletic," Amber said as the others began rolling tires out of the shed. "But it sounds like fun."

"It is fun." Dash leaned closer. "But if you'd rather not join in, it's okay."

"I'd like to," she reassured him. "But I don't have sneakers."

"I'll get you some!" Andi exclaimed. "This will be so fun. But you might want to keep Reno away from the madness."

"He can stay with me," Mitch offered.

They helped set up tires to run through, flagpoles to weave around, and balls to throw into buckets. Their mother lent Amber a pair of sneakers, and she and their grandmother came outside to watch the fun.

"All right, this is how it's going to work," Dash announced. "There'll be two teams, and two people will go at once, starting on opposite ends of the course. Team one will start at the tires, then weave around the flags, climb the rope, scale the rock wall, slide down the pole, and end by tossing three balls into the buckets. Team two will start with the buckets and work backward."

"Girls against boys!" Dawn hollered. "You have to wait until the person before you finishes the first obstacle before the next person goes. That way we won't run into each other."

Amber leaned closer to Dash, talking quietly. "We have to climb the rope *and* scale the rock wall?"

Dash pulled her closer and kissed her temple. "I'll help you—don't worry."

She didn't look convinced. "I've never done either, and we're on opposite teams."

"I'm *always* on your team, babe. I've got your back. Trust me." He kissed her again, then clapped his hands. "Let's go! Gramps, you want to get us started?"

"You've got it!" His grandfather stepped into the yard as they took their places at opposite ends of the obstacle course, hooting and hollering challenges back and forth.

"I've got to get this on video." His mother pulled out her phone.

Dash watched Amber insisting she wanted to go last, moving behind his sisters. He moved between his brothers.

Damon sized him up. "How did it end up being boys against girls? I wanted to kick your ass."

Dash clapped a hand on his shoulder. "You're going against Dawn. You have a better chance of winning."

"I could totally take you," Damon insisted.

Hawk leaned between them. "Can you girls stop bickering and get ready? You're up, Damon."

"Woo-hoo! Girl power!" Dawn yelled, and high-fived Amber and Andi.

Their grandfather held up a napkin like a flag. "On your

marks. Get set. *Go!*"

Dawn and Damon exploded onto the course. Everyone cheered and clapped, screaming, "Go, go, go!" Damon went as fast as lightning through the tires, while Dawn gunned the balls into the buckets. Dash took off after Damon, and he heard Amber's cheers above all the others as Andi came onto the course.

Dash finished in record time and cheered Amber on. "That's it, baby! You've got this!" It took her about seven tries to get the balls in the bucket, but she cracked up, taking it in stride as she ran through the tires and weaved around the flags, squealing with excitement when she finished and grabbed the rope like a champ. He didn't have the heart to tell her she was going in the wrong order, and nobody else seemed to notice. She jumped, trying to wrap her legs around the rope, and slid back down with a giggle. She grabbed it again, trying to wrap her legs around it as everyone shouted encouragement.

When she dropped again, Dash ran over and lifted her by the waist. "Grab the rope!" He put his hands on her butt, pushing her up as far as he could reach while Reno barked and everyone cheered her on.

"Now what?" Amber called out nervously from the top of the rope.

"Let go!" he shouted.

She closed her eyes and let go with a squeal. He caught her, stealing a quick kiss, and then they ran hand in hand to the rock wall, climbing it together. "You've got it! That's my girl!"

She ran to the pole, and as she slid down, more cheers rang out. Dash hugged her and spun her around. The minute her feet hit the ground, Dawn and Andi crushed her in a group hug, jumping up and down, the three of them squealing and laughing. Hawk took pictures as Damon pushed his way in for a hug, and his grandparents, his mother, and Mitch got in on the fun. With everyone laughing and chatting, Amber looked over their heads, her eyes catching Dash's, and his heart beat triple time.

His grandfather slung an arm over his shoulder. "I don't think I've ever seen you this happy."

He looked at the man who had taught him what being a man really meant and saw the man he wanted to be. "I want to light up the sky for her, Gramps."

"Well, son, if anyone can do that, it's you."

DINNER WAS AS loud as ever as they tossed teasing barbs and playful banter. Dash had never heard Amber laugh so much. She and his family got along famously. He'd even caught her talking with his grandfather and Damon about business and to Hawk about the Dark Knights motorcycle club, of which he was a member. His mother must have told him she loved Amber at least a dozen times. He felt the same way about Mitch. It was wonderful to see his mother with a man who looked at her with loving eyes and appreciated the amazing woman she was. Amber had talked with them for a long time about her bookstore. His mother had even tried to convince her to move to Port Hudson and open another one. Dash had seen a glimmer of interest in Amber's eyes, but he knew she'd never move away from Oak Falls, and after the way her family and the community had rallied around her after her seizure, he would never ask her to.

Amber raved about his family the whole way home, and as

they rode the elevator up to his condo, she was still talking a mile a minute. "It was so nice of your mom to invite me for Thanksgiving. Are you sure you want to spend it with my family? You'll be just coming off your tour. We can spend it here with your family and then see my family for Christmas. Graham's brother Zev is getting married over the holidays in Maryland. We could spend Christmas with my family and then go to the wedding together. That is, if you want to. Oh gosh, were you just being nice? Do you want time alone with your family over the holidays?"

The emotions he'd kept in check all night clawed for release. "Do you have any idea how cute you are when you ramble?" He kissed her jaw, backing her up against the elevator wall, and her eyes darkened. "I want to be with *you* for the holidays, and I didn't want you to feel pressure to spend it with mine." He brushed his nose along her cheek, inhaling her intoxicating scent, unleashing twelve days of pent-up desire. He gripped her hips, kissing the corner of her mouth, earning a long, seductive sigh, her soft curves melting into him. He needed her naked in his arms, and trailed kisses up her neck to her ear, whispering, "I'm happy to do whatever you want."

Her fingers dug into his sides, and she rubbed against him like a needy cat. *"Kiss me."*

He crushed his mouth to hers, rougher and greedier than he'd meant to, but she was just as feverish, grabbing at his arms, his back, rocking against his hard length. There was no holding back the passion surging between them as they made out desperate and greedy. He pushed his hands beneath her sweater, branded by the heat of her skin, and sank his teeth into her neck.

"Yesyesyes." She went up on her toes, holding his mouth there as the elevator stopped and they stumbled into his condo

in a tangle of moans and kisses. She tore her mouth away, panting out, "My *luggage*."

Fuck. His arm shot between the elevator doors, and he hauled her bags into the condo, barely registering Reno watching them.

"He's *fine*." She pulled his mouth back to hers.

Fire seared through his veins, desire pounding, swelling, *taking over*. He kissed her harder, deeper, and she stumbled back, hitting the door with a *thud*. He broke away, searching her face for pain. "You okay?"

Without a word, she yanked his mouth back to hers and sucked his tongue into her mouth. *Holy fucking hell.* His cock wept for her incredible mouth, but he was desperate to be buried deep inside her, to feel their bodies as one. He fumbled with the button on her jeans, and she did the same with his. Shoes and clothing flew, her seizure-alert necklace set aside between hungry kisses and wanton pleas. Finally naked, he lifted her into his arms, lowering her onto his cock. She was so tight, so hot and perfect, he could barely think, and she was moving, grinding, driving him out of his mind. He gripped her hips, matching her every move with one of his own. He captured her mouth, pounding into her. He was going to die right there, buried deep inside her, and he didn't care, because nothing had ever felt so exquisite. Reality hit him like a sucker punch, and he stilled them both. "*Fuuck.* Condom. Sorry, baby. *Sorry.*"

His body shook with restraint as he grabbed her hips to lift her off, but she tightened her legs around his waist, her nails digging into his shoulders. "I'm on the pill. I swear. I'd never try to trap you like that other girl did. We don't have to stop."

Heart attack averted, a relieved laugh tumbled out. "I know you wouldn't. That's the least of my worries. Are you sure?"

A wicked grin slid across her face. "I'm your wild thing, aren't I?"

"Hell *yeah* you are," he gritted out, and reclaimed her mouth.

Sounds of their lovemaking filled the room, flesh against flesh, moans and whimpers, as they lost themselves in each other. Their breaths came faster, their skin growing slick. Dash intensified his efforts, holding her tight against him as he thrust faster, harder, their hearts thundering as one.

"Don't stop," she pleaded, her *need* driving his.

He recaptured her mouth, her fingernails digging deeper into his skin, pain and pleasure spiking through him. He felt her muscles tense and knew she was close, his own release gathering inside him like a cyclone, thunder booming, waves churning. She tore her mouth away with a stream of indiscernible sounds, her slick heat tightening around him. Every pulse pushed him closer to the edge, teeth clenched, muscles rigid, hips pumping. Just when he was about to give in, she grabbed his shoulders, catching a second wind, riding him harder, until they surrendered to the pleasures crashing over them. He rasped against her neck, a curse and a plea, as they rode the waves of their love.

When she went boneless in his arms, her cheek resting on his shoulder, she giggled. "We have our socks on."

Socks? He ran his hand down her leg to her ruffled sock. "You know how much I love you in ruffles," he teased, turning her giggles to full-on laughter, making him laugh, too.

"We barely made it out of the elevator." She lifted her head and looked around. "Nice entranceway." More laughter bubbled out. "Your wild thing has turned into a sex fiend."

So fucking cute. "In that case, let me give you the tour of the bedroom."

Chapter Nineteen

AMBER STOOD AT the windows in Dash's living room as he took a call. They'd had a wonderful morning, sleeping in, taking a long, steamy shower, walking Reno, and making breakfast together. Dash had pulled her into his arms to dance while breakfast was cooking, and she'd tried to teach him a line dance, but they'd ended up laughing and kissing.

If only they had a week together instead of just the weekend.

From the safety of his opulent penthouse, with the morning sun reflecting off the windows of other buildings and glittering off the water like diamonds, it was easy to pretend they were far away from the hustle and bustle of the city. She'd love to curl up with Dash on the couch and spend the day locked away from the rest of the world. But they didn't have more time, and she *was* excited to see the Big Apple through his eyes. She'd only ventured into the city once while she was at Boyer, when Charlotte and Aubrey had dragged her there. It was loud, exciting, and a little terrifying. But she knew it would look and feel different with Dash.

She reached down to pet Reno as Dash's arms circled her from behind. She'd been surprised to see that in addition to dog food, he'd bought Reno bowls with his name on them and toys. He'd even arranged for someone he trusted to walk Reno while they were out. He still hadn't told her what he'd planned for them, but she'd worn her most comfortable flat-heeled boots.

"How's my girl?" his minty breath whispered over her skin.

She turned in his arms. "How can I be anything but great when I'm here with you?"

"I was asking myself the same thing." He kissed her. "Are you ready to go?"

"Mm-hm." She crouched to love up Reno, her seizure-alert necklace falling forward as she petted him. She really didn't need it since she was with Dash, but she felt safer wearing it. "Be a good boy. I love you."

Dash petted him, and then they grabbed their jackets and headed downstairs. "That's our ride," he said as they stepped outside. Putting his hand on her back, he led her toward a shiny black sedan. A man dressed in a suit was standing by the back door.

"Our *ride*? Doesn't everyone walk or take the subway here?"

"We'll walk a bit, but we've got a big night ahead of us. I don't want to tire you out." He leaned closer, lowering his voice. "I prefer to tire you out when you're safe and naked in my bed."

Her body shuddered with the delicious memories of last night, when he'd done just that.

"Good morning, Mr. Pennington, Ms. Montgomery," the man in the suit said as he opened the back door.

"Good morning." Amber felt funny having someone drive them around. "You can call me Amber. What's your name?"

The driver looked at Dash, who nodded. "Chuck Marx, ma'am."

"It's nice to meet you, Chuck. But if you call me *ma'am* again, you'll make me feel old."

"Sorry, ma—*Amber*."

Amber climbed into the car and scooted over for Dash to get in beside her. As Chuck went around to the driver's side, she whispered, "We don't need a driver."

"Just go with it." He took her hand and kissed the back of it.

As they drove, the sidewalks and streets became busier. The driver pulled over in front of Strand Bookstore and got out to open the door for them. "We're going to the Strand?" she asked as they climbed out of the car, knowing the store's rich history. The city had once been home to a whopping forty-eight bookstores in only a five-block stretch of what was then Fourth Avenue and had been known as Book Row. The Strand, founded in 1927 by a Lithuanian immigrant, was now the only remaining bookstore from Book Row, though it had been moved in the 1950s to its current location on Broadway and Twelfth Street.

"Just for you, baby. It's one of the ten most famous bookstores in the world. At some point I'll take you to see the others in Paris, San Francisco, Venice…"

"Dash!" She threw her arms around him, her heart sprinting in her chest. She marveled at the famous red awning, boasting 18 MILES OF BOOKS. "Are you sure you want to take me in there? I might never come out."

"Sweetheart, if you're happy, I'm happy. We have all day."

As they headed inside, she said, "I'm serious. They have a huge selection of used and rare books."

Amber tried to be mindful of their time, but she and Dash were having too much fun. When Dash found out she didn't own a leather-bound edition of her favorite book, *Pride and Prejudice*, he insisted on spoiling her with a stunning 1894 trade edition. It had all one-hundred-and-sixty Hugh Thomson illustrations and the beautiful peacock cover. After spending far too long checking out every inch of the store, they picked up a few children's books for Emma, and Amber bought one of Hawk's coffee table books despite Dash telling her Hawk would give her one. Hawk's work was gorgeous, and she liked supporting his efforts.

When they finally left the store, Chuck was right there waiting to take them to Times Square, where they held hands as they strolled down the sidewalk, admiring the holiday decorations. They bought an adorable outfit for Emma with pink-and-white ruffles around the ankles and wrists, and they stopped at a café for lunch, where they had soup and shared a sandwich. They got hot chocolate to go, and Chuck whisked them away again.

As they climbed out of the car, Amber spotted an elaborate white horse-drawn carriage ride at the end of the street. "Dash, *look*."

"Your chariot awaits, sweetheart."

"*My* chariot?" She looked at the carriage again, then back at Dash, her heart skipping a beat. "Really?"

"You've walked, and now we rest, while enjoying a ride through Central Park." He drew her closer, holding his hot chocolate in his other hand, and kissed her. "I told you I'd take care of you."

"You are the best, most romantic and caring man I've ever met, and you're spoiling me rotten." She went up on her toes to kiss him, and too excited to stand still, she took his hand, pulling him down the sidewalk. "Come on!"

They ran for the carriage, holding their hot chocolates out in front of them. *Thank goodness for lids.* They cuddled close in the carriage, sipping their warm drinks, serenaded by the *clip-clop* of the horse's feet and the voices of people in the park. Amber rested her head on Dash's shoulder, feeling like they were miles away from the real world. The city wasn't scary at all today. It was thrilling and fun, and he really was making sure she didn't get tired out. She imagined traveling with him to see all the famous bookstores. Oh, how she wanted that, to take life by the horns with the man she loved, going places she never thought she'd want to go.

She gazed up at him, seeing flashes of him in the stores in Times Square where they'd tried on funny hats, and picked out Emma's outfit. It was so easy to picture a future together, planning a family, picking out outfits for their own kids, taking them on a horse-drawn carriage. She was getting ahead of herself, but it felt so right, she didn't want to stop the fantasy.

"What are you thinking about, beautiful?"

Oh, just marrying you, that's all. "That every time we're together I think it's the best time of my life, and then you top it with the next one."

"Just you wait, sweetheart. We still have a ball to attend." He kissed her. "I really wanted to call you Cinderella just then, but your life is not anything like hers."

"I could be Belle. She loved books."

"That'd make me a bad beast who locked you in a castle. I'm not digging that."

She laughed. "How about we make our own fairy tale?"

"Like *Dash and the Wildest Thing*? Or *Dash and the Bookish Vixen*?"

"I'm not sure I want anyone reading about me being wild or

a vixen. How about *Amberella and the Dashing Prince* or *The Dashing Prince and the Bookish Belle?*"

"Baby, you can call us anything you want, as long as I get to call you *mine*."

WHEN THEY GOT back to Dash's penthouse, they took Reno for a walk, and then they looked through the things they'd bought. Amber held up the outfit for Emma. "She's going to look adorable in this."

"She'd look cute in anything, but I am partial to ruffles these days."

Thanks to him, she was much fonder of them lately, too. She'd even bought panties with tiny ruffles on them to wear to the fundraiser tonight beneath the elegant old-Hollywood style gown she'd bought from Jillian. "I hope Brindle doesn't mind the ruffles. She's not as girlie as I am." She folded the outfit and put it back in the bag. "I can't wait to have babies and buy them cute little outfits. I picture little girls in frilly dresses and boys in tiny jeans and boots. Or maybe the girls will be tomboys and the boys will be feminine. I don't care either way. I'll love them to pieces."

He ran a hand down her back. "You'll be an amazing mom. How many kids do you want to have?"

"Several. Five, six maybe."

"You'll be pregnant for *years*."

"No, I won't. I'm probably going to adopt or use a surrogate."

His expression turned serious. "You don't want to carry

your babies?"

"I'd love to, but there are risks with seizures and pregnancy. They can decrease oxygen to the fetus or slow the fetal heart rate. I could miscarry or hurt the baby if I have a seizure and fall. I don't think I could ever forgive myself if something happened to my unborn child."

"I hadn't thought about those things."

"Why would you?" She took out the books they'd bought, looking them over as she said, "Lots of people with epilepsy get pregnant and have no trouble carrying their babies or giving birth, but you know me. I always err on the side of caution. I just don't think I'll be comfortable taking the risk." She set the books down, and her stomach sank at Dash's furrowed brow. "What's wrong?"

"I just..." He shrugged. "Ever since last night I've been thinking about what it would be like if you got pregnant. I guess I started to picture you that way, and I liked it."

"You *did?*" Her pulse quickened. She was elated that he was thinking in terms of a future together but worried about what her choices might mean for them.

"It's not like I tried to picture it. But you know how I feel about you. My mind just went there."

"Does it bother you that I prefer not to take that risk?"

"No, I just hadn't thought about it."

The disappointment in his voice stung. "You sound bummed."

He drew her into his arms and set those eyes on her. "I'm not going to lie to you. I *just* started picturing you carrying *our* baby, and you took that away in a few sentences. I need a minute to digest it."

Her throat constricted, and she lowered her eyes, fighting

the wave of sadness engulfing her. "We should probably get ready."

He tightened his arms around her, and she met his penetrating gaze. "Amber, needing to digest it doesn't mean I don't support your decision. It just means I need to wrap my head around the idea that I'll never get to see you round with our babies or experience a pregnancy with you."

"Okay. I'm sorry," she said a little shakily.

"You don't have to be sorry. It's your body, and you need to do what's right for you and the baby. I hadn't thought about what a seizure could do to an unborn child. I just pictured you cute and pregnant and me talking to the round belly like a fool."

"Dash." Her eyes dampened. She could see him doing that, and it wouldn't make him a fool. It would make him a loving father. If they stayed together, would it be fair to take that away from him?

A buzz sounded on the intercom, and a deep voice said, "Mr. Pennington, a Miss Oliver for you."

"That's for you, bookish belle." Dash headed to the intercom and spoke into it, telling the man to send Miss Oliver up.

"For me?" Wishing they hadn't been interrupted, she tried to push her worries away, at least for tonight.

"I *might* have hired Shea's friend Indi Oliver, a hair and makeup artist, to help you get ready for the fundraiser." He held up his hands. "Not that you need it, but I heard you tell my sisters you were worried about how to do your hair and makeup in old-Hollywood style, so I made a few calls."

Holy cow. "*Dash.* I can't believe you did that."

"I told you I wasn't going to let you stress tonight, didn't I?"

He gave her a quick kiss and headed for the door, as if he hadn't just swept her off her feet again.

Chapter Twenty

DASH TUGGED AT his bow tie, pacing the living room in his white tuxedo jacket and black slacks. Amber had gotten ready in the guest room because Indi had insisted she make a grand entrance. But Indi had left half an hour ago, and Amber still hadn't come out. He went to check on her and stopped at the end of the hall, unable to speak past the awe of Amber walking toward him in a long, shimmery midnight-blue gown with a plunging neckline, her fingers trailing over Reno's back. Her hair was gathered over the front of one shoulder in old-Hollywood style cascading waves. She was stunning when she wore little makeup, but with winged eyeliner and red lips, he had no words.

"Do I really have to share you with other men tonight?"

That innocent, sexy smile he loved curved her lips, and she ran her fingers nervously along the exposed skin between her breasts. "It's not too much? I've never worn anything like this."

He took her hand, kissing the back of it. "Sweetheart, you are always gorgeous, but in that dress you literally take my breath away. I might need to wear my football gear to keep hordes of men away from my girl."

She laughed, a melodic, sweet, nervous sound.

"You're just missing one thing." He reached into his pocket, withdrew a long black jewelry box, and opened the top, revealing a gold necklace with a diamond acorn pendant he'd bought her.

Her jaw dropped. "Dash…?"

"I couldn't let this weekend pass without commemorating our first trip to New York City together. And I knew you'd feel a little naked without Reno or your necklace. Hopefully, this will help."

Her eyes teared up. "Thank you." She fanned her face. "I'm going to ruin my makeup."

"You'll still be the most beautiful woman there." He moved behind her to put it on and kissed the sexy freckles on her shoulder. She touched the necklace as he moved beside her, a single tear sliding down her cheek. He reached into his pocket and pulled out a tissue. "I had a feeling this might happen." He dabbed at the wetness and kissed her temple. "Still stunning."

She blinked several times, clearly trying not to cry. "I love it. Thank you so much."

"And I love you." He leaned in for a kiss but stopped short to avoid ruining her lipstick. "You're in for trouble after this event if I have to look at those lips all night and not kiss them."

"I like your brand of trouble, my dashing prince." She tapped her cheek, and he kissed it.

"Shall we go?" He held out his arm. "Your limo awaits."

"Limo?" She hugged him. "You really do make me feel like the belle of the ball." She took his arm as they headed for the elevator. "Do you have extra football gear? I think I might need my own with you looking more handsome than Sean Connery in those old James Bond movies."

"This double-oh-seven only has eyes for you, baby."

THE BAD FAMILY had once again outdone themselves. Dash and Amber followed a red carpet to the entrance of the ballroom, where they had their pictures taken beneath a massive HOLLYWOOD sign with red velvet curtains on either side before entering the crowded event. He couldn't wait to see that picture. He had the woman he loved on his arm, and she'd beamed for the camera. His siblings would have a field day with the unstoppable toddler smile he was surely sporting, but damn...

He was one hell of a happy man.

Men and women decked out in old-Hollywood style mingled as they played blackjack, roulette, slot machines, and other casino games beneath glittering gold and silver stars that dangled from the ceiling. A band was playing, and couples danced on the dance floor just beyond the round dining tables, which were draped in black tablecloths and decorated with elaborate centerpieces of red and white roses and playing cards. Cardboard cutouts of celebrities dressed in long gowns and fancy tuxedos from Hollywood's golden age were scattered around the room, and enormous pictures of Lorelei Bad and other children who had stayed at the Ronald McDonald House decorated the walls.

"There's my favorite guy!" Tiffany hurried over to greet them, her burgeoning baby bump covered by an elegant black gown. Her blond hair was twisted in an elaborate updo. She hugged Dash. "Am I seeing things, or did you bring a gorgeous date?"

His mind trampled back to his earlier conversation with

Amber, but this wasn't the time to get lost in that, and he pushed those thoughts away. "You're seeing things, because I brought the *most* gorgeous date. This is Amber Montgomery, my girlfriend. Amber, this is Tiffany Winters-Bad, the toughest sports agent around."

"It's so nice to meet you," Amber said, offering her hand.

"I've repped this guy for years, and not once has he brought a date to a function or ever used the G-word. This calls for an awkward-pregnancy hug." Tiffany leaned over her belly to hug Amber. "Sorry. I'm still learning to maneuver around this thing. You should have seen me trying on dresses. Talk about a nightmare, but yours is incredible. Who made it?"

"Jillian Braden," Amber said sweetly.

"I knew it. I *love* her designs. She needs to make a maternity line."

"I'll let her know," Amber said. "I love your gown, too."

"You look beautiful, Tiff," Dash said. "I bet Dylan is over the moon. Do you know what you're having yet?"

Tiffany rubbed her belly. "A linebacker probably, based on how hard this baby kicks."

"A boy, then? You're going to name it Dash, right?" Dash teased.

Tiffany arched a brow. "*Dashell?* I don't think so."

"When is your baby due?" Amber asked.

"After the Super Bowl, thank goodness."

"When is that?" Amber whispered.

"Early February." Dash pulled her close again.

"I take it you're not a football fan?" Tiffany asked.

"I've always been more of a bookworm than a sports fan, but Dash is teaching me about football, and I really like watching it with him," Amber answered.

"Amber owns the bookstore in Virginia, where I kicked off my tour," Dash explained.

"I guess that explains the medical emergency that interrupted the signing." Tiffany winked at Amber. "Dash met you and his heart stopped?"

Dash held Amber a little tighter. "Something like that."

"Hey, Dash!" Tiffany's husband called out, waving from across the room, then motioned for Tiffany to join him.

"That's Dylan, Tiffany's husband," Dash explained to Amber. "The guys he's with are Johnny Bad and his older brother Kane."

"I'd better get over there before my husband convinces Johnny to write a song for our baby," Tiffany said. "I think I saw the Brat Pack over by the blackjack table. Go have fun and spend lots of money. It's for a good cause. I'll catch up with you later."

As Tiffany hurried off, Amber said, "Do you think we can meet Johnny later? He's such a big star."

"First let me get my football gear." Dash leaned in for a kiss, then averted her luscious red lips and kissed her cheek. "Your lips are driving me mad. Let's go say hello to my buddies before I haul you into a dark corner."

As he guided her toward the blackjack table, she said, "A dark corner sounds good to me."

It sounded damn good to him, too. "You're going to try my willpower tonight, aren't you?"

"That's the plan," she said sweetly.

"Amber?" Sophie, a petite brunette, and her husband, formidable security expert Brett Bad, sidled up to them dressed to the nines.

"Sophie!" Amber hugged her as Dash greeted Brett. "You

look gorgeous. How's baby Brenna?"

"She's wonderful. Getting too big too fast." Sophie eyed Dash. "This is *new*. I didn't even know you and Dash knew each other."

"We're not *that* new," Dash said, taking Amber's hand. "I went to Oak Falls for a break before starting my book tour about a month ago and met this beautiful woman who set my world on fire."

Sophie and Amber exchanged an appreciative glance that made Dash feel pretty damn good.

"Congratulations on your book. I saw you hit the *New York Times* bestseller list," Brett said as he put his arm around Sophie. "I could have warned you about Oak Falls. That place is the Bermuda Triangle of love. It lulls you in with its small-town charm, but once you get there, you go all in, and there's no turning back."

"I can think of worse fates." Dash brushed another kiss to Amber's cheek. "But that's good to know. I thought it was Marilynn's *special* body wash that made the difference."

Sophie's eyes widened. "She gave you Roxie's love-potion body wash?"

"Yes, and let me tell you, that stuff works," Dash said.

"What are you talking about? I never got any body wash," Brett said.

"Maybe you didn't need it as much as I did." Dash cocked a grin. "I had to use every trick in the book to get Amber's attention. I used the body wash, shampoo, *and* lotion every damn day, and I've already ordered a lifetime supply."

They all laughed.

"We'd better finish making the rounds," Brett said. "Why don't we all get together sometime?"

"We're leaving town tomorrow. Amber's heading home, and my book tour runs until the weekend before Thanksgiving. How about after the holidays?" Dash suggested.

"We'd love that," Sophie said.

"I can't wait to see Brenna." Amber hugged her again.

Brett cocked a grin. "You could always make her a play-mate."

"*Brett,*" Sophie chided. "Let them enjoy each other before they get into diapers and sleepless nights that don't include orgasms. Ignore him, you guys. He's so in love with our baby girl, he thinks everyone should have kids. We'll catch up soon."

As they walked away, Dash drew Amber into his arms. "Are you okay?"

"Great. It's so nice to see them."

"Did Brett's comment bother you?"

"Not at all. They're in baby-making mode. Brett's not thinking about my medical issues."

He was relieved. "Okay. Let's go see my buddies. I'm excited for you to meet them."

As they headed for the blackjack table, Amber asked, "What's the Brat Pack?"

"That's what Tiffany calls me and my buddies: Troy Stewart, Clay Braden, and Tyrell Thompson. She reps all of us, and we all played for the Giants."

"That's Troy, right? In the tux with tails and the ascot?" she asked as they neared the table. "I recognize his crooked smile. Gosh, I think he's even bigger than when I saw him a few years ago."

Dash bit back a sting of jealousy over his burly, dark-haired friend. "Yeah, that's him. Clay is the dark-haired guy next to him, wearing the blue plaid suit, and Tyrell is the African

American guy on the other side of the table, wearing the regular black tuxedo."

"I'm starting to understand why some girls like to watch football."

He slid his hand down her back and squeezed her ass. "You're definitely testing me, aren't you?"

She fluttered her lashes. "Who, me?"

"*Hey*, there's our man." Clay tugged Dash into a manly embrace, clapping him on the back. "It's great to see you."

"You too," Dash said as he gave him a quick hug and was handed off to Troy. "Good to see you." He moved to Tyrell. "How's it going, T?"

"Not as good as it is for you." Tyrell lowered his voice. "Thanks for bringing me a date."

Dash laughed. "You wish."

"Amber? It's been a while." Troy leaned in to hug her.

"Better watch *Slick*," Clay teased. "He's trying to steal your girl."

"It's nice to see you again. How's Dani?" Amber asked. Dani was Troy's three-year-old daughter.

"Cuter than ever. What're you doing with this guy?" Troy hiked a thumb at Dash.

"She's *not* slumming it, like she would be if she was with you." Dash slid his arm around Amber's waist. "Amber, this is Tyrell Thompson and Clay Braden."

"It's a pleasure to meet you." Tyrell held out his hand. "If all I've got to do is quit football to go out with someone as beautiful as you, I'll resign tomorrow."

"I don't know what they're feeding you football players, but y'all are too much." Amber smiled at Clay. "You're Graham and Beau's cousin, right?"

"Sure am. We Bradens are everywhere." Clay leaned in for a hug, prying her away from Dash with a chuckle.

"I can see it's going to be a long night," Dash said, making everyone laugh.

"Are you going to be at Zev and Carly's wedding?" Amber asked Clay.

"I am. Zev's working with my brother Noah at the Real DEAL. My whole family will be there. So will our cousins from Colorado," Clay answered. "I guess I'll see you there?"

"Yes." She beamed at Dash. "Hopefully you'll see Dash, too."

Dash pulled her into his arms. "If you think I'd leave you alone with this guy, you're crazy." He kissed her temple, then turned his attention back to his buddies. "You guys look great out there this season."

"It's not the same without you," Troy said.

Tyrell agreed. "You should come out of retirement next season and blow everyone away."

Clay looked at Dash and Amber and shook his head. "I don't think he's in any hurry to go anywhere."

"You've got that right." Dash tightened his hold on her. "I've got a few irons in the fire to keep myself busy."

"Is that what they're calling it now?" Tyrell teased.

They joked a lot, and the five of them made their way around the room playing casino games. Amber sat on Dash's lap as they played poker, and she foiled nearly every hand with her horrible poker face. She squealed when they got three of a kind and clapped at a full house. But she was so freaking cute, everyone at the table adored her. Dash and the guys cheered her on as she played the slot machines, and when she hit it big, they made a ruckus, inciting a round of applause throughout the ballroom. Amber blushed a red streak, and of course his generous girl gave her winnings as a donation to the event. His buddies stuck with them all evening, and when Tiffany introduced Amber to Johnny Bad, Johnny teased her about having more bodyguards than he did.

She was so personable during dinner, she got to know all about Tyrell's and Clay's families, and Troy shared pictures of his daughter. They laughed a lot, and when Tyrell asked if she had any single sisters, she told them she had one who never left her research laboratory and another who was probably tougher than all of them.

By the time Dash led her to the dance floor after dinner, he was so in love with her, he ached with it. He gazed into her eyes as they swayed to the music. "I'm so glad you're here with me. Are you having fun?"

"I'm having the time of my life. Your friends are so fun, and you guys are so close. I bet you miss them a lot."

"Yeah, I do. But we stay in touch."

He held her closer as Tyrell and Clay sauntered over and began slow dancing with each other next to them. He narrowed his eyes. *What are you up to?*

"Oh, Tyrell," Clay said in a high-pitched voice. "When you look at me like that it makes me all squishy inside."

Amber giggled.

"Baby, I'll make you feel something inside, but it ain't squishy." Tyrell's deep laughter followed.

"I have a brother who might be perfect for you guys," Amber teased.

"Hey, if he's as cute as you, he can be my wingman," Tyrell said.

Clay *tsk*ed, feigning disgust. "Tyrell, you two-timing scoundrel." He spun on his heel and stomped off the dance floor.

"Now I'm in trouble. I better go put my boy's ego back together." Tyrell winked and headed off the dance floor.

"Idiots." Dash shook his head.

"I *adore* them, and they obviously love you to pieces."

"They feel the same about you, sweetheart." Each of his buddies had snuck in a few words about how great Amber was and how happy they were for him.

She looked up at the lights and the stars dangling from the ceiling, and she sighed dreamily. "This has been the best night *ever*. The best day and night. I hope I didn't embarrass you at the card tables. It was just so fun, I couldn't hold in my excitement."

"Baby, what did I tell you before? You could never embarrass me. You outshine everyone in this room. In this state. Hell, on the *planet*."

"There you go, making me feel like the belle of the ball again."

"You'll always be the belle of my ball." He pressed his lips to hers and whispered, "Sorry about your lipstick. I had to do it."

"More, please."

He lowered his lips to hers, and they kissed and danced to several songs, their bodies pressed together, the fire between them growing hotter by the second. "What do you say we get out of here?"

"I thought you'd never ask."

AMBER TRIED TO focus as they made a quick round of

goodbyes, promising to get together with Dash's friends soon, but she was too sidetracked by the lust consuming her. They hurried out to the limo. She craved Dash's touch and couldn't get her lips on him fast enough. Thank goodness for the partition blocking the driver's view of them. Dash lifted her onto his lap, and she gathered her dress around her thighs, straddling him as they made out like long-lost lovers. His arousal was tempting and insistent beneath her. She whimpered into their kisses. His hands moved beneath her dress, over her panties.

"*Ruffles?*" He gritted out, "*God, I love you.*"

Reclaiming her lips more demandingly, he pushed his hands into her panties and palmed her bare ass. She ground against him, his hips rocking urgently and needfully. Even through their clothes, the friction was overwhelming. Her sex swelled and pulsed, heat eating her up like wildfire.

She reached down, frantically working his pants open. She was desperate, greedy, her body igniting at the prospect of taking him right there. It was completely out of the realm of anything she'd ever imagined doing, and she wasn't about to stop. She freed his cock, and their eyes locked as her hand circled his thick shaft and she rose onto her knees. He tugged her panties to the side, and she held his dark and dirty stare as she sank down, taking in every inch of him. She felt her body stretching, squeezing, *needing.* Lightning scorched through her, drawing a needful sound from her lungs.

He grabbed her hair with both hands, dragging her mouth toward his, growling, "How am I going to leave you tomorrow?"

He crushed his mouth to hers, slicing her last thread of restraint. She gripped the back of the seat, riding his cock fast and hard, every stroke earning more hungry, passionate sounds that drilled into her, turning her on even more, making her want to see him lose himself in her. He held her ass so tight, she was sure it would bruise, and she didn't care. She'd wear those marks proudly, remembering every second of the titillating sensations enveloping her, the greed driving her, and the orgasm building inside her, pulsing and pumping, mounting to painful levels. He moved one hand between them, expertly working the sensitive nerves that sent her head reeling back, moans and whimpers escaping through gritted teeth. Her eyes closed as pleasure slammed into her in turbulent waves, taking her up, up, up, then crashing over her, sending her soaring. Just as she caught her breath, she was hit with another relentless wave, pummeling her in a maddening, erotic rhythm like nothing she'd ever known. Dash pushed off the back cushion, fiercely reclaiming her mouth as he gave in to his own magnificent release. He groaned into their kisses, tugging her hair, their teeth gnashing, bodies bucking, a symphony of sexual sounds floating around them, until she collapsed against him, and his head fell to her shoulder, their bodies jerking with sporadic tremors.

When their blissful, hazy state finally started to clear, Amber realized they were stopped at the curb outside his condominium complex. "Ohmygosh. We're *here*." She scrambled off his lap, and he quickly put himself back together, but he didn't move to get out of the car.

His head lolled back. "Damn, baby. You destroy me."

Nervous giggles bubbled out, and he laughed, too, tugging her into another kiss.

She pointed to the driver standing on the sidewalk with his back to the car. "He *knows* what we did."

Dash had a goofy grin on his face.

"Oh God! You've done this before, haven't you? You think I'm being ridiculous."

He shook his head. "No, baby. It's a first for me, too. I was just thinking about how I've gone years protecting my reputation, and when you and I are together, I can't hold back. *Nothing* else matters. Nothing else exists."

"Yeah, well, see these red cheeks?" She pointed to her burning cheeks. "They matter. What now?"

He pulled her closer, whispering, "Now you'll have to make an honest man out of me."

"Stop making jokes." She laughed, because what else could she do? Die from mortification?

"You're right. We have no choice. We have to kill him to protect our secret."

She buried her face in his shoulder. *"Dash."*

"Come on, wild thing. I'll protect you from his evil, knowing gaze."

And Dash did just that. He tucked her beneath his arm, shielding her from the driver as they made their way into the building and straight into the elevator, where she wished she could climb beneath his skin and never have to leave him again.

HOURS LATER AMBER lay in Dash's bed listening to the sure and steady cadence of his breathing as he slept peacefully beside her. Her mind was going a million miles an hour. They'd made love again last night, but it wasn't like it had been in the limo, which she still couldn't believe she'd done but didn't regret one bit. Dash had walked Reno while she'd cleaned up from their limo debauchery, and when he'd returned, he'd slowly undressed her, taking a long, lascivious look at her wearing nothing but her frilly panties and heels. Heat prickled her limbs just thinking about his wolfish grin and the hungry look in his eyes. He'd removed her heels and carried her to the bed, making slow, sweet love to her, neither one wanting it to end.

She glanced at the clock. It was four fifteen. They had to be at the airport in five hours, and then Dash would fly across the country to start the last leg of his tour, and she'd go home, missing him. She held the gorgeous acorn necklace he'd given her between her finger and thumb and closed her eyes, reliving their wonderful evening, from the moment he'd seen her in her dress—she'd never forget the look in his eyes then, either—to meeting Johnny Bad with his slick dark hair and air of arrogance, dancing in Dash's arms and feeling like they were the only two people in the world, and stealing away from the event, desperate for each other. And that painful moment she'd been trying not to think about when she'd told him she didn't want to give birth to her babies.

The disappointment in his voice echoed in her ears. *I just started picturing you carrying our baby, and you took that away in a few sentences.*

She opened her eyes, taking in the beautiful man beside her who had done everything he could just for a chance to be with her. He lived his life like an open book, giving of himself to everyone. He'd never asked her for anything, and in a few unknowing seconds, she'd taken away the one thing he really wanted. She hadn't been thinking about how it would come across when she'd blurted it out. She hadn't thought he was thinking that far into their future. But now she wished she'd been more sensitive in the way she'd said it.

Reno stirred at their feet, inching up between them.

"Keep him warm while I go pee," she whispered, and kissed Reno's head. She slipped from the bed, reaching for the shirt Dash had worn last night. Reno moved to follow her, but she held out her hand. "Stay."

She put on the shirt, which smelled like Dash, as she headed into the bathroom. She used the toilet and turned on the sink, hearing the scratch of Reno's paws at the door just before the world went black.

DASH BOLTED UPRIGHT at the sound of Reno barking and scratching at the bathroom door. *"Amber!"* flew from his lips as understanding slammed into him. He ran across the room and threw the bathroom door open.

"No!" tore from his lungs as he dropped to his knees beside Amber, lying still on the bathroom floor, blood pooling beneath her head.

Chapter Twenty-One

DASH PACED THE emergency room waiting area with Reno by his side, the phone pressed to his ear, fear clawing at his chest, as he explained to Amber's parents what had happened. There had been so much blood on the bathroom floor, in her hair, smeared on her cheek, which he knew was from her head jerking with a seizure. He felt sick thinking about her suffering alone. He fucking *hated* epilepsy and everything that came with it. "They're stitching her up and running tests. MRI, EEG, blood work." She'd been back there for a long time, but he'd had to pull himself together before making the call. "The wound was long but not deep. They didn't see signs of a concussion, and they don't think she lost consciousness from the fall. They said she was in a postictal state when I found her."

"Thank God," Marilynn said, her voice riddled with worry.

Dash's jaw clenched, guilt consuming him. "I'm so sorry." Sorry didn't take away the fact that the woman he loved was behind those doors because of him. He'd heard Reno barking in his dream, two, maybe three times, before he'd realized it wasn't a dream and had bolted out of bed. How long had it taken him to wake up? A minute? Three? "This is all my fault. I shouldn't have taken her out before the fundraiser or kept her up so late."

"This is not your fault, son," Cade said firmly. "There's nothing you could have done to ward off the seizure."

"I could have woken up when she got up to use the bathroom and gotten to her sooner. Maybe I could have prevented her fall. I could have made sure her seizure-alert necklace was in the bedroom, where Reno could have pushed it." She'd left her necklace in the guest room, where she'd gotten ready for the party, and he hadn't given it a thought. But a heavier thought weighed on him. This was Amber's second seizure in two weeks after not having them for years, and the only changes in her life, the recent upheavals to her schedule, the traveling, the late nights, were all because of him.

"All that matters is that she's okay," Marilynn said. "Are you okay? Is there anyone nearby who can be with you while you wait?"

"I'm fine," he lied. He didn't want to be with anyone but Amber. "I'll call you as soon as I have an update."

After they ended the call, Dash lowered himself into a chair with a crushing feeling in his chest and rested his elbows on his knees, letting his face fall into his hands. He silently offered himself up to the powers that be in exchange for...he didn't know what. For Amber to be okay? For her not to hate him?

Reno pushed his snout onto Dash's lap, and Dash draped an arm around him, touching his forehead to the dog's soft fur. "She's going to be okay, buddy. She has to be."

When the nurse finally came through the door, he pushed to his feet with his heart in his throat. "How is she?"

"She's okay. We've given her something for her pain, but she's still pretty shaken up and tired."

"What about the tests?"

"There was nothing of note on the EEG, and her MRI was

clear. Her medications are at therapeutic levels. She's been cleared for discharge, and she should see her doctor when she's back in Virginia. I can take you to see her now."

He grabbed the bag of clothes he'd brought from home, and he and Reno followed the nurse down the hall to see Amber. Dash pushed through the curtain, tears burning at the sight of Amber lying in the hospital bed on her side, eyes closed.

"Sweetheart." Dash's voice cracked as he pressed a kiss to her forehead.

Her eyes fluttered open, and Reno went paws-up on the bed to lick her face.

"I'm so sorry, baby. God, I'm sorry." He put his arm around her, keeping their faces close, wanting to climb in beside her and take her in his arms.

"Will you call my parents?" she asked in a thin voice. "I want to go home."

"I already called them. I brought you clothes. Let me help you get dressed, and we'll go back to my place so you can rest."

As he helped her sit up, she said, "I want to go to home to Virginia."

"I'll take you tomorrow. Today you need to rest."

He started to take off her hospital gown, but she touched his chest, stopping him, tears welling in her eyes. "I want to go home *today*. *Please*. I need to be home."

"Okay, baby. I'll drive you home."

"No. You can't miss your tour because of me. People waited a long time to see you."

"Amber, if you think I'm leaving you, you're crazy." He didn't want her stuck in a fucking car for hours when she should be lying in a comfortable bed sleeping, letting him take care of her, much less leave her side for a second.

Her lower lip trembled, and she curled her fingers into the front of his shirt, but she did it lightly, as if it took all of her energy to hold on. "I will never forgive myself if you miss your tour. Don't do that to me."

He gritted his teeth, Sable's voice trampling through his head. *The minute she thinks she's holding you back is the moment you'll lose her forever.*

"Please?" Tears spilled from her eyes. "Give me your phone. I'll call my parents to come get me." She held out her hand, eyes pleading, breaking his heart in two.

"No," he said firmly. "I'm driving you home. I'll catch a flight out from Virginia tonight."

"Promise?"

"Damn it, Amber." *How can you ask me to leave you again?*

She put her hand on his cheek, slaying him anew with that silent plea. "Dash. I'll be fine. I'll be with my family. Promise me."

He reluctantly nodded and gently gathered her in his arms, trying to escape the feeling that he'd just betrayed the woman he loved.

AMBER SLEPT NEARLY the whole way back to Virginia, and the few times she'd woken up, Dash was quick to make sure she was okay. She'd been so scared when she'd realized what had happened, all she'd wanted was to get home to her family, someplace familiar, where she felt safer. Her head throbbed, her body ached, and now that some of the fear had subsided, all she *really* wanted was to be in Dash's arms and sleep until the sun came up. But as she headed up to her house tucked against his side, she knew she couldn't ask that of him, because he would do it in a heartbeat, and she couldn't live with that.

The front door opened and her parents stepped onto her porch. Her sisters, Trace, and Graham appeared behind them. Amber had a cavalry at the ready, and she loved them to the ends of the earth, but even they weren't enough to heal the gaping wounds she was about to cause.

"Honey." Her mother stepped off the porch and embraced her.

"I'm okay," Amber reassured her, although even she could hear the lie in her words as her sisters surrounded her.

"I'll get your bags, babe." Dash headed for the car.

She was glad her father, Trace, and Graham followed him, because he needed support, too. Sable pulled Amber into her arms, hugging her too tight. Amber endured the oxygen-depriving embrace, because she knew Sable shared the same soul-deep need to protect her as Dash did, and they had something else in common, too—the guilt that swallowed them whole when they couldn't. Sable didn't say a word, just released her and turned away, but not before Amber saw the tears in her toughest sister's eyes.

"We know you have to rest, but we just needed to see that you were okay," Brindle said as they ushered her inside.

Dash carried her bags into the bedroom, while the others doted on her, asking if she needed anything, if she hurt, and what they could do to help. But she was barely holding herself together, and when Dash came out of the bedroom looking as grief-stricken as she felt, it took everything she had not to let her tears flow. The only flight he could get was leaving from Charlottesville, and he'd miss it if he hung around trying to take care of her.

"Can you give us a minute?" Amber said to her family, and they shuffled toward the kitchen. She took Dash's hand and headed to the front door.

"Babe, don't make me leave you."

"You have to. I refuse to be a damsel in distress who ruins the life of the man she loves."

"What are you talking about? The life I love is with you."

She didn't want to argue, and she didn't want her family to hear them, so she stepped onto the porch, closing the door behind them. "I'm only *part* of your life. You worked hard to write your book and get it out there. Thousands of people are excited to meet you, and you deserve to enjoy the fanfare of your accomplishment. I'll be fine with my family."

His jaw tightened, and he shook his head. "You sent me away last time. You can't keep putting me in a box and not letting me help you."

"I'm *not*. I'm keeping you *out* of *my* box. Just for now, so you can finish your tour. Then we can figure all of this out."

"Figure it out?" His harsh tone stung. "Are you *questioning* us now?"

"No, but something has to change, or get fixed, or…" Tears slid down her cheeks, and she choked back a sob. "You need to finish your tour, and I need to see my doctor and figure out if I can ever have a different life than the one I've lived, or if I'll always be…" *The person who holds you back.* "If I'll always have trouble doing new things."

He looked up at the sky, anguish rolling off him as he pulled her into his arms. "Then we won't do new things. I don't care as long as we're together."

"You *do* care, Dash. You love going out and doing things,

and I love doing them with you." Her tears wet his shirt. "But I won't suffocate you."

"You could *never* suffocate me." He tipped her face up, anger and hurt staring back at her. He swallowed hard, and a strained smile started to appear. "I'm planting you an oak-tree forest, remember? It's you and me, babe, and a house full of acorns."

She laughed through her tears, knowing he'd plant a dozen forests if she wanted them. But was any of this fair to him? What if this happened every time they tried to do something new? He might be okay with it now, but how would he feel about it in a year? Two years?

Gathering her courage, she tried to get him to see where she was coming from. "Seeds don't just become wonderful things. They can take root and nurture ugly feelings, too, like doubt and resentment."

"I could never doubt us or resent you."

"You don't *know* that," she snapped, frustration and hurt pummeling her. "Bad seeds take longer to sprout and show themselves, but they start with a *single* seed that gets hurt and burrows deep, and then all the other bad seeds pile on, building over time. You don't even know they're there until it's too late and their roots are too tangled up to get rid of. I already ruined your debut signing. If you cancel the rest of the tour, that's like a dozen more bad seeds just waiting to take root. Add the experiences you saw for yourself that I can't give you on top of all of those bad seeds, and it's a recipe for resentment." The words flew from her lips unexpected, painful shards of glass.

"What are you talking about?" Confusion riddled his brow.

"Seeing your wife *pregnant*." She sobbed. "Talking to the baby while it's in her belly. I don't want to be the one who takes those special things away from you."

His nostrils flared, but it was the anguish in his eyes that made her feel sick. "I told you I just needed to process what you'd said, and I *did*. Why are you doing this?"

"Because I don't want to spin around in a year and realize I've ruined your life," she shouted. She hadn't meant to take it this far, hadn't even known she was that scared about everything that had happened and had been said. But now her painful realities were out there. They were knee-deep in them, and she was sinking fast.

He took her face between his hands, his eyes boring so deeply into her, she could feel him weeding through her thoughts, picking up the hopeful ones and running with them, barreling over the bad ones, refusing to let them stand. "The only way you'll ruin my life is if you're not in it. Running scared isn't going to change that. We can figure this out. I know you love me as much as I love you. I can feel it. I can see it in your eyes."

She gulped air into her lungs, salty tears slipping between her lips. "I do love you, more than anything."

"Then don't push me away."

"I have to. You can't stop living your life because of my epilepsy. You have to go."

"Baby, *please*. You just had a seizure and cracked your head open. You're asking too much of me. Too much of *us*."

Trembling, she choked out, "If I don't, who will?"

"Amber, what is this? Are you trying to break up with me or just get me to finish my tour?"

The worry in his voice shattered her heart into a million painful pieces. But she couldn't be the chains that held him back. "I thought it was just the tour, but now I don't know, and we don't have time to figure it out right now." She had to be strong, despite the torrent of sadness between them. "You have to go or you'll miss your flight. We'll talk when I'm better, when you're back." She went up on her toes and kissed him, her salty tears slipping between their lips. "Goodbye, Dash. I love you."

It took everything she had to walk inside the house. The door clicked shut as her sobs broke free, and through the blur of tears she saw her family rushing toward her.

Chapter Twenty-Two

AMBER WATCHED THE time change from midnight to 12:01 and pulled the collar of Dash's sweatshirt she was wearing up over her nose, breathing in his scent, sadness taking over again. She'd been drifting in and out of sleep and in and out of tears all night, reaching for the phone to call Dash, then thinking better of it. Everything hurt. Especially her heart.

She heard the bedroom door open and lay still, pretending to be asleep. Her sisters hadn't wanted to leave, but eventually she'd convinced them to go. Her parents had stayed, and they'd been checking on her all evening, peeking into her bedroom, whispering to each other, then heading back down the hall.

She felt the mattress dip beside her, her father's aftershave seeping in.

"Hey, princess," he whispered, petting Reno. "I know you're awake."

She rolled over, wincing with pain. "How did you know?"

"I saw the covers move over your feet. Ever since you were a little girl, when you'd pretend to be asleep, you'd close your eyes and your toes would curl under."

"I forgot I did that."

He brushed her hair away from her eyes. "I noticed earlier,

but I had to wait for your mother to fall asleep, because she'd never approve of what we're about to do."

"What's that?"

He set her sweatpants and sweatshirt on the bed. "It's a little cold outside, but I think we could both use a little moonlight magic."

"Thanks, but I just want to lie here and feel sorry for my-self."

"I think that MRI was wrong. That fall must have knocked something loose, because my princess has never wallowed in self-pity a day in her life."

"Maybe I have but you didn't know about it."

He shook his head. "A father knows these things. You've been bummed, but you've never wallowed. You're a fixer, darlin'. When something bothers you, you find a way around it."

"If I was ever a fixer, I sure suck at it now." She sat up. "I ruined my relationship with Dash."

"Maybe," he said casually.

"*Daddy,*" she snapped. "Aren't you supposed to make me feel better?"

"I don't know. Am I? I can't think in here. All your wallow-ing is clouding my brain."

"Way to kick a girl when she's down."

"I'm not kicking you, princess. I love you, and I know you're hurting. But I also know my girl, and I think we need to get you outside and set some of that pain free." He pushed to his feet. "I'll be waiting out front if you want to join me for a stroll, but please don't wake your mother. She'll lecture me for not letting you pretend to sleep."

She smiled at that. Getting up was the last thing she wanted to do, but she knew he was right. She'd slept for hours in the car, and she wasn't doing much sleeping now. A little fresh air would probably do her good. She got up and dressed in the clean clothes he'd brought her, pulling Dash's sweatshirt over her own. She didn't care that she probably looked like the Pillsbury Doughboy. She pulled on socks and shoved her feet into her most comfortable cowgirl boots, remembering they were the boots she'd worn the first time she'd met Dash. Another wave of grief hit her as she and Reno made their way quietly out the front door. The cold air stung her cheeks, and she covered them with her hands.

Her father turned, concern hovering in his sharp blue eyes. He was wearing the same tan jacket with a brown corduroy collar he'd worn forever, and it brought a dose of comfort. "I'm glad you came. I wasn't looking forward to walking alone tonight. Are you going to be warm enough?"

She nodded and lifted the bottom of Dash's sweatshirt, showing him the one beneath. They descended the porch steps, and she took his arm as they made their way down the quiet street. All the houses were dark, the streetlights illuminating their path.

"Do you want to talk about what's going on with you and Dash?" her father asked carefully.

"I don't know. I can't figure out if I messed up or did the right thing."

"About…?"

"*Everything.* He didn't want to leave, and I made him go finish his tour. I said things I don't know if I should have said."

"We all say things we don't mean sometimes." They turned the corner, and he was quiet for a minute before asking, "The seizure aside, did you have a good time in New York?"

"*Yes.* The best time. I loved his family and his friends, and we had a great time in the city, and the fundraiser was incredible. But my seizure was a wake-up call, reminding me that I'm not like everyone else. I can't just pick up and go and do everything I want. I have limitations."

"Darlin', you put those limitations on yourself."

"That's not true. I tried to throw caution to the wind and let myself have fun like a regular girl, and I had *two* seizures in two weeks after not having them for years."

"Yes, and you will have a risk of seizures forever. But epilepsy doesn't define your life, sweetheart. *You* do."

"They go hand in hand."

"Not always. When we first found out you had epilepsy, I didn't want to let you out of my sight. If it were up to me and we could have afforded it, I would have quit my job, taken you out of school, and tied a leash between us. But that wouldn't have been good for you. Thank God your mother knew that and helped me understand why. As much as I wanted to keep you under my thumb, I had to earn a living, and we had six other children who had playdates and activities. Our lives couldn't stop. We still took you kids to the park and festivals, to see Aunt Roxie and your cousins in New York. You all still rode horses and chased each other around."

"I think Dash would like to do that whole leash thing, too."

"Would he? Does he want to put you in a protective bubble? Limit the things you do and the places you go?" His tone softened. "Or does he just want a life with you any way he can have it as long as you're safe?"

"I don't know. All of it?" But he hadn't tried to hide her away from the world in a protective bubble. He'd tried to help her live life to the fullest. "I don't want him to give up his life,

Dad, or limit himself because of my medical disorder."

"I didn't realize he had to. You've always had a good sense of what you need. You found ways to slow down that made you feel more in control, and we allowed it," he said as they turned down another road, heading toward Main Street. "But I worry that somewhere along the way, you got so comfortable living within the confines of your fear of having seizures, you've forgotten what it was like to live your life and experience new things."

"I wondered about that, too, but twelve stitches tell me that the way I was living was better than what I did this weekend."

"Was it? Were you happier before you and Dash got together?"

"*No*, but that fall terrified me, and the only thing that's changed from when I was seizure-free is me and Dash and the person he's uncovered."

"Do you like that person?"

"Yeah," she admitted. "But she's not good for me."

"I don't know about that. You're out there living a more exciting life than you ever have, and yes, you've had seizures during that time. But you seem happier than ever lately, so to say the part of yourself that Dash is discovering is not good for you doesn't seem fair."

He was quiet for a minute, and she knew he was letting his words sink in.

"You and Dash really are something together." He let out a little laugh.

"What're you laughing at? None of this is funny."

"I was just thinking about the night you accidentally tripped the seizure alarm on your necklace."

"Okay, that was funny, and embarrassing."

"And yet you survived it, and Dash protected you from the fallout. When I heard about that, he got my vote. You know, your mother and I did something similar once."

"Oh God. Do I want to hear this?"

"I don't know, but I'm going to tell you anyway. Grace was only about a year old when Sable and Pepper were born, and your mother and I never got time alone. So one day I came home early from work and lucked out. All three of them were napping. It was a miracle. A sign from the heavens above. At least that's what I told your mother when I convinced her that we should take advantage of the peace and quiet. We got a little carried away, and she forgot she had dinner in the oven. It burned to a crisp, and the whole kitchen filled with smoke. The fire alarms went off, and all three girls woke up crying. I was sure that was it, and I'd never be allowed to make love to my wife again."

"She obviously didn't cut you off, since you have seven kids."

"She wanted to, trust me. But some loves are too strong to deny. There was no more nap-time lovin' for us, but I did buy baby monitors, and those suckers went everywhere with us."

"*Dad*, what do baby monitors have to do with it? Don't you think you should have come up with a rule to turn the oven off before you fooled around from then on?"

"*Huh.*" Her father scratched his head. "*But* if we'd heard the first baby wake up, we could have kept her from waking up the others."

"*Dad.*" She shook her head.

"Aw, heck. I guess I got a little rambly with my sage advice and got off course. What can I say? I've got a lot on my mind tonight. The point I was trying to make is that life isn't about avoiding the things you want just because they might cause you trouble. It's about finding ways to have it all and making modifications and compromises despite the fears."

She rested her head on his shoulder as they neared Main Street. "I don't know how to do that with this situation. I don't want to be a burden on Dash."

"A burden? We always taught you that having epilepsy was just another part of who you were, like the color of your hair or the freckles on your shoulders."

"I know, and that's how I live my life. I show people who I am, and if they choose not to accept me, then that's on them."

"That's right, darlin'. Doesn't Dash deserve the same respect?"

"What do you mean?"

"It sounds to me like he's shown you who he is, and instead of taking him for his word, you're trying to decide how he lives his life. What happened was traumatic for *both* of you. You're not setting him free, princess. You climbed back into the cage you built for yourself when you were thirteen years old, and you sent him away with clipped wings."

"Dad, he wanted to give up the rest of his book tour, and for what? To sit at home and take care of me?"

"Darlin, that's what love is. It's putting the person you love ahead of yourself, for better or worse. Quite frankly, if he'd *wanted* to hightail it out of town to finish the tour, I'd have worried that he wasn't the right man for you."

Tears welled in her eyes. "You don't see that as me being a burden on him? Ruining his life?"

"No."

"Oh, *Daddy*." Tears fell down her cheeks. "Love is so confusing. I made a mistake. I need to call him. I need to go see him. I didn't mean to clip his wings. What if he doesn't forgive me?"

"I think he already has." Her father hugged her against his side as they turned onto Main Street.

Amber looked up and saw lanterns hanging in the trees, lighting a path to her bookstore. A yellow pennant hung on a limb closest to them, and paper stars dangled from the trees. Her heart leapt as she grabbed the pennant, tearing it from the limb, and read what Dash had written on it. *Montgomery earns a penalty flag for unnecessary roughness.* She turned it over. *Penalty: 15 kisses and an automatic second base.*

She laughed through her tears and ran to the first star, unhooking it as she read his note. *Amber & Dash's Playbook of Rewritten Stars.* Clutching the pennant and the star, she made her way to the next star, and the next, tearing them down and reading them as she went.

We're on the same team.

No more solo rule making.

Trust your teammate to have your back even when you're scared.

Expand horizons at a gentle pace.

When traveling, take lots of naps (some naughty, some sleeping).

She ran to the next tree, hope and happiness swelling inside her, tears falling like rivers down her cheeks.

Talk everything out.

Wake your teammate if you leave the bed at night.

Love our babies (a lot of them) born by surrogate or adoption.

She ran to the bookstore door, yanking the last star from the handle and reading it.

Open the door before I lose my mind.

She threw the door open, and Reno darted past her, sprinting down another path of lights to Dash, who stood by the couch in the back amid dozens of bouquets of Amber's favorite flowers, each one in a vase full of acorns. Reno went paws-up on Dash, tail wagging. Dash loved him up, his eyes never leaving Amber's as she ran to him, hands full of their rewritten stars, eyes blurry with tears. *"Dash!"*

He gathered her in his arms.

"I'm so sorry," she cried.

"You were scared." He slid his hand down her back. "I am, too, baby." He drew back, gazing into her eyes. "Scared of losing you because you have this warped belief that my tour, or anything else, could possibly be more important than you are. I know you're afraid we can't do things together outside of Oak Falls because you might have a seizure and that I'll resent you for it. I understand your fears, baby, but they don't hold water. I came to Oak Falls looking for a break, and I found the truest, deepest love imaginable with you, my wild thing, the girl who outshines everyone and everything around her."

Her breathing hitched, her face wet with tears.

"If you think I'm walking away because we'll face a few challenges in our lifetime, then you've got another thing coming, Amber Montgomery. I messed up by not waking up when you got up to use the bathroom, but I'll *never* make that mistake again, because now we have rules, our own playbook. You need to wake me up before you leave the bed, and if you drop the ball, we'll punt it to your mother to train a second dog whose only job is to wake me when you get out of bed at night."

She nodded, too choked up to speak.

"There's *nothing* we can't figure out together." He picked up a handful of stars from the coffee table and handed them to her.

She looked down at them. "They're blank."

"We're a team, baby. Those are for you to fill out. That's how love works. You can write any rules you want, but I have veto rights, so don't get any ideas about a hall pass for Zac Efron."

Overwhelmed with love for this incredible man, she could do little more than try to remember how to breathe.

"I want to go with you to talk to your doctor and figure out what we can do to further manage your seizures. If he says we can never travel again, then that's what we'll do. But I hope he doesn't, because you deserve to see the world. I want to show you those famous bookstores and everything else you want to see, in low-key trips that include lots of rest. I don't care if it takes us thirty years to see nine bookstores, as long as we're together, and if I need to follow you like a shadow to keep you safe while we do it, I'm there, baby. I'm *your* man."

"Dash," she choked out.

"Let me finish, please. You got a penalty, remember? Now I have the ball." He took all of the stars and set them on the table. Then he took her left hand in his and dropped to one knee.

She tried to swallow past the lump forming in her throat, fresh tears raining down her cheeks.

"Amber Montgomery, I thought I fell in love with you right here in your bookstore the first night we packaged your dirty books, but I was wrong. I think I fell the first second I saw you at the jam session, and I have fallen deeper in love with you every day since. I want to build a life with you here in Oak Falls where we shared our first kiss and made out under the bleachers. I love your big life in this small town, baby, where everyone knows your name and the dirty grandmas take me to breakfast." He laughed a little. "I want babies any way we can get them, because how they get here isn't nearly as important as how we love them. We'll teach them about acorns and football and keep them away from your naughty book club novels."

She laughed.

"I want to take moonlight walks and collect so many acorns we have to build a second house to hold them all. I gave you the wrong jewelry box last night, sweetheart. I should have given you this one." He grabbed a ring box from behind a vase and opened it, revealing the most gorgeous sparkling diamond engagement ring Amber had ever seen. A stunning square canary diamond sat up high, with several smaller diamonds running down the sides of the band. "My sweet, secret sexy reader, I love you with all that I have and all that I am. Will you make me the happiest man on earth and marry me, so no matter where we are, you'll always be with family?"

With wet cheeks and a giddy heart, she exclaimed, "Yes!"

"Yes?" Dash pushed to his feet, and she threw her arms around him, repeating, "Yes!" as he pressed his lips to hers.

Her office door flew open, and cheers rang out as her entire family, save for Axsel, who was still on tour, and all three of her sisters' husbands ran into the room, clapping and shouting "Congratulations" as Dash twirled her around, kissing her, both of them laughing.

"You brought Pepper and Grace home! What if I said no?"

Dash cocked an arrogant grin. "Have you seen the way you look at me? Baby, we were made for each other." He sealed that truth with a kiss as sweet and everlasting as their love.

Chapter Twenty-Three

THE MANSION AT Hilltop Vineyards had been transformed into a winter wonderland for Zev and Carly's wedding reception. Elegant chandeliers hung from cathedral ceilings, and miles of white silk, sparkling lights, and greenery trailed along exposed wooden rafters. A fire roared in the two-story stone fireplace, flanked with floor-to-ceiling windows offering picturesque views of the snowy vineyard and, just beyond, the small town of Pleasant Hill, Maryland. But those views didn't compare to the woman standing a few feet away from Dash.

He couldn't take his eyes off Amber, feminine and beautiful in a sexy peach lace dress. He pictured her fifty years from now, with gray hair, her face mapped with wrinkles, still outshining everyone else. He knew he'd be even more captivated by her, because their home would be full of acorns and scrawled sentiments, and their hearts would be full of a lifetime of loving memories.

She stood by the dance floor with Pepper and Trixie, but he could tell she was only half listening to them. She had that dreamy look in her eyes that he adored as she watched Zev and Carly slow dancing, surrounded by couples grooving to the fast beat. Was his girl thinking about Christmas night, when it had snowed and they'd gone outside to dance in the moonlight? Or was she dreaming of their wedding day next summer? Dash would marry her tomorrow, but he wanted to give her the most magical wedding that had ever taken place, and that took planning. They'd already enlisted Lindsay's help. Amber had raved about Carly's formfitting gown that Jillian's twin, Jax, an elite wedding-gown designer, had made for her, and he had a feeling a wedding dress took some planning, too.

As he made his way to her, he thought about the whirlwind weeks that had passed since he'd proposed. He'd missed five days of his book tour while they'd spoken with her doctor and figured out their plans, and Amber had insisted that he make those days up at the end of the tour. She'd been right to push him. When he'd announced the rescheduling and their engagement, his fans had rallied in support. The doctor had added another medication to Amber's regimen to try to ward off more seizures. In the month and a half since, she'd been seizure-free, Dash had moved in, and they'd made modifications to their lifestyle with the hopes of Amber eventually being able to forgo the additional medication. They hadn't done anything crazy, but they'd taken her sisters' advice and were going to bed earlier. They still went dancing at JJ's and got together with friends, but when they knew they'd have a busy weekend, they planned more downtime around the events. Like they had today. They'd stayed at the hotel last night, slept in this morning, and after having brunch with some of the Bradens and Amber's family, they'd gone back to the hotel to chill before the wedding.

After resting, they'd snuck in a sexy shower. As he slid his arms around her from behind, he couldn't wait to strip that dress off her again. He kissed her cheek, whispering to keep from interrupting Pepper and Trixie's conversation. "This is pretty magical."

"It sure is," she said breathily.

"But it's not nearly as magical as ours will be. Guess who has a consult with Jax tomorrow for her wedding gown?"

Amber turned in his arms, her eyes dancing with excitement. "Are you kidding?"

"Would I kid about that?"

"Dash!" She threw her arms around him.

Pepper gave them a curious look.

He'd gotten to know Amber's serious-minded, sharp-witted sister when he'd called and asked her to come home for the proposal. They'd talked for nearly two hours, just as he had with Grace, Reed, and Axsel. Although Axsel hadn't been able to make it for the proposal, he'd video chatted with them while they were all celebrating. They'd spent Thanksgiving with his family and Christmas with hers. She'd gotten so close with his sisters, they texted her all the time, and he'd not only gotten to know her family better, but he'd also gotten to know Trixie, Jillian, and Amber's other friends who were like family. He'd thought about planning future visits so those close friendships would never feel too far away for Amber, but he had a feeling with their wedding and Nick and Trixie's coming up, the girls would be in constant contact.

"What did we miss?" Pepper asked.

"We're meeting with Jax tomorrow to talk about my wedding gown!" Amber exclaimed, and the girls all talked at once about how much fun Amber was going to have.

Morgyn and Jillian hurried over, and there was another uproar of excitement. Dash stepped back, giving them space, loving how everyone gushed over his girl.

He felt a heavy hand on his shoulder seconds before Cade appeared by his side with Reed and Graham. He and the guys had gotten tight. But Cade was becoming more like the father he'd always wished he'd had. The evening after Amber's last seizure, when he'd clued Cade and Marilynn in to his plans to propose, he'd worried that they might think he was too much for her, and he'd been ready to fight that battle. But they'd told him that they knew he'd move heaven and earth for her, that their love was meant to be, and they'd be proud to have him as a son-in-law.

"And I thought football huddles got loud," Dash joked.

"Get used to it, son," Cade said. "Women are a whole different species."

"They have homing devices for gossip," Graham said.

"Speaking of gossip, Sin and Clay were telling me that you're thinking about creating some kind of fitness app and looking into buying a facility to open a gym," Reed said.

"Please tell me Dash's Darlings aren't going to lose their morning motivator." Nana had coined that name for their morning workout group. Cade lowered his voice and said, "Those morning workouts have led to more energy in the evenings, if you know what I mean. I'd hate to lose that."

They all chuckled.

"No worries there, Cade. I'll be working out with my ladies until they get sick of me. I'm talking with people about an app, and I would like a better fitness facility that's close to home. But I think for now I'd like to focus on being the best fiancé I can be. Maybe after Maui I'll take the next step." They'd decided to go to Hawaii for their honeymoon, and if they made it through that trip seizure-free, they'd plan the first trip to see another famous bookstore.

He glanced at Amber chatting with her sisters and friends,

and her radiant smile widened, hitting him square in the center of his chest. Taking a break and going to Oak Falls had been the best thing he'd ever done, second only to asking that bookish belle to marry him.

"I'M SO HAPPY for Zev and Carly," Trixie said, watching Zev and Carly make their way around the room after holding hands, kissing, mingling.

They'd cut the cake about an hour ago, and then Amber's father had absconded with her fiancé. *Fiancé.* She loved the sound of that and glanced at her gorgeous engagement ring.

"I remember when I first met Zev. He seemed so unsettled, like he was looking for something," Pepper said. "Which makes sense, since he's a treasure hunter, but I don't get the same vibe from him anymore."

"That's because he finally realized what my family has known all along," Jillian said. "He'd been searching for *Carly,* and he just didn't know it." She looked across the room at her cousin Victoria, Clay's sister, who was waving her over. "I'll be right back."

Amber had never gone searching for love, but she'd spent a lifetime dreaming of it, imagining a future she was never quite sure she'd get. Now her dreams were coming true, and she could see them all so clearly. She glanced across the room at her one true love, who was talking with her father and brothers-in-law. Dash was striking in a black vest and slacks, his muscular arms straining against the material of his dress shirt. He was gorgeous in everything he wore. Even more so wearing nothing at all. Memories of the sexy shower they'd shared that morning rolled in, heating her cheeks. They'd spent the afternoon reading her latest book club novel, which had led to acting out their steamy revisions.

As if Dash sensed her thoughts, he looked over, and a slow grin slid across his handsome face, causing a swarm of the butterflies in her belly that had hit her the first time she'd seen Dash and had never left.

Would she ever get used to being so in love? So utterly and completely happy?

Jillian rejoined the group, grabbing Amber's and Trixie's arms. "You guys! You'll never believe what just happened!"

"One of the hot Whiskeys asked you out?" Trixie asked.

All of Carly's friends from Colorado had come to the wedding, including the Whiskeys, a biker family who owned a therapeutic horse ranch, had helped Carly through some rough times, and had several good-looking siblings.

"Ha! I wish. Sable's dirty dancing with Dare Whiskey. That man has got moves," Jillian said. "If Victoria hadn't just given me the best news *ever*, I would definitely be planning a trip to Colorado right now."

"Is she the one that runs Blank Space Entertainment?" Pepper asked.

"*Yes*. She's the one who hooked me up with Johnny Butthead." Jillian winced. "I mean, Johnny *Bad*. I'd better stop doing that before spring, when I go to New York to *meet* with him!" She let out a little squeal. "His tour is back *on*, and guess who's designing his wardrobe?"

Amber and Trixie exchanged uneasy glances.

"Congratulations," Pepper said. "But didn't he jerk you around before?"

"Yes, and she was pissed at him," Trixie said.

"I still *am*," Jillian said far too happily. "But that's not going to stop me from designing his wardrobe. This is a *huge* boon for my business, and it gives me time to do a little matchmaking for *you know who* before I get swept up in the project." She looked across the room at Jax, talking with Nick. "Apparently sparks flew between Jax and a potential client, and he's been off his game ever since."

"Be careful, Jilly," Trixie said. "You might be twins, but Jax is pretty private about his personal life. He might not appreciate matchmaking."

Jillian smirked. "We'll see about that, and then we'll see about Johnny Bad."

"Well, I'm thrilled about your new endeavor. Congratulations," Amber said. "I hope it works out this time."

Jillian arched a finely manicured brow, looking as fierce as she was petite. "It will. I'm going to march in there and give Johnny a piece of my mind. When I'm done with him, he'll *never* jerk me around again."

"If you came after me like that, I'd behave," Pepper said. "Congratulations."

"He seemed pretty arrogant when I met him," Amber said. "I wouldn't expect him to back off as easily as Pepper. I think you might be about to meet your match."

"Oh, *please.* You've seen me in action. Shutting him down will be like taking candy from a baby." Jillian wrinkled her nose. "Wait, that's not easy, is it? It'll be like…"

"Fireworks!" Pepper exclaimed.

"Right. And *I'm* lighting them!" The band began playing "Single Ladies," and Jillian danced in place. "I need to work off some of this energy. Come on, let's take over the dance floor."

Amber saw Dash heading her way. "Actually, I think my dance partner is on his way over."

"That man looks like a tiger on the prowl. I'm totally jealous," Jillian said, and then she and the others headed to the dance floor.

As Dash approached, his dark eyes said, *I love you* and *I want you*, just as Amber was sure hers did. Her time of sitting on the sidelines, watching life pass her by felt like they'd happened in another lifetime. She loved being the envy of all those single ladies, and her dashing prince was everything she could ever want and so much more.

"Excuse me, beautiful. Is your name Amber?"

"Why, yes, it is," she played along, loving this side of him.

"Your name is written all over my dance card. Think you can fit me in?"

"I'm not sure. My card is kind of full," she teased.

"Damn." He puffed out his chest and rolled up his sleeves, revealing his thick forearms. "Maybe this will convince you." He dipped her over his arm, kissing her sweet and slow, leaving her breathless and Jell-O-legged. He steadied her on her feet, flashing a cocky grin. "What do you say?"

"I can fit you in, if there are more of those on the horizon."

"I think that can be arranged." He led her to the dance floor and spun her around as they danced to the end of the song. When the band began playing "Rewrite the Stars," he held her close, swaying to the music, whisper-singing the lyrics with so much emotion, she got teary-eyed.

"You requested that song, didn't you?" She had a feeling there was nothing he wouldn't do for her. "I feel like the belle of the ball again."

"You're not just the belle of an occasional ball, sweetheart. You're going to be the belle of our entire wonderful life." He twirled her around, then pulled her close again. "Buckle up, my beautiful wild thing. We're just getting started."

Ready for more Bradens & Montgomerys?

Fall in love with Jax Braden and Jordan Lawler
in THEN CAME LOVE

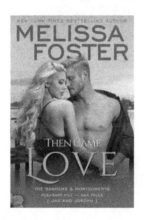

What happens when you find your soul mate but she belongs to someone else?

Famed wedding gown designer Jax Braden faces his toughest competitor yet—his heart. Passion ignites between Jax and soon-to-be bride Jordan Lawler. But honesty is everything to both of them, and neither will cross those lines. Loyalties are tested and hearts are frayed as Jax and Jordan are drawn into a love too strong to deny.

Fall in love with the Steeles on the sandy shores of Silver Island, home to coffee shops, boat races, and midnight rendezvous

Archer Steele is one of the leading vintners on the East Coast. He's arrogant, aggressive, and has never been interested in settling down, which is what makes his hookups with his sister's beautiful blond best friend, hair and makeup artist Indi Oliver, the perfect escape. But Indi's toying with moving to the island, and when she ends their no-strings trysts to focus on her business, Archer isn't ready to let her go…

Ready for hilarity and heat?
Start the Seaside Summers series FREE in digital format
Fall in love at Seaside, featuring a group of fun, sexy friends who gather each summer at their Cape Cod cottages. They're funny, flawed, and will have you begging to enter their circle of friends.

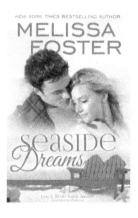

Bella Abbascia has returned to Seaside Cottages in Wellfleet, Massachusetts, as she does every summer. Only this year, Bella has more on her mind than sunbathing and skinny-dipping with her girlfriends. She's quit her job, put her house on the market, and sworn off relationships while she builds a new life in her favorite place on earth. That is, until good-time Bella's prank takes a bad turn and a sinfully sexy police officer appears on the scene.

Single father and police officer Caden Grant left Boston with his fourteen-year-old son, Evan, after his partner was killed in the line of duty. He hopes to find a safer life in the small resort town of Wellfleet, and when he meets Bella during a night patrol shift, he realizes he's found the one thing he'd never allowed himself to hope for—or even realized he was missing.

After fourteen years of focusing solely on his son, Caden cannot resist the intense attraction he feels toward beautiful Bella, and Bella's powerless to fight the heat of their budding romance. But starting over proves more difficult than either of them imagined, and when Evan gets mixed up with the wrong kids, Caden's loyalty is put to the test. Will he give up everything to protect his son—even Bella?

Have you met The Whiskeys: Dark Knights at Peaceful Harbor?

If you're a fan of sexy, alpha heroes, babies, and strong family ties even to those who are not blood related, you'll love Truman Gritt and the Whiskeys.

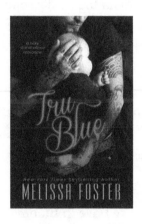

There's nothing Truman Gritt won't do to protect his family—including spending years in prison for a crime he didn't commit. When he's finally released, the life he knew is turned upside down by his mother's overdose, and Truman steps in to raise the children she's left behind. Truman's hard, he's secretive, and he's trying to save a brother who's even more broken than he is. He's never needed help in his life, and when beautiful Gemma Wright tries to step in, he's less than accepting. But Gemma has a way of slithering into people's lives, and eventually she pierces through his ironclad heart. When Truman's dark past collides with his future, his loyalties will be tested, and he'll be faced with his toughest decision yet.

New to the Love in Bloom series?

If this is your first Love in Bloom book, there are many more love stories featuring loyal, sassy, and sexy heroes and heroines waiting for you. The Bradens & Montgomerys is just one of the series in the Love in Bloom big-family romance collection. Each Love in Bloom book is written to be enjoyed as a stand-alone novel or as part of the larger series. There are no cliffhangers and no unresolved issues. Characters from each series make appearances in future books, so you never miss an engagement, wedding, or birth. You might enjoy my other series within the Love in Bloom big-family romance collection, starting with the very first book in the entire Love in Bloom series, SISTERS IN LOVE.

See the Entire Love in Bloom Collection
www.MelissaFoster.com/love-bloom-series

Download Free First-in-Series eBooks
www.MelissaFoster.com/free-ebooks

Download Series Checklists, Family Trees, and Publication Schedules
www.MelissaFoster.com/reader-goodies

More Books By Melissa Foster

LOVE IN BLOOM SERIES

SNOW SISTERS
Sisters in Love
Sisters in Bloom
Sisters in White

THE BRADENS at Weston
Lovers at Heart, Reimagined
Destined for Love
Friendship on Fire
Sea of Love
Bursting with Love
Hearts at Play

THE BRADENS at Trusty
Taken by Love
Fated for Love
Romancing My Love
Flirting with Love
Dreaming of Love
Crashing into Love

THE BRADENS at Peaceful Harbor
Healed by Love
Surrender My Love
River of Love
Crushing on Love
Whisper of Love
Thrill of Love

THE BRADENS & MONTGOMERYS at Pleasant Hill – Oak Falls
Embracing Her Heart
Anything for Love

HARMONY POINTE
Call Her Mine
This is Love
She Loves Me

THE WICKEDS: DARK KNIGHTS AT BAYSIDE
A Little Bit Wicked
The Wicked Aftermath

SILVER HARBOR
Maybe We Will

WILD BOYS AFTER DARK
Logan
Heath
Jackson
Cooper

BAD BOYS AFTER DARK
Mick
Dylan
Carson
Brett

HARBORSIDE NIGHTS SERIES
Includes characters from the Love in Bloom series
Catching Cassidy
Discovering Delilah
Tempting Tristan

More Books by Melissa
Chasing Amanda (mystery/suspense)
Come Back to Me (mystery/suspense)
Have No Shame (historical fiction/romance)
Love, Lies & Mystery (3-book bundle)
Megan's Way (literary fiction)
Traces of Kara (psychological thriller)
Where Petals Fall (suspense)

Acknowledgments

What a joy it was to write Amber and Dash's story and to bring awareness to epilepsy. I am grateful to the many people who shared their experiences with epilepsy with me and answered my endless questions, including, but not limited to, Tonya Hubbard, Ashley Wilcox Taylor, Terren Hoeksema, Patricia Eberhart, and Kelley Ryan Gunther. As always, I have taken a few fictional liberties, and any errors are my own.

I am inspired on a daily basis by my fans and friends, many of whom are in my fan club on Facebook. If you haven't yet joined my fan club, please do. We have a great time chatting about the Love in Bloom hunky heroes and sassy heroines. You never know when you'll inspire a story or a character and end up in one of my books, as several fan club members have already discovered.
www.Facebook.com/groups/MelissaFosterFans

To stay abreast of what's going on in our fictional boyfriends' worlds and sales, like and follow my Facebook fan page.
www.Facebook.com/MelissaFosterAuthor

Sign up for my newsletter to keep up to date with new releases and special promotions and events and to receive an exclusive short story featuring Jack Remington and Savannah Braden.
www.MelissaFoster.com/Newsletter

And don't forget to download your free Reader Goodies! For free ebooks, family trees, publication schedules, series checklists, and more, please visit the special Reader Goodies page that I've set up for you!

www.MelissaFoster.com/Reader-Goodies

As always, loads of gratitude to my incredible team of editors and proofreaders: Kristen Weber, Penina Lopez, Elaini Caruso, Juliette Hill, Lynn Mullan, and Justinn Harrison, and my *last set of eagle eyes*, Lee Fisher.

I am forever grateful to my son Jake for enduring lengthy conversations during the last year of Covid quarantine about my books and characters, and to my other three sons, Noah, Zach, and Jess, who listen from afar. You boys are my heart, my joy, and my world. I love you to pieces.

Meet Melissa

www.MelissaFoster.com

Melissa Foster is a *New York Times, Wall Street Journal,* and *USA Today* bestselling and award-winning author. Her books have been recommended by *USA Today*'s book blog, *Hagerstown* magazine, *The Patriot,* and several other print venues. Melissa has painted and donated several murals to the Hospital for Sick Children in Washington, DC.

Visit Melissa on her website or chat with her on social media. Melissa enjoys discussing her books with book clubs and reader groups and welcomes an invitation to your event. Melissa's books are available through most online retailers in paperback, digital, and audio formats.